C2000003523 2

D1152870

Lc

SHADOWS
OF
GLORY

Also by William Woodruff

Vessel of Sadness

Paradise Galore

*The Rise of the British Rubber Industry
During the Nineteenth Century*

*Impact of Western Man:
A Study of Europe's Role in the World Economy,
1750–1960*

*America's Impact on the World:
A Study of the Role of the United States in the
World Economy, 1750–1970*

The Struggle for World Power, 1500–1980

*The Emergence of an International Economy,
1700–1914*

*A Concise History of the Modern World:
1500 to the Present*

*The Road to Nab End:
An Extraordinary Northern Childhood*

Beyond Nab End

SHADOWS
OF
GLORY

A Novel by

William Woodruff

A *Little, Brown* Book

First published in Great Britain in 2003
by Little, Brown

A CIP catalogue record for this book
is available from the British Library.

ISBN 0 316 72656 7

Typeset in Sabon by
Palimpsest Book Production Limited,
Polmont, Stirlingshire

Printed and bound in Great Britain by
Clays Ltd, St Ives plc

Little, Brown
An imprint of
Time Warner Books UK
Brettenham House
Lancaster Place
London WC2E 7EN

www.TimeWarnerBooks.co.uk

All characters are imaginary. No reference to any living person is intended, nor should any be inferred. The author thanks family and friends who have helped him, especially his wife Helga, Richard Beswick and Catherine Hill of Time Warner Books, and Jane Birkett.

To the students of Oxford University who fought and died in the Second World War, 1939–45

THE CREW

Stern
George Kemp (cox)
Alex Haverfield (stroke)
Charley Bradbury
Roger Blundell
Bill Clark
David Evans
Max Elsfield
Tony Markham
Pat Riley
Prow

THE COACH

Harvey Childers

OTHER CHARACTERS

Beatrix Dekker	A Dutch writer
Hazel Elsfield	Max Elsfield's sister
Lady Elsfield	Max Elsfield's mother
Evelyn Haverfield	Alex Haverfield's mother
Johanna Kemp	Daughter of Herr Krämer
Gloria Markham	Tony Markham's sister
Helen Markham	Tony Markham's sister
Penelope Markham	Tony Markham's sister
Victoria Randall	Daughter of Lord Randall
Hugh Stably	Dean at Arnold College
Evrid Stamboliisky	A Bulgarian refugee
Lydia Turner	Daughter of Lord Turner
Walter Turnbull	Chaplain at Arnold College
Lucy Warner	An actress

Prologue

Sir George Kemp swung the bottle of champagne against the prow of the long, narrow boat. The scattered liquid sparkled in the sun. 'I dedicate this barge to Arnold's rowers, past, present and future,' he called. 'May all those who use it know the joys of rowing; may they know laughter and the love of friends.' His voice rang with sincerity; his furrowed face was earnest; his mass of white hair blew in the wind.

The guard of honour on the bank raised their oars and cheered. Kemp's grandson Thomas and his granddaughter Kate were among them. Members of the college clapped politely. 'Bravo!' somebody shouted. To one side was a knot of Kemp's relatives; beyond lay Christ Church Meadow and the colleges of Oxford University.

The breeze stirred the bunting and the flags; shafts of sunlight played on the barge's many windows. The brightly painted figurehead rose and fell gently. Sir George looked at the face. No one knew that it was that of his wife, as she had looked when he had first met her – sixty-one years ago. With only an old photograph to go on, he marvelled at how well the sculptor had portrayed her features. The joy they had known together echoed in his heart.

'I cannot tell you how much pleasure I have had in watching this boat take shape,' Sir George continued. 'It has brought back memories of the old college barge, where we planned our victories, and consoled each other in defeat. Rowing gave meaning and significance to our lives. The team spirit it bred helped to prepare us for the trials that followed. I know it is increasingly common to say that students nowadays can't spare the time for rowing. Nonsense! I urge you young people to cultivate the art of the oar, and the love of comradeship and loyalty, which rowing inspires.'

With moist eyes, Kemp acknowledged the applause.

'Delightful, delightful,' said Dr Henry Patton, the Master of Arnold College, as he took the place of Sir George on the platform. 'Thanks to Sir George,' he addressed the crowd, 'at a time when many college barges are badly in need of repair, we now have the most handsome and elegant barge on the river.' He waited for the applause to end. 'As some of you know, Sir George was cox of the Arnold team before the war. I'm told he was the best cox Arnold ever had. Some say,' he continued, smiling, 'that rowing was his major undergraduate occupation.' The rowers cheered.

Patton went on to say a word or two about Sir George's contribution to British law. Kemp had been a Queen's Counsel and one of England's leading judges, knighted in 1986 for a lifetime's work in the courts.

As Kemp snipped the ribbon, he noticed a shield with the gilded college crest and a plaque in his name. Everyone surged aboard. Most visitors poured into the lower-deck 'house', with its carpeted floor, couches, easy chairs and a tiny bar. Along a wall were lighted trophy cabinets containing silver plaques, cups, plates and models of the college's most famous boats. Other guests climbed to the deck above to be in the fresh air, where tables were laid out with sandwiches and hors d'oeuvres. There was a popping of champagne corks and much hearty laughter as the young rowers gathered around Kemp to hear tales of past glories.

On returning to college, Patton parted from Kemp at the porter's lodge. 'You did very well, George, the college is greatly in your debt. See you for drinks.' He gently grasped Kemp's shoulder before turning away.

Limping his way past a group led by a student carrying a board proclaiming: STOP THE GENOCIDE IN KOSOVO, Kemp went in search of his old staircase. He turned left at the lodge, then right, then left again, passing the time-worn sculpture of Archibald Arnold, the church dignitary who had founded the college in the seventeenth century. A workman was giving the stern-faced bishop his annual wash. Kemp stopped to watch. He had taken Johanna's picture before the statue in 1939, just after they had become engaged. How beautiful she had looked.

'The bishop's seen a lot,' the man said, rubbing away. 'More than you can tell.'

'I know he has, much of which would be better forgotten.'

'Life is the chanciest business, sir.'

At the foot of staircase four Kemp turned and studied the quad. It looked exactly as it was when he left to go to war in 1939: the same green velvet lawn, the same geraniums in the window boxes, the same sense of age and continuity. Nothing had changed. For a moment he was overcome by memories.

A college porter, who had preceded him with his overnight bag, stood at the bottom of the stairs.

'Here's yer key, sir. Yer bag's on yer bed. Give us a shout if yer need anythin'.'

Kemp was too busy studying the key to answer. Locking doors, he said to himself; what is the college coming to?

He noticed how narrow and steep the stairs had become. He needed to lean heavily on his cane. Generations of pounding feet had left their mark: the stone was pitted, the woodwork chipped and scarred. As the students hurried past him, he recalled the faces and the voices of the young men who had occupied these rooms half a century before. The shouting and the clattering hadn't changed.

'Are you looking for someone?' a passing student asked.

'Only for myself,' Kemp smiled back.

'You must be Sir George. We are proud to have you back on staircase four.'

Weeks before, Kemp had asked Patton if, on this visit,

3

he could stay for a night or two in his old college rooms where he had spent three of the happiest years of his life. 'Dangerous sign of dotage. Comes to us all,' the Master had jested, but had granted his wish.

His old rooms were at the top. For a moment Kemp stood there panting, resting on his cane. He wondered if his decision to return to his rooms had been wise. Slowly, he unlocked the door, pushed it open with his shoulder and stepped inside. The light from the window filled the room. He looked around. Not only had the college shrunk, the room had shrunk too, infinitely so.

On leaving Arnold in 1939, he had carved his initials into the window seat while his fiancée had watched. He crossed the sunlit room and lifted the cushion. The initials were still there and the sight of them moved him. He ran his fingers across the 'G.K.'. How many hours had he spent in that room, occasionally raising his head to take in the river scene and watch a swan glide by? A homing pigeon had tapped politely on his window every day to be fed.

The sitting room was furnished much as he had left it: there was a battered couch and chairs, a table, lamps and rugs. A decorated oar hung above the fireplace. The room even smelled the same. The only unfamiliar thing was the electric fire. He recalled the old smoky coal fire – the chimney drew poorly, as it had done for several hundred years. On wintry days, he and his friends had toasted bread there. As darkness fell, and the walls became cold to the touch, he'd climb into his freezing bed. The thought of it now made him shiver. The rats had occasionally found their way in from the river in search of breadcrumbs and warmth.

On the table stood a bowl of fruit and a vase filled with anemones; against the flowers was a note: 'Welcome back to the college, Granddad,' signed Kate and Thomas.

Sir George hung his hat and coat behind the door and went into the bedroom. The window still looked to the open sky. One night he had climbed through it to sit on the roof. He was young then, and had felt an urge to fly to the stars. As he moved his bag off the bed, his attention was drawn to a photograph above the dresser on which was written: 'Arnold College, First Rowing Eight, 1939.' The eight rowers looked a fine-limbed lot – bright-eyed and bursting with life. Kemp stared at the cox and recognized himself. A large silver cup stood at his feet. Delicately traced across its front were crossed oars. How young he had looked, and how hand-some, even though he wasn't as tall as the others. It took a glance in the mirror to bring him back to his senses – half a century spent in the law courts had taken its toll. There were ten in the photo, including the coach, Harvey Childers. At his feet sat the crew's mascot, his black labrador, Brendan.

Sir George took the picture off the wall. Every one of the faces was etched in his memory. They had all come up to the university in 1936. He, Roger Blundell, Max Elsfield and Tony Markham had rowed together at Eton; Bill Clark had rowed at Harrow; and Alex Haverfield and Pat Riley at Rugby. David Evans had come up from Carmarthen Grammer School. He and Charley Bradbury were scholar-ship boys and the only ones who had not been to a public school. So far as rowing was concerned, Oxford was a finishing school for all of them. They had stood by their trunks with the other freshmen outside the porter's lodge before being sent to look for their rooms. They had answered the first roll-call: 'Blundell, sir; Bradbury, sir; Clark, sir; Elsfield, sir; Evans, sir; Haverfield, sir; Kemp, sir; Markham, sir; Riley, sir.' Except for Pat, who was already twenty-five, they had all been gawky youths.

That first night they had gone to the freshers' dinner. The cold, candlelit hall had filled them with apprehension. They had sat quietly through the Master's call for excellence. 'In war and peace,' he had ended, 'there is no challenge to which Arnold men have not risen, no height they have not scaled,

5

no sacrifice they have not made in the common good. I call upon you to match their greatness.' How still and quiet the hall had been when he finished. Head down, face deep in thought, with a rustle of his gown, the Master had returned to his seat from the rostrum. George had wondered what this greatness was they would be expected to show.

Replacing the photograph, Kemp returned to the window. There was a crew on the water, practising its stroke. 'Take ten,' the cox's voice rang out. His eyes followed the bright rings of water caused by the dipping blades. How quickly the boat sped by. Silver dripped from the oars. Why hadn't he noticed such beauty before?

About seven-thirty Kemp changed and crossed the quad. It was a still evening, the air pleasant and scented. Ancient college clocks struck the half-hour as he approached the brightly-lit Master's Lodgings. Dr and Mrs Patton welcomed him warmly, and introduced him to the other guests. Kemp thanked the Master for the photograph he had found on his bedroom wall. 'I knew you'd like to see the old crew after all this time,' Patton answered. He thought it best to leave it at that.

Just before eight, while still carrying on a conversation, the Master slowly migrated towards the door. The guests straggled after him in a loose line, crossed the quad and entered the crowded, noisy hall. Honoured visitors and the senior members of the college took their places at high table. Candlelight was reflected in the gold and silver plate and crystal. The lighted portraits of past leaders and benefactors of the college looked down wistfully from the dark panelled walls.

Among them, Kemp recognized his old law professor Brower, his face hidden behind an enormous moustache. Brower had spent his life at Arnold College working on an obscure aspect of Byzantine law. Everybody who was anybody in that field had waited with bated breath for his promised magnum opus. The book was always being

6

pronounced as good as finished, but not quite. Brower had even done research in Istanbul, whence – to everyone's surprise – he had returned with a delightful wife. His decision to marry had been wise, for Mrs Brower had later provided the college with a magnificent benefaction. When she first arrived, she gained immediate notoriety by plucking a chicken at her open window above the quad; feathers had drifted down on to the heads of startled staff and students. When Brower died it was discovered that there was no book, and there never had been. Still, there was his smiling portrait on the wall and by the strange way in which these things are decided, Brower had become one of the 'greats'.

About to take his seat, Kemp caught a glimpse of the college's memorial to those who had fallen in the wars of 1914–18 and 1939–45. As his eye moved down the silent list, the horrors and heartaches of the Second World War returned. These men hadn't died of the sum of their years; they had died in the springtide of life – before they had had time to live. He wondered how many students ever gave the names a second thought; no more, he suspected, than he himself had given to the dead of the First World War. For a moment he felt even older than he was. 'Blessed are the peacemakers,' he said to himself, 'for they shall be called the children of God.'

It was almost midnight when Kemp returned to his rooms. Some guests had lingered over their brandy, and he had found it difficult to get away. Staircase four was empty and silent, there was only a mouse about. With its usual shattering whirr and clang, the clock of Arnold College crashed out the hour as he closed his door.

Before retiring, Kemp sat on the window seat above the moonlit river. Irresistibly, he was drawn to the water as he had been in his student days. The trees swayed gently from shadow to light; the night was full of mysterious sounds; a nightingale vibrantly sang its sweet litany; voices of long ago filled the room; memories flooded back. He felt more secure and content than he had in ages. He was glad to be there.

While he was staring at the water he again heard a cox's voice: 'Take ten . . .' He got to his feet and searched for the vessel, but heard only the rattle of boat seats and the swish of oars. Perhaps I've dined unwisely, he thought. Whatever the cause of his hallucination, he decided it would be prudent to go to bed.

Once in bed, Sir George fell to wondering how his life had rushed by since he had slept in this room so long ago. The last thing he saw was the picture of the crew on the wall. The moonlight lit up their faces. He fell asleep in its glint.

A day or two later, having said goodbye to the Master, Sir George took the train to London. No sooner had he left than the original occupant of the rooms on staircase four hurriedly moved back in. When he entered his bedroom, the student was surprised to find a photograph of a rowing crew on the wall. 'Nineteen thirty-nine', he said, as he took it down. 'Whew! That's a long time ago.'

Later that day he gave the photograph to the head porter, Charles Reed. 'Either Sir George left it behind, or it belongs to the Master. Will you please pass it on?'

Reed studied the picture and pursed his lips, which he had a habit of doing. 'Ah, hum!' he said.

'Did you know them?' the student asked.

'Goodness me, no. They were before my time. I didn't come here until the early fifties. But I heard of them – they were Arnold's best. They were famous throughout the university, broke all records, they did. They were trained by a famous coach called . . . er . . . can't remember, doesn't matter.'

'What became of them?'

'What became of them? Well, that's a different story and a long one, too.'

1

George Kemp awoke with a start. Max Elsfield was tugging at his blankets. 'Get up, man! The others are waiting and you're not even dressed.'

Max shot out of the door, crossed the sitting room, and crashed down the stairs. George struggled out of bed, splashed some water on his face, threw on his boating clothes, stumbled over a pile of books, and ran after him. The rest of the crew stood at the foot of staircase four, shivering in the morning cold. The walls of the sleeping college loomed above them, dampness glistening on the stone.

Heavy college scarves around their necks, the crew jogged along the tow-path to their boatshed at Folly Bridge. The sky was still grey, the day had not yet vanquished the night; there was a touch of wind and rain in the air. Pat Riley led, Roger Blundell brought up the rear. Other joggers went by, exchanging a wave. Boats manned by four or eight rowers and several racing sculls were already on the water. Accompanying the creaking of the oars, coxes' voices could be heard as the boats glided by. A sailboat emerged from the mist and, ghost-like, drifted downstream.

Harvey Childers – rowing coach, tutor and father figure combined – had preceded them, wrapped up to his ears, on his squeaking bike. He had already unlocked the shed and was throwing a stick for his dog, Brendan. A stocky middle-aged figure with small twinkling eyes, grizzled eyebrows, broad forehead, strong mouth, grey moustache and a monk-like fringe of greying hair, Childers was the best rowing coach Oxford had produced in a long time. In his youth he had distinguished himself as a rower at Eton. He was one of Oxford's outstanding botanists. Shortly after joining Arnold, he had written several important papers on plant genetics which had caused quite a stir among botanists. Few knew as much as he did about fibrovascular bundles, the professional term for leaf veins. Needless to say, the crew was known as Childers' Bundles.

Amid yawns and light-hearted chatter, the men opened the groaning doors of the shed and lifted the long, frail craft into the water. The dog jumped about under their feet. They took care not to slip on the wet deck. Roger Blundell was telling them about a run-in he'd just had with the university police for flying somebody's underwear on the flagstaff above Magdalen Tower: 'I thought it was about time to shake up such a straitlaced crowd. "Name and college," the "bulldogs" asked, touching their bowlers as I touched the ground. Stung me for £20 they did. Said I'd damaged the walls.'

'That's not much to pay for being a clown,' Max commented. He had a way of demolishing people with his tongue.

While two of the men steadied the boat, the others climbed in and attached their oars to the row locks. George settled in the cox's seat and took up the tiller ropes. The oars were raised out of the water. Bent forward, arms outstretched, the crew awaited his command.

'Get ready. Are you ready? Row!'

Their dipping oars catching the first light, they rowed through patches of mist down the river towards Hinksey Lock. They rowed rhythmically and effortlessly, everybody on time, with maximum power in every stroke. With each pull, the cold turned to warmth. Etched in charcoal against the morning light, the coach and his dog followed on the tow-path, Brendan's spirited barking echoing along the bank. In the distance, the college spires caught the rising sun. Slowly, the mist dispersed.

As the river-bank slipped by, George the cox ran his eye down the boat. Sitting directly in front of him was Alex Haverfield, whose long, leisurely strokes set the rhythm for the crew. Six feet tall in his socks, and the most handsome among them, Alex was all muscle and dark magnificence. The way he knew what those behind him were doing came from a sixth sense. He was superb at setting the pace, and was fiercely self-confident in all he did. A week before he had been dealt a dreadful blow with the death of his father in a car accident in London. It had been a shock to the entire crew.

Behind Alex was Charley Bradbury, a scholarship boy from Scotland. He was powerfully built, of middling height, fresh-faced, brown-eyed and boasted a mop of brown hair. Before coming to Oxford, he had fished for a living. He had handled oars since he was a child, so rowing at the university was a natural choice.

Roger Blundell, who was behind Charley, was tall and thin as a rake, with a long neck, blue eyes and fair hair. He was the type who never seemed to grow up; laughter was never far from his eyes. One wondered what mischief he'd get up to next.

Roger was followed by naval cadet Bill Clark. Bill had a high forehead and unusually bright eyes. He was sparing with words and never asked questions, except when someone was talking about the sea. He was the sort of fellow who tended to get left behind.

After Bill came David Evans, a Welshman with dark eyes, a short, wide nose, a sensuous mouth, and a full black beard. He loved to sing. He was probably the brightest-minded of the lot; some thought him a mathematical genius. He had a habit of talking in riddles.

Max Elsfield, who sat behind David, was fabulously wealthy and a shameless egotist, who radiated energy. He had cold grey eyes, a wide, full-lipped mouth, prominent cheekbones and a narrow chin. His glossy black hair was parted down the middle.

Tony Markham, behind Max, was the right man in the right slot. A big-framed, manly, straightforward character, with steady eyes and a mouth that expressed strength, Tony had a bony, honest face without a shadow of pretence. A landed aristocrat, he was the same man whether he was selling cattle or mixing with the political nobs of Westminster. He wore tweeds so much that they couldn't imagine him wearing anything else – he even had a matching tweed cap. He and Max had shared rooms at Eton. They always backed each other up in their troubles. Tony was the most popular among the nine of them and lucky in everything he did.

Pat Riley, the Irishman in the prow, was tall, lean and sinewy. He had left Rugby by the time Alex arrived. He had long, brown, tousled hair and a lined, masculine face, which was always relaxed. As an oarsman, Childers the coach thought him a gem. Like Charley, he had learned his skills in a rowing boat off the Scottish coast. Why it wasn't the Irish coast was something that puzzled them all, and Pat made no effort to enlighten his friends: there was a hidden dimension to him that none of the crew could fathom. They were close to him despite the fact that he was five years older, and fond of him without really knowing him. Sometime earlier on (he never would say where or when), he must have dabbled in religion, for on Sundays he always went to Mass and there was at least one Irish bishop in his family. Beyond that, Pat kept his beliefs to himself. He had regular meetings with Walter Turnbull, the college chaplain, but none of them knew what they discussed and the crew had given up speculating about it.

George was in his element on the river. He had become cox more by accident than by intent, but had learnt to enjoy the job. It satisfied the bolder part of his nature. He watched the crew as they reached out from both sides of the boat with their long oars, leaving a trail of whirlpools behind. Whether rowing at Eton, where he was a contemporary of Roger, Max and Tony, or at Oxford, it gave him the greatest joy. In the past two years the crew had improved beyond measure. Yet there had been times when they had been sorely tested. He would never forget being in a fierce storm with thunder and lightning above their heads. They had been lucky to get their sinking boat to the bank. George loved the river's eternal movement; he loved the reflections of the overhanging trees; he loved the rhythm and the speed of the vessel and the feeling of a common purpose.

'You're dreaming again, George,' Alex said, smiling.

The cox was a strange mixture of day-dreaming and boldness. Alex and he had gone to different schools, but had become close friends. Next to Tony, Alex was George's favourite.

For the next hour Childers put them through their paces. 'Take twenty!' his deep and unhurried voice rang out from the tow-path. He gave the impression of having all the time in the world.

'Take twenty!' George repeated. 'Get ready. Are you ready?' The vessel skimmed away, the sound of the creaking rowlocks faded. Childers followed on his bike, assessing every move; he had a gift of taking in everything at a glance.

'Not a bad effort at all,' Childers called, coming to a halt, 'but you're not pulling back far enough. You're sitting on your buttocks instead of on your tails. Let's try again.

'Get ready, are you ready? One . . . two . . . three.' Once more, the boat sped away effortlessly.

'Better, much better,' the coach cried, pedalling after them. 'Don't slobber on the feather when coming back; keep your elbows close to your sides; keep your heads up and your shoulders loose. Don't trail the blades.' If he had to criticize an individual rower on the river – which he

13

usually avoided doing – Childers always did it by number. 'Number four,' he'd call out, 'you're leaning to the left.' Always calm, he exercised his authority effortlessly. The crew never questioned his word.

And so it went on, back and forth from Folly Bridge to Hinksey Lock. By then the dawn had given way to a lovely spring day.

After an hour, the rowers were exhausted and running with sweat; their bottoms were cramped. Despite years of rowing, some of them still felt pain in their shoulders, backs and hands. Only Childers seemed fresh. George wondered how anyone as old – he must have been pushing sixty – could pedal up and down the tow-path in all kinds of weather for the sheer joy of it. He knew from college gossip that Childers had been coaching a crew on the same stretch of the river, from the same tow-path, for the past thirty years! He never tired.

When they returned to the boathouse, Alex took two tennis balls out of his pocket. He always threw them for Brendan; the dog had come to expect it. Having rubbed the boat dry and returned it to the shed, the crew jogged back to college, where they shouted and laughed themselves hoarse in the bitterly cold showers – hot showers were provided only once a week. Still shivering, they dashed to breakfast in the freezing hall. Immediately afterwards, Bill and Pat jumped on their bikes and went to lectures; Charley went in search of books; the others worked in their rooms, the double doors of which shut out all sound.

Keeping a promise, George went along the corridor to Max's room to help him prepare his weekly essay. Their Eton days still bound them closely. It took some time before Max was ready to start. How he had ever enrolled for a degree that included history, no one would ever know. His concern was with the here-and-now.

'The first thing you have to realize about the Scientific Revolution, Max . . .'

'I don't give a damn about the Scientific Revolution, I just want to get this wretched essay off my back. I'll work my head off for something that interests me, but I've no time for the dead stuff.'

'But you've got to give a damn about the Scientific Revolution, it's how we all became rich. The way you're going, you'll never get through the exams. Where are your sources?'

'Sources? I make them up. You haven't heard of Professor Horsefutter? Good heavens, man, where have you been?'

'That's cheating, Max. You'll be out on your neck if they catch you. Remember, you are an Eton man.'

Later that day Max returned from his tutorial in high spirits.

'Did you get away with it?' George asked him.

'Of course, he swallowed Horsefutter, hook, line and sinker, but thought him outdated! He was solemn about it. Thank goodness that's done with. Now I face another nightmare: the Industrial Revolution.'

George enjoyed the joke but was appalled at Max's disregard for scholarship. His friend might be sharp and shrewd, but he was no academic.

At four o'clock the crew came together at the Childers's, where they were invited to tea every now and again. Mrs Childers, a plump, homely body, with delicate eyes, a large comb in her silver hair, and a floral print frock, was always ready to welcome them. She enjoyed their visits; the crew was the family the Childers's had never had. Yet they lived a singularly complete life – as calm and natural as the Constable prints on their walls.

No sooner were the young men seated than Mrs Childers pressed on them her muffins, scones and cakes. While rapidly consuming what she offered, they praised her baking to the sky. Brendan was surreptitiously given his share under the table. On special occasions, Mrs Childers set out her home-made bilberry wine.

2

The next afternoon Max Elsfield's mother appeared unexpectedly on staircase four. Lady Elsfield was a tall, thin, autocratic woman with a squeaky voice and an unappealing face. Like an afterglow of the Edwardian age, she wore a headdress of ostrich feathers and clouds of chiffon silk adorned with artificial orchids. A choker of pearls hid the lines on her neck. She was famous not only for her money but also for her soirées, which she held regularly at Elsfield House just off Park Lane. She enjoyed sharing confidences with the famous and those who wielded power; intrigue and secrecy stirred her blood.

Max dreaded his mother's visits and vanished the moment he saw her getting out of her chauffeur-driven car. He looked as if he had just remembered something and dashed off to get it. The crew was puzzled by their odd relationship. They knew that Max and his sister Hazel never went home during the holidays.

The crew lied about Max. She dismissed them with an imperious nod and spent the time visiting her cousin, Hugh Stably, who was dean of the college; he had recently tripped in the quad and bruised his chest. To the relief of all, her chauffeur eventually took her away. Unvanquished, she crossed the quad holding her head high.

No sooner had Lady Elsfield departed, than a thick-set, irritable gentleman, wearing a velvet-trimmed coat, elegant gloves and a bowler hat appeared at the foot of staircase four. This was Sir John Blundell looking for his son Roger. Hearing his father's voice and suspecting that he'd come to pick a bone with him about his latest clash with the dean, Roger rushed back into his rooms, threw up a window, climbed out and fled across the roof.

Sir John Blundell – head of a bank that had emerged from the ashes of the Great War – had discussed with his wife that morning what they should do with a son who involved himself in one fatuous, costly adventure after another. God forbid that he would do such stupid things when he joined the bank. How could he be a buffoon and expect to ever make a living?

Tony Markham offered to look for Roger, while Alex Haverfield engaged Sir John in conversation. Unable to find his son, Sir John paced the corridors, perspired with vexation, consulted his watch and snapped the lid shut. Finally, in a fever of impatience, having paid his compliments to the dean, he left in his glossy chauffeured car as quickly as he'd come – a course welcomed by the crew who feared that his rising colour might lead to apoplexy. The moment he had gone, Roger emerged from cover.

3

As the college clock struck ten the next morning, Tony Markham knocked on the dean's heavy oak door. The corridor was deserted. He and Roger Blundell were 'on the mat': Blundell for climbing Magdalen Tower, Markham because of tutors' complaints.

Tony opened the door to find Dr Stably at his desk, surrounded by books and papers. His face was pale. A white cat sat curled up on a chair beside him.

'Ah, Markham, yes, do take a seat,' the dean began, removing his oval wire-framed glasses and rubbing his watery eyes. 'Markham,' he went on, his voice heavy with thought, 'the college is afraid that you are going to fail your examinations. Your tutors tell me you are devoid of intellectual ambition. I'm told you rarely attend lectures or tutorials, and that your focus seems to be on rowing and politics, neither of which will get you through finals.' Beads of perspiration appeared on the dean's brow. He might have been saving Tony from sin.

Tony took it all in. He knew that Stably was a born grouch whom one had to put up with. Where Stably was concerned, he had learned to keep a still tongue. He had not come to Oxford to shine in examinations. What a thought! He was there because of family tradition and to enrich his mind. He didn't need to distinguish himself at Oxford to represent his county in Parliament; a degree in classics had nothing to do with administering the family estate. If he spent too much time on sport, as the dean insisted, it was because he was built that way. He got a sheer animal joy out of anything physical.

Fifteen minutes later, Tony was shown out of the dean's room. 'Terrible,' he said to Roger who was waiting to go in, 'the man has no blood.' Roger smoothed down his unruly hair. 'Now for it,' he muttered. He wore an expression of agonized culpability as he pushed the door open. He bent his tall figure so as not to overshadow the dean – Stably liked the cowed look. Roger closed the door slowly and sat down. He already felt hot. Did Stably know that the thick flannel underwear he had flown above Magdalen had come from Mrs Stably's washing line?

'Ah-h! Blundell, it's you again,' Stably said, looking up reproachfully. (Earlier, Roger had been 'sent down' for several weeks for blowing a trumpet in the quad in the dead of night.)

'Y-es, sir.'

'Blundell, you're here because you've become completely disconnected from university life. Your climbing of Magdalen College tower does not impress me one bit. I'm told that when the "bullers" tried to silence your singing at the top, you yelled: "I'll make as much racket as I damn well please." It's sad to see a young man like you going to the dogs. You've no respect for authority. Yet I must say I'm amazed at how much you've achieved in your studies with so little effort. Regardless, I can assure you that you'll disgrace yourself and the college when finals come. We simply can't have that, can we? There is such a thing as loyalty to Arnold, you know. Will you never grow up, Blundell?' Stably leaned back in his chair and sighed heavily. 'Hmm,' he answered himself. 'Probably not.'

Roger made no reply. He was too busy coping with the dean's relentless stare to defend himself. What on earth did an honours degree in history matter when his future lay in his father's counting house? But he knew from experience that he would never be allowed to explain anything to Stably. He had tried it once and hadn't succeeded in getting beyond 'Well, er . . .' He took his handkerchief out of his sleeve and wiped his brow.

'There's still time for you to revise your priorities, young man. You're doing too much rowing.'

Roger realized that it was pointless to tell the dean how much he enjoyed a sport where you could win by sliding backwards on your bottom. To be able to look in one direction and travel in the other took his fancy. Instead, he concentrated his attention on the dean's bow tie, which had slipped.

The dean, having talked himself out, showed Roger to the door. Roger knew he wouldn't shine in 'Schools', but he was confident he'd get through his finals. He'd have to – not least to prove the dean wrong. Once in the quad, he lit a cigarette and drew upon it heavily. 'Silly old bugger,' he laughed to himself. 'Worries himself to death.' He went along to Tony's rooms and had a drink.

At lunch in hall that day, George overheard the dean talking to Childers. His voice was a bit shrill.

'Harvey, you've got to get after Markham and Blundell, or they're going to disgrace us. They're on the river when they should be studying. I told them they'll have to leave if they don't pull up their socks. Can't have them failing on us.'

Harvey Childers didn't take Hugh Stably seriously. It was rubbish to talk about expelling a Markham heir, or the son of Sir John Blundell – not as long as the government relied upon Blundell money. Everybody at Arnold looked upon the dean, for whom all sport was a waste of time, as a dry old stick. 'I suppose the Duke of Wellington must have been talking through his hat, Hugh.'

'The Duke of Wellington, through his hat? What's that got to do with it?'

'I think he said that the Battle of Waterloo was won on the playing fields of Eton. Wellington thought it more important to produce character rather than intellect. In exams, he was himself a bit of a duffer.'

'We don't expect these fellows to win the Battle of Waterloo, Harvey. We expect them to pass their examinations. There's a danger of our losing sight of what really matters. They can't make their way in the world as rowers.'

4

Two weeks later, over beer on the college barge, Roger Blundell proudly announced that the Cambridge Cycling Club had accepted his challenge to a bike race. He was elated about it.

'What bike race?'

'Some time ago I read about a six-seater bike used by the Moscow Circus. It intrigued me. Anything done by the Russians, I thought, could be done better by us. So I did some research and got the Cambridge crowd interested.'

'Where will you find such a bike?'

'David and I are working on it. Only someone like David can build a bike like this. I bought six derelict bikes from Sergeant Fletcher – he's the one who booked me for the Magdalen Tower climb. The police have had them in their backyard for ages; they were glad to get rid of them. They're being welded together. We're removing the front forks from five of the bikes, and welding the head tubes to the seat tubes. The chain gave us the very devil of a problem, but David worked out that the cranksets on the middle bikes need chainrings on both sides of the bottom bracket to transfer power. Cambridge has done the same.'

'How many wheels?'

'Only two, and they have to be strengthened to take the weight. This reminds me, we shall have to train for the race.'

'Who's we?'

'Well, you don't expect me to pedal a six-seater all by myself, do you?'

'Haven't you got anything better to do?' Charley asked. 'The whole thing is mad.'

'Nothing wrong with it being mad; a little insanity is a good thing, Charley, as you may one day discover. Better than sitting about poring over books. The race is on All Fool's Day – three weeks on Wednesday.'

'I wonder how you're going to steer such a contraption? You'll have difficulty turning,' Max said.

'That's right, but only when the speed is too slow. Mum's the word though, until the morning of the race. By the time the "bulldogs" react, it will be over.'

Pat Riley, Alex Haverfield, Tony Markham, David Evans

and George Kemp agreed to join Roger. Bill Clark dithered; he didn't like to do things just for the hell of it.

As planned, at eleven-fifty on All Fool's Day, the two teams lined up their six-seater bicycles before the Sheldonian. Supporters had gathered with clappers and whistles. They began to block the morning traffic and fill the street. The Cambridge team had come over in a lorry. The riders all wore dark suits, white ties, gowns and mortar boards. Roger had a white carnation in his buttonhole. Max Elsfield moved slowly through the crowd in his Jaguar to clear the road; his car would lead the race.

At the crack of the starter's pistol, the teams raced across the street and went north on Parks Road. Shouting cyclists and several ragamuffins raced after them.

Cheered by the spectators, the riders gave it all they'd got. At South Parks Road they swerved their elongated contraptions around a scared horse and a cursing cart-driver. With a wobble and a wave, they rounded the corner of Keble College, and, following Max's car, entered Banbury Road. With gowns flapping, they raced neck and neck through the traffic in St Giles, past the Martyrs Memorial and St Mary Magdalen church, until they reached Cornmarket. People on the pavement stopped in surprise as the six-seaters flashed by. At Carfax, a startled policeman waved them on.

By the time they turned into the High, the Cambridge team was leading. But then luck deserted them. Narrowly avoiding a funeral hearse – for a moment the driver held his head in his hands – they ended up in a tangled heap on the pavement. Roger and his friends sped by.

Encouraged by cheering onlookers, Oxford kept its lead down the High. At Holywell, the Cambridge team caught up. By now, the riders were dripping with sweat; it streamed down their faces and into their open mouths.

Roger called for a final effort: 'Keep it up, fellows! Keep it up!' The finishing post was in sight. Max's Jaguar was a few yards ahead.

With a slight lead, Oxford shot out of Holywell on to the Broad. A shouting crowd greeted them. Bill Clark was out there waving. At that moment a highly polished car pulled out from the kerb. There was a crunch of metal and splintered glass as the Oxford six-seater went crashing into it. Roger was thrown across the hood; the rest of them finished up under the bike on the ground.

'Your bloody infantile tricks have ruined my car,' the driver cried. While a bruised Roger was blasting the fellow back again, a policeman came up and saluted smartly.

'Go easy, Roger,' George whispered, 'you're arguing with the chief constable.'

'The chief constable! Oh, my God! . . . I beg your pardon, sir!'

While Roger struggled to recover from his surprise, Cambridge pedalled by to victory.

5

That night the crew members gathered in Tony Markham's rooms; they were spacious, with lofty, ornate ceilings and high windows. Tony's father had used the same rooms many years before. Tony not only had the best rooms, with superior furnishings and carpets; he also had the best servant, aptly named Arthur Weasel. Weasel was one of those men who was as permanent as the chairs. He had won some kind of a decoration in the Great War.

They sat about reading the newspapers, talking sport, drinking and smoking. After their defeat in the bike race, they drank and smoked a little more than usual and had to open a window to let the fog out. Roger was nursing his bruises. Bill was glad he had stayed out of the race but held his tongue.

No sooner had they settled down, than an argument broke out between Charley and Max about the bike race. They were always getting on each other's nerves.

'You're a pain in the neck, Charley,' Max said. 'If we made fools of ourselves, that's our business. We don't tell you what to do. I don't know why the hell they let people like you in here.' Max had disliked Charley from the moment he saw him. He couldn't stand his tiresome harangues about poverty. He had no idea how the poor got by and he didn't want to know – especially not from Charley.

'You can go to hell,' Charley came back. There were times when Charley looked upon the others as a group of spoilt children who ate from a bowl of cherries. They were a good-hearted, misguided group, but deep down he resented their wealth. Yet, if he was going to row, he had to put up with them.

'Steady on, Charley,' said Tony, who always supported Max.

Max set aside the paper he was reading. His heated face turned ugly and twitched. His eyes flashed about restlessly. There was a hush in the room.

'Oh, chuck it, you two,' Roger jumped in. 'You're always at it. You're a wonderful fellow, Charley, and we all love you, but for goodness' sake stop being so serious. I wish everybody well, but I simply don't have your moral and social passion to do good; not on that scale. You're crazy to think that life can be neatly arranged according to your socialist ideals. Life is a farce. How else could we have crashed into the chief constable's car? Hey diddle diddle, The cat and the fiddle . . . And the dish ran away with the spoon.'

24

If the rest of the crew kept their peace, it was because Charley was the best oarsman they'd got. He never let them down; Childers never faulted him.

Several nights later, George and some of the crew came across Charley at an impromptu meeting outside St John's College. A knot of townspeople and students had gathered. Pressure lamps hung from the trees; so did the Red Flag.

The Scot was giving as good as he got when they arrived. His shirt was open at the neck; he wore corduroys and a neckerchief and was red in the face from shouting.

'What's socialism?' somebody bawled at him.

'Socialism means putting everything in its proper place. Greed, selfishness and upper-class privileges will be abolished. Socialism means food and jobs for all. Socialism means fair shares. For our generation, socialism is the only way out. For the world, it's socialism or chaos. Which do you want?'

'Hey, hang on, Charley,' Max interjected. Anybody could see that his blood was up. 'It's stupid to think that you can change society like you change your shirt. The idea that people are overflowing with compassion is absolute poppycock. People don't have time to listen to your pie-in-the-sky talk. They're too busy trying to make a living.' The less control the better, was Max's view of life.

There was a surge of shouts: 'Bravo! Well said.'

'Down with capitalist scum! Up the Red Flag!' somebody countered.

Charley went on to hammer Nazi Germany and praise the Soviet Union.

'If you think that Russia is a better place to live,' Max yelled at him, 'why the hell don't you go there? I'll pay your fare, cash down. The country would be better off to get rid of troublemakers like you.'

Suddenly, it began to rain heavily. Soaked, the two went on shouting wildly at each other through the blinding downpour as everybody else dashed for cover. Only when leaving did Max realize that he was carrying a furled umbrella. It infuriated him for the rest of the evening – he kept looking at the umbrella as if it had assaulted him.

6

A week later, to celebrate Bill Clark's twentieth birthday, the crew rowed the boat up the Thames to swim in one of the weirs. They threw off their clothes and, deaf to the lock-keeper's shout, repeatedly leapt off the weir gate into the seething foam. Later they lay naked in the sunlit meadow, chewing grass, talking about rowing, and yarning about anything that came to mind. Through half-closed eyes, they watched the butterflies flitting about, and the cows ambling by. They laid bets on who could catch a butterfly first – Alex Haverfield, the winner, opened his fist and the brightly coloured insect flew away. They listened to the chorus of birds and bumblebees. David Evans sang; he was the leading chorister at Arnold College.

If the nine crew members were worried about examinations, they didn't show it. Their futures could not have been more reassuring. Bill and Alex would follow their fathers, one into the navy, the other into the army. Roger Blundell would join his father in finance; George Kemp would pursue a legal career, in the family tradition. Max would be absorbed into the Elsfield business empire. Tony Markham and Charley Bradbury would go into politics. David, everyone agreed, would become a professor. Pat Riley was anybody's guess but no one doubted that he would fall on his feet. Except for Charley, peace and affluence were things they took for granted.

A towel fight having broken out, the men jumped to their feet and chased each other through the thick grass, yelling and flicking each others' rumps. Breathlessly, they eventually flung themselves down among the buttercups and daisies, at ease with the world and one another. Theirs was the pure, happy wine of youth.

Among other topics, girlfriends came in for a ribbing. Tony had just surprised them all by announcing his engagement, so he was the first to come under attack.

'Time you started courting, Bill,' Alex called to Bill, who was known for his prudish ways. 'You don't know what you're missing.'

Bill was as shy of women as Alex was bold. They had never known Bill to have a girlfriend. You've got plenty of time, his mother had said. He was one of those odd people who believed in chastity before marriage; the sensual disturbed him.

'Go to Russia, Bill, where love is free,' Charley quipped.

'Nonsense!' Max snapped. 'Love is for the wets. It's money that makes the world go round. Get money and all other things will be added unto you.'

As they rowed home, the setting sun cast its rays across their boat. David began to sing 'This old man . . . he played one . . .' The others joined in: 'he played two, he played nick-nack on my shoe . . .' They caught a glimpse of the university's towers and ancient stone walls; the sound of muffled bells reached them across the fields.

That night, as usual, they came together in Tony's rooms. The ever-resourceful Weasel marched in bearing a cake with twenty burning candles. They all sang 'Happy Birthday, Bill,' and gave him a wristwatch. Bill's face glowed as he stammered his thanks. 'It's jolly decent of you all. I shall always treasure it.' He wasn't good with words, and hated being the centre of attention. Amidst cheers, he blew out the flames.

Several days later Alex Haverfield took the crew for tea at his home in Woodstock, eight miles from Oxford. It was a solid manor house standing among trees at the end of a gravelled drive. Mrs Haverfield was a nervous, grey-haired widow, dressed in black. Alex was her only child. The men expressed their condolences.

'I can't get over the fact that he should have died in a car accident, after all he'd been through in the war,' she said.

Alex showed his friends his father's Victoria Cross hanging in a silver frame in the study. For Britain's highest honour in battle it was surprisingly plain. An impressive portrait of Haverfield senior in his colonel's uniform stood on the desk. On the wall in a glass frame was a quotation from the *Iliad*: 'Glory in war is life's highest honour.' 'God is with us,' someone had written alongside it. One could see why Alex was always on about leadership, duty and honour; and why he was not only bright, but combative. His father had brought him up to believe that Britain had a God-sent mission to rule and redeem the world. Imperialism was in the family blood: Alex's ancestors had planted the British flag around the globe, which Alex thought was a good and proper thing to do.

Evelyn Haverfield without her husband was like a ship without a rudder. The young peoples' talk about the world situation unnerved her. 'What do you think, Alex?' she asked, pulling on her handkerchief. 'Will it come to blows?'

'Of course not, Mother.'

Oblivious of Alex's attempt to protect his mother, David went on to show how the present wars in Spain and China were rehearsals for a much wider war. 'Generals like to test weapons before mass-producing them,' he said.

7

The preliminary rounds of the Head of the River Race, stretching from Wednesday to Wednesday in the middle of

June 1938, left Arnold College where Childers expected it to be: in the final against Exeter College. The two teams had overtaken and bumped more boats than any of the others.

In the final race, despite Arnold's efforts, they had lost. They had rowed magnificently, but Exeter had made an incredible recovery from behind, and had snatched the victory away – in 1938 Exeter was unbeatable and unstoppable. In contrast to its fine show in the early stages, Arnold's final rally had been ragged. It was Exeter's day; the crowd howled their delight.

Max was furious; he couldn't bear to lose, it affected his pride. 'You went out too far on the bend,' he accused George when they were changing on the barge after the race. 'You were blind, deaf and dumb to Exeter's moves. Damned asleep you were. We lost because we didn't have a cox.' He was beside himself with anger.

'Oh shut up, Max, for Christ's sake,' Alex said. 'Things are bad enough without having you going on.'

A flush of anger darkened George's face. There were times when he found Max quite impossible, now and again at Eton there had been ructions between them. Pat had to pin Max's arms to his sides to prevent a fight. 'If you two don't behave I'll bang your heads together,' he threatened, as he struggled to keep them apart. The oldest among them, it fell to him to enforce order.

Secretly, Max's slur bothered George. While he didn't want to broadcast it, he knew he had let the side down. He had not responded quickly enough to Exeter's threat and it worried him.

Childers was disappointed about the race. Kemp had allowed several opportunities to slip by; they'd have to try again next summer. If they had rowed as they had done the day before, when they flew down the river, they would have won easily. It had been a bad day. Even the weather had failed them.

David, as he had a habit of doing, explained their defeat by means of an equation. 'If skin drag is proportional to the square of the velocity . . .' he began, but no one was listening.

Prematurely, the crew had arranged a victory party on the college barge that night and they stuck to it. The barge's blazing lights were reflected in the water, the upper deck had been cleared for dancing. The figurehead of an almost naked nymph was brightly lit. Tony Markham's sisters, Gloria, Helen and Penelope, and his fiancée, Lydia Turner, came skipping along the tow-path in their long dresses, bubbling with excitement and laughter. Nineteen-year-old Lydia was an attractive blonde with a happy, open face. As soon as the guests were assembled on the top deck, the champagne corks popped and everyone toasted Tony and Lydia's engagement. The faces of the betrothed were bright with joy. Tony and Lydia's childhood friendship had become an all-consuming love.

With a flurry, the five-man band began to play. Chatting merrily, Penelope, the youngest of Tony's sisters, followed Pat Riley to the dance floor. A pretty brunette, with nut-brown eyes, her face expressed confidence and self-will. The *enfant terrible* of the Markham family, Penelope was never still, never quiet, never walking when she could run. Her curiosity could be excessive. She was preparing to go to university and couldn't make up her mind what to study. She thought Pat dashing in evening dress. She felt distressingly young alongside him. 'My brother tells me you are a mysterious person,' she giggled.

'He means I'm not dull,' he responded, with half-amused eyes.

She tilted her head and gazed at him with impish delight. She loved to put people on the wrong foot. She had heard that no one knew anything about Pat – except that he had a large private income and property in Ireland, which he never visited.

Helen Markham, the middle sister, was plain. She was as introverted as Penelope was outgoing. A brunette with dreamy eyes and a homely bearing, she accepted David Evans's invitation to dance, blushing and ill at ease. David had met her once at Cambridge where she hoped to study archaeology. She thought him brilliant.

The oldest of Tony's three sisters, Gloria, took the floor with Roger Blundell. An exceptionally good-looking twenty-year-old with a fine figure, Gloria felt responsible for her two sisters. She taught at a kindergarten close to their home and had known Roger for years. A happy-go-lucky young pair with an abundant zest for life, everybody thought them crazy. Nothing pleased them so much as the absurd. Looking at her now under the stars, Roger wondered how Gloria had become such an attractive young woman. Why hadn't he noticed it before? For the first time, he felt possessive towards her. Gloria must have felt the same because she agreed to accompany him to the theatre the following week.

Max had come without a partner: he kept himself free of romantic attachments. Having stood about with a fixed gaze that saw nothing, he danced with his sister Hazel, who had come over from Cambridge where she was studying Slavonic languages. Hazel was a mouse-like creature who dressed indifferently and won all the scholarships. She found the conversation at the party uninteresting, but at least she was not as prickly as her brother.

Bill Clark danced as if he was wearing a wooden suit. He was hopeless at making conversation with women. You could rely on Bill never to get drunk.

Charley Bradbury's arrival in a tuxedo, with Lord Randall's daughter Victoria on his arm, caused quite a stir. Victoria, one of the dark beauties of the university, was also one of the richest young women there. She had a high fore-head and a strong, self-possessed face; there was nothing wishy-washy about her. Tony, who knew her well, contended that she was bored with her upper-class existence. She and Charley had never been seen together before and the crew wondered where they could have met. Charley was always too busy swotting. He looked uncomfortable in evening dress, but Victoria, so the rumour went during the evening, would settle for nothing less. She wore a simple, elegant, grey silk dress; she could have worn anything and still looked aristocratic. In greeting everyone, Charley and Victoria pretended not to notice Max.

'Can't imagine what she sees in that working-class prig. Where the hell did he get those clothes?' Max grumped to those around him. 'First time I've seen him pretending to be a toff.'

'Don't be envious,' George chided. 'Socially speaking they're certainly an odd couple, but you've only got to look at them to see how happy they are together. I must say, a tuxedo makes a world of difference to Charley – he looks like a duke.'

Good-looking Alex was there with a girl no one knew. He often brought along girlfriends, but didn't seem to have more than a superficial acquaintance with any of them.

Pat and Penelope sparked off each other. While the others watched and clapped, they danced a number which Pat had picked up on his travels in America. The more he swung his partner around, the happier she looked. Her chatter didn't interfere with their stride. Their step was so spirited, they went at such a pace, the wonder is they didn't dance right off the barge into the river. Going wild was obviously Penelope's heaven – she always gave the impression that something exciting was about to happen. They never missed a dance, except when Pat took a turn at the drums. This was the beginning of Penelope's first great romance.

Sometime during the evening Roger sat at the piano to sing with Gloria:

> Life is a song, let's sing it together . . .
> Hoping the song lasts for a long, long time . . .
> Let's sing together and make life a song.

The others joined in. They seemed to forget that Exeter had just defeated them on the river. By the interval they were all out of breath. Dancers lingered on the top deck to get some air – a fresh night breeze had sprung up – before joining the crowd for supper downstairs in the 'house'. George talked with Victoria Randall, whom he found pleasant but serious; the idea of putting the world straight seemed to obsess her. He thought it odd that anyone so good-looking should be so wrapped up in politics. She seemed eminently sure of herself. Penelope and Pat, who had overheard some of the conversation, thought Victoria quite dotty – bonkers, in fact.

The second half of the dance was more enjoyable than the first. It was an occasion which, for sheer joy, would linger in their minds for a long time afterwards. To wild cheering, the evening ended with the 'Tiger Rag'. There was a strange stillness once the band and the dancing had stopped.

The ladies were escorted along the tow-path to the Randolph Hotel for a light breakfast. The stars were disappearing, Oxford was beginning to stir. With Pat at her side, Penelope seemed as fresh as ever, jumping about like a cricket. On the Broad they were brought down to earth by a newsagent's placard which read: CHAMBERLAIN WARNS GERMANY NOT TO ATTACK CZECHOSLOVAKIA.

'Time's running out,' Alex said, pointing to the notice. 'Now is the time for all good men to join the OTC.'

'You'll have to run hard to catch me,' Charley told him.

'I'm suspicious of anyone who hopes to make a living out of fighting. Besides, the Officers Training Corps is for the nobs.'

When the time came for the Markham women to return to Ansfield, Penelope protested. 'I'm not going home. I want to stay several more days.'

'You are going home,' said Gloria, 'whether you like it or not. Into the car you go.'

Penelope resented being mothered by her elder sister, but knew better than to defy her. 'Oxford is going to miss me,' she sighed, twirling around, and waving to Pat until the Markham car passed from view.

On returning from their practice session on the river the next morning, George Kemp, Tony Markham and David Evans talked about joining the University Air Squadron. With war looming, they felt an obligation – as everybody did – to join something. To join up was like catching a fever. They didn't need Alex to tell them that it was a matter of duty. They knew that Oxford and Cambridge students were pouring into the RAF. David was pragmatic about it: it was an opportunity to learn to fly. He hoped to find some scientific work later on. George had a strange feeling that the RAF might help him to make his mark in his own way. It was the first time he'd had the chance: his life had been mapped out in detail by his parents since the age of five. The RAF might be a refreshing alternative to the grinding legal career that faced him.

8

Some days later, at the end of June 1938, the crew made their final row before leaving for the summer vacation. At

Childers' request, all of them were expected to do exercises while they were away from Oxford: to become Head of the River, one had to remain on top form. Roger Blundell, Alex Haverfield, Tony Markham and Pat Riley headed for the Swiss Alps to make an attempt on the North Wall of the Eiger, which climbers had been trying to conquer for a hundred years. They'd been planning the climb the whole term.

Bill Clark went back to Portsmouth for further training. For generations, his male ancestors had gone to sea and his father couldn't imagine that his son would do anything else; nor, for that matter, could Bill. His vivid image of success was to be captain of a battleship, as his father had been. He loved naval discipline; he liked its constancy and was happy to be told what to do.

Max Elsfield disappeared with his sister Hazel, leaving no trace.

David Evans stayed in Oxford to prepare for his attempt to win one of the fellowships offered annually by All Souls College to students who had just graduated. Such a fellowship was considered a bull's eye. He felt that he owed it to himself and to his family to try for one – they had put a lot of money into his education, which they couldn't really afford. An added incentive to stay in Oxford was that Helen Markham would be working in the Bodleian Library that summer.

Prompted by their socialist beliefs, Charley Bradbury and Victoria Randall went to work among the Cockney poor at Toynbee Hall in East London. It was known at the university as 'going slumming' – the rest of the crew thought it a strange way to spend a long vacation.

His suitcase loaded with books recommended by Professor Brower, George Kemp staggered off to spend the summer with a German family, the Krämers, in Cologne, where he hoped to improve his German. His father, who handled a good deal of German legal business in London, which he hoped to pass on to George one day, had arranged the visit.

George made the journey overnight from Harwich to the Hook of Holland. He had reserved a sleeping berth and went to bed with a book after dinner but, unable to sleep, he decided to go on deck. The ship's prow cleaving through the water, the pulsating engines, the flashing lights of other vessels excited him, but it was too blustery to stay there. On returning to his berth, he was surprised to find it occupied. When he prodded the snoring figure, the man fought him off. George spent the rest of the night walking round the deck trying to keep warm. It was a relief when the grey dawn came and the coast of Holland, with its long, irregular string of lights, rose out of the sea.

From the Hook, George took the express train to Cologne. He had been to Germany as a boy, but never since the Nazis had come to power. On reaching the frontier he was confronted by an enormous banner proclaiming: EIN VOLK, EIN REICH, EIN FÜHRER. Why do the Germans have to be so strident? he wondered. The uniformed officials on the platform struck him as tight and stiff. From the dining car, where he breakfasted, the countryside looked clean and tidy, there were flowers and flags everywhere. An extraordinary variety of villages, towns, cornfields, meadows, vineyards, orchards, woods, lakes, farms, churches, castles, and the occasional military convoy slipped by. Now and again, workers in the fields waved to the passing train.

Approaching Cologne, George caught a glimpse of the Rhine and the cathedral, whose spire towered above the dark water. He was relieved to find Frau Krämer waiting for him, as arranged, outside the station master's office. Small in stature, she was elegantly dressed in a dark-blue costume, had a soft voice, large, pensive blue eyes and a friendly manner. Unusual for her age, she had pink cheeks, and thick brown hair. '*Herzlich willkommen,*' she greeted

George. In halting German, he thanked her for inviting him, but the noise of passing trains drowned their conversation.

They took a taxi to the Krämers' house, which was not far from the cathedral. On arrival, George was shown to his room, which looked out on to linden trees. A Dürer woodcut of a hare hung on the wall; a bowl of flowers stood on the table; the furniture was heavy and dark. He thought the room comfortable, if slightly formal. By the bed was an English translation of Dostoevsky's *The Brothers Karamazov* in which someone had marked emphatic agreements in the margins.

At lunch George was introduced to the rest of the family; all of them spoke English. Herr Krämer was a small, sandy-haired, bespectacled individual with an extraordinarily fine face, and a friendly manner. He was dressed in a dark suit and a stiff white shirt with a stand-up collar. He taught law at the university, and at one time had worked closely with George's father in London. George knew that Krämer was a much-sought-after legal consultant, who commanded the highest respect.

The Krämers had two daughters – Johanna and Brigitte. Johanna was a student at Cologne University. Small and fair, she had a beautiful oval-shaped face, a delicate nose, the brightest brown eyes and a gentle voice. Her gleaming straw-coloured hair reached down to her shoulders; her breasts pushed invitingly against her silk dress. Johanna was one of the loveliest girls George had met; he stared at her with such fascination that the poor girl blushed.

'*Was studieren Sie?*' he asked.

'*Anglistik.*'

'*Was ist das?*'

Johanna's eyes danced with merriment. 'English,' she said.

It was George's turn to redden. Johanna was sorry she had taken advantage of him. She apologized.

Brigitte was two years younger. She had the same bright

brown eyes, the same fine skin, and the same attractive smile. She also had the grace and comeliness of her mother and sister. The freckles on her nose were becoming; equally beguiling was the pigtail she wore. There was a look of expectancy on her face.

In the weeks that followed, George tried to get down to his vacation reading, but much of it seemed meaningless. He couldn't make up his mind whether he wished to become a lawyer or not; it was something his father wanted him to do. The hours dragged as he tried to make sense of his law books – by the time he had reached Sir William Blackstone's famous *Commentaries*, he found himself day-dreaming.

Now and again, to give George a break from his studies, he and Johanna cycled out to a promontory overlooking the river where they watched the Cologne University crew practising on the water. George thought them splendid, and was glad that they were not competitors at Oxford. He was happiest when talking about boats and for the first time in her life, Johanna tried to show an interest in them, too.

At weekends, the family visited the surrounding country-side with its manicured fields, its scented hay and its vineyards. Often on their travels they'd stop at an inn and dine in its tree-shaded garden. The summer evenings never seemed to end. George's German improved by the day, but the two girls went into fits of laughter at his peculiar accent. They took leisurely cruises on the Rhine, stopping at riverside towns with their ancient buildings. Sometimes they'd be shunted aside, while a cavalcade of Nazis, dressed in black leather jackets, noisily rushed by. Politics was very much in the air in the summer of 1938; the wireless was never silent about the wrongs being done to the Germans in Czechoslovakia. Threats and counter-threats filled the newspapers.

They spent August in a large country house near the Tittisee in the Black Forest, where the Krämers had been going for years. A forest on this scale was something new to George: trees and thickets lined the twisting dirt roads; the sky was sometimes no more than a blue patch in the overhanging branches. He was exhilarated by the beauty of the steep valleys, the round-topped hills, the springs and the pure woodland solitude. It was a relief to get away from banners and demonstrations, and the eternal '*Sieg Heil*', which disturbed George. Yet even in the picturesque little villages Nazi posters were prominently displayed.

George and Johanna took long hikes together. Frau Krämer had balked a little at their going off alone, but had then agreed. One Sunday they attended Mass in Freiburg's cathedral. Small clouds of incense rose from the high altar. Afterwards they climbed the long winding staircase to the top of the magnificent Gothic spire.

The two young people took great joy in helping each other to master another language. Talking about their studies, it emerged that Johanna knew a great deal more about English literature than George did. They also discussed politics. She told him that she had never thought about politics until Hitler came to power. 'At first, the Nazis were like fireworks, they startled us. Processions and rallies were an everyday occurrence; it was all very demanding and very exciting. It gave us young people new hope; everything was going to get better – Germany would become important again. I was brought back to earth one day when a company of brown-shirted Storm Troopers clashed with communist demonstrators in front of our house. The communists – carrying red banners and placards demanding bread and freedom – sang the '*Rote Fahne*'; the Nazis – left hand on belt buckle – sang the '*Horst Wessel Lied*'.

'Cornets blaring, drums beating, belts and buckles flying, there followed the wildest clash between the communists and the Nazis under my bedroom window. The communists got the worst of it. Those that could, fled. The street was littered with kettledrums, cornets and torn flags.

'Later, we joined everybody else to do what we could to help. The brutal way the brown-shirts treated the communists horrified and disgusted me; it turned me against the Nazis for good. I realized that I had nothing in common with them. Fortunately a downpour in the night washed the bloodstained cobblestones clean.'

One day, having raced down a path, George and Johanna stood panting beneath a scented pine. For a moment, they gazed at each other. It was unusual for them to be silent. Johanna's hair blew across her face. George gently parted it and, drawing her close, kissed her smiling lips. He kissed her again. Johanna was overwhelmed, she could do nothing but return his kisses.

'Do you think he loves me?' she asked her sister in the early hours of the next morning.

'Of course,' Brigitte answered, with all the faith and trust of a child. 'You're lucky to have met someone like George. How resourceful of you to have studied English.' Johanna hugged her sister out of sheer delight and the two girls went on talking about the English visitor until dawn. In the next room George passed a sleepless night, too, listening to the sounds in the house and wondering what had come over him.

By the end of August, when they returned to Cologne, George and Johanna had eyes only for each other. Their every word and gesture had come to have meaning; a world was in a glance.

9

George Kemp was not the only one to fall in love that summer. Working together in the slums of East London,

Charley Bradbury and Victoria Randall had become increasingly close. Yet there was a point in their relationship beyond which Charley would not go. Every time Victoria hinted at becoming engaged, he would go off at a tangent and talk about something else. How could he possibly marry a lord's daughter when his pockets were empty? Besides, Victoria's privileged lifestyle would choke him.

Falling in love had come as a surprise to Victoria and she was not going to be put off; she was used to getting her own way. She didn't believe in free love; she had seen what happened to those of her friends who did. She was a socialist, but not where marriage was concerned – strong marriages were just as important to socialist societies as to any other and she felt not to acknowledge this had been one of the more serious mistakes made by the Russian communists. She knew Charley's views; she intended to change them.

On their last day in London, she arranged a picnic in Hyde Park. Sitting on the grass, the pair laughed and talked. As Victoria kept filling Charley's glass with wine they became oblivious to other couples and the passage of time.

As the sun began to sink behind the trees, Victoria gently rested her head on Charley's shoulder. 'Don't you think we should become engaged before we part?' she whispered. 'It would make the rest of the summer easier to bear.' She looked up into his face longingly, and held him with her eyes.

His mind a bit of a blur, Charley forgot his socialist principles about marriages being bourgeois. Under her gaze, he felt his options narrowing. 'You're right, Victoria,' he finally agreed, kissing her. 'I'll buy you a ring. I've enough money for a simple one.'

'Charley, you're wonderful.' Victoria hugged him and they kissed passionately.

They spent the night together in a hotel in the West End, calling themselves Mr and Mrs Ward. Charley felt uncomfortable about it. The hotel was also beyond his means; the money they were asking was outrageous. Despite Charley's protests, Victoria paid the bill without hesitation.

It was the first time they had made love with such abandon; they felt more drawn to each other than ever. Their social status may have been poles apart, but their love united them.

The next morning Charley sent a telegram to his parents telling them of his engagement and saying that he was bringing Victoria home to meet them. They had never heard of her before.

Instead of Victoria returning to her home at Charlton Manor in Hampshire, the couple took the overnight train to Inverness. They shared a sleeper; she again insisted on paying the bill. Lost in their dream world, they were oblivious to the drumming of the wheels and the engine's whistle, which pierced the night, as well as to the flashing lights of the stations through which they passed. A rattling bus took them from Inverness to the coast; the last leg of the journey was across a yellow, gorse-covered moor.

'There's Castleton,' Charley pointed from the crest of a hill. Victoria looked down towards the shore and was overwhelmed by the light and space. The village consisted of several streets of slate-roofed, squat, grey cottages and a tiny church. Some houses appeared to be within reach of the sea-spray and even though it was summer, coils of smoke rose above their roofs. Men were sitting on upturned boats mending nets; other nets were drying on poles. Children and barking dogs chased each other across the beach. For the first time, Charley saw Castleton with different eyes. How small it was! How confining! How remote!

The Bradburys' cottage was one of four in a narrow,

unpaved street. Its rough, unfinished stone, low door, small bottle-glass windows and gaunt, ugly chimney gave it an uninviting look. From behind the lace curtains – where they had stood for some time – Jane Bradbury and her husband Ben watched the couple coming down the street. The hardy Bradburys were ill at ease in their Sunday best. Ben's face was pitted and stained by the weather; so too were his hands. The deep wrinkles round his sea-grey eyes spoke of the sun's glare. By the time Charley and Victoria reached the cottage, the door was wide open. Charley was their only child, and they'd welcome any woman he brought home.

Although Victoria received a warm reception, there was a temporary awkwardness. 'I don't know whether I should curtsey or give you a good handshake,' said the older woman. She looked directly into Victoria's eyes.

'A handshake would be delightful.'

The first thing they did was to toast the couple's engagement with home-made wine. 'We hope you'll be very happy,' said Charley's mother. Victoria found Jane's sunny disposition, her glorious black hair and her soft voice attractive. Ben, pipe in hand, apart from uttering 'ach' and 'aye', and giving the odd slow smile, said little. He had returned from the Great War almost dumb. He was the most peacefully satisfied man Victoria had ever met. Unlike his son, he had no desire to change the world.

Charley's mother showed Victoria around the cottage, which consisted of a small living room, two bedrooms and a tiny kitchen. The flagged floor was covered with woollen rugs; on the whitewashed walls was a framed quotation from the Bible: 'My house is built upon a rock.' Two shiny pottery dogs stared down from the mantelpiece; a brown cat sat on one of the two rocking chairs; a peat fire burned in the grate; on the hob a kettle steamed. A grocer's calendar decorated the whitewashed kitchen wall. The mast of Ben's boat, its furled sail and his fishing tackle could be seen through the back window.

Sitting by the fire that night Jane spoke of the hardships and joys of living in Castleton. 'Our living comes from the sea, but we have to pay for it,' she said. 'Boats are wrecked, villagers drowned. Some the sea gives back, others it keeps. It took Charley's younger brother.' There was a pause as she remembered the dark, winding cortège moving silently across the sand. 'Sometimes the sea roars and rages for days on end. The chimneys here may look ugly, but they are the only kind that can withstand the howling winter gales. But there's a brighter side: the calm comes, the tide gently washes in and out, the mists clear and the boats are launched. It is a great day when the Isle of Lewis suddenly appears on the horizon.'

'I can't speak ill of the sea,' said Ben. 'Her wickedness is not intended.'

They slept that night to the low thunder of the surf and the wind's lament. Charley's parents went to sleep talking about the young lovers. His mother wept silently for her only child; to link their family with an aristocrat's was too much for Jane to grasp.

Charley had given up his bed to Victoria, and slept on the hearth rug before the fire. When she looked out of the window the next morning, there were wisps of mist about and the waves were still crashing on the beach. An endless grey ocean stretched into the distance; the wind whistled through the cracks in the window-pane. The hoarse cries of seagulls mingled with the wailing of the sea.

During the next two days, the news got around that Charley Bradbury had brought home a lord's daughter, to whom he was engaged. 'Ha' ye ever heard of sich?' the locals said. Many a curtain was twitched to catch a glimpse of Victoria. Her wealth was exaggerated a hundred times. Some said it wouldn't be long before Charley reached Westminster. He was the bright one of the village.

When they met the white-haired vicar of Castleton, he congratulated them on their engagement. He was truly joyful for their sake. Charley thanked him for helping him to get to Oxford but, not wanting to hurt the man's feelings, avoided telling him that he had stopped going to church. There were times in the conversation when Victoria feared that the truth would emerge, but it didn't. Charley was spared telling the vicar that he had abandoned the idea that salvation can only come through God's grace. He now believed that human changes would right human wrongs, that a life of reason would replace a life of faith. It had come to him as a revelation during a lecture on philosophy, when he had suddenly realized that he couldn't be an ardent Christian and an ardent socialist at the same time. Victoria knew that socialism was a vision to which Charley was totally committed. The chaplain of Arnold College, Walter Turnbull, had taken great pains to rid him of such false notions. 'Faith, not reason, must always come first,' he had told Charley. 'Heart first, mind next, my dear boy; passion, not intellect. Where would the Bible be without passion?' Charley didn't reveal his loss of faith to his parents either, both of whom were Christian to the bottom of their hearts.

It was a relief to Charley when the vicar steered the conversation towards rowing. As an old Oxford rower, he couldn't hear enough about Arnold's chances of becoming Head of the River. Other topics were dismissed; even the growing threat of war passed without comment.

On the fourth day, Victoria rang up for a taxi to take her back to Inverness. She was beginning to feel a burden to the Bradburys in their tiny cottage. When she tried to leave a small gift to offset the extra cost of her visit, neither Jane nor Ben would hear of it. She embraced Charley and waved from the taxi as it drove away. Charley remained behind to get down to his summer reading; he owed it to his parents and the vicar to do well at Oxford.

As the train headed south, Victoria reflected on her visit to Castleton. Charley's people were simple, but not without true pride. They had a natural vitality which she found enviable. Charley himself was a bit rough on the outside, but completely sound within, indeed she looked upon it as a sign of strength. Nobody could equal him with oars in his hands. She preferred his rough edges to the superciliousness of other suitors. When she had first heard him speaking to the Labour Club at Oxford she had found his talk remarkably refreshing; indeed, she had been captivated by it. His Scottish accent made Charley even more attractive. For the first time, she had fallen deeply in love.

She particularly liked Charley's habit of saying what he thought. Only with the vicar and his parents had he shown discretion. She had been brought up to believe that it was bad form to say what you thought. When you did, you were shushed. You always had to say what was fitting, and that depended on many things. She also admired Charley for the way in which he expressed his thoughts as they came to him, not after the life had gone out of them. How such a man had withstood the scrutiny of the Admissions' Board at Oxford was anybody's guess. He had got used to people saying 'My God, what are you doing here?' with their eyes. A few years earlier, a rigid social hierarchy would have excluded him altogether. The main thing was that he possessed the sense of action which Victoria sought. What greater purpose than to join Charley in his efforts to create a socialist commonwealth of the world? She knew in her heart and mind that he would rise to prominence in the Labour movement – he had the talent, the strength and the vision. What couldn't they achieve together!

A rude awakening awaited Victoria when she arrived home. Her parents refused to recognize the engagement. There was a harrowing meeting between father and daughter in Lord Randall's book-lined study. 'A man without family and property is unthinkable,' he fumed. 'We'd be the object of ridicule. Have you thought about it? Do you realize what you're doing?' He cocked his head to one side and stared at her. 'We Randalls are not free to do as we like, or have what we want. The richer you are, you will discover, the more difficult life is. Rarely have I had what I wanted in life. We didn't send you to Oxford to marry a poor fisherman, Victoria. We never dreamt you'd meet such a man there. He might be the best rower and a fine man, as you say, but he's not our kind. You're letting your emotions run away with you, my dear.'

Victoria listened tearfully. 'I'm not a child any more,' she struck back. 'I'm tired of being paired off with some society drip. Charley Bradbury will outstrip all of them in time. In your fear of the working class, you're a prisoner of the past.' In a temper, she ran out of the room.

The family scenes were too much for Lady Randall, who took to her bed. She was delighted at the idea of a wedding, but family rows struck her dumb.

A special meeting of the wider Randall family was convened. They arrived wagging their serious heads – none of them approved of Charley. 'A socialist who dreams of rooting out evil in the world! A man of no property! What is the family coming to?'

Later on, there was a fractious meeting in Lord Randall's London office between himself and Charley. Beak-nosed, with hands clasped behind him and his jaw set, Lord Randall paced the floor like a tiger. Charley thought him appalling.

'If my daughter marries you, I'll cut her off without a penny,' he threatened. To ensure that his point was taken, he slapped the palm of one hand sharply against the other. 'You're not going to climb the political ladder on the strength of my name.' Not for a moment did he share his daughter's belief that Charley would go on to do great things, neither was he impressed with Charley's feats on the river. Being an outstanding rower didn't necessarily mean that he would make a good son-in-law. He frowned at the thought.

'Keep your penny,' Charley answered and walked out.

Victoria was undeterred by her parents' attitude. The prospect of marrying Charley was the most exciting thing she could imagine. 'He is the strongest and most interesting man I've ever met,' she told them, 'and is totally committed to what he is doing. I have never met a man with such promise. He means everything to me, I've never felt so alive. No matter what you say, I wouldn't dream of giving him up. I don't measure him by class – over which he had no choice – I measure him by the affection that exists between us. I would have eloped with him earlier if he had been willing. Yes, he's that good.'

10

Meanwhile, the crew's mountain climbers Roger Blundell, Alex Haverfield, Tony Markham and Pat Riley – had reached the Eiger. They were staying in a whitewashed inn at Grindelwald in the Bernese Oberland, from which they looked out on to the unassailable North Wall, soaring thirteen thousand feet above them. The snow-covered peak reflected the bright sunshine. Two highly skilled Italian climbers had been trapped by a blizzard on the exposed face, and had plunged to their deaths only days before: weather was everything on the Eiger. Tony and Roger occupied the room these climbers had used; the maid eyed them darkly. But the deaths did not cause the Oxford men to change their plans. The innkeeper – keeping his thoughts to himself – insisted on taking their photograph before they climbed.

Once they had decided on a strategy, the four left Grindelwald to pitch a cluster of tents in a meadow close to the wall. They were never free of a gaggle of summer onlookers. Brimming with confidence and new-found energy, they made exploratory climbs and portaged what supplies they would need. They left ropes in place to regain height later. They planned to make four bivouacs to the top and two coming down. Some stores were left at the foot of the wall, others were carried farther up the mountain. Humping stores and gear was a back-breaking chore which none of them enjoyed but, thanks to Childers, they were as fit as they ever would be.

In the early hours of 18 June, they began their ascent. The moonlit wall loomed above them. Each climbed independently, unroped, with a heavy backpack. Their aim was to spend the night at a campsite used by previous climbers. Everything around them looked grey. Pat led; he was the finest climber among them. None of them understood him completely, but they all admired him. In scaling the mountain's first defences, he never broke his stride or his rhythm. He knew which move to make; where to find handholds and footholds. The swing of his axe never faltered. His companions followed, impressed by his skill and his resourcefulness.

Early in the day Riley met with an impassable crevice. It left him frustrated and gasping for breath. They watched as he struggled to make his way out of the gully and up the wall. The other three roped up together and braced themselves to stop his fall if he slipped. There were moments when they could neither hear his voice nor see him.

Minutes later, a great 'Yahoo!' sounded above them as the Irishman succeeded in scaling the wall. 'Up you come!' he shouted as he pulled his companions up and over a particularly sharp-looking overhang. The last one up was Roger, who got stuck halfway. The rope was in danger of fraying against the jagged rock. He dangled perilously in the air until they freed him.

'A marvellous view,' was all he said.

With the weather holding, they climbed higher, Roger now roped with Tony, Alex with Pat. The first two had been together at Eton; the other two were linked through schooldays at Rugby. As they gained height, the rising sun flooded the wall with light. The remaining patches of fog quickly disappeared. In places the rock turned to orange and gold. It reminded Tony of the sun playing upon the walls of a cathedral. There followed a particularly difficult chimney, where they had to belay each other and their packs to the top.

With crampons clamped to their boots, they began to traverse their first icefield. 'Slow down,' Pat called back. 'There's nothing to hang on to here and the ice is too hard for pitons. Watch your feet,' he repeated. A piece of rock came away in his hand. Now and again a stone went hissing by. Danger was ever-present – it kept them on the alert.

Shortly after Alex had taken over the lead in the afternoon of the first day, they reached a dead end among the overhanging rocks and slowed to a crawl. 'Almost impossible here,' Alex called back, as he tried to inch his way forward. 'There are no handholds.' He was a strong, skilled and fearless climber, and a natural leader, but his muscles were beginning to cramp; his stamina was not what it had been several hours earlier. Breathing became more difficult.

It was Tony who eventually found a way around. With

the help of a piton driven in before the overhang, sometimes swinging like a pendulum, he worked his way foot
by foot into the overhanging cliff. It was an incredible
performance, which the others cheered. He anchored a line
for his friends to follow; from there, they climbed straight
up an icefield running with water and threatened by falling
stones.

Later in the day, they found a sheltered ledge where they
stopped to rest, eat and melt ice for much-needed drinks.
Only then did they have the opportunity to marvel at the
sun-dazzled view of the valley below. Perched as they were,
they might have been eagles. In the far distance, a train was
trailing a wisp of smoke. They studied the bright sky and
kept their fingers crossed.

By the time they reached their first night's bivouac they
were exhausted and wet through. The last patches of
sunlight on the snow had long since disappeared. The choice
lay between sleeping under an overhanging rock from which
water dripped, or fastening themselves to a ledge and taking
their chances with the falling stones. On the Eiger stones
fell all the time.

Despite hot food and drink, and the shelter of their tent-
sacks, the night was long and miserable. The biting cold
pierced everything – feet, hands, nose and ears were the worst.

A storm struck the next day. It began with dark clouds,
deafening thunder and lurid flashes of lightning. Within
minutes, the sky was in tumult. The wind's growing roar
blotted out the noise of avalanches and falling stones. All
they could do was hang on grimly and wait for the turbu-
lence to pass.

When the storm unleashed a barrage of hail, Alex lost
his balance. 'My God,' Pat shouted, as the falling figure
missed him by inches. A line snaked past. They waited for
a shout and prepared to take the strain on the rope. When

it came, it dug deeply into their shoulders and gloved hands. They repeatedly called 'Are you all right, Alex?' but received no answer. They feared he might have broken his neck.

Pat went back in search of him; Tony and Roger paid out the rope. After a long wait, to their huge relief they saw the two men climbing painfully towards them. Alex had landed in a patch of deep snow and was extricated by Riley, unhurt. A headache was his only complaint. 'Give us notice next time you intend to fall, Alex,' Pat shouted into the wind. 'It can happen to any of us, Pat,' Tony shouted back. They pushed on as soon as the storm abated.

They spent the next night in their tent-sacks fastened to a ledge not much more than an arm's length across. Their vision reduced to a few feet, they somehow managed to clear the ledge and prepare hot porridge and scalding tea. Hanging on to the cliff in their tent-sacks, with some coughing and tightness of the throat, they once more saw the shivering night through. Again, apart from the odd cussing, there was little talk. Even Roger kept his jokes to himself.

At dawn, they filled themselves with hot food and drink again. As the light improved, they pushed on; they still had a third of the way to go. 'The higher we get, the safer we will be,' Roger declared. 'There are too many damned stones about for my liking.'

At that moment there was a thump and a loud cry. Alex stood bent over, dripping blood. Despite his light helmet and snow-glasses, a stone had gashed his face between the temple and the upper left cheekbone. Up close, the wound looked forbidding, and would need stitching. Yet the stone had not damaged his eye; there were no broken bones.

While Pat and Tony staunched the flow of blood and cleaned the jagged wound, the four men discussed their options.

'You can't stop now,' Alex protested when one of them suggested turning back. 'You must go on. I can get down by myself.' As he complained of feeling dizzy and threw up within minutes, that option was quickly dismissed. He could never get down on his own; in his shaky condition, climbing higher was equally impossible.

'Rotten bloody luck,' he kept saying. 'Fancy a bloody little stone changing everything.' He looked pale.

'Oh, Alex, shut up,' Pat exploded. 'There's trouble enough without having to listen to you.'

The irony was that the longer they stood there arguing, the better the weather became. The storm passed; the wind fell to a murmur; the sky promised stable weather.

'Let's have a hot drink,' Tony proposed. 'If you feel fit enough after resting, Alex, we'll go on. If you don't, we'll retreat. It will take the three of us to get you down.'

After hunkering down for half an hour on a ledge, Alex was still nauseated and confused. Pat reluctantly gave the order to retreat.

'Your job is to go on,' Alex protested.

'I'm in charge here, Alex.'

'Damn you, Pat.'

'Damn you too, Alex.' The tension between the two would-be leaders was palpable.

They returned the way they had come, rappelling Alex down the worst places. They had to keep him moving against the freezing cold. Although Pat seemed gifted at finding and using the tracks they had made coming up, the descent seemed endless. They couldn't risk a bivouac with Alex as he was. There were times when they were compelled to move an inch at a time. Their hands became swollen and they collected a variety of cuts and bruises. Tempers wore thin, but Pat kept them going. He never lost command, and he could outswear them all.

When they reached the foot of the wall in the early hours of the next day, they could hardly stand. Alex was still disoriented and wearily numb. Disregarding his protests, Pat dragged him to the inn at Grindelwald. From there Pat accompanied him to a hospital at Grimsel, where Alex was stitched up and kept in until the following day for observation.

The following afternoon, their muscles still aching, they took the overnight train from Zürich to the English Channel. They were disappointed at having failed to conquer the Eiger's North Wall, but consoled themselves that they had done the best they could, and had come close to succeeding. They swore they would try again.

On arrival in London, the climbers had a wild night on the town at Pat's expense: he had just won a large sum on a horse in Liverpool. He outdrank them all and, for once, there was no talk of war. Instead, in answer to a question from Roger, Pat opened up for the first time about his past. After the death of his parents, he had found it difficult to settle anywhere. With money to spare, he drifted across Europe and North America. None of the crew had travelled as far as he. Eventually, Scotland had attracted him, especially the Isle of Mull. Mountaineering became the substitute for his adventures on the road.

'What brought you to Oxford?' Tony asked.

'I promised my father I'd try to get there. I also needed the mental discipline.'

George Kemp had no sooner heard from Tony of their failure to reach the top of the Eiger's North Wall than the German papers were full of the triumph of an Austrian team of climbers.

11

Without telling the rest of the crew, Max and Hazel Elsfield had gone to Morocco. Marrakesh was a favourite haunt of his. Down the ages, Phoenicians, Carthaginians, Romans, Arabs, black Africans, Muslims, Jews, indigenous Berbers and European colonizers had all been drawn there. As a result Marrakesh, once the capital of a vast Berber empire, had become a microcosm of many worlds.

By arrangement, they were met at the airport. 'Welcome back,' the driver greeted Max, dipping his head and opening the car door. 'Allah has favoured you. You and your sister are now the honoured guests of the Mamounia Hotel.' Honoured guests, Elsfield knew, were those who never questioned their bills.

Surrounded by braying donkeys and camels, and begging children, who seemed to rise out of the ground, the Elsfields were whisked away past pink clay buildings into a labyrinth of twisting streets and unending alleyways. When the car was brought to a halt by horse-drawn carriages, they caught glimpses of potters, coppersmiths and other metal-workers bending over tasks as old as time. The smell of leather and clay filled the air. Lighted shop windows displayed silver-work, jewellery, bolts of brilliant silk, fine carpets and racks of blue pottery. Blue-veiled women, barefoot children and men wearing the long hooded jellaba were caught in the car's headlights. Veiled men poured water from black sheepskin bags for camels resting under eucalyptus trees. Now and again they passed crowded hovels made of corrugated iron, cardboard and scraps of wood. The sound of drums and reedy pipes accompanied them most of the way.

Marrakesh was hidden behind a high crenellated red wall. Once inside the old city, they joined a stream of vehicles and pedestrians and at last reached the palm-ringed, brightly lit Mamounia, where they were greeted by an elaborately-dressed major-domo. Aromas of saffron and sandalwood met them in the pillared hall, only the sound of splashing water and the low hum of voices could be heard. They were shown to their rooms by one of the hotel staff wearing a striped jellaba and bejewelled slippers.

The first thing Hazel saw on entering her suite was the dark mass of the Atlas Mountains framed in the window. Her brother had insisted on taking rooms from which they could watch the sun's golden light slowly die in the snow-covered mountain passes. The sight was one of the wonders of the world. Before the aide left, he gracefully swung a censer of sandalwood and bowed.

That night they enjoyed the hotel's unmatched cuisine. A dark-eyed Berber played a lute at their table. Hazel found the atmosphere intoxicating. By the time they retired to their rooms, the cold mountain air had begun to creep through the shutters. The tiled floors were heated. Clip-clopping carriages could be heard in the streets.

Each day after that they woke to the muezzin's call: '*Allah akbar, Allah akbar, Allah akbar.*' (God is great.) Four more times during the day the call was repeated. Morocco is unique among the countries of North Africa, in that it was conquered by the Arab word – not by the sword.

Accompanied by the water-pedlar's jingling bells, and the muezzin's cry, Hazel was introduced by her brother to the life of Marrakesh. She couldn't get enough of the colourful markets, some of them hundreds of years old. In the teeming bazaar she bought silver jewellery, leather goods, amber beads and carved wood. As she marvelled at the elaborate Arabic calligraphy on walls and doors, she became conscious of Morocco's artistic soul.

Each night the main square came alive. There were musicians, dancers with their swirling veils, story- and fortune-tellers, fire-eaters, acrobats and spell-binders. For a price, you could buy a spell that would wreak havoc in an enemy's life. With grimy hands extended, beggars sat quietly in corners awaiting alms. On impulse, Max and his sister decided to have their fortunes told. Silver was exchanged.

Looking at their hands, the fortune-teller suddenly feigned illness. 'You will both be very happy,' he croaked, all the while gently ushering them out of his tent. 'Death will brush past you, but the heavens will defend you. You will marry for love.'

'You're a lying bastard,' Max accused him. The man bowed deeply. When he raised his head, he gave Max such a piercing look that he felt it in his bones. His face twitched. He was shocked into silence.

Hazel was so intrigued by the tall minarets she could see from her window, that Max took her to the Koutoubia Mosque. Its massive inscribed doors dated back five hundred years. Not far from the mosque were the churches and temples of other faiths. They strolled through the Majorelle Garden, which they both thought an earthly paradise. The sound of running water refreshed them in the heat.

In the chauffeured limousine, brother and sister penetrated the bare foothills to go skiing in the mountains. Later they made trips to ancient Fez with its crenellated walls, and to the metropolis of Casablanca, where they spoke French and dined to the sound of Flamenco guitars. At Rabat they watched the monarch leading the weekly prayers – *bismillah* – in Allah's name. Wherever they went, life was vibrant. They became accustomed to Morocco's red earth, to its colourful fields of ripe barley and wheat, to its date and olive groves, to its vineyards and cork forests, and to the many scents of which saffron and sandalwood were prominent. Once they rode across a flat stony plain to the edge of the Sahara, where sand and silence filled the parched air. On the way back they were halted by a burial party carrying a wrapped corpse on their shoulders. The Mamounia Hotel remained a restful oasis to which they were always glad to return.

It was at the Mamounia that Max and Hazel became

acquainted with a middle-aged Bulgarian count. He had sent a bottle of the finest wine to their table, and claimed to have known their father. He introduced himself as Evrid Stamboliisky. The charm and grace he displayed, his luminous blue eyes, and his rich head of grey hair attracted Hazel, who conversed with him in Russian. He wore an eyeglass. He was always on hand whenever Hazel wanted to dance. His attentions added excitement to her stay. He gave the impression of great wealth so Max was surprised when Stamboliisky took the same plane as Hazel to London, where he was to take up a university appointment in Bulgarian studies. The man was quite boastful about it. Max didn't know what to make of him.

Just prior to Max's departure from Marrakesh he met a friend of his mother's, the actress Lucy Warner.

12

Throughout the summer of 1938 George kept in touch with Bill Clark who was at Naval Headquarters in Portsmouth, where he had joined his Cambridge friend, Peter Fry. They had trained together the previous summer, and had been trying to get together ever since. Both men were about the same age and build. They shared a stifling cabin on the training ship *Endeavour* lying in the crowded harbour, a stone's throw from Nelson's flagship, *HMS Victory*. Whenever they could get away, they went rowing up the coast.

At the end of the summer Bill and Peter made a trial voyage in a destroyer to Scapa Flow in the Orkney Islands off the north coast of Scotland; other warships took part. Their commission as sub-lieutenants depended on it. A hawk-faced, formidable ruffian, Captain Talbot RN, was the chief examiner.

Conditions were rough; training and discipline relentless. Daily they fired their guns at targets towed by tugs. The flashes of the guns at night staggered them. They also hunted a friendly RN submarine. One night 'Action Stations' was sounded. Alarm bells rang, ladders and decks echoed to running feet, the crew took up their positions, awaiting command. In the mock battle that followed, Bill and Peter fought off the attacking submarines and aircraft, rescued survivors from a supposedly sinking ship, provided first aid to the 'wounded', and guarded the convoy from further attack. As they struggled to exercise command, penetrating criticism from Talbot filled the air. 'It's preferable to make your decisions before the ship sinks, gentlemen,' he'd cry. Bill was glad to have Peter to rely on; he was the more mature and decisive of the two, and Bill knew it.

Quiet watches followed, under a star-filled sky. With the purple shadows gathering, and their ship gently ploughing its way through a phosphorescent sea, the dark outline of islands and hills to port slipped by.

Their make-believe war ended at Scapa Flow, where they anchored among the guardians of Britain's lifelines to the world. The mobilization of the British fleet was under way. Bill had never seen such sea power before, emotion and awe overwhelmed him. It made him feel proud to be part of it; this was where he belonged.

One night Bill watched his father's old ship, the mighty *Hood*, going to sea, its lamp winking at the land. Low in the water, its decks awash, it quickly slid out of sight. It was the pride of the Royal Navy, and Bill had a secret ambition to join it. Peter already had a posting to the vessel.

Captain Talbot reluctantly conceded to the resident admiral at Scapa that Bill and Peter had done well in the exercises. Bill was proud to have satisfied the navy, and quickly sent a telegram to his father: 'I've won my commission!' Knowing what his success would mean to his family, he thanked God for it.

One morning that autumn, with war threatening over Czechoslovakia, Bill and Peter were mobilized to active duty. The prospect of being suddenly thrown into action gave Bill a jolt. 'It's the first time that the threat of war has come home to me,' he told Peter. 'I got so used to practising that I thought it was the real thing.' He and Peter remained with the fleet in port until the crisis between Germany and Czechoslovakia over the Sudetenland was resolved. At least there was plenty to drink and few dull dogs at Scapa.

13

The longer George stayed in Germany, the more surprised he was by the vibrancy and brightness he found everywhere. There were none of the sad, sullen faces that Alex had predicted. On the contrary, there was a feeling of newborn strength. Everyday life in Germany expressed pride in a fresh beginning; nobody was out of a job; confidence filled the air.

While in Cologne, George made his first serious attempt to keep a diary. He not only recorded the extraordinary vitality of the German people, but now and again expressed his misgivings. 'There's a note of hysteria in the press,' he wrote. 'Fear of another war is much greater here than in Britain, Nazi demonstrations are unending, like a drumbeat. You can't go far in Cologne without meeting parades of one kind or another. Nazi doctrine holds that superior Aryan people have the right to crush lesser humans. Jews, communists, and anybody else who happens to get in the way are considered *Untermenschen* (lesser humans). Flesh and blood are what matter – not intellectual reasoning. There's a lot of vague talk about creating a master race, but nothing about compassion and the brotherhood of man. It puzzles me rather than frightens me; most of it is above my head.'

As the days passed, George and Johanna grew closer and closer. They were delighted with each other. 'I don't know how I ever lived without you,' he told her one day. Her answer was to embrace him. Neither had been so happy before.

One night a middle-aged clergyman came bursting in on the Krämers as they were sitting down to their evening meal. The man appeared confused and agitated; his lined face gave the impression of carrying a heavy burden. '*Verzeit mir dass ich Euch so ins Haus falle.*' (Forgive me for coming unannounced.)

'Bernd!' Herr Krämer exclaimed, jumping up from the dining table and embracing the cleric. 'Yes, yes, of course,' he muttered and then waved the man upstairs where they could talk privately. Frau Krämer seemed bewildered. The visit was obviously embarrassing to her. 'It's my uncle,' Johanna whispered to George.

That night, the family gathered in the living room. 'Bernd has been sheltering Jews and other dissidents and is on the run,' Herr Krämer revealed. 'He's in danger of his life and doesn't know where to turn. The trouble with Bernd is that he is too trusting. In the beginning, he didn't think the worst of Hitler. I did. Any man who believes that he has an exalted destiny to fulfil, and does not hesitate to use force to attain it, needs watching.'

'Then how do you explain why there is such tremendous enthusiasm for him?' George asked.

'Hitler expresses strength, and a strong man is always

preferred. His book is called *Mein Kampf*. The Germans' one desire in 1933, when Hitler came to power, was to escape the chaos that ravaged our country. He put into words what many Germans were thinking. His magnetic personality made people follow him blindly. As a corporal with two Iron Crosses, he also has the support of the military. Under his leadership, there's been a resurgence of national pride and prosperity. Millions of people have found work. The Nazi policy of bread and circuses, and work for everybody, has carried all before it. The main thing influencing public opinion is Hitler's promise that he will not go to war, and the Germans believe him.'

'And the price?'

'The price, of course, is fear and the loss of freedom. What bothers me is the way some people rejoice at being enslaved.'

Frau Krämer was fearful of her husband's unburdening himself to George, her face reflected her anxiety. 'It is dangerous to talk to a foreigner like that,' she said to him when they were alone. Before they retired that night, she asked George not to repeat outside the house anything her husband had said.

'You have my word,' he promised.

The visitor stayed upstairs for several days. Ilse, the housekeeper, took him his meals and kept a closed mouth. Several strangers came and went. There were no introductions, no questions asked. Everybody was relieved when Bernd left the house. He was not mentioned again.

A few days later, the Krämers and George were invited to the home of Graf Böll, a lifelong friend of Frau Krämer and a senior member of the Department of Foreign Affairs. He was fiftyish and a bachelor, and was reputed to be tight-lipped and sharp. Herr Krämer was reluctant to accept the invitation. 'You're too hard on Böll,' his wife scolded him. 'It's foolish not to keep a friend at court.'

'I want nothing to do with him. To curry favour with those I loathe is unacceptable. Somebody has to take a stand.'

'I know him better than you. He's not a true Nazi. Like so many others, he's guarding his job.'

'I'll come to the dinner party, but I doubt I'll enjoy it.'

Despite growing shortages, the meal was a lavish affair, beautifully served. During the meal, Böll made passing reference to Krämer's recently published paper on democracy and the rule of law. 'What you say is better left unsaid,' he advised. 'Authority is the basis of the state. The Nazis will look upon you as someone who prefers anarchy to order.'

'Time will bear me out,' Krämer observed.

After all he had heard about him, George was interested to meet Böll. Although a man of few words, he found him unusually gracious. Böll's intelligence and elegance were impressive. Before the party broke up he asked George a few shrewd questions about conditions in Britain. 'A heavy-weight,' Kemp wrote in his diary later on.

Herr Krämer ignored Böll's 'Heil Hitler' when they left. At Böll's feet was his inseparable dachshund Fifi.

The Sudetenland crisis at the end of the summer of 1938 brought George's summer reading to an end. War loomed. The British consul in Cologne told him to return to England. He couldn't make up his mind about it. Instead, he sat around day after day with Johanna and her family, reading the papers, listening to the radio, and hoping that peace would prevail. Johanna helped him make sense of what was going on in the press.

'Every war begins by wearing a mask,' Herr Krämer explained. 'The difficulty in life, as you will discover, is distinguishing what *is* from what *seems to be*.'

'It doesn't help to talk to George in riddles, Harald,' Frau Krämer scolded.

George knew from BBC broadcasts and telephone

messages from home that war was close. His parents had urged him to return at once, on the telephone they sounded afraid.

The two lovers thought the growing war fever utterly mad – especially as they were on opposite sides.

At the end of September 1938, when George was due to return to Oxford, the British, the Germans, the French and the Italians met at Munich to find an alternative to war. When a jubilant Prime Minister Chamberlain returned to Britain waving a piece of paper that promised 'peace in our time', the whole world expressed relief. Chamberlain's picture was in every newspaper. At long last he had turned back the tide of war. The British and the Germans sang his praises in the streets; the press in both countries called him a hero. That night George went out with Johanna and other students to celebrate – the town went mad. With peace at hand, nobody wanted to go home to sleep.

Munich was the end of innocence for Herr Krämer and many of his kind; the war he had thought inconceivable had almost come about. In spite of the celebrations, the Krämers, like many Germans, now swung from one extreme to the other: from thinking that war was impossible to thinking that it was imminent. Hurriedly, they began to store food.

The Czech crisis solved, George could no longer put off his departure. Johanna and Brigitte saw him off at Cologne railway station. Their fresh young faces and their striking light-coloured dresses made them conspicuous among the hurrying crowd. A military band was playing on the platform; steam rose above the engine. It was hard for him to leave – doubly hard for him to say goodbye to Johanna. Much to his embarrassment, she gave him a red rose as he climbed aboard the train. As an Englishman, George was too self-conscious to know what to do with it – it never occurred to him to put it in his buttonhole. Instead, he hung on to it, awkwardly.

With the train hooting and about to depart, and last-minute passengers scrambling aboard, George wondered how he could possibly leave Johanna behind. As long as they were together they were immortal; their love would conquer all, and last for ever. She had become his world. He was tempted to reach down, gather her up in his arms, and carry her off to England; the expectant look on Johanna's face convinced him that that was what she was hoping he would do.

Johanna's hand remained in his until the moving train parted them. After that (with Brigitte trailing behind) she kept up with the train's slow, lumbering movements, refusing to be left behind. '*Gute Reise und auf Wiedersehen, George*,' she called from the steam-shrouded platform. Above her head hung a large swastika. He waved back with his rose. 'Goodbye Johanna, I'll be back soon.' Her brave, tear-stained face and waving handkerchief faded in the distance.

14

On the crew's return to Oxford at the beginning of October 1938, they found Childers waiting for them. Almost before they had unpacked, he launched them on a new training programme. His bike began to creak along the river-bank again. Weather permitting, they were in the boat most dawns and dusks. June 1939 would be their last chance to win the Head-of-the-River Race. That month they would graduate and leave Childers and the university for good.

After an initial surge of activity with the coach, the crew

managed to get together on the college barge to exchange news. Over drinks, George told his friends about his experiences in Cologne, though to avoid arguments with Alex, he toned down his enthusiasm for much of what he had seen. Pat Riley was back from Mull in the Inner Hebrides, he looked fit. The gossip was that he and Penelope Markham were meeting regularly in London, but when asked, Tony knew nothing about it. Pat was tight-lipped. All they knew was that he had gone from one mountain to another, with plenty of money to spare. Roger had had enough of the Eiger. 'We were mad to take it on.' To Pat's annoyance, Alex still had a guilty conscience about having let the side down.

'It's over, Alex, for God's sake. You're not the only one to be hit by a stone. We didn't reach the top and that's that. Let's forget it. We'll try again.' Apart from a small scar on his temple, Alex was none the worse for the mishap. Bill Clark returned to Oxford with salt blisters on his hands; the navy still used ropes. He was never quite at ease once he'd left the sea behind. Max Elsfield had come home bronzed. David Evans had stayed in Oxford. He had had a very happy summer with Helen Markham.

All except Max congratulated Victoria and Charley on their engagement. They knew them so well that they could only wish them great happiness, the social difficulties that faced them were their own affair. Max resented Charley marrying into one of the richest families in England and sulked.

Overriding everything else was the growing threat of war. Recruiting posters were on every college noticeboard. It pleased Alex that the OTC had begun to fill up. 'We'll be at war within a year,' he predicted.

Some time in November 1938 George Kemp, Tony Markham and David Evans volunteered to join the University Air

Squadron at Kidlington, a few miles outside Oxford. After a lot of vague talk and heart-searching, they had made up their minds. There was an aura about the RAF that drew the three. Evans hoped that his pilot training would only be temporary, and that his scientific ability would be made use of elsewhere. George did not seek his parents' approval; he feared they would have other plans for him.

At the air base they were put into a machine that spun them around. As none of them got dizzy or experienced double vision, they were accepted. Commitment, skill, intelligence, courage, stamina, sharp eyesight and quick reflexes were what the RAF was looking for. During the week that followed, with scores of other recruits, they filled out masses of forms, underwent medical and dental examinations, were inoculated against all kinds of diseases, and staggered about under mountains of newly issued kit, including drab uniforms. They were required to be at Kidlington on Monday and Friday afternoons.

They began their training by grappling with devices that measured speed, climb, descent, turn, bank, balance, brakes, height and direction. Information about fuel supply, oil pressure and engine temperature was considered child's play and was dismissed in an afternoon. As the weeks passed, with mental energies sagging, they also did crash courses in map-reading, navigation, aerial photography, communications and reconnaissance. David was obsessed with the boring detail and did not hesitate to pick holes in it; he shone at solving problems. All the others wanted to do was to fly. The thunder of arriving and departing aircraft at the base grew as Britain prepared for war.

Alex Haverfield got a certain satisfaction out of the war fever. He was the only one who talked about heroism. If he ever gave a thought to the havoc war causes, he never mentioned it. He spent an increasing amount of time on the firing range, he did extra drills, and he was forever quoting from the OTC's *Manual of Arms*. Head up, shoulders braced, brasses polished, he looked gallant in his uniform. David Evans accused him of strutting. 'Pride goeth before destruction,' he joked.

Roger Blundell looked upon the threat as a bore, but was persuaded by Alex to join the OTC. 'No choice, old boy: members of the upper crust are expected to lead; it's what our fathers did. Either you make up your own mind, or the army will make it up for you; Hobson's choice, old boy. We'll defend Britain and earn a little glory on the side, you'll see. "Oh talk not to me of a name great in story; the days of our youth are the days of our glory."'

'I do believe you're slightly mad, Alex. I don't see anything thrilling in the prospect of war,' Roger retorted sharply.

Bill Clark knew that he could be called up at a moment's notice. Max held back, so did Pat Riley. 'What the heck,' Pat shrugged when he was pressed at one of their meetings, 'I haven't made up my mind. Don't worry about me. The Irish are not likely to stay out of a fight.' Max knew how to fly and was sure the RAF would accept him for training.

'You'll be taken by the nose as they took our fathers in 1914,' Charley Bradbury told them. 'It will be another capitalist war.' He was unable to disguise his contempt for the military.

'Better to be taken by the nose than to be cowardly and shirk our duty,' was Max's reply. Childers remained silent when the matter of military obligations was brought up. He knew that they didn't have the slightest idea what they were letting themselves in for; like all young people, they weren't interested in what might happen to them after they had joined up. He recalled sadly what had happened to those who had gone to France with him in 1914: a vision of creating a better world had lured most of them to their deaths.

The crew's days were over-full, studying to pass their exams, rowing, exercising, and training for a possible war.

15

Day after day, through October, November and into December, the crew was hard at work on the river. Childers seemed oblivious to the wet and the cold.

It was just as well George was kept busy – as the days passed, he realized that he could not wait until next summer to see Johanna again. He day-dreamed so much about her that his work suffered.

Except for telling Tony – George trusted him completely – he kept his love affair to himself. British sympathies with the Germans had gone into a sharp decline following the Nazi's open violence against the German Jewish community in November. The press had begun to paint the Germans in a totally derogatory light: they were responsible for every problem in foreign affairs. Alex was really nasty about them, calling them 'Huns'. George wondered how his friends would react if he revealed that he was planning to marry a German. He knew his family was not happy about it, but they could think what they liked: Johanna was his heart's desire. Asleep or awake, she was always in his thoughts.

The moment he was free to leave Oxford in December 1938, against his parents' wishes, George took the first ship across the Channel. He carried with him a list of exercises that Childers expected him to do every day. The sea was heavy and leaden, its spray stinging cold. The air was raw and sharp and got colder all the time. He reserved a sleeping berth and this time he refused to leave it, however warm the cabin became.

He was met at the Hook by a dazzlingly white landscape that merged into a lowering grey sky. Day was breaking. The quay and the dock buildings were covered with snow, so was the steaming train. From the stained restaurant car window he caught sight of a line of birch trees of the purest white; red and gold birch leaves were still clinging to the snow-covered branches. The waterways had a crust of ice and snow; a thin white mist lay across the land.

An excited, red-cheeked Johanna awaited him on the platform in Cologne. She was wearing a woollen hat with gloves and scarf to match. She had spotted him through the window before the train had shuddered to a halt, and called his name when he began to clamber down the steps. Dropping his luggage, George picked her up and, to her delight, his head against hers, swung her round and round. 'Oh, Johanna,' he kept saying. 'I nearly died without you.'

'Me too.'

They seemed oblivious to the other passengers. 'You're more beautiful than ever,' he told her. 'How can anyone be so lovely?' She took his head in her hands and kissed him. 'Johanna,' he said breathlessly, 'I've come to ask if you will marry me.' A pent-up emotion flooded his being. Johanna's answer was lost in her kisses and her tears. Laughing and talking, they made their way along the platform draped with Nazi flags. In the street, snow was being trodden into slush; steam rose through the gratings. As they passed the cathedral, George noticed that the jutting gargoyles were wearing tall hats of snow. They avoided talking about his air-force training.

The Krämers welcomed him warmly. At dinner that night, Herr Krämer declared that he had shed his last illusions of Nazism. 'I'm appalled how easy it is to inflame a crowd beyond the bounds of common sense and decency. Something has set the masses in motion, which I find difficult to explain. I had this feeling in August 1914 and it frightens me. *Die Welt ist verrückt!*' (The world is mad!)

'*Ja, es ist schrecklich, Harald*' (Yes, it is terrible), Frau Krämer added, 'yet there's no way of telling the young people that. They don't know what we're talking about; they don't have our fears. Drink your coffee, dear, and let's hope for the best. We mustn't give up hope.'

George quickly settled down in his old room. The linden trees outside his window were now heavy with ice. A cold light lay over the street. Inside, things were exactly as he'd left them. Dostoevsky's *The Brothers Karamazov* still lay on the bedside table. I really must make an effort to read that book, he thought. His conscience bothered him.

In a whirl of activities, the family took George to a performance of Bach's Christmas Oratorio at the university, which was seasonal and moving. They returned home on foot with the snow pricking their faces. Friendly voices in the streets wished each other peace on earth; a wish that this year had added significance.

Bearing gifts, the Krämers and George visited family and friends. Candles flickered through frost-covered windows. They passed crowded shops and walked through the brightly-lit Christmas market full of Christmas trees and wreaths, tinsel and toys, and other good things. The breeze rang the bells hanging from the stalls. '*Fröhliche Weihnachten!*' the red-faced salesfolk called out.

On Christmas Eve the happy couple brought in the tree; its fragrance filled the sitting room. They carried boxes of decorations down from the attic and, with Brigitte, they trimmed the tree with silver tinsel, ornaments and candles. A silver star sparkled at the top. Johanna unpacked the nativity figures and arranged them around the crib. They were a family heirloom and George admired their exquisite workmanship. An Advent wreath with four red candles hung above the dining table, the snow-frosted windows completed the Christmas scene.

That night they attended High Mass in the crowded cathedral, its interior radiant with lights and heavy with incense. The clear, pure voices of the children's choir cast a spell over the congregation; the chanting of the priests in their heavy vestments echoed among the stone pillars. A glint of gold reached them from the raised chalice and the opening and closing of the tabernacle door. 'This is my body . . . this is my blood . . .' A hush fell upon the congregation when the Host was raised. The service ended with the bishop giving his blessing. '*Gloria in excelsis deo. Et in terra pax hominibus bonae voluntatis.*' (Glory be to God on high, and on earth peace, good will towards men), he intoned, as he made the sign of the cross. The organ burst out triumphantly as they filed into the street.

On coming home, they lit the candles on the Christmas tree. The flickering lights filled the room with magic. George exchanged presents with the family. His gift to Johanna was an elaborate musical box that played '*O Tannenbaum*'. Her gift to him was a fine pair of leather gloves. Everybody admired each other's presents and there was much good-hearted laughter and talk and singing of carols. George began 'Silent Night' in English, Johanna ended it in German.

Before dinner on Christmas Day the young people had a snowball fight in the garden. 'Watch my windows,' Frau Krämer called from the kitchen. The dinner was a joyful occasion. The table was festively dressed, with the candle-light reflected in the long-stemmed glasses. Everybody wore their best and was in the highest spirits. During the meal George and Johanna announced their engagement. Herr Krämer responded happily, lifting his glass: 'To George and Johanna, may they have a long and happy life together.' George embraced his fiancée, presented her with a sapphire and diamond engagement ring, and kissed her tenderly. Frau

Krämer seemed heavy with thought as she clinked glasses with George and Johanna, but made an effort to appear cheerful.

Early the next morning Johanna climbed into her mother's bed. 'I'm so happy,' she sighed.

'Good, but don't rush things. You're still a child. I'm not persuaded by your "Love will find a way." There are times in marriage when romance goes out of the window.'

'But Mutti, you agreed to the wedding next July.'

'Yes, but it worries me.'

'Mutti, I love him and he loves me. After all the studying I've done, I'm very happy to marry an Englishman.'

'You could wait a little longer, you're only twenty.'

'But you got married when you were twenty.'

'Yes, but that was different.'

'Why?'

'Because you'll be living in another country. You'll face difficulties that I never had to contend with. Your father and I also worry about your marrying a Protestant, it makes us uneasy.'

'You can't blame George for the Reformation. We've discussed it. We both worship the same Christ. George doesn't object to entering my church, I don't object to entering his. We are ecumenical.'

'Oh, my dear child, I'm at a loss to know how best to help you. There is only one true faith: the Roman Catholic religion.'

'The best thing you can do, Mutti, is to stop worrying about me.'

'I wish I could. I worry about our being cut off from each other. You do realize that Germany and Britain are on the brink of war? What will I do if we find ourselves on different sides? What will either of us do without the other if war comes? I've been through one war, you know. It changed us all. Life was never the same again.' She sighed deeply.

'Ach Mutti!' Silently, they held each other and rocked gently.

The parents of the two families spoke to each other on the telephone that night. They were more cautious about the arrangements than were the engaged couple. Frau Krämer worried about their future constantly. She thought Johanna had her head in the clouds.

'The war and the fantastic inflation of the 1920s are to blame for Mutti's worries,' Johanna told George. 'Her parents, the Steinbachs, were once very rich. My grandmother lived in a world where commonplace things became enchanted. She and I used to go for walks around her estate. It was a place to which we could always escape. Everything was firm and assured. But when the stock market crashed in 1929, my grandparents' world melted away. I don't know the circumstances, only that their mansion and its contents finished up on the auctioneer's block; so did their carriage and pair. Mutti never recovered from the shock. How could you be so rich one day and so poor the next? The war and the Depression left her nervous and insecure.' Johanna had never lost her belief in her grandmother's magic kingdom.

George and Johanna celebrated the New Year of 1939 at the Silvester Ball at Schloss Augustusburg in Brühl, outside Cologne. Johanna wore a beautiful pale blue silk gown, with a low neck and puckered sleeves. She couldn't stay away from the mirror: she had never worn anything that displayed her shoulders like that before. She also wore a ruby necklace and matching ring, which her father had given to her mother long ago. Her dancing slippers sparkled with rhinestones.

Wrapped in furs, their breath steaming, they made the last part of the journey in a horse-drawn sleigh, bells ringing. Deep snowdrifts lined the road. Always there was the whine of the sleigh's runners. Their faces glowed from the frost.

Having climbed an elaborate, red-carpeted marble staircase, the young couple joined the dancers. Johanna was captivated by the magnificence of the eighteenth-century ballroom and the elegance of the occasion. The gleaming chandeliers, the mirrored walls and the swirl of opulent dresses made the atmosphere intoxicating. As they whirled around, she felt herself floating on air. When she left her fiancé to dance with someone else, she reassured George with a playful touch of her hand as she glided by. How had such a handsome stranger entered her life? And now they were engaged to be married! How gloriously complete it was when they were together. She felt part of him, and was happier in his arms than she had ever been. They danced as one, dreamily talking about what was to be.

Supper at the interval was a lavish affair. The tables were crowded with sparkling glasses of champagne, and temptingly arranged platters of hors d'oeuvres and fruit. There were baskets of freshly made bread and rows of starched napkins standing pyramid-like. George was introduced to a number of Johanna's friends.

They began the second half of the ball by dancing a quadrille. The polonaise followed. They never tired. At midnight, when the bells started ringing, they toasted the New Year calling: '*Frohes Neues Jahr!*' Quite out of breath with all the dancing, Johanna raised her glass with wondering innocence. How beautiful life was! Why couldn't it always remain as beautiful as this?

They returned to the Krämers early in the morning through the flickering whiteness of a hushed, snow-filled world.

On George's last evening in Cologne, the Krämer family sang songs around the piano. The two daughters and George took turns at the keys. The evening ended with George singing:

75

I'll see you again, whenever spring breaks through
     again.
Time may lie heavy between, but what has been is
     past forgetting.
These sweet memories across the years will come
     to me,
Though my life may go awry
In my heart will ever lie just the echo of a sigh,
Goodbye.

16

George was back at Oxford in early January 1939. The moment the crew returned, Childers put them to work once more. It was cold and raw on the river, the view across the flat, misty fields was desolate, and there were few mornings without mist. As the dreaded 'Schools' approached, George suddenly realized that he had to do well in his examinations. He couldn't marry Johanna, let alone follow in his father's footsteps, without a good degree behind him.

For the whole of that term, George, Tony and David, in addition to the demands made of them by their tutors and Childers, kept up their training with the RAF. They felt so grown up wearing Air Force blue. George's mother had cried when she first saw her son in uniform. At long last they had their first experience of flying in dual-control planes with an instructor. As spring approached, from the sky the countryside looked soft and inviting. With the sun on the Thames, it was easy to navigate. Oxford and its colleges had a new beauty from the air.

'We revel in every flight,' George recorded in his diary. 'There's something sublime about it; with a roaring engine in front of you, it gives a new sense of power and immediacy; it makes one feel alive and superior to everything on the ground – certainly it beats cramming books on law. I've never felt so satisfied.'

Germany's seizure of the rest of Czechoslovakia in March 1939 threatened to separate Johanna and George once more. There were days when war seemed certain; it upset all George's reckonings. Most people refused to think of war as a serious threat; they were more concerned with arranging their summer holidays. Winston Churchill's warnings of the superiority of the German Luftwaffe were ignored. George's advice to his fiancée was: 'Cheer up, it will all be over soon.' Johanna beseeched the Mother of Christ for help, she knew Mary always protected those who loved her.

Blessedly, the situation improved, except that the newspapers were now full of Hitler's claims against Poland. A strip of German territory on the Baltic had been given to Poland by the Versailles Treaty, and Hitler wanted it back.

Germany's action in Czechoslovakia caused the Oxford Students' Union to arrange an unprecedented debate on peacetime conscription. As Europe edged closer to war, the proposed debate aroused interest throughout the university. Tony Markham headed the Conservative Club, Charley Bradbury the Labour Club, and as both were to take part, the entire crew agreed to be there.

Before going on to the debate, the group had a jolly dinner together at the Mitre. Tony insisted on hosting the meal, to which he had invited his fiancée Lydia and his three sisters. Roger was delighted to be with Gloria again. The previous week – dressed up as a bear – he had clowned before her kindergarten class. George chose the occasion to announce his engagement. He spoke slowly and deliberately; he was nervous. Tony had discreetly prepared the guests for the news, and they all reacted as if they were hearing it for the first time. With happy faces, they tapped their glasses and drank George's health. As far as he could see, there were no odd glances – not even from Alex.

The Students' Union was packed when the crew arrived. Excited voices filled the air; no debate had ever aroused such interest or prompted such strength of feeling. The sea of faces, the large lighted candelabras, the heavy furnishings, and the officers and speakers in evening dress, lent colour and gravitas to the proceedings.

Precisely at 8 p.m. the Speaker rose and called: 'Silence, silence in the House. Silence, I pray.' To a hushed House, one of the officers then read the motion: 'That this House approves the immediate introduction of conscription.' Cheers and boos followed.

The tone of the debate was sombre; there was none of the usual frivolity or word-play. Speakers were badgered, bitter words exchanged, protests alternated with demands for silence, but nothing was done to mar the seriousness of the occasion. With scorching words, Jewish speakers brought home the plight of their fellow Jews under Nazi oppression.

Speaking with a strong northern burr, Bradbury summed up the pacifist case: 'War is a sickness that every now and then seizes our nation. It did so in 1914 and is about to do so again. All the powers are rattling their swords. Yet it's not the sword that will save us, but the love of our neighbour. Young men who went from this chamber to fight the Great War did so with unbounded idealism. They spoke of a purifying storm, of a breath of deliverance. I don't have to remind you that the war ended in desolation, disillusion, domination, repression and cruelty. Europe's belief in itself and the reverence for life were never the same again. The Great War changed our world for the worse. No one knows what another war will do.' Every now and again, Charley hammered his points home on the lectern before him. He lived each word and was at his persuasive best. He mopped his brow as he sat down.

Some cheering followed, but the mixed reactions of the audience and the general atmosphere of the House made it clear that pacifism was no longer as popular as it had once been.

When the House was called to order Tony rose. In his evening dress, he cut a splendid figure and gave the impression of being completely in charge. He didn't strike one as a clever man, or as an intellectual, but he had an easy, patient manner of speech, which inspired confidence and sounded entirely trustworthy. He had always respected his opponent and made no effort to score off his friend now. He responded to Charley not by appealing to party politics or jingoism but by calling for national preservation.

'An immediate increase in our armed forces is vital,' he urged. 'Nazi Germany has had conscription for three years. Our continuing weakness is an invitation for Hitler to do greater harm. Our present policy of collective security under the League of Nations is a sham if we do not have the necessary power to enforce it. Conscription in Britain will send a message to Germany that there is a point beyond which it must not go. Democracy, liberty and freedom can never be saved if we are weak and divided.' His voice was firm but restrained; there were no histrionics, no waving of hands.

'We're not going to fight a capitalist war as my honourable friend has suggested,' Tony proceeded. 'Nor does glory come into it. If we fight, we will fight against oppression, tyranny and fear. Above all, we will fight for self-preservation and to defend our way of life. If the Nazis are allowed to rule Europe, tyranny will triumph. Few of us ever dreamed that we would find ourselves in as dangerous a situation as we are in today. Yet justice must be upheld; no sacrifice is too great to preserve liberty.'

Tony waited for the applause to die down – his words had cast a spell over his listeners. 'Many rulers have tried to destroy liberty. None have succeeded, nor will Adolf Hitler. In this cause, we will each have to do our bit; it's expected of us; our conscience gives us no other choice. Unless we are to bind our hands, pacifism should be abandoned now.'

His final words were drawn from the speech of Polonius to Laertes in *Hamlet*:

> This above all: to thine own self be true,
> And it must follow, as the night the day,
> Thou canst not then be false to any man.

Many students were on their feet applauding before Tony had finished. It was evident that a sea change had taken place in their views on conscription.

With a great hubbub, the vote was taken. There was cheering and cap-throwing when the count was declared in favour of military service.

Victoria was not upset at Charley's defeat. 'Madness is taking over,' she said darkly. 'The Conservative Party will take us to war.'

Following the debate, the crew retired to Tony's rooms. 'So much for those who said they wouldn't fight for King and Country,' Tony started the conversation, while handing round drinks and cigars. 'They were not conspicuous tonight.'

'Without the crisis in Czechoslovakia, Britain would still be asleep,' Alex added. 'Now, thank God, we are awake to our responsibilities and our traditions.'

'Traditions!' Charley cried incredulously. 'Tradition is the dead hand of history.'

'On the contrary,' Lydia answered, 'if we lose our traditions, we lose our souls.'

'Respect for traditions,' Tony added, 'marks us out as human beings. There's very little we value that we don't draw from the past. In part at least, we are always what we have been.'

'Which regiment in the British Army can fight without tradition?' Alex demanded.

No one answered.

'The only good thing about a war is that it will keep me out of the old man's counting house,' Roger laughed.

'This isn't the time for laughing,' Victoria reproached him. 'Nobody here has any idea what will become of us if war breaks out.'

'God does,' Tony interjected. 'Without us realizing it, our days are numbered. The ancient Greeks believed that a man's life was spun, cut and measured at birth. We don't live or die by accident, or chance, but according to Divine Providence. God decides everything, including our destiny; life is the unfolding of God's will. What will be, will be.'

'Rubbish, Tony,' Max protested. 'If life is the unfolding of God's will, then why is there so much evil about? The capacity for evil among some human beings is overwhelming. To say that our days are numbered means nothing. You don't have to go to ancient Greece to prove that your days are numbered. We all have to die. To hell with your talk about Divine Providence and destiny. You can blame anything on them, and shift them any way you want. I'm not a puppet following a destiny laid down by somebody else, I'm a living being, free to choose. What I do is not God's will, but mine. I'll run my life my own way, thank you. I only believe in what I can touch and see.'

'You can believe whatever you like, Max, but the last word is with God,' Tony came back.

'Men make their history, not God,' Charley spoke up. 'Man has the power to make a better world. It's ironic that a socialist should find himself supporting anything that Max suggests.'

'You might make a better world, if you were master of your fate,' Tony answered, 'but you're not, and can't be. Plan as you like, God will decide.'

'What about chance?' Roger broke in. 'Training to be a soldier never crossed my mind. I once had a professor who said that England was saved from the Spanish Armada by a change in the wind. Chance decides the circumstances of our birth, and for most of us our death. Chance stands all our calculations on their head. Need I go on? You can plan to your heart's content, but chance – whatever you call it – will intervene.' He emptied his glass and looked around for support. Gloria had listened to his every word.

'Only fools believe in chance,' Max snapped.

'I'm out of my depth,' Bill admitted. 'I don't pretend to understand what's going on. Philosophy is taboo to a sailor. The Great War made my old man a senior captain – what's wrong with that?'

'There's nothing like a war for promotion, Alex, you might become a colonel, like your father,' Charley taunted.

'Only people like you, Charley, know what is coming. I hope that another war will not bring in a socialist government with you at its head. Even as a professional soldier, I can't imagine fighting for a socialist prime minister.'

'Professional soldiers who don't follow orders are considered reactionaries and shot,' jested Charley.

'Charley's threat, Alex, might not turn out to be as funny as you think,' said David. 'Look at Russia. Stalin has slaughtered the old Communist leaders and half the officer corps.'

'That's a pack of lies,' retorted Victoria. 'What the Russian experiment should have taught us is that we must change our way of thinking. Wrong thinking is how we got into the present mess. We need to adopt the scientific method. If Russia can establish a society free from hunger and want, where all are treated equally, so can we. Our contribution to humanity can be just as great. We must put injustice and inequality behind us.' She was determined to work for a better world.

'What do you think of destiny, George?' Tony asked unexpectedly.

George had been day-dreaming about Johanna. 'I don't know what to think,' he answered. 'I prefer to go on dreaming, and hope that my dreams will come true.'

'I need another drink,' Pat groaned. 'You talk like a lot of old men. The joy of life is in living it, not talking about it.'

'Agreed,' Gloria called.

'It's too much for me,' Lydia said. 'One of you should write a book.'

'Meeting adjourned,' said Roger, yawning.

Gloria suddenly realized that Helen and Penelope had slipped out, and so had David and Pat.

17

In May 1939, the crew belatedly took up an invitation to spend a night at Ansfield House, Tony Markham's ancestral home in Berkshire. Childers was not happy about them taking a couple of days off so close to the final race but he compromised by giving them a fierce workout on the river before they left.

Ansfield was less than an hour's drive from Oxford. George had been there when he and Tony were schoolboys, and had been looking forward to another visit. Those who had not been before were impressed by the wooded approach and the great turreted dwelling, surrounded by flower-beds and shrubberies. Dogs and domestic servants – headed by a butler – hurried out to meet them.

Lord and Lady Markham received them in the Great Hall. Well-built, clean-shaven, upright in bearing, affable in manner and quietly spoken, Lord Markham shared the fresh complexion of his children. Dressed in a heavy, tan-coloured suit, he evidently lived a quiet, rural, patriarchal life and was happiest when talking about crops, horses, dogs and the chase. He rejoiced in the sound of the huntsman's horn. A portrait of him in hunting pink hung in the entrance hall. Unlike Tony, who hoped to serve in public life, he had wisely kept the vexations of politics at bay. Standing next to his father, Tony looked like a chip off the old block. Both had rowed for Arnold College.

Lady Markham was taller than her husband and her piled-up hair made her appear even more so. She was full of life and the source of her daughters' good looks. She kept alive the love of music in the district by holding concerts in the Great Hall at Ansfield, and took an active part in the religious and social activities of the village church. She was the brains of the family. No one guarded the Markham interests as closely as she.

There was an informal tea party soon after the crew's arrival at which Lady Markham made a point of speaking with each visitor. Afterwards, some guests played croquet. Helen went to show David the library. Penelope couldn't get away fast enough; she had eyes only for Pat and the two went horse-riding. Gloria and Roger took off aimlessly across the quiet fields followed by her favourite retriever.

As they walked along, Roger decided to get off his chest something he'd been worrying about for days. 'My dear Gloria,' he began, handing her a daisy, 'I've been wanting to ask if you could be mad enough to marry me?'

Gloria's lips trembled. 'Oh, you great big silly bear! Of

course I will. I've always loved you.' Her face was damp with tears.

'Dear, dear Gloria,' Roger said as he embraced her.

'You'd better get Papa's support. Don't worry. He'll bark, but he won't bite.'

They walked on hand in hand; Roger noticed how warm their hands had become.

Chatting merrily, George, Tony and Lydia wandered off under the oak trees, eventually finding a secluded bench against a wall. All around them were the garden's summer scents. Squirrels scurried across the brick walk. The click of croquet balls and the blur of voices came from the other side of the wall. Tony talked about his childhood. He spoke in a low voice, completely at ease. 'Other than the seasons, nothing ever changed here. Everything and everybody had a proper place, with my father at the head. At the harvest festival everyone came together to feast, dance and play games. I thought that this was the way it was and always would be. The idea that gardeners and pantry maids should run the country, as Charley Bradbury insists, never crossed my mind. Now there is the threat of war and rising taxation, we might have to sell some land to keep going.'

'Nonsense, Tony,' Lydia laughed. 'You know that the Markhams never part with land.'

'You love Ansfield, Tony, don't you?' said George, 'I've always known that.'

'It means everything to me. As a boy, I lived in these woods and fields. I was free. Judd the game warden was like a father to me. He played a great part in moulding my character. He knew where to find the best hares and the best fish. He could catch anything with a piece of string. He always met me at the railway station when I came home from school. I can see him now, with his bony mottled face, leaning forward in the gig and flicking a fly off the rump of the pony with

85

his whip as we rattled home on a hot summer's day. I was so glad to be returning to Ansfield that I used to shout "Hurry Judd, hurry!" How wonderful it was when I saw the turrets and the ivy-covered walls of the house. It was even more wonderful to be welcomed home by everyone.'

On returning to the house, Tony and Lydia introduced George to the stiff, flat portraits of his ancestors hanging in the pillared hall. They had the Markham face, stamped with distinction and self-confidence, if not superiority. The Markham line went back deep into British history. The family was wedded to English soil.

Tony pointed to the picture of a red-faced gentleman in uniform with sash, cocked hat and sword. 'His bugle kept the family and staff in order. The household rose with his reveille and retired when he sounded "Lights out" from the roof. In the army he was known as General Tally-Ho.'

There was a whole wall covered with Markham soldiers, ending with Tony's uncle Andrew who had been killed in France in October 1917, aged twenty-two. If ever anyone looked in the fullness of life, Andrew did; joy was written all over his face.

Ansfield House dazzled Charley. He had never seen such brazen private wealth before. His fiancée's family, the Randalls, was probably equally rich, but they had never given Charley the chance to find out; they had kept him at bay. Charley suspected that like all great fortunes, the Markham wealth had come off the backs of the workers.

If the Markhams were falling on hard times, there was no sign of it at dinner that night, when they dined in splendour. Even though it was May, a great fire burned in the grate; the dogs lay before it.

Penelope, carefully dressed for the occasion, came rushing in late, bubbling with news, to be chastised by her father. Still giggling, she sat down next to Pat. Soon they were both laughing together: since their meetings at Oxford and in

London, their friendship had flourished. The servants bustled to serve her.

David sat next to Helen. They too were at ease with each other; they talked about music.

While Lord Markham laughed with his guests and talked rowing, his wife mentioned a charity ball she was helping to organize. She was on edge about her unfinished dress. 'You'll have to go in a barrel,' Penelope tittered.

Neither Lord nor Lady Markham gave the slightest hint that in Charley they were entertaining a rabid socialist who intended to tax them out of existence. He was a guest and had to be treated as such. The Markhams might have been in the habit of entertaining socialists, so perfect was their behaviour. However, George overheard Lady Markham say, 'It's unwise to have people like Bradbury about, Tony. He'll soil the linen, my dear, you'll see.'

'My dear mother, Charley is engaged to Lord Randall's daughter, Victoria. She was coming here today with Charley, but something else cropped up. I told her that you would be delighted for her to visit.'

'Oh!' Lady Markham exclaimed, her face changing. 'Not *the* Randalls? The Charlton Randalls? Good God, Tony, what is the world coming to? I must have missed the notice in *The Times*.'

The old man couldn't have enough of Pat's stories of his life as a drifter in America; nor could Penelope. On one occasion, he had escaped from the Texas police by the skin of his teeth. 'They fired at my tyres as if they were at a shooting gallery.'

'Bless my soul, sir! You don't say so,' Lord Markham said. 'They'd have devoured you if they had caught you.'

'And my money.'

Lord Markham polished his monocle the better to see Pat whom he regarded as a latter-day Drake. They were about to leave the table when champagne was served. Lord

Markham tapped his glass; the noise was stilled. 'I've delayed this toast,' he said, rising, 'because I was only approached about the matter before dinner. I want to send you away with the wonderful news that our daughter Gloria has become engaged to Roger Blundell.' He raised his glass. 'To Gloria and Roger, our warm congratulations. God bless them.' His words rang in the great room. The whole company stood and heartily toasted the couple. 'Hear, hear!' they called, with good heart, and touched glasses. Eyes sparkling, their faces reflecting the candlelight, Roger and Gloria embraced.

In choosing Roger, Gloria had disappointed her mother greatly. All the Blundells had was money, not a title or land. Talent and merit didn't count. Roger was not what Lady Markham had hoped for – there were several much more eligible young heirs in the county, but he had his good points and with a war coming on, one had to make do. Gloria had set her heart on Roger and stuck by him. She was not a person who was easily moved.

Looking pleased with himself, Lord Markham took up his glass once more, 'Let me give you another toast which I should have given earlier. To the crew that will be Head of the River. God bless them all. God speed! May we have the pleasure of seeing you all here again as victors.'

The servants having drawn back the heavy, high-backed chairs, the company retired to the drawing room, where some played cards, while others talked, smoked and laughed together. Enjoying his cigar, their host spoke readily about conditions on the estate, and the way things had been in 'the good old days'. Charley admired the way Lord Markham foiled Alex's attempts to turn the talk into a criticism of Nazi Germany. He refused to reveal his feelings.

Later that night, George and Tony took a stroll outside. With no curtains drawn, the light from the French windows flooded out into the dark night. The trees cast shadows; the parkland lay quiet all around; the sound of a gramophone drifted out of a downstairs window. Pat and Penelope were dancing on the grass. They came across David and Helen sitting on a bench in the rose garden holding hands. The sky was a canopy of stars.

The next morning, family and guests were photographed on one of the lawns. The photographer was all ready for them with his large camera, a tripod, and a cape he threw over his head. The dogs upset everything by running about barking with excitement. There was a lot of laughter and teasing.

'Don't forget what I said about your returning here as victors,' Lord Markham called as they departed. As the cars pulled away, George looked back and waved. He was struck by the self-assured bearing of the family; it expressed strength. The vast house appeared equally proud and lasting.

That night Lady Markham could not sleep. 'I'm at a loss to know what is going on,' she confessed to her husband. 'Have we ever, in all our lives, heard of a Randall – *the* Randalls – marrying a penniless fisherman, as Victoria is about to do? The paradox of what is going on among these young people today overwhelms me. Gloria and Roger get on very well, but you know as well as I do that the Blundells haven't the slightest idea what it is to be a Markham. Helen tells me that she has lost her heart to a teacher's son, and from what I could learn from talking to him, not a very interesting one at that. He struck me as being out-of-elbows. Helen has always been simple, always doing good works, so easily swayed. There are times when I lose patience with her dreaming. Only she could put up with an eccentric like Evans. He's much too narrow and self-opinionated. As for Penelope and Riley, I don't know what to make of them. We've never been rid of him since Penelope met him at Oxford. At seventeen, she is too young to lose her heart to anyone and Riley must be at least ten years older. But then, we've never known what she would do next, she's always been the headstrong one in the family. On top of which they tell me that Kemp is about to marry a German. What is going on, Cecil, I ask you? God knows I've done my best, with little to show for it. What worries me more than anything else is Riley's secretiveness. I sense something odd about him. He is not to be drawn out where Penelope is concerned – I know because I've tried. Where does his wealth come from? What *is* he worth? Nobody seems to know. All I can say is thank God for Lydia Turner. At least one union has worked out right. The perfect marriage: an aristocrat like ourselves, with lots of land, and right next door.'

'Stop worrying about marriages and go to sleep, Betty. Since the Great War lineage and privilege have either gone, or are going, out of the window. Everybody now thinks they can be a duke or a duchess. We must just hang on and try to be what we are. At least no one is cutting our throats as they did to our kind in Russia not long ago. Now get some sleep.'

'But what are we going to do about Riley? I repeat. Penelope is so young. We must protect her.'

'Penelope is the one member of the family able to protect herself. If she is determined to marry a scalliwag, there's not much we can do about it. It's odd that you should speak of Riley as you do. I find him a straightforward character, if a bit of an adventurer. According to Tony, he is a first-class rower, you know. Of course, I haven't asked him where he keeps his money. My opinion is that Pat and Penelope are both wild. Take my advice, don't worry about those two.'

The next morning Lady Markham drew her daughter Helen aside. 'I found David Evans engaging when I talked to him yesterday,' she said. 'Do you really like him or is he just a passing fancy?'

'Oh no, Mother, I really like him. It's the first time I've

been courted seriously, and I enjoy it. I'd begun to think that I was the Cinderella of the county. Gloria and Penelope have the good looks of the family, I don't. David is a fine man and completely trustworthy. We are lucky to have met.'

'What do you think he might do when he leaves Oxford?'

'There's no telling. He's so bright. He's concerned with the search for truth in physics, which is not easy to convey. He's not so much clever as gifted. I'm one of the few who understand him. I don't know how or when he'll climb the academic ladder, but I'm sure he will. If he gets the All Souls Fellowship, he's sure to get a good job.'

'At a low salary, I suspect. A come-down after Ansfield. You don't think you're stepping down, do you?'

'Of course not, I don't want to stay at Ansfield for ever. I want to set up a home of my own. Our beginnings will be modest, but that's a small price to pay for happiness. Tony and Gloria are different; it would break their hearts to leave Ansfield; they live for it. Penelope and I have the urge to fly away.'

'You've always been a dreamer, Helen. Where would we be if the rest of the family wanted to fly away too?'

In paradise, Helen thought, but she didn't say it out loud.

18

The crew were out on the river, using every minute they could spare to prepare for the crucial test. Childers had them turn out regardless of rain, mist or wind. He worked them with few 'easies' until they ached all over. One day they glided through the water, the next they struggled against a turgid chop, or cold gusts of rain, which lashed their hands and faces. Sometimes they returned exhausted with their shoes full of water. 'Rowing at the highest level is a gruelling business,' was all the coach said. He dismissed their aches and pains, with 'You can't expect to win without them.' He also insisted on their spending an hour a day in the gym; weight-lifting was his favourite activity. He did everything to improve their performance and boost their morale. Sometimes the practice sessions went on and on until they had to put their boat away in the dark. Childers' dog Brendan would be in their midst, wagging his tail off, barking. They'd make up for their hardship by drinking a shandy before running back to college.

Walter Turnbull, the college chaplain, also appeared on the tow-path to cheer them on. 'Come on, Arnold, put your backs into it.' His deep-throated voice had a clerical ring. Hands lost in his black cassock, patches on his elbows, black belt flapping, a convict-haircut, reddish beard, and feet pointing east and west, he was oblivious to the peculiar figure he cut. Everybody knew him as a romping Christian, shorn of doubt. Tony Markham, whom he had trained in boxing, swore by him. Turnbull had fought alongside Childers in the Great War. On one occasion he had carried him, severely wounded, out of harm's way. They had been inseparable friends ever since.

The preliminary rounds in the Head-of-the-River Race, stretching from Wednesday to Wednesday in the middle of June 1939, left Arnold College where Childers expected it to be: in the final against Christ Church. The two teams had overtaken and bumped more boats than any other college. Christ Church was the undoubted favourite. It was rumoured that they were on a strict diet.

'Forget the college chatter,' Childers told them, 'and make up your mind that you're going to win.' He put his hands on George's shoulders. His eyes twinkled, but his manner was unusually serious. 'Everything depends on what you do, Kemp. You have to seize every opportunity you can. If you are able to get the crew to reach down and discover resources that you thought were already spent, especially in the final moments, we'll win. Luck matters; skill and resolution even more.'

'I'll do my best, sir. I'm sure the crew will do the same. You can bet on that.' George felt the strain immensely. The closer they got to the race, the worse they rowed. He began to sleep badly.

Childers' secret worry all along had been that one of the crew would break an arm or a leg on the eve of the vital day. Either that, or someone would lose his oar during the race.

That weekend they varnished their boat again. On Childers' orders, they slacked off before the race. Of even greater concern, George's head was filled with his fiancée's arrival the next day.

Johanna arrived at Oxford station accompanied by George's mother. It was her first visit to England. He welcomed them and hugged his fiancée. Her radiant face was full of life and expectation. He had never known her look so beautiful. He couldn't take his eyes off her, and never let go of her hand. They had come dressed for the sun. Mrs Kemp wore a strikingly blue, light costume. Johanna wore a pretty lace blouse, a long white skirt, a straw hat trimmed with a red ribbon, white stockings and dainty white shoes. Her blonde hair protruded from beneath her hat.

The next morning everybody was up at first light. After studying the sky, Childers announced that the weather would hold. There was a slight breeze, and a few light clouds hanging about, otherwise conditions were ideal. The race was not until the afternoon, but nobody could stay in bed, not when the most important and spectacular sporting event of the year was about to take place.

By breakfast-time all the barges on the river were decked out with flags and bunting. As the day warmed, crowds

93

began to fill the barges and the tow-path. They came with banners, streamers, clappers and whistles. They waved their caps and straw hats and called from the barges and the banks. White parasols bobbed about among the spectators. The air was filled with a gala spirit; there was a great sense of occasion.

The Arnold and Christ Church crews, accompanied by senior members of both colleges, were already on the top deck of their barges prior to the launching of their boats. Pushing his way through the press of bodies, George introduced his mother and Johanna to the crew and their guests. Above their heads the flags flapped.

'So you're George's hidden treasure, are you?' Alex Haverfield greeted Johanna. He was surprised at her excellent English. She found the tall, dark, young man cool but polite. He was one of the most handsome men she had met. Tony's sisters, and his fiancée Lydia, came forward to meet Johanna and George's mother. Lady Elsfield, lustrously dressed and wearing far too much rouge, left the company in no doubt about the vital contribution being made by her son, Max. The Markhams thought such remarks improper, but held their peace; to rebuff the woman in public was out of the question. They couldn't stand her overbearing manner and tried to avoid her.

Against a background of poplar trees and college spires, and cheered on by shouting crowds, both crews took up their positions formally beside their boats. They followed a procedure decided upon generations before. The crews wore white sleeveless shirts and shorts, and long patterned stockings. Only the coxes wore caps. Harvey Childers and his dog Brendan – a ribbon around his neck – stood silently by Arnold's boat. 'Make a fast start, find a pace close to the crew's limits and stay there,' were his last words to George. Arnold won the toss and chose the inside position. The crews would have their backs to the sun.

With much cheering, the boats were launched. The river surged past the jetty posts, the wooden deck was warm to the feet from the summer's sun. George caught a fleeting glimpse of Johanna waving from the barge, her straw hat shielding her face from the sun. He waved back. Everything depended on his getting Arnold in front and staying there. At the end, it was up to him to make the right calls at the right moment. He sweated over it, tense and anxious.

The crews moved a mile down-river to the starting post, turned, and jockeyed for position. While trying to keep in line, they studied each other. The Christ Church crew looked relaxed and confident: they'd been Head before. Except for the slapping and murmuring of the water and the rustle of the trees, the river was hushed. After signals from the two coxes, the decorated oars were raised. The blades were touching the water. Both crews sat stock-still, ready to shoot forward.

'Are you ready?' the starter called. Silence answered. The tension grew. The rowers' hearts pounded. They gripped their oars until it hurt. The minute gun sounded. The coxes took up the slack in the tiller ropes. 'Come forward! . . . three, two, one.' Crack! The pistol shot echoed along the bank, disturbing the birds in the trees. They were off! The crews bent forward, arms outstretched; the river was churned into foam; the water glittered in the sun. The pace quickened as they picked up speed. All the skill, the muscle and the stamina they'd built up over the years were now subjected to the final, crucial test. Each team was determined to leave the other behind. The trees flew by.

Deafening shouts came from the crowd on the bank. The knife-like prows sliced past each other. With a long, relaxed rhythm, Arnold led by a third of a length. Christ Church rallied. Arnold fell behind. Half a length separated the two boats. Alex, pulling like a fiend, increased the stroke. The crew backed him up. The boats were now neck and neck, slicing through the water at great speed. Splashed by each other's oars, they remained neck-and-neck for hundreds of yards. It was difficult to say who was leading. No one had seen the two boats quite as close as this before. The rowers glistened with sweat. Mouths open, their breathing was harder; their faces showed the strain. That eight men could achieve such harmony, unity, rhythm, power and speed all at the same time was nothing short of miraculous.

More than halfway down the course, with an intelligent piece of coxing, Kemp took advantage by cutting the inside of a bend. Christ Church responded by accelerating. Some minutes later, with the blades of the two crews almost touching again, George decided that this was the moment when Arnold had to make the supreme effort. 'Now!' he demanded of the stroke. Gasping for breath, Alex obeyed. Stretched to breaking point, Arnold forged ahead on the inside of the last bend; Christ Church rallied, the barges slipped by. Excited spectators began to run towards the finishing post. Shouts, rattles and whistles filled the air, the excitement was unbearable. In a breathtaking moment, Arnold shot past the finishing line first.

They had won by several feet; they had really won! There was a roar from the crowd. Some of the crew collapsed on their oars. Their wrists, forearms and knees trembled. Bill Clark held his head between his knees. David flung his outstretched arms to the sky. Roger trailed a leg in the water. Alex reached across and grasped George's wrist. Uppermost in George's mind was the fact that he had vindicated himself as cox. In the stern, Tony and Pat hugged each other and waved to the crowd. The spectators on Arnold's barge gesticulated wildly.

The Arnold crew clumsily paddled back to the boat-house, where a bright-eyed Childers was waiting to congratulate them. Smiling broadly, he solemnly shook the hand of each crew member. His shake was like a formal nod.

There was no slapping of shoulders; certainly no hugging. Brendan jumped and barked around them on their return.

Back on the barge, amid congratulations and toasts, George kissed his delighted Johanna – for which he was thrown into the river. Boisterous laughter broke out – the single most expressive gesture in that wild moment of success was for the crew to throw each other into the water. One after another they were pitched over the side of the barge. Like the good sports they were, the Christ Church crew joined in the celebrations. The crews toasted each other with champagne before running to change.

Johanna was thrilled that Arnold and George had won. '*Fabelhaft! Ganz fantastisch!*' She clapped her hands. How much more exciting it all was than filling her notebooks with absurdities at lectures in Cologne.

There was loud cheering on the university barge that night when Harvey Childers accepted the silver cup on the crew's behalf. This time he was in evening dress. Not one of his few grey hairs was out of place. They detected a tear. For Childers, it was a proud moment in the life of a proud man. A little fuzzy-headed, the crew then went to the victory dinner in Arnold Hall.

They entered the hall singing the Eton boating song:

> Jolly boating weather,
> And a hay harvest breeze,
> Blade on the feather,
> Shade off the trees;
> Swing, swing together,
> With your bodies between your knees.

With a noise like growing thunder, the song was taken up by everyone in the hall.

High silver candlesticks had replaced the electric wall

lights; the candlelight trembled against the stained-glass windows; the beamed ceiling was lost in darkness. The crew more white shirts with white bow ties, white-lined rowing jackets, and white trousers and shoes. Everybody else wore formal evening dress. The honoured guests, including relatives and fiancées, and the more senior members of the college, took their places at high table. Everything was done as it had been done for a hundred years; there was a sense of continuity and belonging. Johanna loved the formality of it all.

The crew sat together at one of the long polished tables in the middle of the hall. Theirs was a group victory, not an individual triumph. George was grateful that the egotistical Max had not claimed the victory as his own. 'There was no hey diddle diddle about this race,' Max challenged Roger Blundell, 'we won it the hard way.'

'It was our lucky day,' Roger smiled. 'Chance was on our side.'

David expressed the victory as an equation on his menu card, but no one was interested.

The silver cup with the engraved crossed oars had pride of place on their table. It was surrounded by bottles of champagne. Childers and the junior college dons sat proudly with the crew.

The Latin grace 'Benedictus benedicat . . .' caused a hush to fall upon the hall; the hubbub of laughter and shouting was stilled. Before the dinner began, the Master welcomed the guests. He was followed by Walter Turnbull, the chaplain, who proposed a toast to Childers and his crew. A great cheer rang out when Childers – responding to the toast – announced that Arnold's crew had set a record in the history of Oxford rowing. No previous racing eight had achieved Arnold's speed. The event had placed a final seal of approval on his work as coach.

With the dinner under way, at a signal from George, all

the crew stood up. Glasses in hand, they turned towards Childers and sang 'For He's a Jolly Good Fellow . . .' Everyone joined in. They banged on the tables and rattled the cutlery when the final line was reached: '. . . which no one can deny.' Childers was visibly moved. For a moment, his serenity failed him.

Much later that evening there followed the ritual burning of the boat. By then Lord and Lady Markham had gone home. There was talk of their daughter Penelope returning with them, but she wouldn't hear of it. She joined Pat Riley in the crowd of spectators. With great care the boat was carried into the quad, where it was doused with petrol. George threw in a blazing torch – there was a boom and a flash of flame. Those watching covered their eyes and hurriedly backed away. Great shadows began to dance on the college walls. The tall windows were bathed in a golden light.

As the fire took hold, flames and showers of sparks filled the quad; black smoke stung their eyes; the starlit sky darkened. With the blaze reflected in their faces, the crew watched a great friend die. It had brought them victory; it had challenged and defeated the best boats on the river. Both sacred and secret, the ceremony expressed a cleansing finality. Some great act had happened which could not be repeated. The victorious boat must not be allowed to rot at the river side, fade dismally with age, or suffer the disgrace of being turned into scrap. Better for it to die in the fullness of its glory. David knew that the origin of the custom was Viking. Tony recalled a bullfight he had seen as a small boy in Spain, which had claimed the lives of both bull and matador. It was his first encounter with death and with courage.

At the other side of the crackling, burning pyre stood Harvey Childers. Through the smoke and the flames, he looked like a wavering reflection in water. There was a touch of sadness in his face. On the spur of the moment, as the flames lapped their shoes and trousers, the crew leapt across the fire, some singly, others together, and stood at the coach's side. Their faces glowed with victory. Childers smiled at each man as he arrived. 'This is what it's all about,' he said, looking first into their faces and then into the flames, 'a blaze of glory.' All held hands; they might have been his sons. They stayed together until all was done.

They held a wake for the boat on the barge that night. Only Pat and Penelope were missing. Gloria had been left in charge of her younger sister and was furious that Pat had tricked her for the second time.

The next day the official photograph of the crew was taken. The procedure was always the same: couch and chairs were set out on the lawn before the winning staircase, the cup was prominently displayed at George's feet. There were ten of them including Childers and the cox, eleven counting Brendan. Joy and gladness were written on every face. Turnbull gave thanks for their victory at morning chapel. David sang a solo, 'Worship Him, God most high', accompanied by the choir.

All that now remained was to pass their final examinations.

19

Dressed in dark suits and white ties, the crew spent the mornings and afternoons of the next two weeks in 'Schools'. The examinations were an ordeal for all of them and, except for Pat, their faces showed it. David had worked out the odds on which questions were likely to appear. When the results were announced, they were much as they'd expected. After a shaky start, George had managed to squeeze through his law exams. Roger and Tony got the pass degrees they had hoped for. Tony was also awarded a rowing 'blue', which meant much more to him than the degree. (Childers had recommended Pat and Charley for this, but Pat had trodden on too many toes, and Charley was looked upon as a firebrand.) Alex, Bill and Max all did well. David (who led the field), Charley and, to the surprise of all, Pat (who was critical of the conventional views of history), did brilliantly.

The next morning there was a farewell party for the crew on the barge. They thought Tony's servant, Weasel, a magician the way he produced refreshments. Alex and Roger planned to spend the summer with the army on Salisbury Plain. Alex was excited about it, but Roger shuddered at the thought. George, Tony and David were to continue their RAF training. Bill was to report for duty at Portsmouth. He was happy at the thought of going back to sea. Max and his sister Hazel intended to spend the summer in Scandinavia 'before all hell lets loose'. Pat planned to go climbing on Mull.

In the autumn – if he were successful with the All Souls Fellowship – only David would return to Oxford. 'I'll think of you fellows when you're all out in the slave pens,' he jested. Alex would begin his career in the army. Charley and Victoria were to resume their work at Toynbee Hall in East London. Johanna was to leave for Germany in a couple of days' time. If all went well, George would join her for their wedding in July.

Haltingly, Tony gave a toast: 'God grant,' he said, raising his glass, 'that peace prevails, and that our friendship may last for ever. God guard you all.' They clinked glasses. Their voices echoed throughout the barge.

On their last day the crew went to say goodbye to the

Childers's. Mrs Childers had laid on high tea. The crew expressed their affection for the coach by giving him a brand-new, three-speed Raleigh bike. He had worn out his old one chasing them up and down the river. He was over-whelmed by the gift. 'I say,' he stammered, rising and putting his reading glasses aside, 'this is awfully decent of you, but it's completely undeserved. Whatever shall I do with a three-speed?' he asked his wife. His face lit up with a smile. There was such a twinkle in his eye that the company burst out laughing. 'Hip, hip, hooray for the coach!' George called. 'And for Brendan!' Alex added.

Without giving him time to decline their gift, the crew broke up and went their different ways. 'Easy oars,' he called after them. They hated parting from the Childers's and their dog.

George and Johanna wandered around Arnold after their friends had gone. For a few moments they sat together quietly in the chapel, which Johanna loved. Before leaving the college, they collected some last things from George's rooms; his heavier baggage was already at the porter's lodge. Johanna thought the rooms primitive; only then did George realize that he had spent three happy years with a sunken couch and broken chairs. About to close his door for the last time, he rushed back and carved his initials into the window seat. Johanna looked on, amused.

20

Two days later, George saw Johanna off at Victoria Station; it was hard to say goodbye. 'What am I going to do without you?' he asked. The long, grey platforms and soot-stained roofs gave no hint that it was summer outside. Except for some men who were stacking piles of sandbags, the platform was strangely quiet; there was none of the usual bustle. George stood against the window of the boat train holding Johanna's hand. The newspapers he had bought for her were full of the growing danger of war. Slowly, with the guard's whistle, the train pulled out.

Having waved to his fiancée until she passed from view, George went home to Wimbledon to say goodbye to his parents and then left for Oxford. He felt lost without Johanna. The next day, with Tony and David, he reported for summer training with the RAF at Kidlington. He didn't look forward to barrack life.

They were surprised to find that the base was now on a war footing; the whole tone had changed. Reveille had been moved forward from 7.00 to 6.00 a.m. The buildings had been camouflaged; everything had become much more austere; there were many more cadets and many more iron cots to accommodate them. There were far more planes coming and going; the sky above the base was never quiet.

Drilled by a new contingent of regular NCOs, the three men threw themselves into their training. From dawn to dusk they attended lectures, sometimes in the classroom, other times in the cockpit, and marched about the base 'at the double' until their feet ached.

Now and again, they would go to Oxford for an hour or two and sit over tea and buns. Oxford had become another world to them and going back gave them a feeling of anticlimax. They already felt old among the young faces. More often, they were too tired after a day at the base to go anywhere except to the mess and bed.

At Kidlington they began to reconcile themselves to the new military discipline. The newly-appointed, ramrod-backed Warrant Officer Morgan took a sadistic delight in introducing them to the more oppressive aspects of military life. There were more parades, more guard duties and more spit-and-polish than they'd bargained for. On parade Morgan was spotless from head to foot, some poor devil had spent hours cleaning his tunic, his brasses and his boots. With his shaved head, waxed moustache, tiny yellow eyes, and swagger cane, Morgan's presence invariably meant trouble. His method of communicating was to bring the cadets to attention, select a victim, give a brief and disapproving dress inspection, then bawl directly into his face: 'How in hell's name did you get into a uniform? Types like you are going to lose the bloody war. Is that clear, airman . . . do you understand . . . ?' George thought the procedure cruel and tyrannical.

As long as Morgan was on parade, he never mellowed or showed any warmth. It was the first time they had had to submit to coercion; the first time they had realized how important it was to obey; the first time they had to answer 'sir' instead of 'you'. This time, Morgan was 'sir'. At least when they returned to civilian life at the end of the summer they would be rid of him.

As the days passed, they learnt how to obey without answering back, how to address a senior non-commissioned officer, how to click heels when saluting, how to stand in a queue and wait, how to scrub floors, how to make beds, and how to peel mounds of potatoes. In all such tasks David was hopeless. He resisted coercion of any kind and rebelled against Morgan's strait-jacketing tactics. Having to line up his thumbs with the seams of his trousers when on parade, or march past in slow motion, or go through the charade of presenting arms to some pipsqueak of an officer who had come to inspect them, he thought sheer lunacy. The crowning insult came when he was ordered to shave off his beard. The stupidity of some of the NCOs, who now lorded it over him, he found intolerable. 'Why is it that military life brings out the worst in people?'

'Because unchecked power thrives in the military. For the

weak, the first taste of power opens the door to tyranny,' George replied.

'If Cadet Evans would oblige . . .' a red-faced Morgan bawled across the square.

What made Morgan such a horror on the base and such a genial fellow in the village pub, they never understood. No one could change their facial expression, from benign to grimly displeased, as quickly as he did. The three men weathered the storm together and, when necessary, connived to outwit him. The good side of their summer training was that they did some more flying.

There was more than Morgan to worry about in the summer of 1939. WAR IN ASIA, EUROPE ON THE BRINK, GERMANY THREATENS POLAND, the newspaper headlines blared. The peaceful lanes around Kidlington began to echo to the sound of marching feet; soldiers appeared in their thousands; vast new military camps sprang up around Oxford overnight.

Because of the growing threat of war, George was not allowed to leave Kidlington for his wedding in mid-July. He never gave up trying to get through to the much-distraught Johanna on the telephone. 'A fine pickle you're in, Kemp, marrying a German,' Warrant Officer Morgan declared. 'They're a no-good people. We're just about to go to war with them, didn't you know?'

At the Krämers', all the preparations for the wedding had to be called off. To Frau Krämer's anguish, the scores of elaborate invitations she had sent out had to be followed by a letter of cancellation.

In late August, long after his planned wedding date, George was given a week's leave. 'Run while you've got it,' the orderly-room officer told him, handing him his leave slip. 'I expect all leave to be cancelled at any moment.' George got off the base as fast as he could, sent a telegram to inform Johanna that he was on his way to marry her, and telephoned his parents. They worried about him getting married on the eve of war.

On leaving the camp, he ran into an excited David Evans. 'I've won the All Souls Fellowship,' David shouted triumphantly. George congratulated him and shook his hand heartily, before climbing into a taxi.

Wearing civilian clothes, George crossed the Channel in an empty ship. The link between Britain and Germany was almost broken. There was an air of uncertainty among the few passengers who eyed each other uneasily. From the Hook of Holland he took the train to Cologne.

'What is the purpose of your visit?' the German immigration official asked him at the border.

'To get married.'

The official handed back the passport with a smile. '*Herzliche Glückwünsche!* It's a relief to know that the world has not gone completely mad.'

The German scene was ominous: everywhere troops were hurrying to join their regiments. The railway platforms and trains were crowded with them; the walls of the railway stations were plastered with notices about the military call-ups. On the roads, endless military convoys were on the move; air-raid shelters were being dug. In the towns, anti-aircraft crews were taking up positions surrounded by endless sandbagged defences. On the bright side, the bands continued to march and play; the heavy ears of wheat, which one could see from the train, promised a bumper harvest.

On arrival in Cologne, George was greeted by Johanna who rushed along the platform to meet him. '*Gott sei Dank dass Du hier bist*' (Thank God you've come), she said, throwing her arms around him and holding him tight. 'I've had nightmares about your getting here.'

'We've both had nightmares. Thank God I made it.'

Herr Krämer's face wore a worried look when they met him at lunch. He was convinced that war was only a matter of days away. 'I can feel it in the air. It horrifies me that the tragedy of the Great War will be repeated: *Armes Deutschland, arme Menschheit.*' (Poor Germany, poor humanity).

Johanna spent the evening pacifying her mother, who couldn't accept the idea of a rushed wedding with nobody but the family present. She had spent weeks with her daughter preparing for it; she had dreamt of helping Johanna to dress. The imminence of war, and the fact that George had to be back in England in five days' time, she refused to acknowledge. She went on wanting and not wanting the wedding to take place, dabbing her eyes with her handkerchief, sighing and regretting, until George's head spun. He was glad when bedtime came.

Not that he got much sleep, he was too much on edge. He spent a long, restless night watching the high beams of searchlights criss-crossing the sky. Most beams were white, but some were pale green and violet. This was his last night as a single man. The clock downstairs continued to chime throughout the night. At first light, he got up to close the window. The room had grown chilly.

George and Johanna were married in the Rathaus, the town hall. On arrival, all the family gave the Nazi salute. 'This is not the time and place for a scene,' Krämer cautioned George in a low voice, '*Hand hoch!*' (Hand up!) Having waited their turn, they went before an official wearing a tight-fitting dark suit whose expression alternated between a smile and a grimace. He greeted the Englishman with a suspicious stare. Johanna's parents and her sister Brigitte were the only witnesses. Johanna wore a rich brown velvet wedding dress ornamented with yellow roses, and her mother's necklace. She carried a bible and a bouquet of lilies. Her golden hair cascaded down her back.

The Rathaus ceremony was as bleak as only political fanaticism could make it. Directly in front of them on the wall was an enormous coloured picture of Hitler with his hypnotic stare. There were flowers on the table, but otherwise the room was cold and unfriendly. The windows were blocked out with sandbags. Briefly the official lectured the couple on the responsibilities of man and wife, and on the importance of complying with the will of the state. There was no mention of God, mystery, or union. They exchanged vows, George placed the ring on Johanna's finger; they kissed, signed the register, accepted the official's congratulations, thanked him, said '*Heil Hitler*' and left.

There followed a nuptial mass in a Catholic church, where the couple knelt before the altar. The organ played softly. Contrary to Frau Krämer's original plans, there were few guests. George had long since accepted the conditions laid down by the Church regarding the offspring of a mixed marriage: they would be brought up as Catholics. From a star-studded ceiling, saints, cherubim and angels looked down; a glint of sunshine filtered through the stained glass in the apse; the sacristan swung his censer; the altar bell rang; the white-robed altar boys chanted. There was an indescribable sense of the sacred. Accompanied by an audible sob from Johanna's mother, the couple pledged their troth for the second time.

As George and Johanna left the church, two little girls dressed in white threw flower petals in their path.

From the church they were driven through crowded streets to the Krämers. Before entering the house, the bride and groom were halted by neighbourhood children who had stretched a ribbon across the gate. Only after George had tossed coins to them were they given scissors to cut the ribbon and pass.

The wedding dinner began with many toasts to health

108

and welfare. Photographs were taken of the bridal party and friends. There were telephone calls to and from George's family in England. From Ansfield came a warm congratulatory telegram from Tony Markham: 'Every best wish for a long and happy life together.' Other messages were received from the crew.

'The world can do its worst now,' Johanna beamed at her husband, 'we are married.'

'For always,' George said, kissing her.

'I never dreamt I'd be so happy,' the bride whispered to her sister. 'I have found someone with whom I can share my heart.'

'Then why are you crying?'

'Because I am so happy that it frightens me.'

'What is there to be afraid of?'

The wedding accomplished, Johanna packed her worldly goods, including her favourite doll and some of the presents she had received, then she unpacked them and packed them again – to the point where she became bewildered. The floor was covered with presents, wrapping paper, scissors and string. She couldn't make up her mind what to take and what to leave.

By nightfall Johanna had surrendered her German passport. Having made prior arrangements with the British consul in Cologne, she received a British passport in exchange. 'Not a bad swap,' the consul volunteered. 'Let's hope there's peace.' He talked quietly to George about the threat of war. They would have stayed longer, but they had to prepare for their departure.

That night George and Johanna slept in the bed that Johanna's grandmother had used on her own wedding night long before. It was a carved oak four-poster with large pillows of handmade lace and starched white sheets. In a world divided, they became one. The future stretched before them, bright with promise and hope. They were not the same human beings when they came down to breakfast the next day. The world felt so new that it might have been the first day of creation. George recalled what Pascal had written about happiness: 'We always aspire to happiness but never really experience it.' Pascal was wrong; reasoning had taken advantage of him. They would remember that night all their lives.

The next day, the young couple received visits from family and close friends; Frau Krämer had insisted on it. A long line of them came clumping up the stairs carrying gifts and flowers, their lively voices echoed throughout the house. The housekeeper and the maid scampered up and down the staircase letting them in and out. Nobody could get in or out of the house without passing Hitler's portrait, which hung in the entrance hall where a large wooden crucifix used to be. Frau Krämer had put it there. 'It doesn't do to irritate the Nazis,' she said. Herr Krämer closed his eyes every time he passed it. A knot of Johanna's university friends came. They offered her their compliments and congratulations, addressing her as Mrs Kemp, which pleased her greatly. How wonderful it was to be married, how wholly right, how final. All that she asked was to have as happy a marriage as her parents had had. Love and trust had always existed between them.

Graf Böll was the last guest. His face was expressionless when he entered the house, a Nazi badge in his lapel. He had his dog with him. He declined Ilse's offer to take his hat and coat. He congratulated the young couple and wished them every happiness. Böll then took Frau Krämer aside. He sat with her at the end of the room talking heatedly. She looked pale. After some moments he kissed her hand and took his leave. She excused herself and left the room.

Everybody was woken early the next morning. At breakfast, the Krämers announced that they would accompany

110

George and Johanna as far as the Hook of Holland. Johanna hugged her mother at the suggestion. It would delay their parting. There was a last-minute scramble opening and closing the suitcases. Before leaving the house Herr and Frau Krämer walked slowly, hand in hand, from room to room, touching the polished furniture as they passed, opening and closing drawers. Johanna was puzzled by her parents' behaviour. She heard her mother say, 'I must be dreaming.' There were tears in her eyes.

Having told the housekeeper to expect the Krämers and Brigitte the following day, the five of them left the house. The taxi driver threw up his hands when he saw Johanna's mountain of luggage. '*Himmel, wo soll man das verstauen?*' (Heavens, where can I put all that?) As it was hot and sultry, with thunderstorms threatening, everyone was lightly dressed. At the station, they boarded the train to find that it was surprisingly full. There were none of the usual bands playing on the platforms. Instead, soldiers were building walls of sandbags. Everyone was discussing the recently announced Berlin-Moscow Pact, of which the Krämers were still unaware. Hitler and Stalin – hitherto deadly enemies – had suddenly become firm friends. Paper boys shouted the news and the papers were full of it. Herr Krämer thought this abrupt reversal in foreign policy absurd. 'The truth is they hate each other.'

In giant headlines, the newspapers also reported Hitler's latest threat against Poland. Of course, the present crisis, like all the other crises, was Poland's doing. Appeals for peace from President Roosevelt and the Pope were also front-page news.

While they were discussing these things, the train shuddered and inched forward in a cloud of steam. As it pulled out of the station, Cologne tested its air-raid sirens; the eerie blast shut out the grinding of the wheels.

The newly married couple sat close together. For the first

time, Johanna had an awful feeling that she was leaving Germany for good. Deep down, she felt a wrench at severing her roots. She loved her homeland, and had never dreamt that she would live anywhere else. She studied her parents' faces; they looked worn out and it worried her. She sought George's arm.

Later, as they ate lunch in the restaurant car, a terrible thunderstorm overtook the train. The torrential downpour was accompanied by great claps of thunder; flashes of lightning lit the rain-streaked windows. A startled fly landed on the edge of Herr Krämer's plate and was brushed off immediately by an apologetic waiter.

On approaching the Dutch frontier, Krämer gave his wife a glance that was heavy with meaning. She raised her eyebrows and shrugged. She looked uneasy, as if a sickness was on her. Slowly, the train clanged to a halt at Kaldenkirchen station. The station was on a war footing; sandbags covered the walls of the main building. Several passengers alighted. By then the worst of the storm had passed; the damp platform and train steamed in the summer heat; the surrounding fields breathed heavily under a dense mist. After one or two announcements, immigration and customs officials, accompanied by border police, leisurely came aboard. They chatted among themselves amiably.

The officials could not have been more co-operative – affability reigned. There was an air of detachment about the entire proceedings. No difficulties were raised about the Krämers entering Holland, or about Brigitte crossing the frontier. Papers and passports were shown, stamped and returned; reasons for the journey were given; it was all routine.

The inspection over, the officials drifted away one after another until there was only an old, wizen-faced officer left. The piping on his tunic was red – border police. He stood at Herr Krämer's side, looking at his papers through thick lenses, muttering to himself and seemingly undecided about what to do. Minutes passed; the other officials had by now left the train. George wondered why the man didn't go away. Out of the corner of his eye he could see the creased trousers and the polished boots; they never moved. Now and again, Krämer turned and gave the man a sharp look.

Instead of going away, the man leaned over. '*Es tut mir leid, Herr Krämer, würden Sie bitte mitkommen.*' (I'm sorry Herr Krämer, would you please accompany me.) The voice sounded conspicuously childlike. Frau Krämer's face became ashen.

'And my family?'

'They should come too.'

Burdened with Johanna's luggage, they followed the official to the stationmaster's office. Passengers pressed their faces against the windows to see what was going on. One never knew these days.

While the others sat on the luggage outside, Herr Krämer and his son-in-law disappeared into a room marked '*Privat*'. (Krämer had asked George to accompany him.) Two members of the Sicherheitsdienst – Security Police – sat at a table facing the door. No light came from the windows. They greeted Krämer and George with a fixed stare. Their eyes were cold and penetrating. Incongruously, a large bowl of flowers stood before them. Except for two other chairs, the room was bare.

'Identification papers,' the senior of the two officers demanded of Krämer. His manner was brusque, his voice devoid of feeling. He nodded hastily at George, whose identity he already knew. 'Herr Krämer,' he continued as he studied the papers, 'it is my duty to tell you that it will be necessary for you to return with us to Cologne. If you refuse, we will have to take you back under armed guard.' His gaze held Krämer's eyes intently; it never wavered. The atmosphere suddenly became oppressive; George was shocked.

For several moments Krämer remained silent, while studying the man's face. 'On what charges am I apprehended?' he asked grimly.

'You're charged with being an accomplice in the crime of your brother Bernd, whom you sheltered recently. He is now under arrest for conspiring with political enemies of the state. I'm sure there are no legal aspects of a case such as this with which, in your profession, you're not already familiar.'

'Hmm, well, probably not.' Krämer removed his glasses and held the lenses to the light. 'But why in the world you should pick on that incident is beyond me.'

The officer made notes, but did not reply.

'May I explain to my family what has happened without arousing their fears?'

'Certainly, but do not reveal what I've said. It would be better for everyone if your wife and daughter continued their journey. There will be plenty of time to explain matters to Frau Krämer when she returns to Cologne.' The officer coughed into his handkerchief. The sound of trains coupling and uncoupling, shunting and whistling, could be heard.

Accompanied by the two officers, Krämer returned to his wife. Her eyes were fearful. She took one look at her husband's face. 'Oh, my God,' she said and fainted. While trying to revive her, Krämer explained to Johanna that he had to return to Cologne because of a problem that had cropped up. He flatly refused to allow her to go back with him. 'We're dealing with a minor legal detail,' he persisted. 'We'll visit you in Britain as soon as the matter is settled.' Taking George aside, he urged him in an undertone to persuade Johanna to go on. 'Do as I say. It's vital.' George noticed that the life had drained from his father-in-law's face.

After a tearful discussion, Johanna finally agreed to

114

continue her journey to England. A porter brought his trolley. She said goodbye to each of her family in tears. The parting from her mother was particularly distressing. They stood at one side of the platform, whispering and consoling each other. 'Mutti! Mutti!' Johanna sobbed. Minutes later Johanna and George climbed into the train for Holland. It departed with a piercing whistle.

The last that Johanna saw of her parents and sister were three small pathetic figures waving their handkerchiefs. For a moment, the hissing engine shrouded them in steam. Overcome by grief, Johanna waved back. The poignancy of that moment would stay with her for the rest of her life. Standing behind the Krämers, the two security police officers watched the proceedings with dead eyes, indifferent to other people's sorrows.

Later that day Johanna told George that Graf Böll had urged her parents to flee. Had they reached the Netherlands, they would have sought political refuge in Britain.

George and Johanna reached the Hook several hours before the night ferry left for England; a subdued crowd was waiting to go onboard. Before embarking, George phoned his parents in London to tell them of Krämer's arrest. They were dumbfounded at the news. Johanna tried to ring Ilse the housekeeper in Cologne, but the phone rang and rang without anyone answering.

Alarm bells must have sounded in Europe, for the quayside became more and more crowded. Families clung to each other. The children were quiet. There were sad partings; Johanna was not the only one weeping. The fear of war and separation was tangible; it filled every mouth. One couple, having embarked, turned around and, with loud cries, amid a great commotion, fought their way off the boat at the very last moment. The gangway removed, the steamer slowly made its way into deeper water. Those on board continued to wave to those on shore.

The journey to England seemed to last for ever. To make matters worse, the wind and tides were at odds and it was a rough crossing. It was as if the weather was determined to add to people's sorrows. Many, including Johanna, were seasick.

On arrival at Victoria Station the next day, they were engulfed by hundreds of bewildered schoolchildren being evacuated from London. Each child wore an identity label and carried a gas mask in a cardboard box; some were crying. They had little idea what was happening, except that they were being sent away from their families and homes. Their teachers looked tense and on edge. Tired barrage balloons hung in the sky; anti-aircraft guns and military transports rumbled by. There was the same rush and hurry in the movement of troops and military equipment as they had witnessed in Germany; there were a lot of worried faces about.

George's parents were as kind as they could be to Johanna on her arrival at the Kemps' home in Wimbledon. They embraced her and congratulated the newlyweds on their marriage with a glass of wine. They commiserated with Johanna about her father's arrest. Mr Kemp had already been on to a colleague in the Foreign Office; Krämer, he was told, was too well known in legal circles in Britain for Whitehall to ignore the matter.

The next week was spent in trying to keep track of Herr Krämer's movements; Johanna was blind, deaf and dumb to anything else. Her father had always been her hero – it had never crossed her mind that he might be arrested. Urged on by George's father and his political and professional associates, the British government and the Bar Council made formal protests to Berlin. The matter was raised in the House of Commons and mentioned in the press. According to British sources, Krämer had been questioned in Cologne and Berlin and was now in detention in Cologne awaiting trial. Although all telephone communication with the Krämer residence had been severed, Frau Krämer, Brigitte and Ilse were apparently still living there. The British embassy had tried to deliver letters from Johanna to her parents – but there had been no reply.

Johanna remained completely dejected. Her old world had crumbled; her new world was alien to her. Sorrow gripped her heart. Every time she thought of her parents and her sister, she broke down in tears. 'What a terrible way to begin a marriage,' George's mother confided to her husband. 'And such a child, too.'

21

After an extra week's leave on compassionate grounds, George returned to duty at Kidlington. Johanna was to follow as soon as he could find suitable accommodation. The parting from his young wife was hard.

On his arrival at the now camouflaged air base, which was all of a bustle in preparing for war, Tony and David congratulated George on his marriage and listened sympathetically to his news. They found Krämer's arrest hard to believe.

Early the next morning, 1 September, they were awoken by a cadet hammering on their door. 'Get up!' he yelled. 'We're at war! Germany has just attacked Poland.' They scrambled out of bed, dressed and hurried to the mess. Everybody was hovering over the wireless. A feeling of climax was in the air.

'Thank God,' shouted one of the cadets. 'Berlin, here we come!'

117

'Oh hell!' said another. 'I'm getting married this week. Bugger it!'

Two days later, they joined a crowd around the camp wireless to hear Prime Minister Chamberlain declare war on Germany. 'We must commit our cause to God,' he ended. His voice was strained; there was no cheering; tension filled the room. The war that everybody had feared was upon them. The cadets were now subject to military law. Their lives had changed; so had their voices: they spoke quietly with a more serious air. There was no going back, no going home at the end of the summer; a door in their lives had slammed shut.

Chamberlain had hardly stopped speaking when London's air-raid sirens were heard on the wireless. As the camp's sirens began to howl, George, Tony and David joined in a wild scramble for the air-raid shelters. German planes were expected to bomb Britain on the outbreak of war. After all the rehearsals, this was the real thing; everyone had his gas mask ready.

It was a false alarm; the only air battle that took place that day over Britain was between British planes. Tragically, two Spitfires shot down two Hurricanes.

Max phoned that afternoon to tell George that Roger and his regiment were on their way to France. The British were keeping a promise to help France resist a feared German attack. That night George spent an hour trying to call Johanna, but couldn't get through; the lines remained jammed. He sat up late in the mess drinking beer and talking about the war. The click of billiard balls went on; there were shouts from the card tables; smoke hung in the air.

The next day training was renewed with added purpose.

A couple of weeks after Britain's declaration of war, Max visited his friends at Kidlington. He was in RAF uniform and, as he already knew how to fly, was about to win his wings. 'I've heard rumours that Russia is about to invade

Poland,' he said. None of them knew what to make of it. In a way that they had never anticipated, their lives had been stood on end; very little made sense.

Shortly after the outbreak of war, George, Tony and David were ordered to join an Initial Training Wing at an RAF military air base at Addem in north-east Scotland. George was grateful that they were not being packed off, as other cadets were, to Canada, South Africa or Southern Rhodesia. He didn't know how he would be able to explain to his young wife that he was going to the other end of Britain without her.

That night he managed to get through to Johanna and attempted to tell her – without violating RAF security – what was happening to him. She sounded lonely despite having the support of George's parents. They wept together and tried to cheer each other up; the war might end soon.

The last thing the cadets did the next morning before leaving was to rig up a bucket of water above Warrant Officer Morgan's barrack-room door. Hopefully, when he stepped out later, it would drown him.

In the plane, David opened a letter from All Souls College. 'We sincerely regret what has happened, and hope that you will be able to take up your fellowship after the war,' the college wrote. David looked a bit crushed. The open letter still in his hand, he didn't speak again until they were well on their way.

Later that day they flew over Aberdeen, its stone buildings gleaming in the sun. They caught flashes of silver from the rivers below. Shortly afterwards they were looking down on Addem airfield. It was heavily camouflaged. It stood on a low coastal plain, marshland and rolling countryside to the west and a wide sweep of grey-blue sea to the east. Hurricanes and Spitfires were parked well away from the tarmac and hangars; aircrews could be seen moving among the planes; anti-aircraft defences were scattered about. There were few trees: the surrounding fields were given over to cattle and crops. Running along the shore was what looked like a toy train going north, blowing smoke. Low hills rose in the distance; beyond them were purple peaks. Lying between sea and mountains, the base didn't look so bad.

Any illusions the three harboured of becoming instant air aces were quickly shattered the moment they touched down. With the doors flung back, they were met by a jarring chorus of: 'Out you get! Form up! Look lively! Let's be 'avin' you! At the double! Atten-shun! By the right, qui-ick march! 'Eft 'ight! 'Eft 'ight! 'Alt! Stand easy!'

Five minutes after landing, still clutching their duffel bags, they were lined up before their new boss, the air ace, Group Captain Barnaby. Small, trim and unsmiling, with deep-set eyes, white hair and strong features, he was famous for his exploits as a flight lieutenant in the Great War. At his feet was a black Labrador; it might have been Childers' dog.

Barnaby eyed the cadets slowly and wasted no words: 'Welcome, gentlemen, to Addem. You've been sent here to become fighter pilots. In the time available, it is an almost impossible task, as you will discover. Give of your best because your life and that of your fellow pilots depends on it. For the first time in history, our island is about to be besieged from the air. Upon your shoulders our freedom rests. I hope that your conduct in battle will do honour to yourself and your country. You won't know how good or bad a fighter pilot you are until you face the enemy. Only then will you discover who you are and what you're worth. The motto of the RAF is *Per Ardua ad Astra* – by effort to the stars. I recommend it to you. You will never reach the stars, but it is a road to follow – enough to have tried. Thank you, gentlemen.'

A sergeant took over. 'Atten-shun! By the right, qui-ick march! 'Eft 'ight! 'Eft 'ight! Swing your arms! Pull back your shoulders.'

One of the first things George did was to file an application to live off-base with his wife. That night, as on most nights, he wrote to Johanna telling her of his love. Talk of love was one of the few things never censored in the post.

The prospect for the Oxford men was forbidding. In one wrenching moment the privileges of university life fell away: they suddenly became no worse and no better than any other cadet. There was no scout to clean up after them, fetch and carry for them, make their beds, clean their shoes, press their clothes, bring their shaving water and tell them that they had ten minutes before breakfast was done. Tony's Arthur Weasel was already in France.

The cadets were expected to run or march everywhere; there was a weekly inspection parade when their kit was expected to glitter; physical training was daily; sports were compulsory; discipline was unrelenting. Pleasing oneself belonged to another world. Anyone questioning rules, let alone disobeying them, was in for trouble – and that included David Evans. Answering back was a thing of the past. After several days they felt run off their feet.

Having gone through the name, address and religion business again, they were issued with baggy flying-suits, sheepskin boots, leather helmets, goggles, gloves and a parachute. All they had to do now was to win their wings.

Shortly after their arrival at Addem, the three men were billeted at the back of a cold, scrubbed lodging-house on the seafront, owned by a bird-like Calvinistic landlady called Miss Fogg. She had a deeply lined face and melancholy eyes. Her brown cat ignored the lodgers. The beds and the chairs were as hard as rocks; they smelt of salt and seaweed, and had had much wear and tear. The only thing hanging on the whitewashed walls was a plain wooden crucifix. Outlined in the bedroom window was a black-faced church and a graveyard with its withered wreaths and flowers. A thick hedge with berries and sparrows separated them from the crooked crosses and the black headstones. The leaves were bright with autumn cold.

From the window that afternoon they had a front-row view of a burial. First came the minister and the Cross, then the coffin carried by six solemn men, whose steps were hesitant and slow. The mourners followed, handkerchiefs to faces, shuffling haphazardly like sheep, some of them clinging to each other as if they might fall over. The coffin was lowered into the ground, clods of earth rained down, and the click of the gravediggers' spades brought the funeral to an end. 'The poor bairn,' Miss Fogg said to her lodgers. 'We are all one in death. It is as God wills.' She had a great liking for the dead. There was in fact a faintly funereal smell about her.

On returning to their lodgings at night, they'd catch a glimpse of their landlady in the kitchen. She was forever sewing and she treated them like children. 'You ought to be at home in your parents' care. Get along with you,' she scolded them, with a suspicion of a smile. Some nights her neighbour Mr Tattin – a squat, bald fellow, with a heavy chin – would be there talking Gaelic and drinking tea.

One day on the air base was much like the next. With tunics spick and span and boots polished, they marched through the swirling mist to breakfast at 7 a.m. The food was revolting, but they learnt to eat it. The noise in the dining room was deafening. Raucous laughter was always breaking out. They were expected to be on the tarmac with the flying instructors at 8 a.m. prompt – no excuses, no shilly-shallying. By then the gulls were active; later the sun would disperse the lingering mist. The day was spent in the basic flight-trainers and in the classrooms going over – in monotonous detail – what they had learnt earlier.

At the end of the day the airmen would go over to the sandbagged mess – the place was always filled with tobacco smoke – and phone home. The building was a wartime tar-and-paper job; icy draughts were everywhere. Littered with newspapers, boots, jackets, scarves, cigarette ends, and parcels from home, it hummed with voices. There was always a chess set in use; the billiard table was crowded; the recruits thumped on the battered piano. From the mess's cold walls, pictures of air aces of the Great War looked down. The cadets came from countries across the world. No one said it, but everyone knew that, as far as flying was concerned, they were a superior crowd.

When free of chores, George and his friends wandered down to the dispersal hut where they sat with the pilots and smoked and talked and drank coffee and watched the real flyers coming from battle and going out to fight again. German planes regularly flew over northern Scotland, many of them finishing up in the sea. With its sizzling oil-and-water stove, its nudes, its phones, its model planes, books, magazines and old broken chairs, the dispersal point was where the real action took place.

Sometimes, pilots who had made their first 'kill' would return to do a wild dance in that confined space. Faces alight, they were as noisy and excited as later on they would be silent and exhausted. Now and again, a pilot would break down completely. Others would flood rooms with water, set fire to furniture, or remain drunk from one day to the next. Except for the odd pilot who was trying to spoof his way out of combat duty, rest was the only cure.

When the mess radio wasn't playing morale-boosting songs like 'When the Lights Go On Again All Over the World,' or 'We'll Meet Again, Don't Know Where, Don't Know When', the Oxford men would listen to discussions about Germany's and Russia's joint conquest of Poland, Russia's invasion of Finland, or the course of the 'phoney war' in France. Much of it was gibberish to them. Despite unbearably heavy British losses at sea, the BBC narrator's voice exuded confidence and superiority.

123

From Johanna, George learned that the US had joined Britain in denouncing the arrest of her father, but nothing had come of it. No one knew where he was being held.

Sometimes, afire with life, and on the principle that a short life should be a merry one, George and his friends would go on a drinking spree in Addem. What fears they had could be drunk away, though it didn't take them long to realize that flying and drinking don't go together. At weekends, they would fish for trout or salmon, or hunt hares with borrowed shotguns. George and David were hopeless at finding food; Tony excelled at it. Always hungry, they quickly cooked and ate what they'd caught. Local fishermen and hunters, who had the air of a race apart, resented their poaching. 'Bloody foreigners!' they protested indignantly. Every Saturday night there was a dance at the air base. It was an opportunity to shed the tensions built up during the week. Local girls were brought in by the truckload. All in their teens, many were hungry for love. The courting went on in the interval, in the shadows outside the building. War bred recklessness in everything; tomorrow you might be dead.

David was sometimes roped in to sing during the intermission. On one occasion, he received overwhelming applause for singing that great favourite, '*J'attendrai*'. Drunk or sober, everybody rose to their feet for the National Anthem at the end of the evening.

22

Although the station commander frowned on it, cut-throat gambling took place in the mess every night. Gambling was meat and drink to some; the chants 'Pass,' 'Raise you,'

'Double you,' 'See you,' went on and on. Poker was the favourite, some were addicted to it. The greater the stakes, the greater the crowd, and the greater the need to be on guard. There were times when the stakes were so high that everyone in the room froze until the next call.

Of the three, only Tony Markham could afford to go in up to his eyes. Betting on horses and cards was an Ansfield tradition. He enjoyed the risk. But it was David who won most. A cautious player, he never spoke at the table, nor did he drink. He knew when to stay, raise, see, or drop out of the game. He loved working out the odds and the sequence of cards, he knew mathematically the relative expectancy of every kind of hand. They thought him a wizard. Such knowledge didn't stop him from losing, but over time it gave him more wins than losses. He won so much that he could have managed without his Air Force pay.

Late one night they played for particularly high stakes. One of the players was a twenty-year-old called Steve Newton. Newton was strangely disliked, perhaps because of the downcast look he always wore. Tony, forever generous, had paid for the round of drinks. George had opted out; he didn't have David's skill or Tony's money, and had already lost enough for one night. After the cards were shuffled, cut and dealt, Newton began an extraordinary run of luck. He won the first three rounds with a flush, a straight hand, and three of a kind. He continued to win, either with unusually strong hands or by bluffing. The more 'pots' he won, the greater the pile of money in front of him, the more quarrelsome and hotheaded he became. Hidden by clouds of smoke, spilling his matches and cigarette ends on the floor, he went on talking of things nobody wanted to hear about.

An hour later David had dropped out and there was a stand-off between Tony and Steve Newton. It was to be the

125

last game of the evening. Newton's winnings had been whittled down, but there was still a lot of money in the 'pot'. Tony had raised Newton by five pounds. There was an expectant pause while his opponent took a quick glance at his hand, and studied Tony's face. Tony returned his long, cautious stare. 'I'll raise you,' Newton said, increasing the stakes. Unusually for him, he was smiling. Tony took his time; he lit another cigarette and sipped his whisky. He wondered if the fellow was bluffing, or did he have a straight flush? He matched the bet. 'I'll see you.'

Slowly Newton revealed his hand: three queens. He never took his eyes off his opponent's face; there was defiance in his look. Quietly, Tony turned his cards over: three kings.

Newton's confidence vanished; he blanched. Bursting into tears, he picked up his cigarettes and what money he had left and hurried out of the room without saying goodnight.

'A bad loser,' someone remarked.

The next day, on full throttle, Newton slammed his plane into a hill. He had left a note behind. Tony was detailed to go out as one of the recovery party. He felt bad about winning the man's money; in a way, he'd killed him. There was an unspoken wrong about Steve Newton's death. Tony helped to extract the body from the wreckage and didn't like what he saw. Charred and jammed into the confined space of the cockpit, it looked like a burned log. They had difficulty finding the head with its embedded goggles.

Newton was posted as killed in action. His comrades passed silent judgement on him. He had borrowed money until he could borrow no more; a long run of ill-fortune at the gaming table had brought him to the begging stage. There was a fuss about his death, but in the mess the gambling continued, even while his sealed coffin was in the morgue.

They tossed a coin for pall-bearers. It fell to George and others to bury what was left of Newton in the snow-covered churchyard, where all sounds, times, shapes and spaces were muffled. Over the past weeks, George had watched him fall apart and would have gladly avoided the funeral. Slowly, those bearing the coffin shuffled their way through the snow to the grave. Even in death, their dislike of the man remained unchanged. Newton's mother and Miss Fogg were the only mourners. Only his mother cried at the graveside. To be killed in action was acceptable; to be killed by deliberately slamming yourself and your plane into a hillside was not. It was too cold for flowers. A holly wreath with bright red berries lay on the coffin.

23

The pace of life at Addem was so fast that Newton was soon forgotten. After his locker had been cleaned out; not a trace of him remained. George and his companions, using American Miles Master dual-control fighter-trainers, were in the air every day. Endlessly, they climbed into the cockpit, their parachutes buckled across their chests, strapped themselves in, tested the controls, and with the help of the corporal fitter, took off. If all went well, the planes suddenly and miraculously rose into the sky. Exhilarated, adjusting helmet, goggles and ear straps, they'd soar like birds, gaining new views of the earth, the heavens and the sea. They'd flip on their radios and listen to the crackling world around them.

No sooner were they airborne than instruction began: 'Keep your eye on the artificial horizon; keep it level; watch the altimeter; line yourself up with a cloud . . .' and on and on. There was no familiarity between instructor and cadet. There couldn't be as the instructor demanded immediate obedience. A cadet's chance of a commission depended on the instructors' reports.

As always, David Evans proved to be a problem. He'd hum on the intercom. 'There's nothing to bloody well hum about, Evans.' When he wasn't humming, he went on about angles and spins and prop revolutions until he confused the instructors and everybody else. His passion for logic and maths caused him to be fanatical over matters of minor importance. Where maths was concerned, his trainers could not keep up with him. There were times when he took advantage of them and led them by the nose. He was always theorizing, always stressing fundamental laws. He accepted nothing that wasn't thought through. If other people's heads were not up to it, that wasn't his fault. The instructors' 'Damn it, man, it's an order,' meant nothing to David, who defied convention on principle. Their threats about practical consequences left him unperturbed; their appeals to God only appalled his Welsh soul. He refused to be browbeaten. He never listened to Tony's warnings that he was in danger of being thrown out. 'Sooner the better,' he would answer. He didn't seem to have his heart in the game. There were times when the instructors wondered what they'd caught. Laughing among themselves, they called him 'professor'.

At the outset of the training, it was rise, circle, land; rise, circle, land, *ad infinitum*. Later, the cadets would chase each other down great valleys of cloud with endless shadows and rainbows. It called for both daring and discipline.

The sky could be a lonely place and they all experienced the horror of being lost in murk and mist. Ordered to land, George sometimes failed to find the right field. Through the mist, every field looked the same. Unfamiliar woods, heaths, farms, groups of houses, ditches and rivers, ploughland and pasture glided by. With obscene mutterings from the instructor in the rear of the plane, he'd go back to the

128

railway line and the sea, or to Balmoral or Braemar Castle to get his bearings.

The instructors were a highly skilled lot, with years of experience behind them. Nothing surprised them. 'Don't panic' was their maxim. 'No use getting fussed.' Pilots made of ice were what they were looking for. Yet it was not unknown for the odd instructor to explode: 'How many times must I tell you, you bloody idiot . . . You're bloody well wet behind the ears.' Even the best instructors had a habit of muttering from the rear about being cursed with an imbecile who was determined to kill them. Such outcries were never taken seriously; everyone was under strain.

The stress increased when they began to bring their planes in at the end of the flight. Gingerly, they felt their way down to the airfield, throttling back as it came up to meet them. Flaps down, they'd ease the stick back and then, at what they'd been taught was the right moment, slam the stick against their stomach and ease the nose into the wind. There'd be an awful wobble. If the fates were kind, they'd bounce a bit on landing – invariably forgetting to see-saw the rudder bar. Foot pressing lightly on the brakes, they'd taxi slowly to a halt. If the fates were unkind – with the mutterings from the rear growing more insistent – they'd slew and weave their way down to the ground, drop like a stone on the runway, bounce high into the air, bounce twice more for good measure, and grind to a halt. 'You're bloody well determined to kill me,' a shaken instructor would shout, hurriedly climbing out of the cockpit. Sometimes a cadet did.

Night flying was particularly grim. They'd line up their planes in the pitch dark – sometimes with the aid of a torch – at the end of the runway. The moment the runway lights were switched on, the leading plane would lunge forward, struggling to rise from the darkened earth. With the runway lights going on and off, the others followed one by one.

There was no room for error. Silhouettes of the camp buildings flashed by on either side; once up, the lights went out.

Landing in the dark could be equally hazardous. On the ghostly, dimly-lit runway, distances could be deceptive. They watched one pilot misjudge his landing, veer off and prang his plane into a building, killing himself. They saw another overshoot the flare path and the aerodrome, plough across fields and crash into a stone wall. These accidental deaths were honourable, yet it was sickening to watch a friend end his flying career this way. Miss Fogg was never short of a burial to attend.

Of the three, George was the last to fly solo. It hurt his pride and his self-respect. Despite all his enthusiasm to begin a new life, he'd had a rough time in training, something which he kept from his wife and family. Tasks that came easily to Tony and David came hard to George. He lacked Tony's enormous self-confidence and David's skills. For some reason, he never seemed to get the feel of a plane: he couldn't watch his instruments while co-ordinating his feet on the rudder and his hands on the stick and the throttle at the same time. The instructors had taught him what to do, but he kept forgetting. 'Relax,' they told him. 'You'll never "twig" it if you don't.' At one point there was doubt if he'd win his wings. 'Lacks resolve,' reported one instructor. 'Inwardly weak,' said another. The comments, relayed to George, touched him to the quick.

'"It's all yours, Kemp, take it up," the chief instructor ordered me today,' George recorded in his diary. 'I swear the fellow was grinning. I hated him for it. Determined not to show fear, I climbed into the cockpit and took off. I was convinced that everybody else had chosen to take off at the same time,' he wrote. 'Once up, I made a wide sweep of the airfield. I was surprised how much better I flew without the instructor on my neck. I began to enjoy myself; the sense of triumph was almost intoxicating. My earlier fears of giving way were absurd.

'After fifteen minutes I was back over the base. With the instructor watching, with wheels and flaps down, I put the machine into a gliding turn about the hangars. After that I made a wide sweep, throttled back and approached the hedgerow at the end of the runway. The hydraulic pump groaned and rattled to an extraordinary degree as I put my wheels down. With the ground coming up at me unusually quickly, I waited for the right moment before pulling heavily on the stick. The plane hit the runway and ran on at a great speed. I jerked up the flaps, waited a second and then gently applied the brakes. I still ran on until the last yard of the runway and finished up with the hedgerow touching the plane. Shaken, I turned, taxied back to the hangar and cut the engine. "Seen worse," the instructor scoffed, as I climbed out. He seemed to be enjoying my troubles.'

George didn't take the criticism to heart; instructors were known to be hard and craggy. It only increased his determination to succeed. 'One day, I swear, I'll beat them at their own game,' he wrote. 'I'll make them eat their words, damn them! It's only a matter of time before I distinguish myself.' Always he was fighting his own fears.

The three men continued to fly solo every day. The aim now was how to kill, or at least how to survive under stress. Pushed deep into their seats by terrific pressure, thrown this way then that, head driven into the body, with the plane on its belly and then on its back, held in only by their harnesses, the cadets frantically manoeuvred to get each other in their gun sights. To survive, they needed eyes all around their heads.

With the instructors buzzing around them, they were taught every trick of combat. Aggression was the key.

'There's only one way to deal with an attack: turn and face it. If you begin to think in terms of defence, you're dead.' Fights were broken off only to start again. Using blank cartridges, there would be endless dogfights and pretend 'kills'. Tony enjoyed it. He called it jousting in the sky. Somehow, he never got fussed.

Time and again, the instructors, playing the part of Germans, would suddenly appear out of nowhere to make a 'kill'. 'Number One, you're on fire. You've had it. You're on the way down.' Sometimes they would warn pilots of the dangers in the sky: 'Look to the right; the sods are coming up at you. There's more of them below to port! . . . Watch the bugger behind . . . Break! Break! Don't hang around. For Christ's sake, break! . . . Watch for flak coming up at three o'clock.'

One instructor, Sergeant Haughton, had a macabre streak. He revelled in each 'kill'. 'You've bought it, Evans, you have.' As far as he was concerned, the more 'kills' the better. '"Who saw him die? 'I,' said the Fly. 'With my little eye, I saw him die.'" Ah!' he'd say before switching off. 'Ah!' He was downright creepy. He was the only instructor with a natural tendency to laziness. Once out of the cockpit, he moved with a slow, heavy motion. He wanted the war over so that he could sit around and yarn, and smoke an atrocious number of cigarettes.

David got the hang of the killing game before George and Tony. The instructors had to agree that he was smart under pressure. He was not only a 'professor', but a man of action. In an air duel he was deadly; when he fired, he killed.

Victory went to the most skilled and the sharpest-witted. 'You must be quick and decisive,' the instructors urged. 'React ten seconds after the German, dive too steeply, fail to spot the Hun in the sun, indulge in a moment's absence of mind, and you're dead.' Always they stressed stealth and the pre-emptive strike. 'A dogfight is a killing matter; it ends with death. You've got to get in there and knock him dead. There is no time for pity or mercy. Winning is all that counts.'

The instructors displayed superb airmanship, which they tried to teach. Each had developed his own technique of combat. They showed the cadets how to straighten up behind the target, and how to fire their guns in short, sharp bursts before rolling away. They called it 'getting off a squirt'. 'At one hundred yards astern, you just.can't miss.'

It was an exhausting procedure: the cadets' hearts pounded, they became drenched with sweat; all of them felt the pressure. To ease the burden, some of them carried lucky charms and actually believed in them. Tony carried a tiny silver horse on a chain round his neck, which Lydia had given him; George's talisman was a picture of Johanna. It had been taken on a beach somewhere in Germany. She was wearing a swimming costume, which revealed her lovely figure; her bright face was turned to the camera. One Irish Catholic wouldn't fly unless he had a tiny statue of the Virgin Mary in his cockpit. David had a little brass replica of St Bernardino, a famous saint, from his birthplace in Wales. All those who had carried it in the Great War had returned to the village unscathed, or so he said. Of course, he was too much of a scientist to believe in supernatural means of protection.

Occasionally, the trainers escorted the cadets out to sea to fire live ammunition at targets moored in the water. One touch of the button with the ball of the thumb would cause a shattering roar and send a solid stream of metal at the target. Here again, David excelled. When it was time to head for home, the trainers would fall upon them out of the clouds and round them up like shepherd dogs. Only when they'd climbed out of their planes at the end of the day could they afford to smoke and relax. Always there was a post-mortem of the day's flying, which was taken seriously. They knew that the Germans would not play mock battles with them.

David would sometimes make a nuisance of himself at these meetings. He'd challenge the instructors' arguments and show, usually through a cloud of smoke, where they were wrong with calculations on the back of an envelope. He dealt with square roots and kinetic energy and centre of gravity and speed variations until their heads spun. He was the first to spot the flaw in the new speed indicator they were using. By his reckoning, it was exactly five per cent out of line. He was always annoyingly right. 'The only way to convince that bugger Evans,' one of the instructors threatened, 'is to use real bloody bullets. That would shut him up.' The wonder is they didn't.

In time, the three men graduated from Miles Master training planes to flying hunch-backed Hurricanes, and finally to the most wonderful plane of all, the Spitfire. A strange mystique had grown up at Addem about the sleek, nimble 'Spit'. It was faster and lighter and had a legend in its favour.

24

Weary of the Addem regime, some time in early November, while the weather was still favourable, the three took two days off to hike the forty miles from Aviemore to the village of Blair Atholl. The hike was a favourite of Group Captain Barnaby, who hunted deer there. In the mess, the walk was always referred to as 'Barnaby's Death March'. He was forever recommending it to new cadets: 'Do you a world of good, young man. Toughen you up.'

'Well,' Barnaby approached George in the mess one day, 'What about it? Is it on?' He gave him a look that defied him to say no.

'It's on,' George said. He welcomed the chance to get away from the base.

Early on the first day, a friendly RAF driver dropped the three men off at Aviemore. He was to pick them up two days later. With the parting words, 'Yer don't know wot ye're in fer,' he left them at the foot of the hills. Kit strapped to their backs, sticks in hand, compasses and maps in pockets, they began to climb the wild, muddy upward track leading to a pass seven or eight miles away. Wild water, the colour of beer, rushed and plunged past them downhill; a skimming grouse was the only living creature they saw.

Without warning, a weak sun suddenly penetrated the mist; the air cleared. All around them were endless uplands of purple-brown heather and blue-grey mountains – the Cairngorms and the Grampians – whose peaks were lost in cloud. The meeting of mountain and sky was as spectacular and as inspiring as anything they had seen in the Swiss Alps.

After three hours of upward march through fields awash with mist-drenched heather, with the sun now gone and the clouds low above their heads, they sheltered under a crag from a heavy shower, which started with a drizzle and ended with a fury of hailstones.

The rain gone, they climbed an unending, twisting, stony track, which brought them to a gloomy pass, where they had to jump from rock to rock across the ice-patched streams. By now their feet were wet through. After a while the trail disappeared altogether, and they had to slip and slide over boulders. Peat bogs and yawning potholes followed.

With Tony leading, they walked under overhanging rocks, a yawning abyss at their side. Now and again they halted to adjust their kit, enjoy the view and study the map. They felt their old selves again and rejoiced at having escaped from RAF discipline – especially David.

As they trudged on, they swapped news. 'I spoke on the phone to Bill Clark before leaving Addem,' George said. 'He's in Glasgow. He's been assigned to duty on a destroyer and is on the point of sailing down the Clyde with a green crew on convoy duty in the North Atlantic. He sounded proud. He's a sublieutenant. It's his first step up the ladder.'

'I'll let you in on a secret,' Tony put in. 'Lydia and I have decided to get married during the Christmas holidays. We hope you'll turn up.' There was a subdued cheer. It had been a love match from the start, but everyone also knew that Lydia would bring a lot of land to the marriage. Later, Tony asked George to be his best man.

Several miles farther on they emerged from the dark pass and descended to open grassy country where the turf was as thick and soft as fur. Completely exhausted, they collapsed by the side of a river edged with stones. The water was clear and quiet. They were wet to the skin, cold and aching all over. George wondered what David found to sing about. When he wasn't singing he was smoking his pipe.

They bathed their chafed feet, smoked a cigarette and forded the river; the icy water reached to their knees. On the other side they put on dry socks. After another eight miles, with the light fading, they threw off their packs and collapsed on a heather-covered hill by a fallen Scots fir. Nothing stirred. With tufts of heather, pine needles, dead branches, and rich brown peat they soon had a roaring fire going and crowded close to the heat.

After eating great quantities of hot baked beans and pork sausages, accompanied by scalding tea, they hung their clothes and boots to dry, then gathered pine branches to make into beds. In time the mist cleared, and the moon and stars shone brightly above the hills. The now black pinewoods rose dimly in the distance. Rarely had they known such peace.

They fell asleep watching the sparks rising from the glowing embers of the fire.

During the night they awoke shivering and threw on fresh wood, enough to make the fire crackle.

'Are you asleep?' George asked David in the early hours.

'No.'

'Are you still looking forward to becoming an academic?'

'I did once. Now go back to sleep.'

'How can you sleep on such a cold, clear night and with such a moon above your head? I wonder if the god of war is supreme up there?'

'Oh, shut up, George – there's a good chap.'

Light came grudgingly the next day. After scalding tea, more beans and biscuits, they made an early start for Blair Atholl, twenty miles to the south.

The air was crisp, the mountains fresh in the morning light. The miles seemed shorter, the hills less steep. As the clouds drifted across the peaks, the ribbed heights changed from light to dark. Capped by snow, all stood out against the blue sky in naked distinction; the mist lying across the moors turned to gold. A hawk hovered above them. 'Was there ever such a morning in the world before?' Tony asked. 'Now you know why Walter Turnbull used to quote Keats saying that beauty is truth, truth beauty.'

'Only God could make such beauty,' answered David, and broke into song about the mountains of his native Wales. George took pictures of their surroundings. Thus far, they had not met a soul. For the first time since coming to Addem they felt the emotions of solitude.

Several times they stopped and gazed at the scenery, each of them occupied with his own thoughts. With binoculars, they could see heavy snow on the summits that would never melt, and glacial holes where Tony said the deer were inclined to lie. They caught a glimpse of red deer grazing on the distant hills – their bodies small and elegant enough to be mystical. Their bugling came down the wind. All was peaceful and wild. Tony thought of the deer that would sometimes graze on the lawn outside Ansfield House.

While he was studying the deer, he saw one animal collapse. A shot rang out, followed by a rolling echo. 'Trouble in Paradise,' mused George. 'I hope he died quickly. Deer are lucky; they die without any idea of death – nor do they worry about eternal life. I've read somewhere that death is a problem peculiar to man alone.'

They also saw their first golden eagle majestically patrolling the sky. It flew with a sublime air no pilot could match.

While sitting on their packs, gunfire reached them on the wind. They became aware of an air battle some distance away; an explosion sounded from deep in the mountains; a parachute appeared in the sky. Fascinated, they watched as the white dot drifted in their direction. They wondered whether it was friend or foe. The closer it got, the greater their concern.

The parachute landed about a quarter of a mile away. An RAF plane flashed above it across the moor. 'I wonder if it's a German,' said Tony, peering through his field glasses.

'We'd better go and see,' George said.

'Leave him alone,' said David. 'If he's a German, he'll be armed and perhaps a bit crazy.'

'This is where your German comes in, George. I'm sure you'll be able to calm him down; after all, you are a lawyer.'

'We'll meet enough Germans later on and we're not armed,' said David.

Tony thought it unfitting to walk away from a downed pilot – so the three of them went to look.

'Hello,' called George as they approached. The pilot had freed himself of his parachute and his helmet and was standing with a revolver in his hand. He was tall and fair-haired, with a moustache, and about the same age as themselves. He was dressed in Luftwaffe uniform: he wore high boots, black trousers and a short dark jacket bearing his epaulettes and his wings. He looked a well-built, tough fellow. For a few moments he stood there, eyes flashing from one to the other of them. He gave the impression of someone about to bolt for cover.

'George, tell him that to stand with a gun in his hand is a certain way to get killed,' said Tony. 'Tell him that he has the choice of surrendering to us, or staying here with the risk of being shot. If he hasn't made up his mind in a couple of minutes, we'll leave him to his fate.'

George shouted in German for the fellow to hand over his pistol. The man didn't move. He still held his gun before him. There was nothing to stop him shooting the three of them. The tension was unbearable. After standing there seemingly at a loss to know what to do, he suddenly replaced his pistol in its holster, stepped forward sharply and saluted: '*Heil Hitler*. Leutnant Karl Steglitz.'

Everybody breathed a sigh of relief.

They formed up, with the German between them, and continued their march across a long, flat stretch of heather. George carried the pistol in his belt; he hoped that the prisoner would not take it into his head to bolt; he'd hate to have to shoot him. He wondered what Johanna would have thought of it all.

With their eye on the prisoner, they continued across the open moors. The sweep of the terrain delighted them. After the hardships of the previous day, all was joy. At the end of a mile-long gorge, they came upon another river, splashing and cascading its peaty waters to the sea. Some of the beeches and oaks were still blazing with late red and yellow leaves. They knew from the map that the river led to their journey's end at Blair Atholl. Once more they bathed their feet, changed their socks, and had a mouthful of food. Cloud shadows drifted over the hills.

The German was reluctant to share their rations; what he did accept, he ate awkwardly. He seemed to have reconciled himself to his fate. He talked with George, who told him that he had recently been married in Cologne.

'What does he say?' asked Tony.

'He agrees that there would not be much point in making a dash for it here.'

'What's he doing here anyway?' asked David.

'He's been reconnoitring Scapa, and the Firth. He wonders what the Luftwaffe will think of his bailing out. It might damage his career.'

'Ask him who's going to win the war.'

'*Deutschland, natürlich.*' There was an arrogant note.

'Why are you so sure?' Tony asked through George.

'Göring is confident that the Luftwaffe will bring England to its knees. In the air, you are inferior. Besides, it's Germany's destiny to rule Europe.'

'That's what Napoleon thought,' David replied. 'The result was a bloodbath. Believe me, you're lucky that events have tossed you out of the war.'

'*Es wird im Kampf entschieden.* (War will decide.) The *Sitzkrieg* (phoney war) can't go on for ever. I shall be home for Christmas, you'll see.'

Their hostility towards him lessened when George revealed that Karl had rowed on the Neckar for Heidelberg university. The German was not only a fellow pilot, he was a fellow rower.

Later that day, they saw white flecks of sheep on the sloping mountainside. They heard their cries. Quite suddenly, they disturbed a doe in the bracken. Men and beast regarded each other with questioning eyes. The deer

140

remained frozen to the spot for a moment, then gently yet swiftly made off. Later they zigzagged down through the trees to the river again with its reddish, washed stones. By now the earlier glowing peaks were capped with cloud.

As they hurried forward the miles became longer, the hills steeper, the gorges deeper, their backpacks heavier. They didn't try to conceal their fatigue; they were so tired that they didn't stop to talk to anyone they met. Tony's concern was to get to Blair Atholl before the driver got tired of waiting and went back to Addem.

In the final hours of the march, they talked about nothing but food. Dismissing war rationing, they spoke of feasts they'd known. Tony talked about the lovely sausages he'd eaten in Switzerland – twenty kinds. The German said that in Munich there were thirty. 'A good slice of beef will do me,' Tony decided. They made reckless promises about what they'd do for the driver if he was still waiting. They were prepared to promise anything to avoid a gruelling train ride. They knew that the 'up' train idled at every station. All they wanted was to hand over the German to the police, fill themselves with food and drink, and be driven back to their beds.

The sun was now low. With the light almost gone and gusts of wind at their backs, the imposing white façade of Blair Castle at last came into view. Even Tony, the toughest and most experienced of the four, felt the ordeal. 'One last effort,' he called to George who was straggling behind with the prisoner. With trailing feet and aching bodies, they eventually tumbled into the inn. A boy stood transfixed at the door as the German passed him. Blessedly, they found the driver sitting in the narrow bar with a couple of farmers. The three were astonished at the sight of the German, but responded eagerly to Tony's call for drinks all round.

Before going in to eat, George called the police. After which, despite wartime regulations about 'fraternizing with the enemy', and muted protests from the prisoner, they all sat down together in the empty dining room. The presence of the German upset the waiter. 'Dash it all,' Tony said, 'we can't leave the fellow in the corridor, and we're all starving.' It troubled him that a uniform could make all the difference. The German could have been a student from Oxford instead of Heidelberg. Before the war, they would have welcomed his company.

Alas, they had hardly swallowed their soup when a confused, red-faced constable appeared. He was armed and carried handcuffs. He was startled at the sight of the German eating with the others.

'I'm not sure that this kind of thing is allowed, gentlemen.'

'I'm sure it isn't,' Tony agreed.

'Good luck,' they called as Karl was led away.

'And you also. *Auf Wiedersehen und danke*.' He looked back and waved with his handcuffed hands.

The next day George phoned Johanna and told her all that had happened. Although he phoned and wrote to her at every opportunity, she could not hide her loneliness from him. She had heard nothing more about her family in Germany. She told him that Bill Clark had sent them a letter from Newfoundland. She couldn't imagine where the letter had been – it was dated September.

25

Bill Clark had left Bath in early September. His mother had seen him off on the train to Glasgow, waving bravely as it pulled out of the station.

The train was packed with RN personnel reporting for duty. There was a lot of laughing and shouting and knee-slapping. Together, they were going to give Hitler hell. There was talk about when the first bombs would drop on London.

From Glasgow, Bill took a bus to Greenock on the Clyde. After searching the crowded quays, he found HMS *Exeter* anchored close to the aircraft carrier *Ark Royal*. Although dwarfed by the larger ship, the *Exeter*'s long, lean, clean-cut lines impressed him. He was the last officer to board.

Two days later, the *Exeter* put out to sea. With other warships, it took charge of a convoy of more than forty merchant marine vessels forming up off Liverpool. Stretching over several miles, Bill's convoy gradually made its way down the choppy Irish Sea beneath a low, grey sky. He could just discern the mist-covered Irish coast; there was no war there. 'Darken ship!' was the command as they left Ireland behind.

Day after day, the convoy battled its way across the Atlantic. Bill became accustomed to being dragged out of his bunk at all hours of the night. Half asleep, he stumbled up the ladder to the bridge to do his four-hour stint. He was proud to do so. Under the supervision of a first lieutenant, he learned how to keep the *Exeter* on course, guarding that part of the convoy for which his ship was responsible. Often he found Captain Rodney wedged in a corner of the bridge, watching and smoking. He wondered if he ever slept.

Sometimes, on dark nights, Bill felt that the *Exeter* was moving in the company of 'ghost' ships. When zigzagging, the 'ghosts' slipped away, only to magically reappear. Ghostly voices spoke to him on the wireless from the ships around him. He was surprised that – except for the odd ship that fell behind and had to be chased back into place – the convoy managed to stay together. Come dawn, the 'ghosts' disappeared and real ships and a real horizon took their place. It might have been a different convoy.

As long as Clark was on the bridge, his eyes and ears were always on guard. At any moment the sky could turn red with flames. It was a time of watching, waiting and hoping that the worst would not happen. He was never out of the sound of the Asdic U-boat detector and the crunch of a head sea. There were nights when he was hypnotized by the Asdic's ping, as its sound waves came and went. The pinging stayed with him long after he had returned to his bunk. He was always fighting sleep.

After nine days at sea, at a pinpoint in the Atlantic, in a wilderness of water and biting rain, the British met the Canadians, and exchanged convoys, and mail. There were dozens of ships, all with flags flying. Looking on the two convoys, Bill was thrilled to be there. He watched as the America-bound convoy disappeared into the night. The *Exeter* turned around and tailed the new convoy home.

There were U-boat alarms and rumours of surface raiders on the way back, but nothing came of them. The routine tasks and the routine sounds continued; the lookouts on the *Exeter* watched their appointed arcs, without catching a glimpse of enemy vessels.

The day after they turned around, a storm hit – it was one of the worst storms the 'old hands' had seen. It scattered the convoy and turned life on the *Exeter* into a groaning, creaking, clattering hell. Bill wondered how the rivets held. Fittings were smashed; cuts and bruises were common; climbing up and down the ship's slanting ladders was nerve-racking for him. There was no communication except by bawling. The bridge seemed to swing in the air; only by wedging himself did Bill avoid injury. Several times the screaming wind forced him to his knees. Without a lifeline, he would have been washed away. It was always a relief when the ship's bells signalled the end of the watch and he could crawl back to his bunk and smoke a cigarette.

For two days the convoy hove-to, its ships sinking beneath the white foam, only to rise again. Gradually, Bill's body adapted to the strain. Roiling clouds and a storm-filled sky were preferable to a torpedo attack.

As if to make amends, the sea became calm once Scotland

and the mouth of the Clyde were sighted. After a hot shower and a change of clothing, it was hard to recall that there had been a storm. Bill phoned his mother on reaching shore. When he got home, his father couldn't hear enough of his experiences in the Atlantic.

The *Exeter* continued its work in the North Atlantic during September and October. There was a lot of talk about submarines, but peace reigned. Now and again, the convoys were routed away from areas where submarines were thought to be. Bill had just concluded that the U-boat menace was exaggerated, when one struck.

It was about midnight; Bill was on watch. The convoy was on its way eastwards with another five days to go. There was a three-quarters moon, a slight wind and a slight swell. The upper deck and the helmeted men on guard were bathed in a cold light. The Asdic was pinging away; the *Exeter*'s section of the convoy was in place. No problems.

Bill heard the explosion, saw the towering ball of orange flame and smoke, and felt the hot blast simultaneously. A red glow lit the sea and the sky. For a moment he was horrified and bewildered. 'Oh, my God,' he kept repeating. What he'd feared since first coming aboard had happened. Instead of reacting with commands, he stood there, mesmerized, and broke into a sweat, his heart beat like a drum.

While Bill stared disbelievingly at the sinking tanker, the first lieutenant took command. A half-dressed Captain Rodney appeared through the smoke; the alarm was sounded; orders were shouted. With a tremendous rush of feet from below, the entire crew took up their Action Stations. The *Exeter* began its search for the submarine.

The attack caused an uproar throughout the convoy. Alarm sirens shrieked; ships moved away from the burning tanker; a thick smell of oil filled the air. The water was littered with debris and the dead and dying.

The hunt for the submarine continued without success; the Asdic never changed its tone. With the tanker sinking – its prow was gone, its screws were out of the water, survivors were clinging to its towering stern – the *Exeter* returned to help those who were still shouting and thrashing about in the oil-covered sea. Rubber life rafts were thrown to swimmers; scrambling nets were lowered for those who could climb aboard. The more seriously wounded were lifted over the side on stretchers. No attempt was made to recover those presumed dead – with a submarine in the vicinity, every second's delay was perilous. The moment the survivors were on deck, with a roar of its engines, the destroyer lunged forward again.

The wounded were treated on the forecastle and the mess deck. Fewer than a quarter of the tanker's crew had survived and most of these were black with oil or red with blood. Bill came close to vomiting. Nothing could be done for many of the men until their oil-soaked clothing had been cut away. Some suffered unbearable pain at the slightest touch. Several with burns and smoke-contaminated lungs died within minutes of being rescued. Why did some of the men die with a sigh, while others died in endless torment? Bill asked himself. It was a question he was never able to answer.

His first experience of war was worse than his most fearful imaginings. Later that day he experienced an acute attack of diarrhoea and had to take to his bunk.

The next day the *Exeter* held a burial service. Unslept and unshaved, Bill prayed with the rest. 'Forasmuch as it hath pleased Almighty God of his great mercy to take unto himself the soul of our dear brother here departed, we therefore commit his body to the deep . . .' At a nod from the captain, the weighted bodies were slid, one at a time, from a rough bier over the rail. They were Bill Clark's first burials at sea and the sight was to haunt him.

26

While the *Exeter* was making its way up the Clyde to Greenock, George, Tony and David were on an RAF flight from Addem to London. They had been given leave to attend Tony's wedding, and were in the highest of spirits. The good sport that he was, Tony took their ribbing cheerfully. Momentarily, the war was forgotten.

From London, David went on with Tony to Ansfield where Lydia and Helen awaited them. George went home to Wimbledon. When Johanna saw her husband coming down the street, she ran out to meet him and they threw themselves into each other's arms. Three dreadfully long months had passed since they were together. Their emotions bewitched them; everything else in the world was forgotten. Johanna clung to him until they were inside. 'I refuse to be parted from you again,' she said.

'Tonight,' George recorded in his diary, 'I listened while Johanna quietly unburdened herself. How very much I love her. She seems so young and innocent. She cannot rid herself of the fear of what may be happening to her father. She told me that every effort had been made to discover what had become of her parents and sister. There's been nothing but silence.'

George and Johanna made the journey to Ansfield in a train swamped by the military. They had to be up before dawn to catch it. Until then he hadn't realized how packed the trains were. Johanna was so happy to be with her husband that she didn't mind sitting on her suitcase. At the stations, women wearing braided caps and armbands had replaced the men who had been called up. The sandbagged stations had an unkempt look.

They arrived to find Ansfield House and the surrounding fields covered with snow. Its oak-lined drive and parkland were as impressive as ever; in a war-stricken world, peace reigned. The air and land war that everyone had predicted had not materialized. The house was packed with family, relatives and friends. Great log fires burned in the grates and the dogs roasted themselves in front of them; wreaths of holly and mistletoe hung from the ceilings and walls; an impressively decorated Christmas tree stood in the Great Hall. From a large table against the wall, the butler served hot toddies, coffee and cake. The clink of china and cutlery was drowned by the hubbub of voices as Lord and Lady Markham met their guests. Helen and Penelope Markham were there in uniform, brasses shining. They'd just joined up and were enjoying their new freedom.

George and Johanna greeted the other crew members with laughter and cheers. They were all delighted to be together again. Every arrival brought more snow and cold into the vast house. Putting down a present he was carrying, Pat Riley made a lunge at Tony, pretending to throw him down. Penelope threw her arms around his neck. Lydia and Gloria quietly took charge of Johanna. They knew what had happened to her family, and went out of their way to be kind to her. Gloria spoke of the difficulties they were having with the London children who had been evacuated to Ansfield; some of them had become terribly homesick. Roger had turned up at her school the day before in his bear suit to cheer up the children. They had built an enormous snowman together.

After a dinner party that matched peacetime standards, the crew and their friends retired to a corner of the Great Hall where they sat and talked. Max was sporting his wings and spoke enthusiastically of the action he had seen over the south of England. His sister, Hazel, had abandoned her

Slavic studies and was now training to be a nurse. She talked about the growing RAF casualties. 'It's just as well that we don't have time to think about it,' she said as an aside to Lydia, shaking her head.

Pat – now a second lieutenant in the commandos – joked about a survivors' course he'd just finished on the island of Rum in the Outer Hebrides. 'My God, it was pure agony: running, burrowing, jumping, climbing, clawing, sliding, and crawling through barbed wire and snow-covered mud, accompanied by live ammunition and drumming rain. Never a dull moment. I enjoyed it.' Penelope never took her eyes off him.

Bill Clark was just back from South American waters. They noticed that he had lost weight. He was flustered and slow of tongue when he became the centre of attention. His words were few and deliberate as he talked about flying fish and dolphins. He didn't tell them that his first real taste of action had left him inert in his bunk. He did mention that he hoped to get a posting on HMS *Hood*, the greatest battle cruiser ever built. Tony remembered the newspaper clippings about the six-foot-long model of the ship which Bill's father had built in his retirement. It stood on a special table in a glass case. Bill's mother hated it, not least because it took up most of her sitting room.

Charley Bradbury was the only member of the crew in civilian clothes. His head had not been shorn. As a conscientious objector, with Victoria's help, he had become an agricultural labourer on her father's estate. Lord Randall had not spoken to him since their London meeting, he acknowledged his presence only with an expressionless stare when riding past him in his fields. Meanwhile Charley grew sugar beet for Lord Randall and studied Russian in his spare time.

'Well, Charley, what do you think of your chances of establishing a utopia now?' Max's face was flushed with drink; his voice had a hard edge to it.

'I've not lost hope. Socialism will arise out of the ashes of war.'

'You haven't changed, Bradbury, you're still all words. Put your money down and I'll take your bet.'

'I've never been able to get it into your noddle, Max, that sooner or later capitalism will fail.'

'Sheer bloody rubbish,' Max snorted. 'You with your "pie-in-the-sky" and your love of the Russians, and Bill with his love of the sea. You're both crazy.'

'Not as crazy as you,' Victoria broke in impatiently.

All smiles, Roger cheered them up with his tales about the British Expeditionary Force and the 'phoney war' in France. He was the same old jester. 'While waiting for the Germans, we march this way then that, and get blisters. Anything to kill time. I'm convinced that people at the top don't know what they're doing. There seem to be as many opinions and strategies as there are generals. I'd be much happier if those who started the war actually fought it. It's no good leaving it all to me.' Gloria laughed with him. There was a new light in her eyes.

With Helen sitting next to him, David Evans remained strangely silent. Lady Markham was civil to him, but not overly warm.

The most popular man there was Harvey Childers who had come across from Oxford with Walter Turnbull, the college chaplain. Childers still treated the crew as if they were his sons. It was some time since they had seen him, and they found him in an expansive mood. They congratulated him on his promotion to acting head of Arnold. The Master had been called away on war work.

Later, George related how there had been a fight over the headship. Hugh Stably, the dean, had assumed that the position would fall to him. There had been an election of the senior members of the college, accompanied by the usual intrigues, plotting and back-biting, from which Childers had emerged the clear winner. Shamefaced, Mrs Stably had had to remove the curtains she had prematurely hung in the Master's lodgings.

Childers took Roger's comments about the army in France with good grace. He had probably felt the same way twenty-five years earlier. A shrewd observer of life, he realized that a joker often has an uncanny way of speaking the truth. George asked Childers how long he thought the war would last. 'As long as the Great War?'

'Longer,' he replied, gravely; his face darkened.

'I dined with Alex and his mother in London a week ago,' Roger put in. 'He's two inches taller since he put on battle-dress. He was about to embark for Egypt to take on the Italians in Libya. He can't get into battle fast enough. I told him that he could have my share.' Everyone laughed again.

With the windows heavily curtained, the crew sat up talking and drinking with Childers until the early hours. George and Johanna went outside for a breath of air before turning in. Searchlights were feeling their way across the distant sky. Max and Roger went on playing billiards until dawn.

27

The next day they all drove across wooded fields to the parish church, the spire of which could be seen rising from a clump of trees. Because of the war, its bells were stilled. Founded in medieval times, its famous stone carvings of the Stations of the Cross had been defaced by icon smashers during the Reformation. The altar was crowded with lighted candles and silver gifts of bygone ages. From the family pew, which was centuries old, Lady Markham beamed with happiness.

The congregation seated, Tony and George took up their positions before the altar. The scent of pine boughs lay heavily on the air. Tony wore his Air Force uniform and glowed with health. As George nervously felt in his pocket for the ring, he recalled his own wedding.

When Lydia and her father entered the church, the curious began to stretch their necks. Attired in white, with a glittering diamond necklace, the bride looked radiant; there was about her a self-assured grace, an inner serenity; her eyes were bright. For the moment, colour, light and extravagance had returned to life. Two little girls dressed in white carried Lydia's train.

The ceremony was performed by the sombre-faced village vicar; Walter Turnbull, assisted. All went well: the choirboys, faces shining in the candlelight, sang 'The God of Love my Shepherd is'; the pageboy, covered with satin frills, fell asleep; a difficult child was finally hushed.

In strong voices, the bride and bridegroom pledged their troth. 'In the sight of God, and in the face of this congregation,' their commitment was made: 'To have and to hold . . . till death us do part.' Lady Markham touched her eyes with her handkerchief. The seriousness of such a commitment in wartime was reflected on her face. She remembered similar promises being made during the Great War. She knew that the present generation of young people were too scatterbrained to give a thought to the hazards confronting them. While Tony and Lydia signed the church register, Helen and David, accompanied by the organ, sang 'Blessed be the tie that binds'. Their voices were well matched, their harmony perfect.

'A blessed pair,' said Walter Turnbull as Tony and his bride left the church. To their complete surprise, they had to pass beneath an arch of rowing oars that the crew had smuggled in. There were lots of cheers.

Perhaps intended, Tony's sister Gloria caught Lydia's bouquet. Her face was wreathed in smiles. 'Watch out,' everybody called to Roger, pointing to a sign on the inside of the church door: '*Amor Vincit Omnia!*' After the inevitable photographs, everybody returned to Ansfield House for the reception. A trio played Elizabethan love songs during the meal; a fire crackled in the hearth. Afterwards, led by the bride and groom, everyone danced.

> It is sweet to dance to violins
> When love and life are fair.

In the afternoon Tony and Lydia left on a forty-eight-hour honeymoon. Graciously, they took leave of everybody. Towards evening, the party broke up with the report of enemy aircraft. Lights were put out, the curtains opened. Outside, long fingers of light erratically searched the heavens. Across the field, an anti-aircraft battery was silhouetted against the sky by the flash of its guns. Several guests hurriedly took shelter in the deep cellars of the house while some – including Pat and Penelope – went outside to watch the gunfire. Unharmed, the enemy planes droned on. 'Thank God they didn't ruin a wedding day,' said Johanna to her husband.

Before dispersing, the guests viewed the wedding presents set out on tables in the Great Hall. The gifts expressed the promise of a new life. Somebody had given the couple a silver coffee pot, though everybody knew that there was no good coffee available.

The last thing the company did was to sing Christmas carols around the piano. When they had finished, Roger continued to sit at the piano, absentmindedly fingering the keys. Playing more to himself than to anyone else, he struck up the tune of the wartime song: 'We'll meet again, don't know where, don't know when, but I know we'll meet again some sunny day . . .' Gradually, led by David and Helen, the guests took up the song until the room rang with their voices. It was more than a song they sang, it was a hope and a promise.

28

From Ansfield, George and Johanna returned to London. George was glad to be home again. Addem and its pilots belonged to another world.

'The city has changed,' he wrote in his diary. 'London is still unravaged by war, but it has become a coarser place. Dress is drabber, uniforms are everywhere; there is a colourless, shabby, regimented air about it all. People move about with a quieter step, like in Germany on the eve of war; they look more concerned. I run into refugees all the time.

'At the same time the bars are packed,' he went on, 'restaurants and nightclubs are full; theatres and cinemas are doing a brisk trade. Not even the harsh winter keeps people off the streets. The fear of being killed has made people snatch pleasure now before it is too late.'

If there was a moon, the Kemps had no difficulty in getting around in the blackout. With dim lights, taxis, buses and the underground never stopped running – even after people began to use its stations to shelter from the bombing. There was no shortage of anything if you had the money and the right connections. If the worst came to the worst, and the enemy started bombing, there was an air-raid shelter in your own back garden or at the end of the street. Londoners had developed the mentality of burrowing rodents, ready to dive underground at the first warning. Some people had also developed a fear of lights. They were forever switching them off and drawing curtains tighter.

Walking home arm in arm in the moonlight, Johanna and George passed shop windows boarded up, or plastered with ugly tape or wire netting against bomb-blast. Sandbags and diggings, emergency water tanks and air-raid shelters lined their path.

For Johanna's sake, they visited the museums and walked in Hyde Park, feeding the seagulls, the pigeons and the ducks. Hideous wartime huts now occupied its lawns. Equally ugly barrage balloons hung in the sky. They visited Tower Bridge, Buckingham Palace, St Paul's Cathedral and Westminster Abbey. They saw some of the sights of Dickens' novels. One day they walked through St James's Park and had lunch in a little café in Soho. They listened to a Salvation Army band playing outside, bringing warmth and colour to a bleak setting.

Moving about London, George found that his uniform acted like a magnet to those who wanted to launch a verbal attack on Hitler and the Germans. There was always someone ready to tell him how to bring the war to a victorious end in a manner that would cost the speaker nothing. They dismissed George's protests as modesty: what could an ordinary airman know? One night, while dining in Piccadilly, an uninvited, red-faced drunk joined them at their table. He brought a bottle of wine, and thanked George profusely for 'killing Huns'. 'The Hun has taken on the wrong fellow this time. Oh, my good laddie, has he! We're going to give him hell, aren't we? What!'

Johanna regarded the stranger pityingly. Finally, she lowered her eyes to avoid his glistening face. It wasn't the first time in her life that she wondered if the world had gone mad. She thought of her family and home.

29

George and Johanna spent Christmas with his parents. Everybody did their best to celebrate the occasion but the festivities of 1939 struck a sombre note. Men were being killed at sea and in the air. People's lives had been disrupted. There was nothing settled, nothing stable, nothing safe.

Towards the end of December, George and Johanna took the train to Addem. Group Captain Barnaby had finally agreed to the Kemps living off base. George wasn't sorry to be going back. He had found it difficult to return to civilian life – deep down there was a feeling of not belonging there. Of course, everybody was friendly to a man in uniform, but they weren't friendly because of who you were; it was because of what you were doing. The centre of one's life had shifted. Civilian life was a strange façade; reality was preparing for battle.

Exhausted by the conditions of wartime travel, they finished their journey in a freezing, rattling bus, arriving in the empty town square as the wintry day was drawing to a close. The shops and the cluster of houses were tightly shut; there was not a coloured light or a winking Christmas tree to be seen. Snow lay thick on the cobbles; icicles hung from the eves of the fretted roofs; stillness filled the air. The white bulk of the lonely fields and hills lay hushed beyond the town.

Carrying their few possessions, the Kemps crunched their way to their lodgings, where they kicked off the thick chunks of snow clinging to their shoes. Their landlady greeted them with food and hospitality, though she found it a bit odd when George introduced his German wife. 'Well, in war you never know what next, do you? I mean to say.' She knitted her brow as if perplexed.

The accommodation was frugal, the rooms were dingy and ill-lit, but in wartime one was glad of anything. Nothing was bad if it could be shared. It was the first time they had lived alone together. Johanna was only too glad to have left the loneliness of London behind. Through their windows they could hear the sound of the sea and the broken shutter banging fitfully.

* * *

Johanna would always remember Addem as the place where she discovered what it was like not to fit in. Disillusionment came slowly. She noticed that the landlady was always cautious with her – never open, always serious. When she entered the village shop – the doorbell ringing – the chatter would cease. Empty faces turned towards her; she had an awful feeling that they'd been discussing her. Sometimes the snubbing was too pointed to disregard and she felt embarrassed. Eventually, she asked George to do the shopping for her.

Even when trying to make polite conversation outside the church on a Sunday morning, she was ill at ease. There was a great difference between what the villagers were saying to her and what their eyes and their mouths expressed. They were visibly confused when the conversation turned to the war. She knew that they called her 'The German'. The odd thing was that Father Bauer of St Thomas's, where Johanna worshipped, was also a German, but no one dreamt of snubbing him.

Johanna came home one sunny day to find the washing she had put out in the sun had dirt on it. 'Which side are you on?' someone had written in ink on her best sheet. For a moment she was bewildered. These people didn't realize how difficult it was for her to decide. She couldn't tear out her roots and stop being a German; she couldn't blame her people for everything, as those around her did. How could she tell them how much she missed her family and her country, and how frightened she was? Being cut off from her roots weighed heavily on her: for the first time in her life, Johanna felt that she didn't belong anywhere. She was a woman without a country. Life was difficult enough when dealing with the familiar; it became impossible when you didn't understand what was going on around you and your neighbours were unfriendly. How right her mother had been!

No matter how hard she tried, she was always misunderstood. She despaired of finding common ground between herself and those around her. Father Bauer was the only one who understood her plight. 'Be patient,' he advised her. 'It's not too great a burden to carry while others are dying.' There were times when she wept.

On New Year's Eve the Kemps entertained Tony Markham and David Evans. Tony had been refused leave to join Lydia. David sang for them, and they drank and laughed and talked, while keeping an eye on the clock. Muffled up against the cold, they went outside at midnight to hear people cheering and the trains hooting, and to watch the glimmer of searchlights flickering from cloud to cloud. 'To 1940,' they toasted, gripping each other's hands. Who knew what the future held? David thought that 1940 would see the end of the war; he'd worked it all out. 'Then I'll get back to All Souls.' Across the road, an unrelenting sea crashed on the shore. The Scots were celebrating their greatest night of the year, people of all ages were in the streets. The greeting 'A guid New Year to ye a',' rang on the cold night air. In bed that night Johanna remembered the New Year's Eves she had shared with her family.

Early in January, George and his colleagues were back in the air, flying above the mountains and the sea. The Air Force had come to dominate their lives again. Unlike George's feelings about London, this life was real. They flew in all weathers and would sometimes land with wheezing voices and frost on their faces. The wonder is that they could fly in such freezing temperatures. A thermos flask of coffee helped to keep them awake and banish the cold. By now they were accustomed to flying in tight formation, their wings tucked in beneath those of the squadron leader. 'Tuck in, boys,' he'd say, 'tuck in.' It was not easy, but they got better all the time.

Sometimes they flew over the long, deserted beaches far out to sea. On a cloudless day, they could see for thirty miles.

Below them, the sea looked like an endless corrugated sheet. Once they caught sight of stepped-up layers of German bombers and fighters coming their way. They recognized the Junker 88s, the Heinkel 111s, and the Me 109s. Their excitement died when they were ordered out of the area; fighting was not for them yet.

Pilots who had returned from operations sat about in the mess, tunics unbuttoned, talking to each other in soft voices. They smoked and drank beer with shaking hands, while waiting for the next sortie. When it came, they went out together cheerfully, and took their chance. Nothing seemed impossible, nothing was beyond their reach. Of course pilots crashed, but never today, never tomorrow, and never them. To speak of dying or of the dead in the mess was taboo; instinctively, death was kept at bay. To joke about it was worse. Unwritten, unspoken, there was a way to die, as there was a way to live. Those who didn't return were hardly mentioned; there was no brooding, no outward show of sorrow, no reminiscences. Somebody would announce matter-of-factly that Bertie had 'bought it'. 'Poor Bertie, poor sod. Damned rotten luck!' It wasn't callousness; it was the only way to keep one's sanity.

By March, the three men had won their wings and were proud to wear them. To celebrate, they danced a wild jig together. In their elegant new uniforms, they had their pictures taken. Once they had got their wings, they no longer belonged to the mob; they had risen in the ranks. No one shouted at them any more, no one put them on fatigue duties, no one bullied them. Instead they were saluted by subordinates and given five days' leave. In late March the three of them were declared 'operational' and were held in reserve, awaiting postings to fighter squadrons outside London. In a month they'd be gone.

30

George and Johanna and Tony and Lydia decided to spend the five-day leave on the island of Mull. They had wanted to go there ever since they'd heard Pat Riley talking about it. Lydia, still at Ansfield, was overjoyed at the idea of joining them.

David Evans chose to spend his leave with Helen at Ansfield House, which pleased Tony. Roger Blundell and Pat Riley were hoping to be there at the same time.

After much coming and going, the leave tickets were issued, a fast car was hired from a fellow pilot, petrol was finagled, food coupons obtained. Tony, Johanna and George met Lydia as she got off the train from Aberdeen. Despite the long journey, she was in top form. It was a great reunion not only for Tony and his wife, but for the two women. Johanna and Lydia were both wholeheartedly committed to life, and were always happy together. Their spirits rose and fell to the other's buoyancy.

The four of them left Addem the next morning. For the moment, they felt free of the war. There were few cars on the road, the day was sunny and clear and promised to remain fine. Tony knew the way and was at the wheel. The men wore their pilot's uniforms. They were all in such high spirits that they sang as they went along. Before reaching Inverness, they turned off at a sign marked Culloden. They drove past shaggy red Highland cattle until they came to the memorial to the Scots who had died there in their last futile battle against the English in 1746. The huge cairn was in the middle of a misty field, surrounded by gentle hills and gaunt, snow-streaked mountains. The faint note of a piper's lament could be heard in the distance. '"The Flowers of the Forest"', Tony explained.

At Inverness, they turned south towards Oban, running alongside the dark-coloured waters of Loch Ness. There were cultivated fields on one side of the loch, and rough hills, with ribs of rock and patches of golden broom, on the other. Larch and pine lined the water's edge, their buds bursting; mountain peaks shouldered the sky.

At Oban, a cosy, cheerful seaside town with houses built of stone and capped with grey slate, they walked up and down the seafront to stretch their legs. The harbour bustled with fishing vessels and the smell of fish filled the air. Red-faced, aproned girls chattered and laughed as they cleaned the fish; gulls and cats scouted for scraps. Oban looked westward to the Hebrides and the New World. From here one could joyfully set out on journeys to places with unimaginably enchanting names.

Late that afternoon, with the clang of a bell, they sailed to Tobermory on the Isle of Mull. The boat was filled with Gaelic-speaking farmers and crofters. Favoured by the weather, the two-hour journey took them across a blue-green, leaden sea; gulls accompanied them, as did the wind's song. As they approached the island's indented coast, they were struck by its dramatic cliffs and myriads of birds.

They arrived at Tobermory as the golden sheen of the setting sun lit the trembling waters of the sea-carved bay. A knot of curious old women greeted them on the pier. The inn was close by.

'We're late for dinner,' said Tony apologetically to the innkeeper.

'It's never too late for a good meal,' he reassured him with a smile. 'In Mull, it would be sinful for a guest to go to bed hungry.' Doubly sinful, he might have added, to refuse anything to a guest wearing fighter pilot's wings.

Having dined on lobster and lamb – no one mentioned

161

rationing regulations – with a toddy of Scotch whisky in which there was a hint of heather, the four of them walked along the quayside enjoying the keen night air. It touched their wartime conscience to have eaten so well.

The next day they woke to a sunlit sky. They were lucky, they were told, to have such bright sunshine; Mull's usual chill wind had warmed. Yet fires still crackled in the grates. After a hearty breakfast of porridge with thick, yellow cream, they went out to look at a world of startling beauty. The island was dominated by mountains; Pat Riley had been climbing them for years.

Later they drove along a dirt track between the clear waters of two great lochs, both burnished by the sun. Their journey took them past fields where the crops were just starting to sprout, past seams of black peat, and white-washed cottages whose thatched roofs were held down by heavy stones. Always there was a bluster of wind. Now and again a horse and cart went by filled with people clinging to its sides as it jolted over the potholes. Here and there were roofless, abandoned crofts. A tangle of bracken-covered hills separated the visitors from the sea. Yet, on one occasion, they caught sight of the ever-changing line of foam among the rocks and basalt columns along the coast. They looked down on caves and arches in the cliffs and endless dark ledges of rock; they heard the thunder of the tide.

They were surprised to come across a well-preserved windmill, which stood in a boulder-strewn field, peppered with late daffodils. Although the mill seemed brightly new, the vanes were still. On the steps, facing the ocean, sat a beautiful young woman combing her hair. Not wishing to intrude, they waved and passed by. She waved back.

They did a lot of walking that day, sitting down and contemplating the scene when weary. They met simple crofters and fisher-folk, dressed in coarse, homely clothing. 'The old ways are going,' one old man told them. 'And so is the Gaelic. If we lose our tongue, it will be an unholy thing. Money is the curse. Och, there's truth in that.' The visitors wondered what the future of the children, with their fair hair and laughing blue eyes, would be. The islanders knew little about the outside world, except what soldiers wrote home. 'Everybody on the island has somebody at the war,' one woman said. 'We dream of them and pray for their safety.'

On returning to the inn that night the Kemps and the Markhams feasted on seafood, a rich fruit dumpling, and fruit and cheese. There was plenty to drink.

George and Johanna went to bed in a room flooded with moonlight – so much so that George had to get up in the night to close the curtains. He gazed through the window at the neighbouring roofs whose tiles glistened. The weather was unusually calm. Silvered fields and hedgerows lay beyond the houses; no wind disturbed the overhanging trees. A full moon rode above the sleeping town; a thin white mist lay low over the sea. George thought it an incredibly peaceful sight and paused before returning to his wife. There was a quotation above the bed, worked in coloured wools, which said. 'The beauties of Mull are surely the work of God. The works of man perish, the beauty of Mull remains.'

In the morning they drove to the south coast of the island. Sea birds drifted above them. To the west were several rough-cut, gem-like islands; to the north were dark, brooding peaks. From the western tip they looked across an exquisite purple sea to the tiny island of Iona. The first Christian monastery and chapel in Scotland had been built there. From Iona, Gaelic-speaking monks had carried the word of the Christian God to Europe and the wider world. Johanna knew that they had carried it to Germany. There was a statue of the Irish St Killian on the bridge at Würzburg. Throughout the day, subtle changes of colour took place, ending with the mountains framed in the flaming gold of the setting sun.

They spent their last evening with Pat Riley's friends, the

McTavishes, who were a delightful couple. Edward McTavish was a prosperous London merchant who had retired with his wife to Mull. Their large house offered spectacular views of the sea. As they dined, the setting sun cast a diffused glow on the water; ships passed by.

Over dinner, there was talk about Mull, the war, and Pat. A chance remark by McTavish told the visitors that Pat's father – an Irish lord – had died years before while climbing Everest, and that his mother had died shortly afterwards.

'Where does Pat stay on Mull?' Kemp asked.

'He lives in a windmill at the western end of the island.'

'We passed it on our first day.'

'It's known to the locals as "The Wind's Song".'

'Who's the woman we saw?'

'Ah, now, there lies a long story. Her name is Beatrix Dekker. She came to Mull from Amsterdam. She is an accomplished writer who's recently begun to earn a good living. Her books are all about make-believe worlds; she likes to dream. She and Pat have done a beautiful job of restoration. The mill used to smell of mould. It cost Pat a lot of money – more than he could afford. Her work, Pat, and the mill are all she lives for. By the way, you've got to watch out. She sees nothing wrong in telling you the most far-fetched stories for fun. She caught me out several times when I first met her. She's been Pat's girlfriend for years. But you know that.'

The visitors stared at the floor. Nobody spoke. Tony was furious that Pat was deceiving his sister. He returned George's stare with an angry shrug.

'Beatrix is a bit of a recluse, she likes to keep herself to herself. But we're all grateful to her,' McTavish went on, 'for bringing Pat back to the straight and narrow. He'd have been in trouble without her.'

'Drink?'

'In a way, you might say. I've known Pat since he was a boy. He's always been wild, sometimes disappearing for long periods. In his search for happiness he's tried one thing after another, including drink. He was called "Mad Pat" when he was younger. Climbing mountains is his present means of seeking freedom and happiness. Irresponsible? Perhaps. Cowardly? Never.'

After dinner, George played the piano, accompanying McTavish on the violin. One of the guests had brought his fiddle and played and sang such Scottish airs as 'Highland Lassie' and 'Ae Fond Kiss'. For an encore, Lydia and Johanna tried to join in. The fiddle's gentle notes, coupled with the firelight dancing on the walls, created a poignant moment. The spell was only broken when the music ceased.

Warmed by a good meal and the best whisky, by friendship, song and music, the visitors eventually set out for their inn through the dark night. The man with the fiddle was unsteady on his feet so Tony offered to drive him home.

As Tony and George helped him through his cottage door, the fellow turned round and placed an unsteady finger against his nose. 'Patrick smuggles,' he confided in an undertone. 'Runs a pack. At it all the time.'

'Does he, indeed,' Markham answered, dubiously.

'Not in a dishonest way.'

'Of course not.'

'For excitement . . . and he needs the money.'

'Naturally.'

'Got away with it by the skin of his teeth, so far. Came close to being caught. A storm saved him.'

'Really.'

'Not something you or I would choose to do.'

'No.'

'Not a word to McTavish. He's touchy about Pat.'

'Of course not.'

With a vacuous grin, the man thanked them, bowed his bald head and shut the door. Tony and George exchanged a heavy glance.

They arrived at their inn just as the porter was putting out the lights.

'What on earth are we to think of Pat Riley?' Johanna asked George, when they'd reached their room.

'Smuggling is something I would never have associated with Pat. No wonder he's rich. As for Beatrix and Penelope, the fellow obviously doesn't know his own mind.'

Johanna was horrified by the idea of such deception. 'I don't know what I'll do when I see him next,' she murmured.

They woke on Sunday to a different world: pouring rain, wet cobblestones, a white-streaked sea and low, scudding black clouds. Having made up their minds to move on, they drove to the ferry through a howling wind and fearsome rain. The captain doubted whether it would sail that day. A few passengers made up their own minds and returned to the inn; they'd try again later. Those for Oban were asked to wait on benches below deck. An hour later, the decision was made to sail; the car was hoisted aboard and the ship cast off. The crossing was so rough that George and the women were seasick.

Later that day, a much subdued, rain-soaked party drove along a twisting track across the moors. They spent the night at a hotel by the side of a loch. Early the next morning, they drove the curving miles back to Addem. For much of the way they had mountains on both sides of them. They arrived a day late; the weather proved to be a sufficient excuse. However fleeting their glimpse of Scotland had been, it had left them with a lasting memory of the solitude and rugged grandeur of the Highlands. The beauty of Mull would remain in their dreams.

Lydia was happy to stay with her husband for another week. Increasingly, with Gloria teaching, and Helen and Penelope in the army, Tony's parents had come to depend upon their new daughter-in-law. Tony was loath to see her

166

go when, after many embraces, she climbed into the train wearing the woollen suit he had bought for her on Mull.

31

The next week there was a party in the mess for the pilots who had won their wings. Amid the general clamour, a concertina accompanied the singing. Everyone drank too much and some of the songs were bawdy; the party went on till late.

Johanna did not enjoy mess parties – too often there was a false jollity – and she stayed away. She felt that she was not really welcome. The day before, one of the officers, whose brother had been killed in a dogfight, had deliberately snubbed her. 'We're at war with your kind,' he had said, darkly. The remark hurt; it was an effort for her to remain silent. She held herself in check by clenching her fists.

The party over, Tony and David left the mess to drive George home. Although it was late, they were going to discuss a trip they were proposing to make with Johanna to a Spitfire squadron at Turnhouse near Edinburgh. The night was wet and gloomy.

David sat next to Tony in the front of the open car, George was in the back. With dimmed lights, they were tearing down a narrow, winding country lane leading to the coast, when David suddenly shouted, 'Look out, Tony, there's a body on the road!' Tony swerved and slammed on the brakes. With a squeal the car pitched to one side, felled a couple of small trees and landed upside down in a ditch, its wheels spinning helplessly. Tony and David were thrown free; George was trapped in the back seat. As the car rolled over, he had felt a bone in his leg snap with the brittle sound of a dry stick. With a red mist swirling before his eyes, and increasingly aware of the smell of petrol, he struggled to get out. He knew he was in danger of being burnt alive.

Tony and David came to his rescue at once. Gradually they pulled him out from beneath the car. Each pull left George sick with pain. Having dragged him away from the burning wreck, David went back to deal with the body on the road. 'It's a bloody sack of coal,' he reported.

Tony threw his coat over George and ran back to the base for help. George lay by the roadside in David's care. Drenched by rain, with his teeth chattering, heart thumping, and an acute pain in his leg, he felt battered all over and shivered uncontrollably. Other than the dripping of leaves and the gurgle of a brook, nothing stirred. George was sick with anger about the senselessness of what had happened. He didn't have the Germans to thank for his troubles, but a sack of coal. 'Not now,' he kept saying to David, 'not when I've just won my wings. Damn! Damn! Damn!' He went on muttering distractedly.

'Oh, for God's sake, George, shut up!'

After what seemed like an eternity, they heard a car approaching. It was Tony with an ambulance and an RAF doctor. 'You chose an out-of-the-way place to have an accident,' the doctor started. George didn't appreciate his humour. Having been given an injection to kill the pain, he was shipped to a military hospital in Aberdeen. Tony and David were dropped off in Addem to report the accident and break the bad news to Johanna.

That night, George lived in a daze. His extensive cuts and bruises were treated; he had more injections; his body was X-rayed; his right leg was reset and placed in plaster and then in a harness. He was glad when they had finished with him and he could get some sleep.

When he awoke the next morning Johanna was sitting beside him, holding his hand. He felt her presence the moment he opened his eyes. 'Hello, darling,' he mumbled, still feeling faint. Johanna looked as if she was bearing great news. George guessed what it was from her radiant face and moist eyes: they were going to have their first child. They had been talking about it the day before, and now it was confirmed. They hugged each other with joy. 'I shall never let you out of my sight again,' she teased him. Overwrought, George thought he was going to weep.

Later, after Johanna had gone, he noticed the strong smell of antiseptic in the ward. He watched the orderlies moving about with towels, bottles and pails. Patients were sleeping or talking in low voices. At the end of the ward a man suffering from gangrene was sobbing. Even at that distance George found the smell repellent. Visitors came and went. Every now and then a relative would become distressed at a bedside. The nurses took it in their stride. Compared with the other airmen in the ward, George knew that his injuries were minor. He expected to be back in the air before long – what had happened was another challenge to be surmounted. Next day, Tony and David brought him news from the base. They roundly cursed his bad luck and continued to visit him whenever they could get away.

After ten days George was back at Addem with Johanna. The plaster on his leg was covered with signatures. Dr Crowder, who had treated him, had promised him a full recovery within three months; which is what would have happened had he not begun to run a fever. He had a feeling of being wrung out; the pain in his leg got worse. The RAF doctor on the base thought it better for him to return to hospital. 'No problems, but better to take precautions.' He studied George thoughtfully. There followed more X-rays and tests. George's temperature remained high. He watched the comings and goings in the ward with burning eyes.

Shortly after returning to hospital, George caught sight of Dr Crowder coming down the ward with the X-rays. He looked concerned. 'I'm afraid you've had some jolly bad luck, Kemp,' he began. 'You've developed an infection of the bone marrow: osteomyelitis. Very rare. It can spread. If it doesn't respond to treatment, the leg will have to come off; either that or it will kill you in double-quick time. I'm sorry to be so frank, but the occasion demands it. A week's time and we will know either way.'

At first George couldn't grasp what the doctor was saying. When he did, he refused to believe it. The idea that he might lose his leg struck him as preposterous. What was to become of the heroic career in the RAF that he had planned for himself? 'Christ,' was all he could say.

Crowder gathered up his papers to leave. 'Cheer up! All is not lost. With X-rays we'll trace the progress of the infection and with medication we'll try to stop it.' He tapped George's good leg. 'We'll soon have you back in the air.'

'It's not the end of everything,' Johanna consoled him. It seemed that she was always at his side when he awoke. She stitched and knitted for the coming child while her husband slept. She was convinced it would be a girl; he was certain it would be a boy. 'You need to rest,' he told her. 'Stop fussing,' she laughed. Sometimes she read to him in a low voice, or they'd talk about their trip to Mull. Always she was supportive and sound in her ideas. She was as strong as she had been when she had said goodbye to her family at the German frontier. George wondered how he had ever managed without her.

More disappointing news followed: Tony and David were suddenly posted to a fighter squadron at West Hadding, south of London. George should have gone with them. Tony came clumping down the ward, clad in combat gear. 'We're off!' he called. 'Shh!' the nurses reprimanded him. Excited about the chance of front-line fighting, he behaved like a

170

schoolboy breaking up for the long summer vacation. There was the same wild feeling about him, the same youthful ardour, the same air of innocence. David was more subdued when he came in later.

It was a black moment for George when they shook his hand and said goodbye.

'Goodbye,' he answered with dismay.

'You'll be with us in no time at all,' they called as they left. 'We'll keep a special place for you.' George found it difficult not to hold back his tears. Why did he have such bad luck? In spite of his ambition, was it his lot to fail? After that, despite the efforts of the doctors and the support of Johanna, his condition worsened. No matter what they did for him, his fever continued to rise. There was no controlling the pain. Several times a day, they had to change his sweat-drenched sheets. He was becoming too ill to care.

When further X-rays showed deterioration, Crowder made the decision to amputate George's leg above the knee.

George's mind could not accept what was happening. It was all a bad dream. Was he going to be like those other patients he had seen hobbling about?

He knew that the fateful moment had arrived when an orderly came to give him a sedative, shave his leg, and clean him up. Johanna held his hand until his stretcher was wheeled into the operating theatre. Weeping, she then went to the hospital chapel to beseech God to spare her husband's life. She prayed alone in a room so bare that she thought it bleak. The lonely candle against the wall had gone out. She longed for her mother. Johanna was with George when he came round from his general anaesthetic. Dr Crowder was there too. 'You're lucky,' he said to George. 'We thought we might have to take off the lot.'

There followed the weariness of recovery. Despite all that his wife and his mother did for him (the latter had joined

171

Johanna in Addem), George became terribly depressed and difficult. 'I said things I never intended,' he later recorded in his diary. 'My injury is bad enough, my loss of pride is worse. My wife is only twenty and here I am without a leg. How can I live with her as a cripple? The loss of my limb has made me less of a man. Why do I have to be frustrated all the time? Why does it happen to me?'

He hated the sight of his flying boots, one lying on top of the other on the floor. There would have been several takers in the ward if he had wanted to part with them. The orderly who polished the floor had pushed his hand into one of them to feel the wool lining, but had been too decent to mention them. Thankfully, Johanna took the boots away.

One day Group Captain Barnaby visited the ward. He had his dog with him. He went from bed to bed, tactfully saying something to each patient. When he reached George he stood and eyed him for a moment. 'Ah, Kemp, yes,' he began, brushing his face with his hand, 'you're the fellow who picked up a German pilot on the Blair Atholl hike. Tell that German wife of yours that I'll arrange another trek for you when you're well enough.'

It wasn't like Barnaby to be so light-hearted. 'I shouldn't take the loss of your leg too seriously,' he continued. 'It doesn't mean you're useless. I've fought alongside pilots much worse off than you. Come and see me when you get back.' He smiled faintly and moved on.

George began to have difficulty sleeping; his fears gave him nightmares. In the middle of the night he would suddenly experience the horror of his accident all over again, except in his dream he'd been burned to a cinder. He would start up trembling, in a sweat, and stare terrified at the ceiling. His face became haggard and worn; he even stopped thinking about their coming child. 'Sometimes I find myself sitting up in bed staring aimlessly around the ward,' he wrote in his diary. 'Why do visitors – in an attempt to cheer

172

me up – talk the nonsense they do? I've begun to notice the bullies among the nurses. I resent being called a "boy". I've stopped taking communion on Sundays. The way the vicar darts in with the Host, and darts out again, disgusts me. There is something furtive about it. It's odd that I hadn't noticed these things before.'

On another occasion he wrote, 'I'm tired of the daily routine. Each day is the same. After troubled snatches of sleep, I watch the blackout curtains being drawn back; I smoke the first cigarette of the day; I hear the stirrings of patients around me, the retching and the coughing; I see the night nurses and orderlies go off duty, the day shift come on. There follows the inevitable bed-making, washing and new dressings. There's always water being poured in and out of bowls, the noise suggests a soothing finality. Breakfast follows, then the doctor's visit, then an attempt to look at the newspapers and catch up on sleep. Trying to talk to the patients on either side of me has proved futile: one of them is dumb from shock, the other has been wounded in the neck and can only whisper. I wonder where Tony and David have got to and why they haven't written. The war and the world are going on without me. I feel as if I don't count any more. So much for my dreams of recognition and fame.'

Johanna saved him. She was there every day, full of loving warmth and good cheer. She faced their joint crisis better than George did. With Crowder's co-operation, she had him transferred to the glassed-in balcony at the end of the building. Everything was different out there: noises, space, air, light, shadows – everything. On crutches, George became quite mobile. His first faltering movements on crutches lasted only a day or two.

News of his accident had by now reached the other crew members. Roger Blundell wrote from France to say that the British Expeditionary Force was still hanging out its washing on the Siegfried Line, adding, 'Sorry, old boy, what damned bad luck.' Max Elsfield sent him a case of Scotland's best whisky; among their many properties, the family owned a distillery. It was smuggled into the hospital and everybody who wanted it got a tot. It surprised George that Max should have taken the trouble – it wasn't like him. Alex Haverfield wrote from Cairo. His letter was full of talk about the desert. Tony and David finally wrote from their new air base: they were up to their eyes fighting the Germans. Pat Riley wrote from the depths of Scotland. There were also letters from Charley and Victoria. They told George that they hoped to go to Russia and were reading all they could on the Soviet Union. Despite Max's bad-mouthing of the pair, everybody said that they were more in love than ever. Gradually George's old self returned; his wound healed; X-rays showed that his life had been spared.

The day George left the hospital for his lodgings in Addem, he received a letter from Harvey Childers, who had now been confirmed as the new Master of Arnold. 'Why not convalesce with us in Oxford?' he wrote. 'For treatment, you cannot do better than that offered by the Radcliffe. As several flats are empty, we can put you up at Arnold without any trouble. If you wish, you can both dine in hall. To keep your mind active, there are one or two things you could do for us here. I've checked with the Air Force and they'll be glad of a hand with the officer cadets who are to be billeted at Arnold any day. Even on crutches you can help. There'll be no more boat races until the war is over, but there are young men here who are still eager to learn how to row. Running the college doesn't give me the time to show them. It would be a useful way of earning your keep. Of course, if you wish to advance your law studies at the same time, either here or in London, you will be free to do so. Think about it and let me know.'

On the same day, 4 April, Germany invaded Norway and Denmark.

After discussing the letter with Johanna, George accepted Childers' offer until the Air Force decided what to do with him. The alternative was for him to go to an RAF convalescent home, which would have meant being separated from his wife. The RAF had already scheduled a medical examination for June.

32

Johanna was especially glad to get away from Addem. The community didn't want her among them – she felt it in her bones and regretted it. Calvinist Scottish Sundays depressed her. She had definitely liked what she saw of Oxford at the time of the boat race: it would be a good place to have their child, if they were still there in November. She welcomed the change.

At the end of April 1940, after a good deal of string-pulling in Addem and Oxford, George left Dr Crowder's care to become an outpatient of Dr Carter at the Radcliffe Infirmary in Oxford, where his artificial limb would be fitted. He was on crutches and would be on sick leave from the RAF for the next three months.

The crowded train journey from Aberdeen to Peterborough was long and tiring; even harder for the children cooped up in the carriages. There was no dining car and the carriages were unheated. Johanna bought endless cups of stewed tea and rock-like buns on railway platforms. But it was spring and there was new life in the air. From one of the platforms they watched a flock of migrating birds – they looked so free, flying above a world at war. Always there were aircraft on patrol. By now British troops had been defeated in their first clash with the Germans in Scandinavia.

No one begrudged George anything on the journey; to his embarrassment, he was treated as if he was a fighter pilot who had come off worst in battle. 'I reckon you've done your bit,' one passenger said to him, 'God bless you.' If only I had, George thought. An elderly lady insisted on giving him her seat: 'Fancy the poor boy being without a leg.' She willingly sat with Johanna on the suitcases. She was convinced that the war would soon be over: 'Neither Britain nor Germany want a war on their hands. It will all be settled peacefully, you'll see. Then you young people can get on with your lives.' In the absence of porters, she helped Johanna with the luggage. To have to hobble along behind the two women hurt George's pride. He was no longer self-reliant.

Childers picked them up at Peterborough and brought them to Oxford by car. He greeted them with a warm handshake and a shy glance; there were few words. Dusk was falling by the time they arrived at Arnold. As George entered the college, he couldn't help thinking of all the pains he had taken to escape from legal studies ten months earlier.

The Childers and Walter Turnbull did everything possible to help the Kemps settle into their flat. Johanna was delighted to have a place of her own overlooking the river. Plain as it was, it was heaven compared to what they'd had to put up with at Addem.

Most of the dons George had known had gone, but some of the old gardeners were still there, moving about in the bushes and mowing the lawns. The flower beds were aglow with spring blooms. College gardening couldn't stop for a war. One or two of them recognized him with a touch of the cap or a wave of the hand, and smiled. Students he met lived in another world. No one commented on his crutches or missing leg – not that that reduced his embarrassment.

The flight of scholars and staff from the university had been offset by an influx of continental refugees and political exiles, many of them Jews fleeing persecution. Johanna

176

often followed their conversations in German in shops and cafés; she thought it wonderful to hear German spoken again. In Oxford, no one showed surprise at the sound of a German voice; she was never snubbed. There were also many Cockney evacuees, and all kinds of civil servants – including some from the Foreign Office. In contrast, the number of undergraduates had declined; more of them were women and younger men, who had military as well as academic obligations to fulfil. The RAF cadets were expected to arrive at Arnold college any day.

While George realized how lucky they both were to return to Oxford – doubly lucky that they had the Childers to fall back on – he felt that some of the university's graciousness and stability had gone. Much of the university had tunnelled its way underground; ugly emergency tanks of water stood in the quads; air-raid shelter signs desecrated its ancient walls.

33

A couple of weeks after the Kemps moved to Oxford, their world fell apart. George had been sleeping late when a worried-looking Johanna burst into the bedroom and handed him the newspaper – it was dated 10 May 1940. The headline 'GERMANY STRIKES!' was the biggest he had seen. German troops were pouring across Belgium and Holland; the British Expeditionary Force (BEF), leaving their prepared positions in France, had crossed into Belgium to help repel the German attack. The Germans had also pierced the Luxembourg and the Ardennes defences and were throwing back the French. That day, Winston Churchill replaced Neville Chamberlain as Prime Minister.

'In the name of God, go!' a Member of Parliament had hurled at Chamberlain the day before.

For the next few days the Kemps remained glued to their wireless; every hour mattered. At first the news was vague and contradictory, but each day it got worse. Protected by the Luftwaffe, German armoured divisions were charging across France and Belgium on their way to the Channel ports; the BEF, Britain's 'invincible army', was in flight. Any hopes that the RAF might stop the German tide were abandoned after a disastrous air battle above the River Meuse several days after the invasion had begun; a third of the British planes were shot down. The speed of events left everyone stunned: in a week – despite heroic resistance – Holland was overrun; Belgium had capitulated. In ten days the Germans were at the Channel; the British Army was fighting a rearguard action to Dunkirk; Paris was threatened; the invasion of Britain was imminent. The American ambassador advised all Americans in Britain to leave at once.

The shattering news of the British Army's retreat to Dunkirk confounded everybody; at first it was too serious to grasp: the British Army was in deadly peril of being destroyed. Only gradually did it dawn on people that Britain's situation was much more desperate than they realized, and that there was no easy way out. Some members of the Senior Common Room at Arnold suspected Belgium and Holland of treachery; the Commander in Chief, General Gort, was also blamed. Something had gone wrong at the top. All that Churchill could offer was 'blood, toil, tears and sweat'. Once again Johanna had to watch her every word in case people took offence. As the news of the German advance poured in, she agonized about her family.

After making several attempts, George finally managed to reach Tony Markham on the telephone at his air base at West Hadding. Tony confirmed Britain's desperate situation. He told George that David, Max and himself – were now in the same squadron, and were in the thick of the fighting over France. George could not conceal from Tony his feelings of being left out. 'David Evans made two "kills",' Tony reported. 'Max Elsfield made four. He is on the way to becoming an instant ace; air warfare is evidently what he's been looking for. I've never seen anyone so fearless. He's not a man for quarters and halves; with Max it's all or nothing.' George didn't tell Tony that they had already heard from Lady Elsfield about her son's successes. The last thing he asked before being cut off was the whereabouts of Roger Blundell.

34

Unknown to either man, Roger was at that moment fighting for his life in France. German armour had smashed into Holland, wheeled left into Belgium, and threatened to cut the Allied forces in two. The BEF had rushed from France to Belgium's aid. Roger's men were tired of waiting for something to happen and were glad to go. They sang as they left on a beautiful May day, with Roger wondering whether racing into Belgium wasn't racing into a trap. 'Orders,' the brigadier commanded, 'is orders.'

The Germans were halfway across Belgium when Roger's formation met them head-on. As his convoy came over a rise in the tree-lined road he was astonished to see several grey beetles crawling down the hills a mile or two away. Panzers! Through his binoculars he saw truckloads of German infantry following the armour – the first enemy troops he'd seen. There had been no warning that they were in the vicinity. Under a clear blue sky, German cannons began to bark. The crash of the first shells was nerve-racking, the heaviest made deep furrows in the ground before exploding.

With the rest of the brigade, Roger and his men dismounted from their lorries to face the oncoming troops. The anti-tank guns were dug in. White puffs of shrapnel and grey-black smoke from bursting shells began to appear among the Germans. Through his field glasses, Roger could see the shell bursts. One of the shells exploded among a group of men and horses. The growl of shellfire quickened to a dull roar; there was a loud drumming of the earth. Not a moment too soon, British armour arrived. With the ground shaking beneath them, the two sides closed.

Roger knew he was in deadly danger when he saw his first soldiers stumble and fall. For the first time fear gripped him by the throat. Some men hollered when they were hit; others didn't make a sound. The soldier he had been talking to was lying on his side with a ghastly stump for a leg. The man was still conscious. 'Had my bloody number on it,' he gasped. Most believed that either God or a godless fate decided their lot. Another soldier had been cut in two; the head and shoulders were missing. Roger was terrified. His heart beat violently. For the first time he gazed upon the repulsive face of death.

The Germans continued to advance like an irresistible tide, attacking from the air and the ground. After bitter fighting across fields of young grain, Roger's brigade was driven back. In the dense smoke of battle, units got lost, were overrun or were fired on by their own side. Equipment was abandoned, leaders were killed, communications broke down. Roger's unit was always in danger of being cut off by the Germans.

Having recovered from the shock of the attack, trading blow for blow, Roger's men made a stand on some high ground overlooking a shallow river. Accompanied by the crack of anti-tank guns, the bark of mortars, the crackle of rifles, and the stutter of Bren guns, they drove the Germans back. Using bayonets and hand grenades, in hand-to-hand fighting, they regained all the ground they had lost and more. He was amazed at their bravery and self-sacrifice; he was doubly amazed at the loving care which the roughest of them showed towards their wounded comrades. They were ordinary fellows whom he might never have met, but he was proud to lead them. British anti-aircraft guns even brought down a low-flying Me 109. It stood on its nose in a field and burned, crackled and sparked like a great funeral pyre. The pilot hung upside down, sizzling among the flames. Everybody cheered, hopes rose.

At one point Roger had a dying German corporal on his hands. All he could do was to give him a cigarette. In broken English the German told Roger to surrender, and then died.

Roger had worried how he could steel himself to kill. Necessity taught him; he killed to survive – the instinct for self-preservation drowned every other feeling. Without hesitation, he shot a German rushing at him through the smoke with a grenade in his hand. The youth had got close enough for Roger to see the ginger stubble on his chin and cheeks. Without thinking, he pointed his revolver and fired. A crack, a hoarse choking sound, and it was done. It was his first kill at close quarters and he felt remorse. Yet had he not fired, he would be dead himself. He left the German sprawled on his back in the bloodstained grass, still gripping the grenade.

Convinced that they'd thrashed the enemy good and proper, Roger was amazed to see the Germans fording the river in greater numbers than ever. Even when the British poured their fire into them – some of the shots stuttering and hissing in the water, others tearing the bushes and trees apart – the soldiers kept coming on. They simply took up where the dead left off, one relentless wave after another. Despite the desperate resistance put up by his regiment, in a deafening uproar, the German armour and infantry eventually broke through.

Roger and his unit fled through clouds of smoke to positions in a cemetery behind a village church; his men were red-eyed and shaking with fright. Expecting another frontal assault, they clawed their way into the earth, seeking what cover they could. As the mortars found them, clods of earth and shattered corpses mangled with filth rained down; shell splinters rattled against the headstones; the church steeple took a direct hit and came thundering down in a cloud of dust. Cries came from the rubble. Later, some of the injured had to be evacuated on coffin lids.

Crouching and crawling, and running from cover to cover through the smoke, Roger retreated from the cemetery to an apple orchard, where dead British and German soldiers – their eyes and mouths open – already lay under the trees. Some had an accusing look; others were resigned to their fate. A small stream burbled through the orchard. In the background was the barking of dogs and the lowing of cattle. Once he was surprised to hear a cuckoo's call; it gave him new hope. Spring was about and promised new life. Every now and again, stray shrapnel shook the trees.

The next night, with a general retreat under way, British troops were led along the wrong road. Unsuspecting, Roger followed the jiggling glow-worm axle light of the truck in front of him. The Germans must have thought the British mad. They were right on top of the enemy when the night erupted with fire. Suddenly the air boomed and crackled; death hissed and howled.

Blinded by popping white and coloured flares which turned night into day, dazzled by gun flashes and tracer fire, with bullets hissing about their ears, deafened by the din, Roger and his men – some too crazed to know which way to run – dodged and crashed about until, helped by the light of burning vehicles, they picked their way back to the right road. For a moment, fear had turned into panic; it was every man for himself and the devil take the hindmost.

Even when they had taken to their heels, they never felt safe. A deafening metallic shriek, a blinding flash, and Roger was lying face down in the mud, stunned. It was a miracle that he wasn't dead. Alongside him was a decapitated soldier whose blood was coming out in spurts. Some of it washed on to him; the smell sickened him. 'Jesus Christ,' someone said, crossing himself. Roger was deeply shaken. How degrading is the fear of death, he thought as he struggled to get up; how it bares the soul. For some minutes he rocked like a drunk trying to get his balance. No matter how hard he tried not to cry, the tears trickled down his pale face.

The flickering of shellbursts went on throughout the night; the clank of passing armour was heard. The murmur of battle in the distance was never stilled. Come daylight, they were strafed and bombed by the Luftwaffe all over again. The enemy never allowed them to recover their breath. '*Blitzkrieg*' the Germans called it – lightning war. Where was the RAF? everybody asked.

Roger's unit fled along scorched roads blocked for miles by troops and distraught refugees, whose faces reflected bewilderment and misery. Some women carried their babies on their backs in shawls. The boys and girls who ran alongside the column were cowed. Frantic mothers shouted after their children. The refugees had no idea where they were going, all they wanted was to get away from the fighting. Their appeals to God to save them never ceased.

Here and there was a goat, a cow, a horse or a melancholy dog trailing after its owner. The pitiful whinnying of a wounded horse could be heard through the din. Eyes gleaming, mouth open in fear, the mortally wounded animal sank humbly to the ground. Dead horses joined dead men. Another horse reared on its hind legs and stampeded with its rider hanging on. The ring of its metal shoes echoed in the night.

Roger spoke with a family of refugees whose world had

collapsed. Several days earlier hundreds of retreating troops had swarmed across their fields. In an explosion of shouts and screams, with the soldiers racing here and there, there had been a terrible pillage. Only the pigeons, who flew away, escaped. The ducks, the hens, and the turkeys were carried off. The farmer had tried to defend his family with a pitch-fork and a lame dog. In less than an hour his farm had been stripped bare.

'Soldiers are like locusts,' he cried out in grief; 'they leave nothing behind.' His face reflected his despair. They parted company at a crossroads, where there was a statue of the Madonna and Child.

The boom of the 'heavies', and the clatter of British gun carriages hurrying by, never ceased. Coming under the hellish crash of shellfire again, amid an uproar of shouts, trucks bumped each other, became entangled, crashed off the road and burst into flames.

Roger's burnt-out vehicles had to be abandoned, along with the field kitchen and much of the food. The retreat continued on foot. Blankets, backpacks, rifles, ammunition and trenching tools were all the soldiers took with them in their flight.

Roger and his men fled across a checker-board of flat green fields, by dykes and misty canals, past stone cottages with red-tiled roofs, and burning farms. Some were heaps of smouldering rubble with black chimneys pointing to the sky. Others, with doors and gates swinging in the wind, were empty of life and as silent as the grave. They sheltered in silent barns – what bliss to sleep on warm, dry hay – where the peasants' tools hung in neat array. The harrows and the rakes, the picks and the shovels spoke of the art of peace. Light came from a silvery moon, shining through the holes in the roof. They broke into cottages from which the occu-pants had fled but found little food; most of it had been looted already. The livestock had gone, broken pottery, smashed furniture and rubbish was all that was left. In one cottage the corpse of an old man was sitting in a chair facing the door. He wore a dark suit, shirt and tie, a flattened cap covered his head. Challenged by his dead eyes, they left.

The flight to the coast went on day after day. Sometimes Roger's group overtook other units on the run; other times they were overtaken themselves. Always there was the incessant rumble and roar of vehicles, the tramp of feet, the unending columns of men with rifles at the ready, lurching wagons filled with the wounded, the clink of metal, the rattle of mess tins, and the shouting and cursing of those trying to escape. The smell of dead animals was overwhelming. Not a day passed when they didn't have to bury one of their comrades, the men standing around silently with bent heads.

Whenever Roger's unit stopped to rest and regroup, the Germans would reappear on their flanks or in the sky. No sooner had the troops grabbed a tin of bully beef and a mess tin of tea, than they had to drop them and run. 'Hurry! Hurry!' Roger ordered, 'or you'll be cut off.' Men who had fallen asleep by the roadside had to be shaken awake again. Life was lived so intensely that the wild flowers, the apple blossom, the blue sky and the magic of spring largely passed unnoticed; so did the birdsong. They trod down grain that would never be harvested. Uppermost in everyone's mind was flight, first by road and then, because of growing Luftwaffe attacks, across the open countryside. There was a constant battle against sleep. After each frenzied retreat, they became lathered with sweat, too breathless to speak.

In the pandemonium no one seemed to know what to do. Every kind of rumour was abroad: that the British Army had been destroyed, that the soldiers had mutinied, that traitors and spies had undone the Allies. 'What's the truth?' Roger asked a passing senior staff officer. 'Are we surrounded?'

'Come, come, lieutenant! Of course not. For the moment, the army is engaged in a successful tactical withdrawal. You don't believe me, do you? I can tell it from your face. You think that you got into this pickle because of us. That's because you know absolutely nothing about handling troops on this scale. It's not a matter of rushing around with rifles and bayonets, it's a matter of great precision and foresight. My advice is that you do your bit, and leave the rest to us. All will be well in the end, you'll see. Chin up, now.' Roger suspected that the officer knew as little about the retreat as he did himself.

Roger was told to get his men to Dunkirk – a black pillar of smoke on the skyline – and he wasted no time in trying to get there. Once they had outstripped the Germans, and the gunfire became distant, the troops relaxed and made fun of their predicament. Those who had recently feared for their lives, slapped their knees, shouted riotously, chattered and exploded in laughter. Some indulged in recounting adventures which were obviously transparent lies. Mouth stuffed with food, one comic frisked about with a false nose he had picked up in a bombed house. 'I'm alive, ain't I?' he babbled. Hysterical laughter took the place of uncontrolled fear.

Roger's company had to cross a series of canals before threading its way through the British and French defences surrounding Dunkirk. Accompanied by the shouting of orders, masses of troops struggled to reach the sands. The men were stupefied with exhaustion, their faces drawn from lack of sleep. They knew that the Germans were not far behind. In the town, hundreds of civilians lay dead. Looters were shot on the spot. Mountains of abandoned equipment blocked the streets and miles of warehouses were on fire. With a smothered roar, buildings collapsed; oil tanks exploded, releasing clouds of acrid smoke which tasted bitter on the tongue, but softened the sun's glare. The fires added to the already torrid heat. Every now and again a blast of suffocating heat would overtake them.

Several drunken soldiers belonging to his regiment jeered as Roger and his men marched by.

'Have you no shame?' Roger yelled, on edge.

'Shame? With shit falling everywhere? Go and get yourself killed, you silly bugger.'

Roger marched on; arresting drunks during a rout was futile.

With dragging legs, he and his men eventually jostled and pushed their way on to the pearl-grey sand. In peacetime, it would have been wonderful to stop and picnic there in such glorious weather. He was happy to see the sea, which was crowded with rescue vessels and British warships. Bombs fell among the ships with an iron clang, producing a waterspout a hundred feet high; dogfights filled the sky. Long lines of men – British and French – were embarking by the thousand. In all the chaos, dozens of beach commanders kept control.

He reported to a group of staff officers who were trying to work out which units had arrived and which were missing. 'We'd given you up,' one of them told Roger. 'I don't suppose you realize that your mob was surrounded.'

Roger joined a group of soldiers gathered around a field wireless listening to a service of intercession and prayer that was being broadcast from Westminster Abbey. 'Oh most powerful and gracious Lord God, save them for Thy mercy's sake in Jesus Christ Thy Son our Lord, Amen.'

'That's the old cock, the Archbishop of Canterbury,' somebody said.

The avalanche of bodies pouring on to the sand never ceased. Some regiments arrived in perfect formation, moving in great curving, endless khaki-coloured lines, as if on parade. Other units straggled in, heads down, swaying from fatigue. Those swathed in bloodstained bandages were past caring.

Roger and his men collapsed on the sand, awaiting help

from the sea. Many soldiers fell into an exhausted sleep, their helmets over their faces; others watched as bombed and mined ships exploded or veered in wide circles before sinking. One ship that had already keeled over was like a giant blowtorch. Men frantically ran about the burning decks, and leapt from the rails.

One of the previous occupants of Roger's burrow had been left behind. He was standing resting against the trench wall, staring into the distance. Roger was about to speak to him when he noticed his stark, set face and his vacant eyes. A stray bullet had caught him, the blood on his face was congealed and black. He could only close the man's eyes, feel pity for him and bury him in the sand, using the soldier's upturned rifle and helmet as a marker. They had prayed over their first dead; Roger had even quoted from the New Testament. Now death was too common to fuss over. 'Rest in peace,' was all they had time for.

The pounding of the beach went on throughout the day. Some of the troops scattered like frightened sheep every time a bomb fell; others just lay in the sand and took their chance. With almost no anti-aircraft guns to defend them, angry soldiers fired their rifles at attacking planes amid scenes of anguish and death. Blessedly, the soft sand absorbed much of the bomb-blast, but smothered those who had dug in too deeply. Bullets from enemy aircraft screamed across the sand, tearing into anyone who got in the way. The medics and other good Samaritans did their best for the wounded, but they didn't have the resources; it was guesswork diagnosis. Holding the hand of a seriously wounded man did more good than trying to retrieve a bullet. Here and there, the army chaplains administered the last rites. The nightmare scene was shared by lost children, who didn't know which way to run, stray, bewildered dogs and startled birds. A bedraggled, solitary cavalryman, holding a fluttering pennant, rode his weary horse through the dust and the heat. He might have come from another world.

That night they ate well from food that had been brought from England. During the long, wakeful hours that followed, Roger watched the flicker of shellbursts on the horizon, the gentle blinking of Addis lamps far out to sea, and the red dots of soldiers' cigarettes pricking the darkness. Heavy guns were at work down the coast. He wondered what his family and Gloria were doing. Fear of death – that he might never see them or England again – dominated his thoughts. He dreaded the idea of becoming a prisoner. England was so close, yet so far away.

In the misty light of morning, two of his soldiers tried to swim out to a rescue ship and were drowned. Other frantic men stormed the small boats in the surf and had to be driven back. There were outbreaks of temper, but nothing serious enough to threaten the retreat. 'Make sure your men don't rush the boats!' a pistol-toting beach commander warned Roger. 'Discipline is all that's left. Without it we're lost.' The man wouldn't have hesitated to enforce order with his gun. Less desperate men sat and watched; others stood in clusters, talking in subdued tones. Everyone cursed his own bad luck; strangely, no one cursed the generals. Few of the men had abandoned hope. Had they been ordered to turn around and fight again, Roger was confident they would do so. With unruffled calm, a few played cricket. They dispersed under fire, only to renew their game once the enemy planes had passed. One fellow played his cornet to an admiring crowd. Couriers came and went, making their way through the chaos as if from a different war.

Endlessly, the troops awaited evacuation; they agonized over when their turn would come. A narrow, ramshackle jetty was the chief place of embarkation. Others were ferried out from the beach. Some said the Germans had broken through and that there was little hope of holding them back; others said the Germans had halted outside the town; it was odd that they hadn't already appeared. Throughout the campaign the enemy's greatest weapon had been its speed of attack. Until now there had been no pauses. Never did he escape the stench of the dead, which the heat and the stillness of the air made worse. Roger made all sorts of promises to himself as to what he would do if he was rescued.

Roger shut his eyes and tried to think of other things. He recalled the peaceful day he had spent on a beach in England the previous September. He had heard the rattle of buckets and spades, children's cries and the sound of the waves as, from a deck chair, with half-closed eyes, he had drowsily studied the sea. Incoming channels of water gleamed like silver in the sun. It had been a moment of infinite peace; the fear of death couldn't have been farther away. He had been dozing off again when he heard the shout of a paper boy on the promenade behind him: 'Britain declares war!'

After three days of hell, Roger's unit was ordered to embark at dusk on 1 June, a date he never forgot. A lifetime seemed to pass before he got the actual order to move. His severely wounded men had to be left behind; several medics volunteered to take care of them until the Germans came. Hope went out of their eyes when they were told this – the bond that had kept them going and had been strengthened under fire was about to be broken. 'Don't leave us,' one of them pleaded. Soldiers hung on to each other when the time came to say goodbye.

Dodging bomb-bursts and fountains of sand, Roger's group ran to the water where they were ferried out to an armed merchantman. The weather was perfect; the sea was like a millpond. Around them were frigates, corvettes, destroyers, paddle steamers, cross-Channel ferries, flat-bottomed Dutch barges, yachts, pleasure boats, fishing boats, tugs, motor boats, river craft, lifeboats – vessels of all shapes and sizes, some not much larger than a bathtub.

As Roger climbed the treacherous rope ladder, he turned to look at the man on his left and was astonished to see Sergeant Weasel, Tony Markham's servant, grinning at him. 'Blimey, not you sir?' Weasel said, as he leaned over and pinched Roger's arm.

No sooner had they greeted each other on deck, than German planes dived on the harbour. 'It's a funny old world, sir,' Weasel called as he ran to join his men. Roger noticed that the sergeant was wearing his Great War decorations.

Guns flaring, decks awash, with its ghastly siren sounding, a British destroyer packed with soldiers took a direct hit. Following a monumental explosion, the vessel disintegrated; flames and smoke billowed from the debris. Weighed down by kit and heavy clothing, many of the soldiers slid beneath the waves before anyone could reach them. Roger's ship – its deck already slippery with blood and oil – shivered and shook. Revulsion swept over him when he looked upon the torn bodies heaving in the sea. 'Jesus,' he exclaimed.

Picking its way through the wreckage, his ship got away as the light was fading. Once out at sea, some of the dazed and grimy survivors fell on their knees, crossed themselves and prayed aloud: 'Lord have mercy, Christ have mercy . . .' In mortal danger, they clung to God. Others were content to throw themselves down in the hold and sleep beneath the eerie blue battle lights; every inch of the ship was occupied.

As the English coast loomed up out of the dark, a stationary object was sighted to port. The captain saw it and signalled it with his lamp. A torpedo replied; it narrowly missed them. A flood of curses was poured out upon the enemy. Passing a blazing wreck, the ship arrived at Dover in a stench of gunpowder and blood. Roger was thankful to feel the soil of England under his boots again. Teeming humanity, in every stage of fatigue, crowded the dock.

Only half of his company answered the roll-call; a bleak silence spoke for the rest. Roger felt responsible; his men had died for nothing. What a waste of young lives. He felt bound to these youths as he had never felt bound to anything before. In spite of all the men around him, he was lonely and sad.

Later, after bolting down some food and drink, he fought his way on to a crowded troop train, while a band on the platform crashed out 'Tipperary'. Good God, not 'Tipperary', he thought. His father had marched to the same song in 1914. Paper boys yelled the latest news. Among all the tumult, Roger heard shouted commands, the slapping of rifles and the presenting of arms; it sounded as if some-body was celebrating a victory. Nothing could surprise him now – not even an invasion of Britain, which a French staff officer on the train assured him would take place within the next few days. 'You are almost naked on the coast,' he told Roger. The possibility of surrender was never mentioned; it would have been improper.

The train continued to wind its way through the English countryside. Never had he seen it so beautiful. He looked upon an English sky, an English sun, English fields and English flowers, thankfully. He didn't fall asleep until he was hours from the coast. Every station he passed through was crowded with soldiers. They waved their caps. You'd think they'd just won the war.

The evacuation of British and French troops from Dunkirk ended two days later. Most of the British troops were brought home to England; thousands more were taken prisoner. After that Roger never lost his belief in miracles.

35

On 2 June, the Kemps were startled out of their sleep by someone knocking at the door. With an effort, George threw on his dressing gown, took his crutches and hobbled out on his one leg to find Roger Blundell standing there. He hardly recognized him. It was six months since they had been together at Tony's wedding. Roger was filthy and had a heavy beard; he looked pale and sickly. He had been on the run from the Germans, chiefly without sleep and food, for three weeks. The remnants of his brigade were bivouacked on Port Meadow in North Oxford, little more than a mile away.

'Roger!'

'Sorry to wake you, old boy. Told you we'd meet again, "don't know where, don't know when". Well, here I am and I need a bath and a stiff glass of brandy. Hard luck about your leg,' he added.

The first thing Roger did was to phone Gloria and his family to tell them that he had survived Dunkirk. He almost wept while speaking.

While Roger was bathing and shaving, Johanna prepared some food and a drink. Then she busied herself cleaning Roger's tunic; George gave him clean underwear.

In Johanna's absence, Roger blurted out whatever came into his head: 'War at close quarters, George, takes you back to the beginning of time; back to tooth and claw; back to what some of us have been hiding. It turns the head. Everything was bloody, ruthless, brutal and cruel. It was the cruelty I hated most. Reality was to kill or be killed. I'd no idea that fear could dominate me; that anger could give way to bloodlust. War is stark raving mad, George. It's a crazy, ugly business, I tell you . . . meaningless. I don't know how anyone could call it glorious. Glory in war is fine if you don't have to discover the truth for yourself in combat. Virtues don't count one bit. Nor does the idea of fair play upon which you and I were reared at school. An Oxford education in the classics is about the last thing one needs. Do you remember the lectures we went to on European progress? Progress my foot! No one thinks of civilization, or morals, or ethics, or progress when he's fighting for his life. Conscience doesn't come into it, either. I never realized until now how civilized life is in my father's bank. We never saw the RAF. God knows where they were.'

Every now and then, having got something off his chest, Roger lapsed into silence, fidgeted in his chair, or got up and strode about the room. He was stunned by the normality of George's life. 'What peacefulness! What unbelievable calm!' he exclaimed. The windows were open, a gentle breeze from the river filled the room, a nightingale sang.

George was appalled. Where was the jovial, merry fellow he'd known – the fellow with the frivolous wit and the perfect composure? Except for giving a nod or a gesture, he did not try to answer his friend's gabbling.

Roger fell asleep while talking. George covered him with a blanket and left him to sleep the night away. He told Johanna that he would sleep for the next twenty-four hours. He was wrong; for all the sleep Roger got, he might just as well have stayed on Port Meadow. From their bed, the Kemps heard him walking about talking to himself.

The next day Roger slept so soundly that he had to be wakened when Gloria arrived from Ansfield. For a moment, he lay back with glazed eyes, not seeming to understand where he was. He wept with joy when he realized who was beside him. Through the blur of tears, Gloria clung to him and wouldn't let go. 'Oh, my God,' she kept saying. It was as if a dam had burst. 'Yesterday we heard you were missing in action. It's as if a life has been given back.' When Roger got up, he stood leaning against the bed. They had breakfast together. Later Gloria took him back to his unit bivouacked by the river. His voice betrayed him when he said goodbye.

He rested by the Thames for a week and then was drafted to duty elsewhere.

36

Shortly after Roger's return from France, Tony Markham rang the Kemps to tell them that Max Elsfield's plane had been shot down over the Channel on returning from Dunkirk. 'He managed to bail out and is now in the burns division of the military hospital at Canterbury. He's been awarded the Distinguished Flying Cross. I never knew anybody who enjoyed combat so much.'

George told him about Roger's visit. 'He seems to have lost his nerve. He was critical of the RAF. The only planes he saw were the Luftwaffe.'

'We know there's criticism and we resent it. I fought over the beach repeatedly, sometimes four times a day, often out of sight of the troops stranded there. Had we not done so, the men would have been slaughtered. We were over and around the port every day until dark. Even when resting, we stayed on "cockpit alert".'

When George telephoned Max's mother, Lady Elsfield, he was relieved to learn that her son's injuries were not serious. His helmet had caught fire and he had lost some skin and most of his hair, but his sight was unimpaired. His goggles, gloves and boots had protected him. The Kemps went to Canterbury to visit him.

On entering the crowded hospital ward, the Kemps passed a young man lying on his bed unconscious and almost naked. He had been roasted from head to foot. Death, they thought, would have been more merciful. His parents were sitting beside him, holding hands and weeping. From the coughing going on, it seemed that some pilots had been burned inside as well as out. Other patients were sitting up in bed dressed like mummies. Even though the windows were open, the smell of carbolic soap and burned flesh was overpowering.

They had difficulty finding Max until he greeted them from his bed. His face and hands were heavily bandaged, but he brushed his injuries aside. He seemed glad to have someone to talk to. He told them that his sister Hazel had been to see him earlier and that she was being courted by a Count Stamboliisky whom they had met on holiday in Morocco. His mother had visited the ward the day before; he knew from overheard conversations that the nurses had poked fun at her.

Max didn't mention George's missing leg. He was much happier talking about himself, and was in his glory talking about combat; he'd never felt so alive. While Johanna went to look for a vase for the flowers she'd brought, he told Kemp how he came to be shot down.

'Bloody clot, I was. I shouldn't have followed the plane down.' He was furious that he had let a Hun get the better of him.

'All I can remember was a shattering explosion. I lost control and my kite went into a spin. There was a panicky moment when I couldn't get the hood open. It was torture to breathe. I struggled so much and cursed the hood so hard, that I wasn't aware that the skin was peeling off my face. It's surprising what you'll do when your life is threatened – nothing concentrates the mind so much as the fear of death. I eventually got the hood back and bailed out. I landed in the water with the parachute as a shroud. My hands were too burned to throw the switch and get rid of it. It took me some time to break free. Sitting in an icy-cold sea, fighting with your parachute and crying with pain is not the way to die. All good-byes should be brief. What a relief it was to be rescued!'

Invasion or no invasion, Max was certain that Britain would win the war in the end. 'We'll beat the hell out of them in the air and on the ground in the next round, you'll see.' He went on to make all kinds of rash judgements about it. It was obvious that he would be back in the air as fast as he could.

On Johanna's return, they changed the subject.

Before leaving, they congratulated Max on his DFC. He was pleased.

At the entrance to the hospital, George and Johanna ran into Pat Riley and Penelope Markham. Both were in army uniform and in their usual high spirits. Penelope passed on to Johanna the exciting news that her sister-in-law, Lydia, was expecting a baby. The Kemps were surprised that Pat and Penelope were still together; hadn't Tony told Penelope about Beatrix? Johanna was ill at ease with the Irishman; her conversation was strained and she was glad when they parted.

37

Awaiting George on his return to Oxford was a letter from the RAF giving the date and place of his medical examination.

This took place in the Museum building in Parks Road, Oxford shortly after the last British and French troops had left Dunkirk.

He arrived early for his appointment. The dry weather was holding. It was the first time he had worn his artificial limb in public, and he felt uneasy. It wouldn't do what he expected of it; he couldn't trust it. 'That's normal,' they had said at the Radcliffe. As he entered the building, he wondered if he would be able to persuade the board to allow him to return to duty.

George joined other pilots in a depressingly dark waiting-room. Like himself, most of the pilots had canes: they looked fit enough until they tried to stand up. Some were free-and-easy in discussing their troubles while others remained quiet. A conversation sprang up between George and a French pilot sitting next to him. He asked how long he'd been waiting. 'Thirty minutes,' the Frenchman answered. He told George the devastating news that France had just surrendered. Then he began to talk about a new invention called radar which George knew little about. When his name was called, the Frenchman stubbed out his cigarette and limped after the orderly. The inquisitive glance George gave him when he came out was answered by a gesture of hope.

In due course, George followed. Because of his new leg, he made an awkward entrance and was glad to sit down. The Medical Board consisted of three senior RAF doctors. Contrary to what he had been led to expect, they were pleasant and considerate, even fatherly. In a relaxed way, they inquired about his present activities. They had him remove most of his clothing and lie down on a hospital bed. The examination was thorough and painstaking. He knew he was in the hands of first-class physicians.

After examining him, they spoke leisurely of the favourable reports they had received on him from Dr Crowder at Aberdeen and Dr Carter at the Radcliffe. 'The loss of a leg is nothing to worry about,' the chairman reassured him. Their report would be forwarded to the appropriate RAF authority, from whom he would be hearing shortly. George left the room feeling quite confident that he would be recalled to the RAF – if not in the air, then for ground duty. He'd win through his troubles after all. Johanna was waiting to take him home. There were few people about. Except for telling her that he'd be back in the air soon, he hardly spoke.

Three weeks later a letter from the RAF arrived. Johanna handed it to George and watched his unsteady hands open it with a knife. 'We regret' was all that George needed to read. He threw the letter and the knife on to the table. He had been invalided out: he could no longer fly, and there was no offer of a job on the ground. So much for his secret yearning for recognition and fame; so much for his loyalty to the RAF. He cursed his luckless fate.

George fell into a deep melancholy that lasted for days. He became morbidly sensitive, and had fits of timidity. It was one of the few times in his life when he didn't know which way to turn; he simply couldn't make up his mind what to do. He refused to believe that the Air Force no longer needed him.

Johanna saw the change in George's features and secretly breathed a sigh of relief. Almost every week they heard of someone they knew who had been killed; friends just died – one after the other – one lost count. She'd take him as he was: crippled and rejected by the military. She didn't want a dead hero for a husband, she wanted the man she loved. She wasn't interested in anybody winning the war; she just wanted the madness to stop. She certainly didn't want her husband to distinguish himself by killing her German cousins.

George was devastated. His life as a fighter pilot was over; his brightest hope had died. He was left with an officer's uniform, a sheepskin jacket, a pair of wool-lined flying boots and a pistol. The Medical Board must have had doubts about him. Obviously, they'd killed him with kindness. He assumed that the comments of the flying instructors at Addem – 'Lacks resolve' or 'Inwardly weak' – had raised their ugly heads again. Or was it his German wife? There were times when he felt an undercurrent of resentment, not something he could discuss with her. Instead of seeking his wife's help, he shut her out. Isolating himself didn't help either of them; it made them both miserable.

In losing the RAF, George felt he had lost something absolute, like losing truth, or trust, or love, or beauty, or purpose. Instead of the fame he had dreamt of, he'd been rejected. Why did life have to be so cruel? How could he call Tony and the others and tell them that he'd been thrown out of the RAF? Somehow, Max knew already and had sent him more whisky.

Harvey Childers' response to George's troubles was to pile more work on him. As the RAF casualties grew, Childers and Johanna felt that they were saving George from a worse fate. So did George's father, who was unrelenting in his advice that his son should follow him to the Bar by joining the Middle Temple. George would be able to postpone his Bar examination until after the war, but he was not very happy about the dinners he would have to attend under the scrutiny of the senior barristers. Reluctantly, George did as his father advised. Everything he had done to avoid a legal career had failed. Fate had won.

38

From June until October 1940, the Kemps were spellbound by the unceasing battle fought in the sky: the Battle of Britain was under way. A growing stream of German planes appeared in the daytime – five hundred or more at a time. On a visit to London, while walking through Hyde Park they witnessed one of the raids. RAF fighter planes darted in and out of enemy formations; there was a sound like fire-crackers; one German plane tumbled down like a flaming torch. The crowd cheered fiercely, even the children took part. Oxford was not bombed, but almost every night they heard heavy bombers endlessly throbbing their way north.

Emboldened by its success in Europe, Germany called upon Britain to surrender. 'We shall never surrender,' a defiant Churchill answered, instilling his own supreme confidence into his countrymen. It was one thing for Germany to impose its will on Norway, Denmark, Poland, France, Luxembourg, the Netherlands and Belgium, and another thing to subjugate the British Isles. Instead, in deadly peril, the British closed ranks. British defences were strengthened; defence industries worked round the clock; the Home Guard was mobilized; anybody who could load and fire a rifle was recruited; signposts were removed across the country to confuse any invading Germans. In the remoter parts, fire beacons of furze and cordwood were prepared. Everyone was told to stay put and all military leave was cancelled. The whole nation held its breath and waited for the onslaught to begin. There was no panic, no disorder – the nation went about its business as it had always done.

The retaliatory night bombing of Germany brought new worries to Johanna. She was shocked at the heavy bombardment of Cologne. She couldn't suddenly stop worrying about her family and feeling the German losses. For her, the war was doubly mad. Often in the night she would lie awake wondering about her parents and sister. Her pregnancy caused her to yearn for them even more.

'Why did God decide that we should witness all this?' Johanna asked George. 'I don't know how to explain it. It feels like being in the middle of a great maelstrom. What is going on is so huge that it makes me lose my balance. It cannot be the result of Hitler alone. It's too big. And you and I with different loyalties. How can we bridge our differences?' George thought her brave.

The Kemps – like everyone else – prepared for the invasion which they believed was imminent. They went to bed knowing that there might be fighting in the fields around Oxford before morning. Sometimes they would wake up in the night convinced that they had heard the church bells signalling that the Germans had landed.

George knew that the Germans had far more planes and battle-hardened pilots than the British. Only in the seas surrounding Britain could the country hope to hold its own. In the Atlantic, where Bill Clark was fighting, the German U-boats were winning.

Throughout these anxious weeks and months, George fitted his visits to Dr Carter at the Radcliffe and his trips to London to the Middle Temple around his work at Arnold College. He wondered what the study of law had got to do with the deaths that rained down on the city every night. Because of the bombing, moving about London was like crossing a cratered wasteland. Gaping, glassless windows stared from shattered buildings; they reflected George's own shattered dreams. Other windows were blacked out. The stoicism which Londoners had shown earlier was beginning to wear thin: going to and from air-raid shelters in the middle of the night was taking its toll. Throughout the summer and autumn of 1940, there was no let-up in the bombing and the anti-aircraft fire. The air-raid sirens were forever howling; the air was filled with acrid smoke and dust.

George eventually started counselling the RAF officer cadets billeted at Arnold. It wasn't what he had planned to do with his life, but neither was a legal career, and at least it helped to keep him sane. He thought the cadets were even more inno-cent than he had been two years ago. He also helped those studying German, and gave uninspired tutorials in law. Walking with a cane, he limped along the tow-path, recalling the hours he had spent on the water. The river still drew him like a magnet. He was familiar with its smell. 'This is the river that not long ago was ours,' he said to himself. 'We did win; in our moment of triumph everything was ours.' He haunted Arnold's boatshed, and became a lonely figure walking along the bank in all weathers. The 'fours' and the 'eights' that passed were a temporary distraction, but the reflection of the trees in the water he now ignored. There was an emptiness in his life which he was unable to fill. Sometimes an acquaintance stopped him, but he had no desire to talk. Instead of the heroic acts that would have carried him forward in the RAF, he had become a nobody. He felt completely unfulfilled.

In all the gloom, in August 1940, David Evans and Helen Markham became engaged. Helen was now a clerk with RAF Fighter Command. The news delighted the Kemps. 'Well, some things do come as a surprise,' was Johanna's comment. 'I thought David would never make up his mind.'

'You can never tell what David will do,' George replied. 'He can change his mind like quicksilver. The wonder is that Helen has got him as far as she has, she's been pushing him for ages. Anyway, let's celebrate the engagement.'

39

In late September 1940, Johanna visited the Kidlington air base with files for her husband to tutor RAF cadets there. George himself was in London. Leaving the car at the entrance, she set out to walk to the command building. It was a normal day at the base, with personnel going about their business and planes coming and going. A crowded truck stopped to offer her a lift. As the weather was fine, she declined; she needed the fresh air. She halted for a moment in the sunlight to watch a fighter plane take off and then walked on.

Suddenly the truck she was following rose before her eyes and exploded. Bodies and debris were flung in all directions. A chill of terror went through her for her unborn child before the blast threw her across the runway and she lost consciousness.

The first thing she heard when she came to were the air-raid sirens. There was blood on her face. All around her, buildings and planes were on fire; bodies littered the ground. More bombs fell; the anti-aircraft guns opened up. She could hear someone shouting through a megaphone. The command building was hit. Wounded men and women were stumbling about in a daze; airmen dashed out of shelters to drag the injured under cover. Dense black smoke filled the sky.

Getting to her feet, Johanna's first impulse was to help others. For the next hour, through renewed bombing, she continued to assist the medical corps in providing first aid until, in a state of shock, she was taken to the Radcliffe Infirmary, where a miscarriage was feared. George rushed up from London the next day. Two days later, Johanna was sent home. Blessedly, she had not miscarried.

40

Britain under fire meant that the Kemps were forced back on themselves. Gradually, George gained control of his melancholy moods, and largely oblivious of other people, they rejoiced in sharing little things. They took a bus to Wytham Wood to hear the birds and watch the seasons change; they breathed the flower-scented air. The plot of ground allocated to them by the college under the 'Dig for Victory' programme also helped to take their minds off the war. The work was light, and it pleased Johanna to return to their flat smelling of soil and sweat. Her family in Cologne was always on her mind. How they would love to know that she was expecting a child! Harvey Childers encouraged her to attend lectures on the English nineteenth-century novel.

Evensong at Christ Church Cathedral gave the Kemps

the strength to go on. They welcomed Arnold's chapel bell calling them to prayer and were often joined by cadets who were in residence. Living through such chaotic times, the service moved them deeply and gave meaning to their lives. The darker the outlook, the greater the number of deaths, the more the churches and chapels filled. God was real in these perilous times: people clung to prayer when they had little else to cling to.

One night they attended a Beethoven concert in Arnold's candle-lit hall, performed by a distinguished quartet of German refugees. In wartime Oxford such entertainment was rare. The deep, sad note of the cello spoke of the futility of war. There were moments when Johanna was overcome by the music. She recalled the concerts she had attended with her family.

Halfway through the performance the air-raid sirens sounded. Most of the audience dutifully hurried away to the shelters; a few went outside on to the darkened street to watch. Someone raised his hand to stop the quartet, but it played on. Johanna felt the incongruity of German musicians playing German music in the almost empty hall of an English university while German bombers droned overhead.

During night fire-duty at Arnold, which George shared with Walter Turnbull, they watched the owls come and go. They shared a flask of inferior coffee while Walter told stories of another war. The blackout gave a starlit beauty to Oxford which George had never seen before.

41

The closer Johanna got to her confinement, the more sensitive she became. Unlike her old self, she wept at the least provocation and was easily hurt. George had to watch what he said about the Germans. In the heat of the moment, he was apt to say things he later regretted. He'd blurt out, 'Germany intends to enslave us,' or 'The Germans are all fools to allow Hitler to rule them.' An ill-judged word, he discovered, could have a shattering effect on the trust and affection between them. There were occasions when they went for an hour without speaking after George had made a tactless remark; silent mealtimes were the hardest to bear.

One day, after throwing a tantrum, George put his hands on Johanna's shoulders. 'I'm sorry,' he confessed, holding her tightly, 'I don't believe a word I said.'

Sobbing, Johanna flung her arms around his neck. 'Don't let us fight over politics,' she begged him. 'Our love is too precious for that. Have you forgotten? We swore that politics would never be allowed to come between us. It is possible to live together and love each other regardless of nationality. The Germans are human beings like the British – to put all the blame on them is as bad as Hitler putting all the blame on the Jews.' George took his handkerchief to dry her tears. Clinging to him, she laid her head against his chest. 'You are my love and my life,' she whispered.

The palliative for Johanna was to tell long stories about her childhood; after which her mood would lighten visibly. She told them with such innocence and purity of heart that George's ill-disposed remarks seemed worse than ever. Why had God given him such a wonderful, simple-hearted wife? He admired Johanna's growing ability to cope with the setbacks of life. In changing from a girl to a woman, there was a new element of mystery about her.

A visit or a phone call from Lydia and Gloria at Ansfield always restored Johanna to the best of spirits. Lydia was in her element assisting Lady Markham at Ansfield House; Gloria was still teaching at the nursery school. Whenever the three women managed to get together, they would go into a huddle from which George was discreetly excluded. To him, their chatter seemed endless. Gloria told Johanna that she and Roger wanted to be married before Roger left the country again. Everybody approved of Roger with his generous impulses. There was talk, God forbid, of his unit going to Greece.

Following the success of German expansion in the Balkans, the Italians had invaded Albania. Having made a mess of it, they appealed to their German ally for help. The Germans not only restored Italian rule there but also embarked on an invasion of Greece, which had gone to Albania's help. The Greeks began a life-and-death struggle against the Germans. Fulfilling an earlier promise, the British sent troops to resist the German advance through northern Greece.

42

Life went on regardless of the desperate times. In the late autumn of 1940, George was asked by Tony and Lydia to be godfather to their first child. The ceremony was to be at Ansfield. Johanna was recovering from a cold and chose to stay behind. He was saying goodbye to her at the door when the phone rang. Johanna answered it. It was Tony, calling from West Hadding; he wanted to speak to George urgently.

'Hello, Tony, what's up?'

'Thank the Lord I've found you. David has been shot down and killed.'

Tony said it in such a way that George knew he didn't have to question it. In that awful moment, neither of them spoke; life was suspended; a heavy silence reigned. All that

George could hear was Tony's heavy breathing. 'I'll tell you more when we meet,' he said abruptly, and rang off.

George had difficulty controlling his emotions. One of his closest friends had died. It was the first time that the war really struck home and he felt chilled. Why did David, the brightest and most gifted among them, have to die?

'What on earth's the matter?' Johanna asked.

'David Evans is dead.'

'Oh, no!' she gasped, covering her face.

Tony conveyed the news of David's death to his sister Helen on his return to Ansfield the next day. Stunned, she had gone directly to her mother's room. 'You needn't worry about my marrying David Evans any more,' she said.

'I needn't?' Lady Markham's face darkened.

'No, he's dead.'

'Oh, my dear child.' For a moment the two women stood staring at each other, then they flung themselves into each other's arms and wept.

David's death cast a shadow over the baptism of Anthony Richard Markham, at the ancient sandstone font of Ansfield parish church. As Lydia held her child's head above the font, George vowed, in the child's name, 'to renounce the devil and all his works' . . . and to 'constantly believe God's holy word and obediently keep his commandments.' The choir sang 'A Child of God Baptized in Joy'. Held by the proud mother, the baby – its tiny hands waving – was presented to one woman after another, giving to all an assurance of life in an uncertain world. Lord and Lady Markham were delighted; they now had an heir; their line had been given a reprieve.

A reception followed at Ansfield House, much of which was now being used by the RAF as a convalescent home. With vehicles, tents and stores scattered about the grounds, and troops tramping in and out with muddy boots, the building had lost some of its former grandeur. The fields and the woods around were clothed in autumn colours. Lady Markham moved among her guests, her dogs trailing after her. Regardless of the war and all its privations, she remained regally dressed and straight-backed. She had done more than give up part of her home to sick airmen; it had become the centre of the local war effort. Volunteer groups of women sat at long tables knitting for the troops, others packed parcels of food and clothing.

It was heart-easing for George to see Tony, Lydia and Tony's sisters again. The two girls were in uniform. They were laughing about a surprise visit Lord Markham had made to Penelope's unit. He had found her under a vehicle with black grease all over her face. 'You should have been a boy,' he exclaimed.

George thought he saw the fear of losing Tony in Lydia's eyes; outwardly, she was all stiff upper lip.

Max Elsfield was also present, with only a light-blue scar across his cheek to show for his injuries. There was talk of his getting married, which everyone jokingly agreed was absurd. Yet a note had appeared in a London gossip column saying that he was about to marry an actress. They had never seen him with a woman other than his own sister Hazel. Max answered their questions with a smile.

That night, Max related how, in early September when the Battle of Britain had been at its height, he had been in a bunker at Air Vice-Marshal Park's Group Headquarters at Uxbridge when Churchill arrived. On a huge map, little lights flashed on and off, tracing the course of the air battle. 'Churchill watched as the staff plotted British losses. "What fighter reserves do you have left?" he asked Park. "None, sir." The last lamp on the table signifying fighter reserves had just flickered and gone out. Looking grave, Mr Churchill departed.'

The next day, a number of the Ansfield visitors went for a walk in the park. The dogs chased after them. Although it was September, the weather was at its best; an Indian summer someone called it. The ground was dotted with acorns and fallen leaves. All the young male farm workers had long since been called up. Girls from the Women's Land Army were harvesting the crops and tending the cattle. Tony and Penelope fell behind. Ever since he had returned from Mull, Tony had been worrying about his sister's relations with Pat Riley. Their latest caper was to be caught in a storm in their sailing dinghy in waters under naval control. Pat had disregarded both the navy and the storm warnings. The boat swamped, he had somehow dragged and carried Penelope to safety. He was duly reprimanded for his madcap adventure. Penelope thought him more adorable than ever.

'I wonder if you'll forgive me, Pen, if I speak up about Pat Riley,' Tony asked his sister.

She tilted her head and gazed quizzically at him. 'It's difficult to forgive you without knowing what you have to say.'

'I'll come straight to the point. I don't think you are the only one to whom Pat has given his heart.' He had put off warning her several times, to avoid hurting her feelings.

'Tony, it's absurd of you to say that.' Penelope's eyes flashed with anger. 'You can't possibly know Pat as well as I do. We are very much in love; we're going to get married; it's my greatest wish. One thing about Pat, he is true.'

Tony was baffled. Should he tell her about Pat's girl on Mull, or should he let her find out for herself? It would be better if she found out for herself, he decided. It was preferable to hurting her or causing a scene. If anyone could take care of herself, Penelope could. Time would settle the matter. He walked on with his sister in silence.

The conversation kept returning to David Evans, whose loss they felt sorely. Helen drafted a letter of condolence to David's parents in Wales, which they all signed. Gloria talked about Roger; it looked as if her fiancé was bound for Greece. Penelope told them that Pat was doing further commando training at Inverary. He was still climbing mountains, this time with the army.

No one had news of Alex Haverfield or Bill Clark. Alex, they presumed, was still with the Eighth Army in the Western Desert; Bill might be anywhere on the high seas.

Tony had met Charley Bradbury in London. 'Charley is no longer an agricultural labourer working for the Randalls,' he said. 'Thanks to Victoria and her family, he's come up in the world. He's being groomed to serve with a Foreign Office delegation going to Russia. He's become immersed in Russian studies.'

'God help the Russians,' said Max.

43

In a quiet moment, later that night, when the conversation lagged, Tony and George slipped away to the pavilion by the lake, where they could talk and smoke in peace. The moon was reflected in the water. The dogs settled down at their feet. There was a butterfly collection on the table; hip boots and fishing rods stood in a corner. The two men remained silent until their cigars had been lit and were drawing well. Then they talked and talked, desperate as they were in those anxious days to reveal themselves to each other. George couldn't disguise his regret at having been denied a chance to fight.

The subject of night-fighting cropped up.

'It happens all the time,' Tony said. 'I'm always chasing after the blue flame of bomber exhaust pipes. Only last week, we brought down one bomber after another. With their wings torn off, they cartwheeled in flames across the sky. A hit in the bomb bay is always fatal: there is a monumental red-orange flash, and another bomber and its crew are gone. Although the Germans are just as smart as we are, the losses they're suffering are too great for them to continue. In a raid on Lille the other day, for eleven of our bombers, we shot down dozens of their Me 109s.'

Later Tony talked at length about David's death; he never looked at George, and his emotionless voice seemed far away. 'Things went as usual that day,' he began. 'The group captain read a prayer; the odds against us were so great that only God could restore the balance. We sat outside awaiting orders, alone with our nagging thoughts and fears. I'm always tense when about to fly; waiting is always the worst. David was his calm self. He usually hummed a tune when we were sitting about, but that morning he was oddly silent. When he did speak, he sounded listless and indifferent. It was a relief when the controller's voice told us to scramble.

'Following the squadron commander, we emerged through low clouds and levelled out at 25,000 feet. A long straggle of 109s were coming straight at us. One felt the threatening noise and I experienced an extraordinary sharpening of the senses. With David on my right and the sun blazing in a clear sky, we met them head-on. We were twelve, they were twenty. We had no need for orders. In seconds, the sky was full of individual dogfights; it was difficult to separate friend from foe. Among flashes of sunlight, with the usual shouts of warning, we dived, wheeled, climbed and spun. Tracer bullets and burning planes were everywhere; bullets gouged my windscreen. Dead ahead a Messerschmitt became a ball of fire. There were long plumes of grey and black smoke. With little tongues of flame spitting at me and tracers leisurely curling past, I rolled and turned and struggled to gain height. Then I dived back into the fray. More by accident than by intent, my guns struck a plane that fell away streaming smoke. David flashed by, thumb up, on the tail of a Messerschmitt. An enemy plane followed him into the sun. 'David,' I screamed into the intercom, 'watch the sod on your tail.' I guess he was too preoccupied to hear. With dread, I saw a burst of fire rock David's plane. For a moment it hung before my eyes motionless, then it slowly turned over on its back and plunged into the sea. The water itself caught fire. There was no parachute.

'In one wild, baffling moment, David died. It caused me to drop my guard. I had to tell myself to watch out. Except for distant smoke trails, the sky was empty. Every buzzing, swarming hornet had gone. Heavy-hearted, I turned for home. For some odd reason, I heard Sergeant Haughton's horrible whisper, "'Who saw him die?' 'I,' said the Fly. 'With my little eye, I saw him die.'"

'Other deaths were anonymous; David's was different. It left me stunned. I kept saying to myself, David's mind was too sharp to die like that. I was so depressed that I had a close call with a barrage balloon, which suddenly lurched at me out of a low-lying cloud. It made me catch my breath. It was very close and I instinctively felt for the little silver horse that Lydia had given me, and which I kept around my neck. It wasn't there.

'There was a party in the mess that night for Max, who had downed his tenth plane. As a special treat, there was sucking pig and apple sauce for dinner. I couldn't face it. Amid the shouting and toasts, I had to walk out. I was so drained by David's death, that all I could do was to lie on my bunk and think of nothing. I was past feeling – past hunger. Max was as mad as hell when I left the mess, he still had to be told about David. With everybody shaking his hand, it was beyond me to tell him.' Tony relit his cigar; the rooks cawed, the dogs stirred.

'I can't accept that David is dead,' George said.

'Nor can I. David was curious about death. He'd worked

it all out in that extraordinary mind of his. I think he over-complicated the manner in which we get to God, but I suppose it doesn't matter how we reach Him, provided we get there.

'There's something else I have to tell you, George, that I wish I could have been spared. I don't know why I'm telling you, except to get it off my chest. David was to be married quietly on his return from his last flight. He'd met a local girl at a dance at West Hadding and had had a couple of drinks with her. They'd gone back to her place and he had left her pregnant. David was the last man in the world I'd have thought would do that. I find it incredible; he never indulged in bewildering emotions. He undertook to marry the girl, even though he didn't love her. You know that he was engaged to be married to Helen. Papa went along with the engagement, but Mother wasn't keen. I think she told him so.'

'How do you know all this about David?'

'He left a letter to be handed to me if he didn't return. It fell to me to tell that simple woman what had happened. When she opened the door she assumed that I was coming to make final arrangements for the wedding. I didn't say anything until she was sitting down. Then I said, "David is dead." It was one of the most difficult things I've ever had to do. I spoke quietly, but my words sounded like a great bell tolling. She sat quite still, staring at me in disbelief. "David is dead," I repeated. "I'm sorry." She didn't say a word, but I could see the pain and anguish in her eyes. She looked around the room as if seeking help, there was an uncomfortable silence between us. 'Why would God take David now?' she asked finally, close to tears. As she sat there hanging on to her chair, looking into my eyes, I nearly broke down, it was a struggle to control myself. I noticed my hand trembling.

Telling Helen of David's death was even worse. They were to be married in a month's time; it was all arranged. I said nothing to Helen about the West Hadding girl.'

214

There was a pause.

'One other thing puzzles me about David. He left behind several large gaming debts, which he kept secret from Max and me. I suppose most of us have something we don't tell. Max insisted on settling the bills, he said he'd feel better if he did. He always thought of David as a good man who was completely wasted in the war. There have been times when Max's generosity has surprised me.'

'David's luck at the table must have run out.'

'I suppose so.' There was an air of forgiveness in his voice.

'Do you think he killed himself?' George asked, unexpectedly.

A long pause. 'I don't think so . . . no, of course not. The Germans killed him. David wouldn't play God. What you can say is that he experienced a number of setbacks. He never found satisfaction as a fighter pilot. What he wanted was to be involved on the scientific side. He was always waiting for the call that never came. I also regret to say that my mother did not welcome him as a future son-in-law.'

'Poor David, he was so convinced that the war would end quickly.'

'Well, it did for him.'

They were quiet for a minute, until Tony took up the conversation again. 'Have you ever thought, George, how much unrequited love there is in the world? I always felt that Helen's love for David was never really returned.'

'David's death must have been a terrible shock,' George answered.

'It was. She was devastated when I told her. She doesn't sing any more.'

'She doesn't have much to sing about. What a hell is war. It comes out of nowhere and explodes right in your face without the slightest consideration of what you might want or deserve. It impales those who stand in the way.'

Tony nodded. 'Fortunately, one day life will begin again

215

where it left off. The deeper and more enduring currents of life and the slow process of time will reassert themselves. The Hitlers of this life may hasten the process, but life will go on transforming itself as it always has.'

George was not convinced. 'Sometimes I wonder what we'll do with ourselves when the war is over. So far all my fine plans have gone awry. I'm a good pilot wasted. Law's all right, but for some reason it doesn't satisfy me. I feel completely disillusioned. If the war ended tomorrow, I wouldn't know which way to turn. Meanwhile, I keep active at the college in a humdrum sort of way.'

'But you're blessed, as I am, with a wonderful wife, and a child about to be born. You've everything to look forward to. The main thing is to get the war done. Then we'll be able to live our lives as we choose. We must not only defeat the Germans, we must try to build a better world. It's my hope as a would-be political leader that we will rise above the brutality and horror of these years and try to find meaning in it all – it will be the job of our generation to restore faith in humanity and civilization. I'm so appalled by the ghastliness of our times that I'm in danger of losing faith in the goodness of the world. Against the events of today I must sound outdated, but I believe that people are naturally good, not naturally bad. When it's over, I shall come back to Ansfield and the land I love. Ansfield has stood like a rock through all the trials of the past three hundred years. It is a bit of old England expressing a stubborn stability in a war-torn age. To live here with Lydia and my family is all I ask of life. We Markhams are part and parcel of the earth. My worry is that the war will end, but hatred and revenge will go on. They won the last war and they will probably win this one. Love of our fellow men will have no place; the self-righteousness of the victors will prevail. Each nation will believe its own version of events. What has become of the 'Do unto others . . .' creed that

216

was drummed into us when we were young? We were taught that to return hatred is to deserve it. God forbid that evil and the thirst for power should land us in still another war.'

Tony stopped as suddenly as he had started. There was silence in the pavilion. 'Whew! my goodness,' he started again. 'You really must forgive me, George; I got carried away.'

'I don't think so; we need to say these things.'

Tony got up and walked to the window, looking out on the moonlit night. 'I think it's easier to live through war when you're married and have children. It's also easier when you can fall back on a friendship like ours.'

They grasped each other's hands in silence. The depth of their feeling was reflected in their eyes.

George made the journey back to Oxford that night. With other ghostly figures, he waited for the train on a forbiddingly darkened platform. Before the war, railway stations had been cheerful places; now they were places where you shook someone's hand and never saw or heard of them again.

Creaking and rattling, the train eventually arrived. It consisted of one long, open coach. It was unheated and rundown, but the warm autumn weather made the journey bearable. The blue lights in the ceiling showed little of the other passengers' faces; you knew they were there because of the glow of their cigarettes. There was a hullabaloo in the night from a passenger whose pocket had been picked. It struck George as preposterous that while young men were giving their lives for their country, thieves were taking advantage of the wartime conditions.

On the journey home George could not stop thinking about what Tony had told him. Had David really used death as a way out of his dilemmas?

44

In November 1940, the Kemps' child was born at the Radcliffe Infirmary. It was a boy, christened Harold Robert – after the two grandfathers. Walter Turnbull officiated in Arnold College chapel. Many friends turned up; Tony was godfather. Charley Bradbury and Victoria Randall didn't believe in baptism, but they came too; petrol was available for such journeys. 'If we didn't come together for births and marriages,' Johanna exclaimed, 'we'd hardly ever see each other.' She didn't tell her guests how her heart ached for her own family, especially now. Fate had denied her that joy.

Pat Riley and Max Elsfield had driven from London for the day. Earlier in the year, Pat had been on a commando raid in Norway. 'Piece of cake,' he told them, grinning. Penelope was convinced that Pat was the bravest man on earth.

The christening party took place in the Kemps' flat. They toasted the child with champagne – which, unlike bread, was still plentiful. The proudest guests were George's parents, who beamed with delight. George was always worrying about their safety: they spent as much time below ground in London as above it.

Johanna told Lydia that she had gone to the Radcliffe too early and had been sent home again. As George had feared, the second time she had left it too late and had almost had the child in the taxi. 'I thought George and the cab driver were about to have a fit. At least their worries helped me take my mind off myself. I shall never forget the driver's anxious face.'

'Having got her there,' George added, 'I waited in the corridor with all the hospital smells around me and listened to the babies' cries, hoping that my own was among them. In no time at all, a nurse came out with our son wrapped in a blue blanket. "Don't you want to see your beautiful baby?" she asked. I looked and saw the most wonderful chubby infant; I knew immediately that it was ours.

'When I was allowed to see Johanna, we clung to each other in silence; words had no place; time and the world stood still. I was amazed at the brightness of her eyes; she had become a lovely mother. It was fitting that the sombre room should suddenly be flooded with sunshine. We were so thankful to have a healthy child – how wonderful that such a miracle can exist in a world racked by war. I left the hospital walking on air. Our first-born had changed the universe.' George went on and on about his son. Fatherhood had gone to his head.

Charley spoke of his work with the Foreign Office. It surprised the others to see him dressed in Whitehall fashion: black jacket, black waistcoat, pin-striped trousers, white shirt, grey tie. He even arrived with a bowler hat and a furled umbrella. He had nothing in common with the fisherman's son they'd known at Oxford.

'You've become a bloody toff, Bradbury,' Max charged him. 'Even your accent has changed. The next thing I know you'll be one of the upper class, demanding privileges.'

Victoria gave Max a withering look. Charley stayed silent. He knew that whatever he said would not satisfy Max.

In the late afternoon they all gathered in the chapel for a memorial service honouring Arnold's war dead. A sombre Childers, as Master of the college, joined them. There was a sprinkling of cadets. The chapel was cold, dark and silent; the altar was bare. Dressed in the heaviest black, David Evans's parents had come from Wales. Helen was at their side. Everybody went out of their way to be kind to them. Mr Evans was a distinguished schoolmaster who had seen in his son's Oxford career all that he had hoped to achieve himself. Mrs Evans was a silent, sorrowing figure, oblivious to what was going on around her. Her face reflected an aching tenderness and a broken heart. When she wasn't wiping her eyes, she clung to Helen's hand. She was comforted by it.

Turnbull called the roll of the dead and said a few words about the circumstances surrounding each man's death: 'Second Lieutenant John Adams . . . Sublieutenant Percy Cadbury RN . . . Air Force Fighter Pilot David Evans . . .' the list went on and on; no one moved. He gave a quotation from Rupert Brooke: 'Blow out, you bugles, over the rich Dead! . . . poured out the red sweet wine of youth; gave up the years to be of work and joy . . .'

'And so they passed over,' he ended, 'and all the trumpets sounded for them on the other side.'

There was a moment when George thought he heard David's voice soaring to the rafters. He recalled the night of the accident, when David had looked after him in a cold, wet country lane in Scotland. He wondered where David was now; whether the meaning of life had been revealed to him in death. And what would become of the child that David would never see?

Before leaving, they recited the 23rd Psalm: 'The Lord is my shepherd, I shall not want . . .' The words echoed against the walls. 'The Lord bless you, protect you and keep you,' Turnbull ended. 'Amen.' The ceremony was so simple and moving that it left many of them unable to speak.

After the service they sat in Arnold's common room. Overcome by grief, Helen left the company and wandered into the courtyard. She could not get over the loss of David; she grieved over him like a mother for a lost child. Sitting on a bench under a tree, she recalled the summer of 1938 which they had shared. It had been one of the happiest of their lives. Every evening David had waited for her to finish work at the Bodleian. They went out to supper together, or she cooked a meal in her flat. They attended all the music recitals and concerts. At weekends they'd go up the river to picnic at the water's edge; sometimes they borrowed a canoe.

On one rare occasion, lying in the grass, David had talked about himself. 'I shall always be obsessed with physics. I had to work so hard to get to Oxford that I've neglected the social side of things. I suppose you could call me a loner. Until I met you I knew nothing about women. You've changed that. What worries me is that I can't find a suitable equation to express my love!'

When Helen told him that he had come to mean everything to her, David had taken the blade of grass out of his mouth and sat up. He gently placed his hands on her breasts. Their lips met. Slowly they sank down together on the grass, out of sight. They were as alive as it is ever possible to be. Remembering that shared joy gave her the greatest pain.

When Helen returned to the common room, the party was breaking up. Before they left to go their separate ways, photographs were taken. The crew members felt that they belonged to each other; the tragedy of David's death had united them even more. They had become much more aware of the realities of life since leaving Oxford. As they left, lightning shattered the darkness; for a moment it lit up the entire courtyard. Thunder followed; a storm threatened.

Shortly after the birth of his son, George began to take walks with Walter Turnbull early every morning while Oxford was still sleeping. George kept up with the help of a cane. Turnbull was a stabilizing influence on George, but he was always saying things that puzzled the younger man.

'You complain about the war, George, God knows you've a right to. But remember, it will last only for an hour, whereas life will go on. What is happening now has happened before. Struggle, peril, self-sacrifice, pain and death are not new. Like everything else, they come and go.

Time and life will outlive the war. Be grateful, thus far Providence has spared you, and you have a wife and a child to live for.'

When George got home his mind was always wrestling with something Turnbull had said.

That Christmas Johanna and several friends skated together on the frozen Thames. George stood on the snow-covered river-bank. He heard the skates scraping the ice and watched enviously.

45

In the spring of 1941 Roger Blundell and Gloria Markham were married by Walter Turnbull in the chapel of Arnold College. Gloria wore her mother's wedding dress, and carried lilies-of-the-valley. The brightness of her dress contrasted with the groom's dull uniform. Tony was best man. Unobtrusively, Mr and Mrs Childers sat at one side.

Even though it was wartime, a lavish reception was held at the Randolph Hotel. All Sir John's colleagues in the financial world were there, along with Lord Markham's landed friends. Roger and his bride looked proud and happy. As always, Pat and Penelope were inseparable; they never stopped dancing together. Lord Markham wondered aloud why they didn't get married. His daughter Gloria was more discerning; like her mother she had never overcome her dislike of Pat.

Tony and Max Elsfield looked older; their stressful life was taking its toll. Later that night Max remarked to George how Roger had matured during the past year.

It was heart-warming to see the changed relationship between Roger and his father. Arm in arm, faces glowing, they walked about with their heads together as if they had discovered each other for the first time. In the toasts, Roger got a good ribbing, but gave as good as he got; his sense of humour was still intact. In an aside, he told George that he was bound for Greece. As the newly-weds left the reception, in a car marked 'Just Married!', Roger shouted to George, 'I'll keep in touch.' Roger's mother stood outside the hotel weeping and waving long after her son had passed from sight.

Following a short honeymoon, in which the hours raced on to their poignant end, Roger reported to his unit at Greenock on the Clyde. He was waiting to embark for Greece. Ten days later, he spent an hour on the telephone before getting through to Gloria at Ansfield. Afraid of being cut off, he stammered, 'Gloria, I will take you with me in my heart. I shall count the moments until we meet again, I love you.' With a sharp click, they were cut off. He'd been separated from all that truly mattered in his life. He wept. He couldn't sleep that night; he could still hear Gloria's voice. Any further attempt to get through to Ansfield failed.

The next day, Roger climbed the gangplank of his troop ship, his possessions on his back. He was one of an unending stream of men embarking. Once aboard, he drank a stewed cup of tea while a military band on the dockside played 'Auld Lang Syne'. The ship lingered, so the band crashed out 'Land of Hope and Glory'. There was no crowd on the quayside to bid them goodbye. The only wave came from a man and a boy working on the docks and they seemed half-hearted; there were no paper streamers. Eventually, with a blast, the vessel shuddered, cast off its hawsers, and hesitatingly trailed the rest of the convoy out to sea. Roger felt that he was being swept along by forces he neither understood nor controlled. He had joined up to defend the shores of England. Here he was on his way to Greece. Absent-mindedly, he stared at the passing shore and the teeming waste on the water.

46

After a rough voyage, Roger arrived in Greece. A discordant band and a handful of black-clothed women greeted the British convoy at Piraeus. Ominous-looking warships lay about. The women hugged and kissed the soldiers, while shedding tears for their daring. Sobbing, they then sang: 'Greece of our Fathers'. A profound silence followed.

Once they had disembarked, nobody knew what to do with the Allied troops. A general retreat from the advancing Germans was under way. Several times Roger's unit was mobilized to go north, only to have the orders cancelled. It was the battle for France all over again: reinforcements were inadequate; confusion reigned.

Bored with inaction, Roger wandered off to the Acropolis, from where he looked down on the city and out to sea. He never succeeded in shaking off the would-be guides and the beggars. He also visited the museums of Athens. Some meaning, he thought, had to be extracted from his visit. As an English schoolboy he'd been taught to revere the greatness that was Greece. One day he found a copy of Robert Graves' *Count Belisarius* in a cramped bookshop off the main square. He knew the bookseller from an earlier chance encounter in one of the museums. The book was a first edition signed by the author. He thumbed through it and came across a line that delighted him: 'To enjoy the art of war you must willingly serve under stupid superiors.'

'How much?' he asked the Greek.

'In these days of worthless drachma, I'll take a pair of pyjamas.'

Roger later returned with his only pair; the book was his.

'We'll dine on it,' said the bookseller, shutting up his shop and taking Roger to a restaurant in Constitution Square. No sooner were they seated at an outside table, than a shouting, gesticulating mob rushed past in pursuit of a desperate-looking figure. To Roger's horror, the man was overtaken, brought down and kicked to death. The mob disappeared as quickly as it had come.

'*Politika*,' the Greek shrugged. Across the square, a barrel organ played 'Toreador'.

While he was in Athens, Roger received a letter marked 'Most Urgent and Confidential' from his mother-in-law. It was brought by a nephew of hers who was serving on the destroyer *Resolute*, which had just arrived from England. Roger hesitated before opening the envelope. Why would Lady Markham want to write to him? he wondered.

'My dear Roger,' the letter began. 'We all miss you dreadfully and hope you are safe and well.' A good deal of family news followed before Alice arrived at her main point. 'I wonder if you realize that you are living close to an area that provides the most succulent currants in the world. I mean the currants grown at Corinth, close to where I think you are now. I assure you, from having been there, that these currants are beyond compare. I suspect they are one of the reasons why the Romans conquered the Greeks. Nero is known to have stripped the currant vines of Corinth. The point I'm trying to make is that if you are in the neighbourhood, I do hope you will purchase some and give them to my nephew who has promised to get them back to me.

'I trust that I'm not asking too much of you. God keep you. All our love and blessings, Alice.'

Fortunately, Roger's Greek assistant, Constantin

Andreapopolus, a sharp character with bright eyes and an eager face, was moved by Lady Markham's plea. Currants suddenly became of greater importance to him than Germans. He was certain that there were no currants to be had in Athens, but the cellar of his home in Corinth was stuffed with them. His family would consider it an honour to let Roger have some. They could make a quick dash there – say two or three hours – and a quick dash back. He made it sound so easy, and was so eager to please, that Roger allowed himself to be persuaded.

Early the next day Andreapopolus came to Roger looking glum. 'A problem has cropped up,' he said awkwardly. 'The German Army is approaching Corinth. If you want currants, we'll have to leave now.'

An hour later, Roger and his companion were bumping along the deserted road from Athens to Eleusis and Megara. Roger enjoyed the folly of being there, not least because army regulations forbade it. After Eleusis, the road cut through the hills above the Saronic Gulf. On the old road to Corinth, which curled along the shore, they drove past olive groves, fields of grain, and the glowing earth looking its spring-time best.

Just outside Megara, a sprawling white town between two low hills, they were held up by a lively peasant wedding party, which had just left the church and was filing into a field dotted with lemon and olive trees. The narrow lane was filled with singing, dancing, gaily-dressed women in colourful skirts and full-sleeved white blouses, and hot-faced men in tieless white shirts and tight long woollen trousers. Red-faced boys and girls ran to and fro. The bride, wearing a heavy silver necklace, rode on a donkey deco-rated with bright ribbons and beads. The groom walked at her side holding her hand. A black-robed, bearded priest accompanied them. Zither music filled the air.

As a British officer, Roger was expected to join in the

celebrations. His need for haste was brushed aside. 'What is more important than a wedding?' Peasant pride demanded that he and his companion should toast the couple's health, eat some roasted lamb and dance a while. It was afternoon when they got away.

Avoiding the main bridge, Roger and Constantin crossed the Corinth Canal by an unguarded swing-bridge nearby. Close to Corinth, they left the car with relatives of Andreapopolus, who were astonished to see them. 'Don't you know that there are Germans about?' That done, they began to climb a zigzagging track. It was a difficult climb across stretches of stones, in which the Greek excelled. Twice their path was barred by a wild stream. Exhausted, Roger stumbled after the striding figure. Each man walked with his own thoughts and fears. Below them in the afternoon light was a staggering view of the Gulf of Corinth – its piled-up blue hills and its purple sea lapping the rocky shore. 'The most beautiful sight in Greece,' Andreapopolus sang out, pointing. There was the scent of orange and lemon in the air, a perfume of pines and herbs. All around them was the hum of insects.

Below the peak they met an American archaeologist with whom they stopped and talked. He had heard that a few Italians and Germans had reached Corinth but had seen nothing of them; nor had he seen Greek or British troops. His country was neutral, and nobody was likely to dispute the ruins of antiquity with him.

Roger was glad to talk, but was worried about the time; the shadows were lengthening, the sky was overcast. As they said goodbye to the American, he reminded them that the track they were. on was the one used by St Paul.

With Andreapopolus increasing his pace, they staggered on in the dark. Roger had difficulty keeping up. He concentrated on putting one foot before the other. 'How much further?' he kept asking wearily, mopping his brow. His calves were beginning to cramp; his feet were aching; repeatedly he slipped on the stones. 'Not far,' was the invariable reply. Later, they thought they heard German voices. They stood silently, listening. A voice called in their direction. Andreapopolus gripped Roger's arm tightly. 'Don't answer,' he whispered. Roger had a panicky feeling and would have fled if his feet had not been riveted to the spot. Fortunately, the voices faded into the night. After that he was always seeing German soldiers in the shadows.

It was after midnight when the two travellers emerged from a long line of tented vines and slid down a hillside of weeds to Andreapopolus's house. By then the moon had worked its way through the clouds. The house was in darkness. They knocked softly, but no one stirred, no dog barked. The doors were locked and barred. They threw pebbles against the upstairs rear windows. Heads appeared, a hushed conversation took place, a door was thrown back, a cupped hand protecting the flame of a candle waved them in. There was an odour of resin.

The moment they entered the house, an attractive, red-lipped young woman threw herself on Andreapopolus with a cry. The others shook Roger's hand vigorously. '*Kalos orisate!* Welcome!' they chorused. After the ordeal of the mountain, he was too exhausted to respond.

Even though it was one o'clock in the morning and German soldiers were thought to be in the vicinity, the family brought out glasses and wine. Roasted lamb and vine leaves filled with ground meat were served; the bread was sprinkled with sesame seeds. Everyone drank and chatted amid roars of laughter. The wine warmed Roger through. They even brought out a rare vintage that tasted like nectar. 'The best in Greece! *Thavmasios!* Wonderful! Better we drink it than the Germans.' Roger agreed. The more they drank, the redder their faces became.

After several glasses of the precious liquid, Roger began to wonder why he was there at all. His head was beginning to spin, the candlelight had grown strangely fainter, the idea of buying currants got farther and farther from his thoughts. His limbs felt like lead. He hadn't seen Constantin or Maria since they arrived. Every time he asked where they were, the Greeks shrugged and refilled his glass. They told him that the couple had recently become engaged.

Roger was roused from sleep by Andreapopolus and Maria, who, without any explanation, led him down a long stone staircase into a deep cellar. Their wavering candles threw shadows against the cold, whitewashed walls. Piled in a corner was a glistening mound of currants – enough to send Roger's mother-in-law into ecstasy. The smell of so many currants in that confined space was intoxicating. Using flat wooden shovels, they filled two ten-pound boxes. Having forced some money on his hosts, Roger made preparations to leave. It was dangerous to wait until sunrise.

After a last drink, heartfelt handshakes, and lingering embraces between Maria and Constantin, Roger and the Greek began their return journey in a murky light, in a still sleeping world. Feeling their way with slow feet, they made little progress at first. Andreapopolus led – his mind on Maria; Roger followed – his mind on the Germans. As he struggled through the loose dirt, he tried to decide what he should shout in German if they were challenged by a patrol. It seemed ridiculous for him to tell the Germans that he was wandering about the mountain in the dark to buy currants for his mother-in-law in England. With mounting apprehension, they listened to the night's faintest sounds and started at every suspected approach.

Soaked with sweat, the two men reached their car in the silver grey of dawn. By then their walk had been reduced to a shuffle; Roger's legs were trembling. The ten-pound boxes now felt like fifty pounds each. Lights and shadows caused by the rising sun were beginning to fill the mountainside; the night fog on the heights had lifted. Beyond the Bay of Eleusis they caught sight of the Acropolis rising out of the distant plain.

That morning the currants were handed over to Lady Markham's nephew whose destroyer was still at Piraeus. Totally exhausted by his Corinth caper, Roger was happy to see them go. By the time the port of Piraeus was heavily bombed by the Germans in April 1941, Lady Markham's currants were on their way to Britain.

47

At the end of April the Greek northern front suddenly collapsed. With the Germans rapidly approaching Athens, order and public services broke down; the streets were blocked by a retreating army, drunken revellers and fleeing civilians. Everybody joined in a mad effort to escape the oncoming Germans. British and Commonwealth troops retreated from Athens to the small southern port of Kalamata – Piraeus had been bombed out.

To avoid armed bands of deserters, who were seizing whatever transport they could, Andreapopolus led Roger and his men down the back streets of Athens until they were clear of the city. Joining up with other Allied troops, they then made a hectic dust-filled, overland journey past ruins of antiquity to Kalamata. On their approach, the Germans strafed them from the air and barred their access to the town. Only after German armoured cars had been destroyed by anti-tank shells were Roger and his men able to make their way to the sea, where they were quickly ferried out to one of several British men-of-war lying offshore. No sooner were they aboard the crowded vessel than it set sail. Behind them the din of battle continued; the night sky was lit by flames; thousands of Allied troops were captured.

Soon after sunrise the next day Roger's destroyer was attacked by German aircraft. Guns ablaze, it took a direct hit and sank. Pitched into the water without a life jacket, in a state of shock, Roger bobbed to the surface and struck out madly among the dead and the dying.

Without warning, he was seized from behind by the neck. No matter how much he struggled, his attacker silently hung on with frenzied strength. On the point of losing consciousness, Roger clawed at the choking fingers. He twisted and turned to use his last ounce of strength to bash the man's face with his elbow. As the grip loosened, he watched his attacker sink slowly in the dark water. Two staring eyes were the last thing he saw; a trail of bubbles was all that was left. A severe cramp immobilized the hand he had used as a claw.

With water streaming from his clothes, and gasping and struggling for breath, Roger was dragged out of the sea by the crew of another destroyer. By then he was almost past caring. The tide-tossed dead were left behind. Overcome by his experience, his stomach filled with water, his heart pounding, it took him some time to recover; fear of death possessed him. All he could think about was that he might never have seen Gloria again. To all else, his mind was a blank.

En route to Crete, the news came through that the British Navy had just sunk several Italian warships in the Mediterranean. It was considered a great victory. HMS *Hood* had played a leading role. Roger wondered if Bill Clark had been there.

He watched as the coast of Crete rose out of the sea. Spectacular mountain ranges soared above the island in a cloud-filled sky. Screeching German Stukas tumbled out of the clouds as the British convoy entered Suda Bay, their bombs narrowly missing Roger's destroyer.

Having been so close to death, the first thing he did on

landing was to write to his wife and parents. He wrote in the cool shade of an olive grove; springtime scents filled the air. A turquoise sea relentlessly washed the shore. A young Cretan brought him food and drink and ran his errands.

Two weeks after Roger's arrival, in May 1941, the Germans invaded Crete. An attack had been expected; the Allied troops had been on full alert for days. Roger's unit was defending the port of Herakleion on the eastern end of the island.

Hearing an ominous drone that grew louder and louder, Roger dashed out of a portside building to see an air armada of Junker 52 transports, bombers and fighter aircraft filling the cloudless sky. The invaders had flown from Athens, an hour's flight away. There were so many aircraft that they cast a shadow over the ground; the noise was deafening. After orange bomb-bursts had peppered the British positions, thousands of billowing, green, red and yellow parachutes drifted down through the fog and the murk of explosions. Dirty black shellbursts blossomed in the sky. As Roger watched, one plane blew up, another became a flaming torch and plunged into the sea. Bodies tumbled out of the stricken Junkers and gliders. Many para-troopers died while still airborne; others fell into the water and were drowned. Everybody who had a gun was firing; the reek of gunpowder grew. The sky was full of the rushing sound of attacking planes and the whistle of falling bombs.

Despite heavy German losses, scores of gliders and hundreds of parachutists managed to land. A bitter battle ensued in which both sides suffered heavily. The dead and the wounded lay about in heaps. Terrified civilians were caught in the crossfire. The fighting went on through the night, from street to street and house to house. The Germans seemed to be in every house and on every roof. Every now and again, a dead German parachutist fell off a roof with a thud. There was no let-up; no knowing where the next burst of Schmeisser fire would come from; no escaping the buzzing planes with their howling sirens. Roger had no time to eat, sleep, or change his sweat-drenched clothing. In the daytime, the light was blinding, the heat overpowering. There were times when he was past caring who was dead and who was alive. He lived off bully-beef and biscuits, which he carried in his clothing, and wondered if he would survive.

Roger's unit was ordered to hang on to the port at all costs and they did so. Some of his troops managed to defend a neighbouring aerodrome, keeping the Germans at bay. Maleme Airport on the western side of the island, however, fell to the enemy after a couple of days.

Hopelessly outnumbered, without air support, and short of arms and ammunition, Roger and his unit were evacuated by the British Navy one week after the initial German assault. The Cretans who had fought with the English – wearing camouflage jackets they had taken from the dead – fled through the smoke to the hills. On leaving the island, Roger's men fought right down to the water's edge. Some of them went on firing until they were up to their knees in water. Naval gunfire saved them. Thank God for the navy, Roger thought; three times they've saved us from total disaster: France, Greece and now Crete. The last thing he saw, on looking back, was one of his men impaled like a rag doll on the iron spears of the tall dock gates. The Luftwaffe continued to hammer the British and the New Zealand forces until they were well on their way.

The convoy to Alexandria was bombed, but this time Roger's vessel was unharmed. In an unending din, its gunners had brought down an attacking plane. It was a relief when the long line of the North African coast appeared on the horizon. He hoped that he might never see Greece or Crete again. He'd had his fill of defeats and chaos.

Several hours from Alexandria, a long line of tawny-brown cliffs appeared along the coast.

'What is that?' they asked, for they knew that no cliffs existed there.

'It's a sandstorm,' one of the crew said. 'Thank God that we're not in the middle of it.'

Once disembarked in Alexandria, Roger passed through sun-filled streets echoing to children's play and vendors' cries. It felt good to be alive and well – and not to be threatened by imminent death. Domes, turrets and minarets surrounded him. There was a smell of cooking; snatches of strident music came from the alleyways; children kicked a ball around; the crowded streets quivered in the heat. He bought a water melon to quench his thirst. On a dun yellow wall was a faded poster advertising a British concert that had taken place in Alexandria months before. The cultural activities of peacetime seemed so far away.

One of the first things Roger did in Egypt was to write letters of condolence to his dead soldiers' next of kin. He wrote them on an upturned box in a hole in the sand, with the tent flapping above his head. Now and again, he stopped to look at the occasional photograph or letter which had been taken from the pockets of the dead. It unnerved him to intrude on anything so intimate. Time and again, his hand stuck to the paper.

48

While he was recuperating in Mena, at the foot of the pyramids, Roger received a letter from Gloria.

Dearest Roger,
I cannot begin to tell you, my love, how happy I am that our first child is on the way. It will be born at

the end of October. What shall we call it? I feel I am walking on air. For me, the sky is brighter, the days no longer stretch into eternity. Every day was a day wasted after you left, I had no interest in what was going on around me. I even neglected my work at school.

Now our lives have been given new purpose, new hope, new meaning. While I don't know anything about the big questions of the war, I do know that love is the ultimate reason for life: it is the light in our dark world, it is the undying hope. We now have even more to live for. I pray that you will be back with us when the baby arrives, it is my dearest wish. All I ask of life is to be together, sharing the joy and the laughter we knew. One day, the shadows will be lifted, and we'll be able to live in peace and do as we see fit. Nightly, I plead with God to send you back to me. I pray that we will soon be together, in each other's arms. I love you with all my heart, if only you knew how much . . .

Roger read the letter over and over again; Gloria meant everything to him. In friendship and love their two spirits had become one. Without her he would not have survived as long as he had. He was happy at the news – even a little proud. He couldn't afford to get killed now. After that, he carried the letter about with him in his tunic until, with the sweat of his body, it fell apart.

At the end of her letter Gloria mentioned the sinking of HMS *Exeter*, Bill Clark's destroyer, off Iceland. She was worried about it. Had Clark been killed? she asked.

Some days later, to Roger's surprise, Alex Haverfield walked in on him in his dugout in the desert. Until he saw him, Roger had no idea that Alex was in North Africa. It was months since he had heard anything of him. For a moment the two men stood there hardly able to believe their good fortune, their eyes shining with delight, then with a shout they threw themselves at each other.

'What have you been up to?' they both asked at once.

Alex had arrived at dawn and had spent ages trying to find Roger. He was dressed as if he had just come off parade. They had a meal together in a flapping tent (leftover bully-beef rissole with rock-like biscuits soaked in tasteless tea) during which they swapped yarns and talked with longing of home and their Oxford days. The crew, the boat, the river and Childers were their common memories.

They talked about David's death. Alex spoke of an Arnold man, who had died recently in a desert battle. Roger described the battle he'd fought in Crete. British defeats sat ill with Alex.

Sitting over drinks, they exchanged views about the war but found little upon which they could agree.

'The Germans are very much in the wrong,' Alex said. 'The war remains a struggle between the forces of good and evil. We've no choice but to keep on keeping on.' Always self-assured, he never dreamt that he might be wrong.

'Go and ask the troops,' Roger said. 'They'd make peace with the Germans tomorrow, given the chance. War, not the Germans, is the real enemy, Alex – it's the curse. War destroys winners and losers. Its aim is to create hatred and extinguish life.'

'Don't get excited, Roger, war is part of the human lot – it's changed the course of history again and again. Eternal peace is a myth. Wars have shaped our world; there always will be wars.'

'That's the tragedy, but we can't go on like this, fighting, forever fighting, one generation after another, with fear possessing our souls. I don't know how the world will be saved but I do know that it won't be saved by war. There

236

has to be a less degrading, less sickening, less evil way. I think this war should be ended by the generals fighting each other with clubs, while the rest of us go home.'

'Roger, you're hopeless. We didn't start the war, the Germans did. British freedom and our age-old Empire are at stake; a quarter of the world relies on us to be brave and do the right thing. Either we fight or go under. The trouble is that you want the moon and you can't have it. Life is not your sweetness and goodness to all, life is struggle – sometimes brutal. Reality is the eternal conflict of interests.'

'Your problem, Alex, is that you have no sense of tragedy, no sense of compassion or mercy. You are unable to appreciate the terrible suffering going on around you. It outweighs any of your finer motives.'

Alex stiffened; a shadow crossed his face and there was a pause in the conversation. For a few moments neither spoke. This time Roger had overstepped the mark.

'Gloria tells me that Bill Clark's ship has been sunk,' he said, changing the subject.

'It has, but Bill was in hospital in Bath recovering from a leg injury.' The two men went on talking until long after the African sun had sunk into the sand. Only with the greatest reluctance did they release each other's hands and part. The sound of gunfire accompanied Alex all the way back to his unit.

At Mena, Roger received three more letters from Gloria. They usually arrived in bundles. 'We shall have to have more children,' she wrote, 'because I've never felt so well. If only you could come home, darling, before October.' She told him all the family news.

My parents are as well as can be expected, but are forever worrying about Helen and Penelope in the military, as well as about you. Papa wonders what

237

Penelope will do next. She's unpredictable. There's never a shortage of tension when she is about.

Papa still rides, but needs help to mount. He gets very cross about growing old. He's inseparable these days from his favourite dog, Bess. Penelope, of course, worries about the safety of Pat, who has managed to get himself into a pretty scary unit. Helen still mourns David. There are times when I think she will never recover. Ansfield, thank God, remains a peaceful oasis, far from war.

We had a trying visit from Lady Elsfield, who seems to be going to pieces. She is in the clutches of a fortune-teller, who promises her everything but delivers nothing, except frightening predictions of gloom for all the Elsfields. She also talks aloud to herself. Papa found her cantankerous and was glad when she left. I never knew such an unhappy family. Fortunately, after she departed, George and Johanna arrived with baby Harold, who captivated everyone.

Yesterday we ate bananas for the first time in ages. The children had never seen a banana before. They shrieked with laughter when peeling them. Even at Ansfield, rationing is beginning to tell. Most of the able-bodied servants and farm workers have been called up. More and more, we take care of ourselves. You would not recognize the lawns full of nettles and dandelions, or the lake full of rubbery weeds. Papa wages an unceasing war against them without much effect. There is talk of Ansfield being taken over as a military headquarters. The growing number of RAF wounded recuperating here makes that unlikely. I'd hate to think what damage the military would do to the house if they were to take it over entirely. They already have so many cables blocking the gutters that water is pouring down the

library wall. However, compared to others'
suffering, our problems are tiny. Somehow, we
manage. At least the invasion scare has long since
been laid to rest. All at Ansfield sleep undisturbed . . .

Gloria's letters warmed Roger's heart.

The next one he opened was from his mother-in-law,
giving him much the same news. She thanked him for the
currants; all the family had feasted on them. 'If ever you
are in the vicinity of Corinth again . . .' Roger winced at
the thought.

49

In early June, Roger was able to return Alex's visit. By now
they were both in the Western Desert. Alex's unit was close
enough to make a quick trip by car. The catch was that
Roger didn't have a car and nobody was prepared to lend
him one. The only vehicle in sight was the colonel's limousine, standing in front of his empty tent. It was a highly
polished Rolls-Royce, which the old man had used in Cairo.
It had a silver spear that stuck out in front. What could be
easier than borrowing it? Roger thought. The dry old stick
is away overnight and will never know.

The colonel's driver had orders not to let anybody touch
the car, but after much persuasion and a certain consideration, Roger was shown where the keys were kept. It was
an easy trip and he and Alex had a wonderful reunion. So
much so that his friend would not hear of Roger leaving
when the time came to part.

The colour was leaving the sky when Roger finally got
away. With dimmed car lights, and no moon, and the fear

of land mines, he found the return journey nerve-racking. He could just see far enough to avoid crashing into boulders. The darker it got, the slower his progress.

Having slid and skidded to the bottom of a wadi, Roger had difficulty getting out at the other side. The steep incline was full of scree. The car groaned and wobbled as it fought its way up the hill. He feared he might roll back. Instead, the wheels suddenly gripped and hurled him into an object. Thrown heavily against the windscreen, he cut his face.

The obstacle proved to be a stray camel making its solitary way up the hill in front of him in the dark. By the time he had recovered, the animal was sitting on the car bonnet, lashing the vehicle to bits. The demented creature seemed malicious about it. Roger stared disbelievingly at the mountain of flesh pressed against the windscreen. Because of the car's silver spear, car and camel had become inseparably attached. The camel's screams confirmed it.

In desperation, Roger put his hand on the horn. With a wrench, the camel lunged forward into the black night. He sat there trembling, still gripping the steering wheel. He was convinced that the frenzied beast would not stop running until it had reached the coast of Morocco and fallen into the sea.

Several hours later, chilled to the bone, he rattled back to camp. With nowhere better to put the car, Roger left it in front of the colonel's tent. He never recovered from the shock of seeing his vehicle the next morning.

50

In May 1941, Bill Clark had visited George and Johanna in Oxford. For Bill to return to Arnold in such enjoyable company was like coming home. George had set time aside from his college duties to entertain him. The Kemps thought him in high spirits and unusually talkative. George noticed that Bill was still wearing the wristwatch the crew had given him on his twentieth birthday.

While Bill was in Oxford he received his much-sought-after posting as a junior gunnery officer to HMS *Hood*, now lying in Scapa Flow. The posting was 'immediate'. He was jubilant: he'd been angling after a job on the *Hood* for a long time and couldn't believe his luck that he would be joining Peter Fry. His father had done what he could to help. He had given Bill a tiny silver replica of the *Hood* as a lucky charm. Bill dropped everything and rushed to Bath to take leave of his parents. He took a train north only hours after he arrived. Complete with a duffel bag, a duffel coat and a woollen balaclava, he took a boat from the Firth of Forth to the Orkneys. He worried that he would arrive and find the cruiser gone. If that happened, he would be posted to another ship and might never see the *Hood* again.

Clark was relieved to see the familiar silhouette the moment he reached Scapa Flow. His pulse quickened as he picked his way along a quayside littered with empty paint drums, piles of wood and metal shavings. Puddles of water lay about; cranes hung overhead. Accompanied by a cacophony of hoots and whistles, other warships were preparing to leave. With a crowd of high-spirited young officers and men he eventually clambered aboard a lighter as the sunset faded. Once aboard, he was taken in tow by a friendly deck officer, who ordered a rating to take Clark and his baggage to his cabin.

Peter Fry was lying on the upper bunk when Bill opened the cabin door. 'Well, well, well,' he welcomed him, shading his eyes from the light. 'So you've made it at last. I'd given up on you.' He jumped down, clasped Bill heartily, and helped him stow his kit. Bill was delighted to be back with his friend. He felt surer of himself with Peter about.

That evening, Bill wrote several letters: one of them was to George and Johanna, thanking them for their hospitality. 'I've made it at last,' he told them, 'I'm with Peter Fry.' The mail went out the next morning. A photograph of the whole ship's company was taken on deck; Bill was proud to be included. For security reasons, the picture would not be released until the voyage was over.

Bill's first day aboard ship was spent with the chief gunnery officer, a stocky individual whose wrinkled eyes had seen a lot of battles. Although Bill had been around the ship before, he took time to familiarize himself with its armament control. He looked up old sea mates. They thought that he had been lucky to have pulled off the transfer and took it for granted that Bill's father had helped.

Two days after his arrival – as midnight approached – the *Hood*'s great screws suddenly began to turn. A tremor passed through the ship. With a deafening blast of its whistle, it raised anchor, severed the cables, passed through the boom gates and set forth on the dark sea. It was blowing hard and raining heavily, the squalls were growing in strength. The surrounding islands stood dark against the night sky. Gathering speed, it began its patrol of the North Atlantic approaches to Britain.

Throughout 22 May, the *Hood*, accompanied by the battleship *Prince of Wales* and several destroyers, heaved and plunged its way northward through heavy seas. Its prow pointed towards Iceland, where it would refuel. Forecastles and bridges were hidden by fog, sleet, rain and sea-spray. Later snow began to fall, making visibility even poorer; the horizon was scarcely distinguishable from the sky. When night came the ships were darkened, galley fires were damped down.

The next evening, 23 May, Bill learnt from Peter that something big was looming. 'The German warships *Bismarck* and *Prinz Eugen* have been spotted off Iceland.

They're headed for the Atlantic; there'll be a massacre if they get through.' Later that night, at a staff briefing in the wardroom, Bill heard more about the *Bismarck*. It was Germany's greatest warship and it was on its maiden voyage.

Meanwhile the *Hood* increased speed to its maximum, 28 knots. The high-pitched whine of the ship's turbines grew. In such heavy seas, the accompanying destroyers had difficulty keeping up. With everything battened down, the battle group lunged through the waves. Decks awash, a glistening white track in its wake, the *Hood* continued to lead. It became difficult to move about on deck without a safety harness.

At nine that evening, Bill heard the shrill piping of the bosun's mate on the public address system: 'Captain Kerr speaking. Men of the *Hood*, the German warships *Bismarck* and *Prinz Eugen* are on a course that will take them into the Atlantic. Our orders are to intercept and destroy them. On our present course, we shall engage the enemy tomorrow morning. With God's help, and every man doing his duty, we will strike a decisive blow.' The captain ended by giving the order: 'Prepare for action!' Bill thought of Nelson at Trafalgar. He was exalted at the thought of battle. He knew that the *Hood* was invincible. It was a lucky ship, which meant everything to a sailor. Outside, the dark waters hissed by; a rime of frost formed over the upper works. The ship buried its prow beneath the angry waves which shot up and collapsed in confusion.

The *Hood* continued to lead, the *Prince of Wales* followed. Those destroyers still in the race brought up the rear. Every move was followed on the radar screen.

Bill attended a meeting in the wardroom to study a chart that showed the *Bismarck*'s course. It was all very calm and gentlemanly. After that, casualty stations were prepared and manned; anti-flash gloves and hoods were distributed.

As the night wore on, the distance between the German

and the British warships closed steadily. At midnight, the order 'Action Stations' was sounded; there was the hurried tread of feet and much shouting; battle ensigns were hoisted; a clear day was promised for the 24th. This is it, thought Bill, as he hurried through the bowels of the rolling ship. He thought of his parents. He returned the many 'thumbs-up' salutes he was given. As he passed Fry, his friend waved and called out, 'Well, you're going to see the old lady do her stuff.'

Early on the morning of Saturday 24 May, two days after leaving Scapa, the *Hood* sighted the *Bismarck* and the *Prinz Eugen* off the coast of Iceland. They were almost through the Greenland Straits when shrill alarm bells rang. The cry 'Enemy in sight!' went around the ship.

The *Hood* opened fire; the ship shook. Bill exchanged excited glances with his fellow officers. With orange shell flashes, the British shots fell short: columns of water and black smoke covered the enemy vessels. The German response was immediate and much more threatening. The first salvo fell just ahead of the *Hood*; the second astern; the third straddled her. The Germans were concentrating all their firepower on the *Hood*. The British were firing on both the *Bismarck* and the *Prinz Eugen*.

About three minutes after the engagement began, shells from the *Eugen*'s fourteen-inch guns struck the *Hood*. Although deep below deck, Bill felt the blow and heard the boom. 'My God,' he said aloud, as he picked himself up off the floor. Tightness gripped his throat; fear possessed him. For a moment, his instruments went dead. Unknown to him, the *Eugen*'s shells had caused a fire amidships on the starboard side of the boat deck. Red flames and black smoke engulfed the ship. Seconds later, *Bismarck*'s fourth salvo ignited the *Hood*'s ammunition magazines. Enormous explosions followed throughout the ship. With a tremendous roar, pillars of flame shot hundreds of feet into the sky. Guns and gun turrets came splashing down. Bodies littered the decks and the sea. The *Hood* shuddered, shook, and broke in two. A vast pall of smoke enveloped it.

Observers from the other British vessels watched in horror as the *Hood* split and sank. In two or three minutes it was gone. From its opening salvo to the end of the engagement, only six minutes had passed. Bill Clark had no time to contemplate death; his bravery was never tested. In one blinding flash the sea claimed him as its own for ever.

At 0613, twenty minutes after the battle began, and with only two guns still firing, the *Prince of Wales* broke off action and turned away under a smoke-screen.

In Oxford, the Kemps heard of the *Hood* on the wireless; they were stunned. Bill's letter from Scapa had trickled in the day before. 'Some things do go right,' he had written. Of the *Hood*'s crew there were only three survivors; Bill Clark was not one of them.

In Bath, Bill Clark's mother was the first to receive the news of her son's death. For a few moments, she sat on the couch, holding the telegram, head in hands, numb. Before the maid could stop her, in a blinding fit of rage, she jumped up, took the poker, and smashed her husband's model of the *Hood* and its glass case to bits. Then she collapsed, still holding the poker, and wept bitterly. Why had a loving God taken her only child?

For the next forty-eight hours, everybody at Arnold followed the search for the *Bismarck*. If it could sink Britain's leading warship in a matter of minutes, what other damage might it do? Three days after sinking the *Hood*, the *Bismarck* was overtaken by British air and sea forces and sunk. Britain rejoiced.

Several days later, Mrs Clark received from the Admiralty a picture of the *Hood*'s crew, taken before its final voyage. It included her son. A brooding darkness settled on her face; a passive sadness possessed her.

51

George Kemp had written earlier to Alex Haverfield in the Middle East about the death of David Evans; now he wrote about the death of Bill Clark. After a long silence a reply reached him from Alex in Cairo. He had unusually kind things to say about Bill; what a wonderful member of the crew he'd been, how loyal, how modest, how trustworthy. Bill had made the supreme sacrifice for his country. Whatever faults he may have had were now forgiven.

Alex went on to talk about his life in the Western Desert and the coincidence of running into Roger.

Anybody who comes out here thinking that he's going to dodge a harsh British winter for a life in the sun is more likely to be lashed to death with sand or chilled to death by the cold desert night. Failing that, there's always the chance of being robbed or murdered by the fellahin, who resent our presence and curse us darkly at every turn. You never saw such ingratitude! It staggers me that some of my forebears should have felt it necessary to take up the 'White Man's burden' and give up their lives for them. What folly that we should have ever thought that we could save this rabble from heathenism. 'Go, English, go,' they shout hotly, waving their arms, 'go in the name of God, the merciful, the compassionate, but go.' There is fury in their eyes. They no longer think of us as superior. There's a hatred of us here that I never suspected. What has become of Rule Britannia?

The flies hate us every bit as much as the natives do. They are the native's secret weapon. The sicknesses they spread decimate the troops. They get in your mouth, your eyes and your nose. Corpses in the desert are black with them. If disturbed, they'll rise with a loud rasping sound to seek another victim. We call them the devil's torment.

I ran into Roger in Cairo. We dined at Portofiro's Italian restaurant in Gezira. It was crowded and noisy, and we had the misfortune to get a table next to a group of hawk-eyed military police looking for drunks. A lute player and several women with bracelets on wrists and ankles tried to entertain us above the din.

Roger insisted on drinking champagne. After army tack, we plundered the menu for something fresh. It was a jolly meal, until I noticed my legs becoming stiff. My sight was also affected. When I tried to put my weight on my legs, they failed me. I concluded that I was tipsy.

'Roger,' I said, leaning across the table, 'my legs have gone.'

'Gone where?' he asked, blowing smoke.

'They're dead. If I collapse here in front of the Redcaps, they'll have me court-martialled.'

'Don't worry, Alex,' Roger assured me. 'I'll soon get you to the car.' I stole a glance at the Redcaps; they seemed ready to pounce.

Roger paid the bill, got me to my feet and with his arm around me, made for the door. The next thing I remember was Roger lying on top of me on the floor. Neither of us could move. 'Some kind of a bloody friend you are,' I said. Roger shook with laughter.

We were dragged away by a group of fellow officers before the military police could intervene.

Both of us were desperately sick for days. 'A straightforward case of wood alcohol poisoning,' was the camp medical officer's opinion. I hate to think what might have happened to us had we been alone: the other day a fellahin pointed a finger at me and shouted, 'Shaitan,' which means devil.

Alex ended by telling them about climbing the Great Pyramid of Cheops:

I climbed by starlight. It was something I wanted to do. When I reached the summit, I sat there alone, freezing from the sharp chill of the desert night. Imperceptibly, the first shafts of light appeared in the East. A huge ball of fire rose above the horizon. It lit the top of the pyramid, leaving the sands below in the darkest night. I was transfixed as the colours changed from purple to blue, orange, pink, and then red, until the whole world was bathed in a golden light. The scene was so wonderful that I wanted to shout.

Living in the desert has taught me why so many great ideas – such as those of Christ and Mohammed – have sprung from the most desolate areas of the world. Stark surroundings intensify one's imagination and help a man to find his soul. Ideas are the only thing that can take root in sand. The desert sun in the heat of midday not only plays tricks with one's eyes, but with one's head as well.

Johanna was always glad to hear from Alex. She found his letters full of interest and read them several times.

52

In June 1941, two weeks after the loss of HMS *Hood*, Harvey Childers sat down next to George at high table and told him that Germany had just attacked Russia. There had been rumours of a possible Russian–German clash for weeks, but for Germany to break the non-aggression pact and commit several million men surprised everyone. The newspapers and the wireless were full of it; nobody spoke of anything else. The war between Japan and China was momentarily forgotten.

In Britain, news of the German invasion of Russia was the cause of great relief. Germany could not send millions of soldiers to Russia and fight Britain at the same time. GERMAN THREAT DECLINES ran one of the headlines; LUCKY BRITAIN ran another. After that, no one needed to listen for the church bells to warn of an invasion. The centre of war had shifted from Britain to Eastern Europe. The first newspaper reports showed that the Germans were advancing with astonishing speed. Leningrad and Moscow were about to fall; Hitler vowed to drive all Slavs into Siberia.

Grasping at straws, Churchill quickly overcame his prejudices against the Soviet Union and promised aid. Many were puzzled by this decision; atheistic communism was an alien creed. When the British were fighting for their lives, the Soviets had been an ally of the Germans. 'How,' asked Turnbull, 'can we move to God-appointed ends with the help of the devil?'

The first shipments of aid to Russia left the Clyde in August 1941, two months after the German invasion began. Because the convoys were vulnerable to German air and sea forces operating from northern Norway, the losses sustained by the British Navy were heavy.

Oxford's contribution in cementing Anglo–Soviet relations was to fly the Hammer and Sickle and the Union Jack together on the Carfax Tower, play both 'God Save the King' and the 'Internationale' at concerts ('Arise ye prisoners of starvation . . . a new world's in birth . . .'), and call Stalin 'Uncle Joe'.

The Kemps found the whole thing bewildering. Why, at this point, would Germany want to attack Russia? The possibility of a German defeat entered Johanna's head for the first time. She was both sad because Germany would be defeated, and glad because it would mean the end of the war. Now they knew why the bombing of Britain had fallen off markedly since April.

To Charley Bradbury, the Second World War had been an imperialist war until Hitler's attack on Russia. Now he called it 'a just and right war in defence of democracy'.

'Rubbish,' was George's answer.

Guided by Turnbull, George and Johanna followed the course of the German–Russian war closely. Russian losses were enormous. Germany was conquering Russia as swiftly as it had conquered France, Belgium and the Netherlands. 'If Russia collapses we will be in mortal peril,' the chaplain told them. 'If Russia survives and America enters the war, the Allies will triumph. If Russia and the US join forces, however, the Western imperial order in Asia and Africa is doomed. Great Britain will become much less great.'

It was strange to talk like that. The United States was far away. Russia, though a great power, was thought of as a country of peasants.

53

In October 1941, Gloria called the Kemps to announce the birth of a fine healthy daughter, who was subsequently christened Margaret Eleanor. She had wired the news through army channels to her husband Roger fighting in the Western Desert.

The message had to pass through many hands before it reached Roger's headquarters. An orderly picked up the phone.

'You C Company?' he was asked.

'Yes.'

'You've got a lot of din on the line, I can hardly hear you.'

'Been like that all day. Jerry's gone off his rocker. The freak rain we've had hasn't helped either. We're all like drowned rats. Anyway, who are you?'

'Rear echelon. You got a Lieutenant Blundell?'

'Yes. He's one of the drowned rats down the trench.' The rain dripped off the soldier's tin hat on to the phone. 'What do you want with him?'

'Tell him he's got a 505.'

'What does it say?'

'It says "Mother and daughter well."'

'That should please him.'

'Better than a 506.'

'What's a 506?'

'Mother and daughter dead.'

'Jesus! I'll settle for the 505.'

'Nice to talk. Hope you get through the night in one piece.'

Roger was filled with relief and joy at the news. He noticed the smile and the goodness on the face of the man who brought the message down the trench. He should have got drunk, but he felt like crying. The idea of a birth seemed remote from the battle going on around him.

54

One morning in early December 1941, George and Johanna were listening to the wireless when the programme was interrupted with news that the Japanese had attacked the US Pacific Fleet at Pearl Harbor in Hawaii. Many warships had been lost or damaged. The attack came as a complete surprise to everybody. Japan was too far away to seem real – the idea that she might conquer America, as she had conquered China, had never been taken seriously. Those Americans who had sounded a warning were considered cranks. The next day, in support of its ally, Japan, Germany declared war on the United States. 'Hitler's final folly,' Turnbull predicted that night. By a stroke of good luck – a fluke – Britain had been provided with the strongest allies in the world: Russia and America. Its position in the war had been transformed.

In another letter to the Kemps from the Western Desert, written soon after the fall of Hong Kong, Alex expressed shock and concern that the Japanese, a nation he had thought inferior, should have conquered part of the British Empire and defeated the British at sea. 'What on earth is happening?' he asked. 'All over Asia, the British peace is imperilled.'

He also wrote of the setback the British had suffered in the closing days of 1941 at the hands of the German Afrika

Korps that had gone to the aid of the Italians in Libya. Armed by faster and more powerful tanks, Field Marshal Erwin Rommel had broken through the British defences and turned a defeat into a smashing victory. A popular commander, his troops followed his example of daring and speed. Alex hinted darkly that there had been unforgivable panic among the British: 'Not like our side at all.' This was confirmed by Roger Blundell, whose division had also been outflanked. 'Our self-confidence and self-respect – the mainstay of our power – are at risk. Has God deserted us?' Alex asked.

55

In Oxford, Christmas 1941 began with Walter Turnbull leading carol-singing in Arnold College's chapel. In addition to staff, the chapel was crowded with RAF airmen, many of whom regarded the chaplain as a father figure. Outside there was a first flurry of snow. Johanna studied the bright young faces around her and prayed that the war would end before these men too were sacrificed. Some of the cadets already killed had been George's students whom she and her husband had entertained in their flat. It seemed that they graduated overnight and were gone: some to fame, others to death. Happiness was always unfairly distributed.

As the gigantic struggle between Germany and Russia continued, the casualties became unparalleled. So far, Leningrad and Moscow had resisted German attacks. The German Army was not prepared for the terrible Russian winter.

The Kemps sent Christmas greetings to all the members of the crew. Their flat had become the clearing-house for the crew's mail – they were always receiving letters or forwarding them to one or other of their friends.

In December, Johanna became a volunteer nurse at the Radcliffe. Mrs Childers offered to look after Harold, who was getting bigger and stronger by the day. She didn't mind his constant demands and Brendan the dog provided all the entertainment Harold needed.

The Childers's and Walter Turnbull looked in on the Kemps on New Year's Eve to wish them a Happy New Year. Everyone fussed over little Harold; there weren't many other infants about. Johanna insisted that they should stay; she felt in need of their company. She entertained them by playing some Mozart on the piano that George had given her for Christmas. 'I've got a surprise for you,' he had said when she cycled home from the hospital one night. He threw open the living-room door and there was the piano – something she had wanted since leaving Cologne. George was not as fond of classical music as Johanna was, but he enjoyed listening to her play. After the music they talked about the crew. With war raging across the world, none of them looked too far ahead. They had become accustomed to hanging on, living day by day.

When the visitors left, Johanna and George stayed up to see the old year out. As Arnold's clock struck midnight the couple embraced. Their love, understanding and loyalty had surmounted all difficulties and had kept them going. In the second year of war, they had a greater respect for Roger Blundell's talk of 'chance'. Like Tony, Johanna believed that chance events, like everything else, were the work of God. George was no longer sure – doubt had entered his soul.

56

For much of 1942, the news at Oxford was dominated by the battles between the Germans and the Russians on the eastern front. It looked as if they might destroy each other. George was constantly surrounded by RAF cadets asking him to explain what was going on in the world.

In the West, preparations for the launch of a Second Front were under way. On a visit to Oxford in August 1942, Tony told the Kemps about an attack which the British and the Canadians had made on German-held Dieppe. It was meant to test the German defences. He had been in operation above the French coast throughout the battle.

'The Luftwaffe's response far exceeded what we'd expected. There were dozens of dogfights, some of them low above the water. I did little to help the infantry making the landing because I was too busy trying to stay alive. Regardless of our efforts, the Germans continued to bomb the landing craft; the coastal guns went on firing; the beach was covered with bodies. We had to use smoke to get the survivors off. In the end, I skimmed home alone above burning boats and pilots waving from their yellow dinghies. Many would die from exposure before help reached them. Dieppe was a disaster. We lost over a hundred planes with nothing to show for it; the bulk of the troops on the beach were killed or taken prisoner, yet we called it a victory. I was given a medal.

'When it was all over, I was asked if I would visit aircraft factories and RAF training depots to tell them how we had given the Germans hell at Dieppe. It's called "morale boosting". Had I told them what it was really like, they would have locked me up.'

George tried to get Tony to speak to the Arnold cadets about the battle above Dieppe, but Tony did not have the heart.

A few days later, the Kemps heard that Pat Riley's group of seaborne commandos had taken part in the Dieppe raid, and had run into German warships lying off the coast. Pat's landing craft had been blown out of the water and he had lost his left arm. He had been dragged to safety by an army chaplain.

Leaving Harold with Mrs Childers, George and Johanna went to visit Pat at St Mary's Hospital in Roehampton. As they made their way through the unending corridors, patients on crutches hobbled by. Now and again they were given a fixed stare by those recovering from plastic surgery. There was a strong smell of disinfectant.

The Kemps tried several wards before they found Pat. He was asleep when they arrived. His face had aged and his hair was more tousled than ever; his remaining freckled hand twitched nervously on the sheet. It was some minutes before he stirred and noticed them.

'Thanks for coming,' he said. 'You've just missed Tony and Penelope Markham. Penelope is returning later today.' He was surprisingly cheerful. 'Everest will take some climbing now,' he grinned, pointing to his missing arm.

While a nurse was attending to Pat, George approached another patient. He had snow-white hair. 'When were you wounded?' George asked him.

'In 1916.'

George turned to one of the nurses for confirmation.

'That's right,' she said, 'Joe was wounded in the Battle of the Somme, twenty-six years ago. There are patients who've been here even longer. One wounded in August 1914 has been gurgling through a tube ever since. Years ago Joe and he used to have visitors, but nobody visits them now except the Salvation Army.'

George was dumbfounded.

Pat told them later that the little room at the end of the ward was where those who were about to die were placed. 'I went there a couple of days ago to cheer up the occupant. His face was like a skull against the pillow, there was a death rattle in his throat. I was astonished at his heavy breathing. He gasped out that he was going to make a final appeal for help from the surgeon that day. "Give it a go," I said, but he died before the surgeon got to him.'

The hottest rumour in the hospital from those who had just been flown back from the Middle East was that the British were preparing to mount a major offensive against the Germans in North Africa.

A couple of days later the press announced that Lieut.-Gen. Bernard Montgomery had assumed command of the British Eighth Army in the Western Desert. He had fought brilliantly and fearlessly against the Germans in France. His arrival in the Middle East would boost the morale of the British troops. It was rumoured that the British Army was becoming listless in the desert war.

That day George wrote to Alex Haverfield, telling him about Pat Riley's brush with death and enclosing press clippings about Montgomery.

57

Alex received George's letter on the same day that he attended Montgomery's first meeting with his officers. George had enclosed a description of the general he had come across: 'An outstanding battle commander, who is dictatorial, cocky and tactless; a lonely, egotistical man known for his monk-like habits; a bit of an actor before crowds, as well as an irredeemable bible-puncher.' 'Like Calvin,' George wrote, 'he knows that God has some work for him to do. He is concerned with sin and death and life everlasting, yet he is able to impose his personality upon large bodies of men. He used to be famous here for not allowing coughing at his lectures!'

Montgomery, surrounded by his red-tabbed staff, announced that the next clash of arms with Rommel would be decisive. 'I have chosen the place of battle with great care. We have the men, the equipment and the will to deliver an almighty blow and drive the Germans out of Africa. This we will do. There will be no more retreats.' He punctuated his words by stabbing the maps hanging on the wall with his cane. There was a murmur of assent. Here, at last, was a single-minded individual committed to immediate victory – no iffing and butting, no perhaps or maybe. The large tent in which they were gathered rocked in the wind; outside, the waves of the Mediterranean crashed unceasingly against the shore, rolled up the beach, broke and ebbed away.

Alex wondered how it was that this little, sinewy, self-righteous general could arouse such confidence and loyalty.

In October 1942, Alex's brigade took up a position south of El Alamein on the Libyan–Egyptian border. He was excited at the thought of another trial of strength with the Germans. His unit travelled in packed trucks across the moonlit sand, bouncing and bumping in and out of the hollows, with minefields all around them. The deep tracks of those who had preceded them, perhaps the first such tracks ever to appear there, showed black in the moonlight; the horizon was lit by a recurring red glow; aircraft droned in the sky. In the dark, two graceful gazelles hurtled past them, fleeing the area.

For the best part of two days, Alex's men dug in, awaiting the order to attack. During the day they were roasted by the heat; at night they were frozen by the cold, which blessedly banished the flies. As soon as darkness fell, accompanied by the hum of low voices, and the clink of pots and mess tins, steel-helmeted figures squeaked about the sand and the camel scrub distributing rations. The food was hard tack, seasoned by grit; the tea tasted of chlorine. Coughs were stifled; voices silenced; no one smoked; sleep was snatched on a bed of stones and dust.

Until dawn, Alex liaised with the units on his flanks. He stood and watched the murky night-chilled columns trudging into the line.

Wandering among his men, he came across a group of young, raw Lancashire recruits who had arrived from Britain only in the last few days. Two weeks before they had danced all night in the Blackpool Tower ballroom. Those brought up in factory towns couldn't get over the desert's limitless distances. Red-cheeked, bright-eyed, they still had to learn about the terrors of war. Some were talking in whispers and worrying about what the next day would bring; most were joking bravely. Drink had got loose among them – the old-timers had distilled whisky from potatoes – and had encouraged a false cheerfulness; one or two in their teens were befuddled. Their innocence oppressed Alex. He wondered how they would fare in battle. Some would undoubtedly panic; some already had fear on their faces; others would stand as hard as rock. In a few hours a number of them would be dead; the best and the bravest would go first. Perhaps he'd be killed himself; he'd never thought of death like that before. His forebears had always placed their lives in the hands of God.

The British Eighth Army attacked on a moonlit night. It was clear and cold. As zero hour approached, Alex's eyes were glued to the luminous dial of his watch. Blinding flashes of light lit up the anxious faces around him. In a deathly silence, he gave the order to fix bayonets. There was a clicking as the bayonets were pressed home. 'Ten, nine, eight, seven, six . . .' Some moments last for ever. His heart thumped.

The attack began with an opening barrage of more than a thousand guns. The desert shook beneath the drumbeats of the artillery; gun flashes covered the sky; red, white, orange flares, with their multicoloured rain, changed darkness to light; tracer fire criss-crossed the forward area; clouds of dust and smoke veiled everything. For a moment Alex was deafened and confused by the clamour.

After an initial delay, the German and Italian artillery responded with a steady roar. Every gun for miles around was firing. Bombs began to fall. Above the din, Alex caught the wail of bagpipes from a regiment advancing on his right. Only hours before, he had watched a group of them go down on their knees in the sand to receive communion; he had no such solace.

As the barrage moved forward, Alex sprang from the trench and led his men after the tanks making the assault. Broken barbed wire trailed behind them. The thud of exploding mines, the deadly hammering of machine-guns, and the tearing, ripping whoosh of mortars filled the air. Men cried out and fell alongside him. Exploding shells threw up fountains of sand, stones and dirt. Heads, arms and legs went flying with the rest. Directly in front of him, Alex saw a man disembowelled.

With acrid smoke and dust drifting across the battlefield, the attack was brought to a halt. No matter how many times Alex regrouped his men and counter-attacked, no matter how often he shouted 'Advance! Forward! Forward!', no matter how much the British artillery, armour and Air Force attacked, the Germans and Italians fought back and held their line.

Dawn found him in the middle of a minefield reeking with gunpowder. His eyes were stinging with sweat, his lungs were full of dust and smoke; he was overcome by the din and the fighting. His unit had advanced half the distance expected of it. They had pierced the first lines of the enemy's defences, but still had several successive lines to go. Far from racing forward as he had been ordered, it was as much as he and his men could do to dig in and hang on. He knew that something had gone wrong – it often did. He was astonished at the toughness of the enemy's resistance: for every yard gained, they had paid an impossibly heavy toll.

Nothing had changed by the time the huge blood-orange sun slipped out of the darkening sky into the distant dunes. Despite the savagery of combat, the line had hardly moved from where it was the day before. To the left and right of Alex's position, thousands of troops were pinned down. Quivering and floating in the heat, funeral pyres of burning tanks, vehicles and planes spluttered and crackled across the sand. Fanned by the breeze, black smoke had settled in the hollows. Heaps of corpses – behind which the troops sometimes took cover – and pools of blood identified the areas where the fiercest hand-to-hand fighting had taken place. A New Zealand unit on the extreme right had come under particularly heavy fire – hundreds lay dead and dying. Some of the corpses were stacked like firewood. The blazing sun made the smell worse.

Alex had little idea what was happening elsewhere. The news that dribbled in was that greater success had been achieved on the central and northern fronts. An Australian infantry division was about to seize the coastal road.

To hit back, snatch some food and drink, and get the wounded off the battlefield was all Alex could do. They screwed up their faces and clung to the stretchers as they were jostled to the rear. No amount of fighting had inured him to their ghastly wounds or their moaning. Some were mutilated beyond recognition. A long line of walking wounded dragged itself after them, including the panic-stricken, who shook uncontrollably, as well as the cheery patients, who knew that at long last they'd escaped from the war. It was sickening to hear the pathetic cries of those lying in no man's land. In the daylight they were roasted; at night they froze. Some of them called for their mothers; one man, lying across the barbed wire, raged against God. Others died with a sigh as if going to sleep. One of Alex's men had nothing but a small yellow mark on one arm, other than the lack of a pulse, there was nothing else to show that he was dead: no tell-tale queer stillness or bloodless pallor. Sporadically, throughout the night, the din of shell, mortar, machine-gun, hand grenade, and rifle fire rent the air; droning aircraft probed each other's positions; a star-filled sky hung over all.

The strain of continuous fighting told on everybody, especially on those who had not been in battle before. The odd soldier broke down and cried. All breathed a sigh of relief when the glare of the sun gave way to the shadows of night. Having survived a desert-cold night, each new day came as a revelation. It was the 'old sweats' who lasted longest. They were skilled in the use of weapons; they knew from experience how to disable or kill a man quickly, when to duck, when to take cover, when to stand still and when to run; they also knew how to feign death. Raw recruits undergoing their baptism of fire ran about like startled pheasants looking for somebody to cling to, and often paid for it with their lives.

Unable to turn the enemies' flank – the sea was on one side and an impassable desert on the other – the Allied troops and aircraft engaged in a battering match with the Germans and Italians, in which thousands on each side died daily. Bodies were strewn across the battlefield. 'Pound them,' Montgomery ordered, 'and keep on pounding them, don't stop.' Fire! Reload! Fire! Reload! Fire! Reload! There was so much pounding from both sides that the earth trembled; weapons became too hot to touch; men wearied of firing. The ear-splitting noise never stopped; nerves were stretched to breaking point.

Hour after hour, for eleven days, Alex's unit fought almost without pause. Across the battlefield, sheep-like masses of men hurried here and there, only to be shot down or bombed. They knew that some of the German troops opposite them were being drawn off to stem the Allied breakthrough on the northern front. On the twelfth day, after an incredible pounding, Alex became aware of a crucial psychological moment when the Italian section suddenly wavered and turned; weapons were dropped; little figures scuttled madly like a lot of frenzied ants looking for cover; the desert was suddenly filled with gesticulating, panic-stricken men running for their lives; white flags appeared across the front. From the British side came a roar of triumph. They'd won! Enemy soldiers, many of whom were dazed, were quickly disarmed; isolated groups of Germans and Italians who refused to surrender were overrun. Wild shouts accompanied the ensuing slaughter. One of the strongpoints that Alex captured had been bombed from the air; it was a tumult of earth, sand, stones, weapons and mangled bodies.

With RAF bombers and fighters on their heels, the German Afrika Korps and the Italian contingents fled westward towards Tunisia, fifteen hundred miles away. They left behind a battlefield strewn with ruin and death – a paradise for flies and rats. Some of the over-fed rats were as big as cats, and brazen, too. The desert was dotted with bloated bodies, blackened tanks, and shattered guns and planes. What had been healthy men the day before were now putrid bundles of flesh and bone covered with buzzing swarms of flies. Alex was appalled by the deadness of it all; dead bodies lying on dead sand. How small is a corpse, he thought! The devastation was so gruesome that he was at a loss to describe it in his letters to George and Johanna. He felt the full effect of it only when it was over. By then his clothing was black with sweat; his face was coated with grime; his lips were cracked; his eyes reddened with the heat, cold and dust. For a day or two he walked about seeing nothing. He couldn't get his mind off the awful slaughter in which he had been engaged. On the third day he wrote home to say that he was safe.

Having survived, Alex was promoted to captain; he was also awarded the Military Cross. It wasn't the Victoria

Cross he had hoped for, but at least he hadn't let the side down, nor had he yielded to terror. His father could rest in peace. He thought of the brave men who had died alongside him in battle, unrewarded and unrecorded.

At Arnold College, the Kemps had followed the course of the British offensive in the Western Desert. Evelyn Haverfield rang them every day to ask if they had any news of her son. Everybody was asking whether the British victory was the turning of the tide; it was Germany's first important defeat on land.

58

Soon after the British breakthrough at El Alamein in October–November 1942, Roger Blundell took part in a seaborne landing on the coast of French Tunisia. A mile from their landing, German planes suddenly appeared over the coastal hills and caught the British by surprise. 'Prepare to receive torpedoes,' the captain of Roger's destroyer shouted over his megaphone, as if it were a daily occurrence. There was the deafening clanging of alarms and hooters, the pounding of anti-aircraft guns, the hectic, feverish manoeuvring of ships, and the terrifying sight of the long, shiny torpedoes rushing through the calm sea towards them. Packed like sardines on deck, Roger and his men could do nothing but stare wide-eyed at the planes and torpedoes – and hope.

Neither ships nor planes were hit; a sigh of relief went up. Unopposed, the British quickly disembarked and marched inland. In the distance were hills and the outline of mountains. It was a far different terrain than Blundell had been used to in the Western Desert.

Following the landing, Roger's brigade attacked German forces in the vicinity of Medjez-el Bab. At the beginning of December 1942, in hammering rain, the enemy mounted a major counter-offensive, as a result of which Roger's brigade was forced to retreat. The winding Tunisian Majarda river had broken its banks and – sliding and slithering about, with death as their constant companion – they fought ankle-deep in mud. To make matters worse, it was along the Majarda that typhoid and cholera claimed their first victims.

Roger left those at home in no doubt about his loathing for Tunisia. 'It belongs to another age and another century,' he wrote. 'The weather is awful – one either freezes or bakes; the hot dry wind adds to the discomfort. At one place we fought beneath ancient Roman columns still towering in the sun. Wild roses and honeysuckle clustered around their bases. The barbarism of war seemed out of place there. Another day we took cover in a Roman amphitheatre where, engraved on a cracked pillar, were the words: "*Humanitas, Libertas, Felicitas.*" Humanity, liberty and happiness – wars down the centuries have belied the Roman ideal. The amphitheatre sat in the middle of a wild and deserted place, now strewn with ancient blocks of masonry, burnt-out vehicles and tanks; lizards played among the debris. With the Roman past overlooking us, time had no meaning. We ended up dug in before a German position on a Tunisian hillside.'

At night, Bedouin camel trains would sometimes slouch down the valley, coming from God knows where, going to God knows what. He was told that the tribesmen had owed allegiance to no government for years. They came and went as they wished with their camels and their black tents. In the glimmer of a lantern, he sometimes caught a glimpse of a woman in a red robe, or a boy walking alongside the camels. Shouts of 'Halt or I shoot' were wasted; passwords meant nothing to them. Warnings about mines and the tangle of barbed wire went unheard. It unnerved Roger to watch the long, shrouded figures gradually emerge out of the night, chanting a hoarse, half-muffled note. If anything moved at the front, you shot it before it shot you. Not so the Bedouin. Bearded, proud, tall and erect, the tribesmen stood before him. The veil of night made it difficult for him to see their faces properly, but he felt their air of superiority. 'Who are you?' he demanded angrily. '*Nehna abid Allah*' (We are servants of God.)

Without pausing, the camel-drivers – young and old – touched their foreheads, exclaimed '*Allah akbar!*', shouted at their camels and, shadow-like, went their way, singing. Accompanied by the jingle of the bridles and the voices of the drivers floating on the night air, the heavily-clothed figures melted into the dark. Roger suspected that this was how spies drifted across the front. Later that night, a howling pack of wild dogs, their tongues hanging down to the ground, rushed by in pursuit of wild pigs. He listened as their barking faded on the wind. He felt the presence of brooding mountains above him.

A few days later, Roger stopped his vehicle before a burned-out farmhouse. It was one of those brilliantly clear days when one feels glad to be alive. On impulse, he decided to investigate the rear of the building.

The first thing he saw on turning the corner were two military policemen – there was no mistaking the red bands on their helmets – dragging a bedraggled, hand-cuffed civilian to a stake before a broken, blackened wall half concealed by dead bougainvillea. The prisoner looked like a French colonist. His raven-black hair was brushed well back; his face was drained of colour. His white shirt was torn open at the front. A knot of police, rifles at the ready, stood against a jeep. A grave had been dug. There was an air of impropriety about it all.

The victim's eyes immediately fixed on Roger. 'Save me!'

he pleaded in French. His voice rose from a whimper to a frantic shriek. '*Sauvez moi! Sauvez moi!* I am innocent! I have children!' The words tumbled from his mouth.

Roger froze to the spot. He stared at the firing squad. He had seen enough people being killed, but not this way.

The man's burning eyes never left Roger's face; his screaming never stopped.

A British major approached. He wore a short, tight-fitting jacket. On the lapels of his tunic were the badges of the Field Security Police. He was very much in charge. 'You've no business here, Lieutenant. How the hell you've managed to barge in on the execution of a spy, I don't know. But I'm ordering you now to barge out, double-quick. Bugger off.'

Roger saluted and slowly backed away. He passed a wooden toy horse mired in the mud. Everybody's eyes followed him. He heard the rifle shots before he reached the road and experienced a strange feeling of shame; his mouth was dry.

When he passed the burned farmstead again the following day, it was deserted. A mile or so beyond, at the side of the road, was a large fresh mound of earth with a makeshift wooden cross on top of it.

'Whose burial is this?' he asked a group of soldiers.

'Redcaps,' one of them replied. 'Six were killed here yesterday from the air. Poor sods didn't know what hit them. That's their jeep,' he nodded towards a mangled heap of metal.

Roger knew that the executioners of yesterday had themselves been executed.

59

For the best part of a week the Germans on the Tunisian hillside in front of Roger's unit had shown no sign of activity; not a thing moved. It was so quiet that the war might have been over. Some said that the Germans had pulled out. The British did their washing and played cards.

The peace which the battalion was enjoying was suddenly shattered when the brigadier ordered a reconnaissance in strength of the German position. To be overlooked by the enemy was unacceptable to him – the hilltop had to be taken, the enemy flushed out. A whole day was spent deciding who would go and who wouldn't. Eventually, two companies were detailed. Roger knew that the attack had nothing in its favour: it was uphill, in daylight, and across open ground. Apart from the scrub and cactus, there was no cover. An idiot could have told the brigadier that it would be a disaster, but no idiot dared. To have said so was to be guilty of defeatism. Doubters were dangerous; humility has no place in war. Roger gave silent thanks when he and his men were excluded.

As the two companies formed up at first light, he hugged friends who had to go and took their last messages. Their voices were strangely lowered; goodbyes were avoided. 'Good luck, old man,' was as far as Roger could go. In some soldiers he detected the sacredness of duty, of loyalty to the cause. One or two openly crossed themselves before leaving; others expressed a confidence they didn't feel. Most were concerned with their gamble with death. He saw fear in their eyes, especially in the eyes of the young, who shouldn't have been there at all. They were scared. He felt it in their handshakes. Of glory there was none; instead, there was a sense of dread. The much earlier craving of youth for excitement and danger was a thing of the past. His eyes were never off his watch, he prayed that the attack would be called off and held his breath as the silent moments passed. The sense of expectancy was suffocating.

The roar of shellfire from behind dashed his hopes. The barrage was enough to batter the enemy positions to bits.

A terrifying silence followed. Bayonets fixed, the British climbed out of their trenches and raced uphill across the brown, scarred land towards the enemy line. They disappeared into clouds of smoke only to reappear again. Here and there the sparse vegetation clung to their legs. They displayed a courage that, to Roger, only made matters worse.

They had almost reached the trenches at the top when the Germans opened fire – *rattatat rattatat rattatat* – in long sweeping strokes. The air hissed and whistled. The runners wobbled and fell. Frozen in grotesque positions, their arms and legs pointed to the sky. It was awful to watch them fall. Wisps of smoke covered the tragic heaps. Not one of them had got close enough to throw a grenade. Through his field glasses, Roger followed a young officer running on alone, waving his pistol. He couldn't take his eyes off him. The man went through the fire unscathed. Suddenly, he staggered and pointed his pistol in the opposite direction. With his death, only a profound silence and the agony remained.

The brigadier lowered his glasses and grunted. He had stood there, watching, throughout the attack.

When darkness fell, both sides buried the dead. Quickly the corpses were covered. In the light of a wandering moon they made out a shadowy figure dragging itself down the hill towards them. 'I'm the only one left,' the soldier said, apologetically; his face was covered with blood. It was enough to make the bravest man cry. The Last Post sounded on the clear night air.

The brigadier remained silent when they ate that night. His plain, red face shone beneath the hooded light; his bulging eyes had a strange, staring look; he spoke only to his glass. Roger looked at his commander and wondered if he realized that he had just lost the most indispensable element of command: the confidence of his men.

Even an old soldier like Roger was appalled by what he'd seen. It took time for his anger to subside. A suicidal attack such as this should have been led by the obstinate, crack-brained fool who had planned it. After they had eaten, the brigadier's empty-faced aide-de-camp assured Roger that the commander was a pious man who believed only in the will of 'Gaud'. 'I know exactly how you feel, old man, but that's how it is.' He leaned forward to emphasize his words.

'God help us,' was the only retort Roger could make. There were so many deaths that his brigade was pulled out of the line and sent back to rest. It gave him a chance to kill his lice and to write at length to Gloria.

In December 1942, Roger's unit took up a position outside Al Qayrawan in south-eastern Tunisia, the fourth holiest site of Islam. The crenellated brick wall of the Great Mosque and its massive, square minaret stood above the town. Roger knew from a book he had with him that Phoenicians, Romans, Vandals, Byzantines, Arabs, Ottomans, French and Germans had all been there before him. Mohammed's companion Sidi Sahab was buried in the mosque with a pouch containing three hairs of the Prophet's beard. Instead of visiting the mosque as he had hoped, Roger remained holed-up outside the town, besieged by bands of wandering Arab children, looking for anything that they could lay there hands on. He never ceased to wonder where they came from, and how they managed to survive. Sand and wind, and the cold glimmer of starlit nights, remained his lot – that and the snoring of his men.

On Christmas Eve, Roger joined his soldiers going through the motions of Christmas celebrations. War had caused the men to draw closer to each other. He wondered how they could sum up enough courage in the freezing cold to sing carols with a flickering candle for light. To wish them a Happy Christmas – with death in the air – seemed absurd. But he did – the pretence was kept up. Together they sang 'O Come all ye Faithful'. The words poured out: 'O come let us adore Him, Christ the Lord . . .' Like most of his men, Roger thought of home. The carols demanded more than he could give; tears trickled down his cheeks. He was not the only one weeping, he quickly turned away into the shadows.

That day he received a photograph of his baby daughter Margaret which moved him intensely. Muffled up to the ears against the cold, he trimmed the wick of his lamp to see the picture better. He was always calculating how old she was. With her open face, and large pensive eyes, she was the perfect likeness of Gloria. The cheekbones, the dimples, the smile, the shoulders and the neck were all the same. 'God sent me this miracle of consolation,' Gloria had written on the back of the photograph. 'We live for your return. Every day we love you more. God protect you. I'm always dreaming about what the three of us will do together when you come home.' How enduring and bright the future looked.

Gloria had attached a note to the picture. 'Here is something that will cheer you up! Last night Lydia and I bathed the children and got them ready for bed. Having tucked them in, we left them. Imagine our horror on returning to see whether they were asleep to find Anthony exploring the unused fireplace. Lydia hauled a black, grinning baby out of the chimney flue. He was delighted to have a second bath.'

With a map, Roger worked out how many miles separated him from his loved ones, before realizing that distance didn't matter. To get back, he would have to reach a different world. Fifteen months had passed since he had left home. It felt like fifteen years. How much he ached to return. He felt drained by the emptiness and senselessness of war. If only it would end, he would gladly work in his father's bank to have a settled family life. He buried his head in his hands. Was this 'the pride and splendour' of war that Alex had talked about in 1939? When, in his life, would he be able to banish the fear that beset him daily?

271

That night Roger remained awake, staring into the darkness, thinking of home. Gloria and his daughter were his one reality in a mad world. He whispered their names; it gave him solace. He recalled the words: 'When seas divide me from my own, I will look up at the stars' light. And make each one a stepping stone.' The next morning he studied the treasured photograph again.

When Roger was moved from Al Qayrawan to the barren foothills of the mountains in the west of Tunisia, he was glad of the change. This way he could leave some of his ghosts and troubles behind. At the end of January a number of Christmas greetings reached him from Arnold College, including a letter signed by George and Johanna, Mr and Mrs Childers and Turnbull. No manna falling from heaven could raise his spirits as much as mail from home.

60

In early February 1943, almost before he'd had time to settle down in his new location, Roger fell ill with a severe attack of dysentery. He endured the usual gut pains, bleeding, and the feeling of total exhaustion. With a high temperature, he was shipped to the rear in a roasting-hot ambulance. He was too sick to know or care where they were taking him. He had no control of his bowels; his tongue was dry and swollen, and was getting worse. He dimly remembered being lifted out on a stretcher on to a dusty road crowded with military traffic and screaming camels. Flies covered his fevered face. He was too weak to resist.

''E's not goin' to mike it,' said the orderly, studying a thermometer, 'that's wot I say.'

''E don't look too rosy ter me either,' answered the driver.

"'E's goin' ter conk out on us, that's wot 'e'll do. Better get rid of 'im.'

That settled, Roger was lifted back into the ambulance in a cloud of flies. He remembered the vehicle grinding and shaking its way up a steep hill. Dust settled on his face; now and then he heard gunfire. After a while the ambulance stopped and he was lifted out again.

The hospital was in a small hilltop monastery where chaos reigned. While the British medical corps struggled to get into the building, the recently ejected French monks milled around outside. Roger was placed on a stretcher in the shade of palm and pepper trees.

Having at long last been given a drink and a cursory examination, he was carried into a thick-walled cell containing two rusty metal cots within arm's reach of each other. A crucifix hung on the whitewashed wall. A band of light shone between the closed shutters. It was as well there were no sheets, for he was filthy. "'Ang on 'alf a mo,' the orderly told him, putting him to bed, 'we'll git to you right away.'

Roger thought the cell was heavenly. It was cool, quiet – the thick-grimed window was shut – and there was no gunfire, no blinding light, no strength-draining heat, no clouds of dust and flies. He couldn't believe that the war had finally been shut out of his life; the deep silence of the monastery was almost weird. All he could hear from the corridor were muffled conversations, the opening and shutting of doors, and the padding of feet echoing ever more faintly. Better to die here in peace, he thought, than to die outside on the road in the blazing heat. His fevered eyes studied the ceiling and the door. A long column of ants marched up the wall into the rafters. He pulled his grey blanket over him. At long last he could rest.

Roger had no idea how long he had been in the cell when another patient was brought in, an infantry lieutenant like himself, whose tunic was torn and covered with dirt. He had a rough beard, and staggered about like a drunk. Having given Roger a penetrating look, the officer fell head first on to his cot. He began to snore as soon as his head hit the pillow.

That afternoon, with a terrific thud, a bomb hit the building. There was a deafening roar, screams, and the crash of glass. The thick walls shook as if they were made of paper. Roger's room filled with dust and smoke; his door slammed shut; pandemonium broke out in the corridor.

The instant the bomb struck, his companion shot out of bed. Gibbering and shouting, he climbed on top of Roger, who was too weak to resist. Petrified, Roger stared through the dust into his assailant's gloating face. The man then leapt on to the window-sill and tried to climb up the closed door. Failing that, he sat cross-legged on the floor moaning, while rocking to and fro. He twisted and turned like a puppet on a string.

Some time later, Roger felt himself rising to the surface of a deep lake. He heard Gloria calling, 'Roger! Roger!' When he opened his eyes a doctor was leaning over him. A flickering candle stood on the window-sill. 'You did the wisest thing, old chap, you fainted. Luckily for you, your companion came rushing down the corridor, climbed over the rubble like a monkey, and attacked me instead. It took three of us to calm him down.' Roger lost consciousness again.

The next patient to occupy the other cot in the cell was a young Oxford undergraduate, also suffering from severe dysentery. He looked peaky. He was a Trinity man. Trinity was known as an Irish college with 'English lawns'; his rooms had looked out on them. He was quick to show Roger pictures of his family and fiancée, a young bright-faced blonde. In the long hours they spent together they played endless games of patience with a tattered pack of cards the orderly had given them. Between games, the young man went on about his family's farm in the Lake District – about the cupped lakes, the rugged surrounding fells, and the soaring rocks.

As the days passed, the fellow talked less; he even stopped smoking. His fingers began to look spidery; his breathing became shallow. His lips sank back so that his teeth were protruding; his hair hung in wet strands over his forehead; his face became so bloodless as to be transparent. Each day he visibly shrank. Roger couldn't imagine how anyone could become skin and bone so quickly. No one had to tell him that death had entered the room. There was a strange silence, which he was reluctant to break. They exchanged glances but could find nothing to say. Now and again an orderly rushed in, hurriedly cleaned up the young patient – the smell was terrible – took his pulse, briskly told him 'We'll git yer right,' gave him a drink, ran a damp cloth over his face, and rushed out again. The doctors were busy elsewhere.

To cheer him up, Roger told him that he would be sent back to Britain any day soon.

'Do you really think so?'

'On my word; they always do that to patients who don't respond to treatment. From here they'll put you on the train to Algiers; from Algiers you'll embark on a hospital ship for "Blighty". There's sure to be a band to see you off. You'll travel with pretty nurses all the way. Mornings and afternoons, they'll carry you out to sunbathe on deck. When you pass Gibraltar, you'll see the flag on the peak; you might even see apes on the Rock. Once through the Straits, it's all yours to England: no torpedoes, no bombing, the best grub, and nothing to worry about. Once in London they'll have you right in no time. Next time we meet you'll have put on fifty pounds. What bothers me is what you'll do with yourself once you get home.'

'Finish my degree.'

'I don't know how you can face such a thing after being out here. There must be better things to do.'

275

'There are, like taking my girl up the river and pretending there is no war. We'll pick daisies and buttercups and talk about getting married. I can't tell you how happy Betty and I were together.'

'I'll come and see you when we all get home,' Roger promised. 'We'll celebrate your wedding. I won't say a word about the war or Africa.'

Roger woke up the next day to hear his companion quietly sobbing. Chinks of light were creeping into the room. The youth's face was wet with sweat and tears; his eyes had receded even further; there was a blankness in his gaze.

'What's the matter?'

'I know I'm not going home.' (His pulse had become almost imperceptible in the last day or two.) 'I don't blame you for trying to help. Will you give this medal to Betty? Tell her and my parents what became of me. Tell her,' he stammered, 'that I loved her with all my heart. I didn't want to die out here. Promise? Promise?' he kept repeating between sobs.

'As God is my witness.'

The youth reached out and clung to Roger's arm. 'I don't know how to say goodbye,' he gasped.

'Don't try.' Roger stroked his hair and held his hand; it might have been frozen. Specks of dust gleamed in the light coming from the window.

Blundell knew the end had come when the army chaplain arrived with the holy oil. The priest brought grace to a graceless scene. He spoke gently of Christ the Redeemer as he anointed the youth's head, hands, eyes, mouth and ears. Roger lay quietly aside, fighting back his tears.

Later he realized that he was sharing the room with a corpse, whose eyes were staring into the unknown. The last words his cellmate had breathed among his gurgles and rattles were 'Green grass, green grass.' Outside, a sandstorm was blowing. Down the corridor, a wounded German soldier, isolated as if he had the plague, was softly playing '*Ich hatt' einen Kameraden*' on his mouth organ.

Roger wanted to weep, but his eyes remained dry. He felt he'd lost a younger brother. 'Damn the war,' he muttered.

61

In due course, Roger was declared fit and left the monastery. His battledress hung on him; his shoulders stood out like knobs. He seemed taller and thinner. He studied the distant clouds; he saw trees and flowers again, heard the birds sing and smelt the earth. Overcome by the brightness and the blueness of the sky, he pulled down his cap against the light.

Before leaving he took a moment to visit the famous statue of the Mater Dolorosa in the monastery garden. The Mother of Sorrow had a sad face; shrapnel had carried away one of her arms and pierced her heart. Peasants came from miles around to seek comfort and succour from her; there were many instances of the afflicted being cured. Roger sat alone on a bench with the fir-tree branches gently swaying above him; a crow cawed softly. He could hear the sweet sound of water splashing. It was a moment of intense peace. Unaccountably, the statue didn't fill him with a feeling of sorrow and death, but of life and joy. He wondered why. Eventually, he stirred himself and left.

From the monastery he was sent to a railway siding, where he found a train made up of boxcars and open wagons stacked with large-calibre shells. He thought it madness to go straight from a hospital, where one fought to save life, to the front line, where one fought to end it.

Roger marked out his spot with his kit in one of the boxcars, and then joined other officers who were drinking tea in the shade of the square. Sand-gritty rations for the journey were handed out by a quartermaster sergeant with shifty eyes. Kerosene was available for those who wanted to protect themselves against lice.

Idly, a group of Arabs wrapped in long, white jellabas sat watching, droning to each other throughout the sultry day. They shared a pipe, and sometimes chuckled over a hidden joke. Several negresses made the square ring to their unrestrained laughter. They saw something funny in the Englishmen's plight. Ragged children stood and stared; the odd one stuck out his tongue at them and ran away. Hawkers offered fruit; buzzards hopped about the rubbish in the square; donkeys and their riders clattered by, sometimes with jingling bells. Dogs lay, dead-looking, on the stones. A man in a soiled jellaba came and tapped the train wheels. He was followed by a French railway official with a curled moustache and white gloves. He walked the platform smartly, studied the engine and left without saying a word. Shadowy figures looked on from a latticed balcony at the front of a rough stone house.

Other than that the train was going in the general direction of the enemy, no one seemed to know or care where it was headed. The fat, morose driver, with a dark crushed face, never said. When Roger spoke to him, he regarded the Englishman with strange white eyes, which Roger could have sworn were blind. His hands were hidden in his long, loose jellaba.

'Will we leave today?' Roger asked.

'*Insha' Allah!*' (God willing.)

'There's something fishy about that fellow,' Roger remarked to one of the other officers.

'There's something fishy about the whole bloody war if you ask me.'

After sitting in the burning sun the whole day, the train crawled out of the siding as the light faded. Clouds of belching smoke came from its smokestack. A number of

Arabs sitting by the track watched the train leave; their set, sullen faces belonged to another world. Roger shared a corner of a wagon with a dark lieutenant recovering from wounds. He didn't seem friendly. No one knew his name and he didn't offer it.

Once under way, the driver made wrenching starts and grinding halts whenever he felt like it. Anybody who questioned him was answered with a shrug. The train travelled at any speed – or none at all. Whenever it halted near a line of white-washed, dusty hovels, chattering barefoot Arab children selling water, tea, fruit, oranges, mandarins, figs, barley and wheat cakes would board the train like pirates. Eyes dancing, they spoke in gestures. Anything unguarded disappeared into their loose clothing. They eventually jumped down crying, 'God help you, Tommy Englishman.'

'Where is England?' Roger asked one of them. He was answered by a toothless grin.

To kill time, the troops reminisced – war encourages a natural interest in other people's affairs – played cards, killed lice and brewed tea on a small stove on the floor; tea was as vital as air. In the daytime, the doors were thrown back, allowing the warm sunshine to stream in. A sharp lookout was kept for enemy aircraft, which could swoop down like hawks.

From the train, the countryside floated by. Camels, surrounded by a halo of dust, pulled ancient ploughs across the sandy earth. Dogs barked. Packs of shaggy goats grazed on cactus and scrub. Primitive wells provided a trickle of water for irrigation. Occasionally an olive grove or a vine-yard slipped by. Now and again, a turbaned head would appear against a roughcast wall, but there was no waving; this was the Arab–Muslim world, hostile, remote and strange. They saw natives prostrating themselves on the earth. Sometimes they would catch the outline of mountains clear against the sky.

That night Roger lay on the freezing floor in the pitch dark. The use of a torch was not welcomed by those who didn't have one. Candles could not withstand the draught. Periodically, he opened and shut his eyes, and covered his nose. To body smells was added the stench of diarrhoea. Things would have been worse without the ventilators in the roof. He was never free of the monotonous rhythmic rattle of the railway wheels: *da-di-da . . . da-di-da*, and the creaking of the boxcars. Sometimes through a crack between the boards, he saw the dark gleam of water. For men recovering from severe wounds and sicknesses, the cold was hard to bear. Some of them huddled together in an attempt to keep warm. Packing so many men in a boxcar made sure they would share their lice; the soldiers never stopped scratching.

The dreadful snoring, accompanied by the opening and shutting of the sliding door in the night so that someone could piss into the wind didn't help either. To sit and piss with one's legs sticking out of the sliding door was asking for them to be amputated. Too late he discovered that some of the other boxcars had straw, and a bucket for night soil.

With the glimmering dawn, the men began to stir; the night's trials lay behind. Some broke into song. It seemed absurd to have crowded, rattling cattle wagons wandering around Algeria and Tunisia ringing to 'Daisy, Daisy, give me your answer, do; I'm half crazy all for the love of you,' yet there were times when – accompanied by a mouth organ – the men needed to sing; song was a balm.

When he wasn't surveying them with a surly look, or feigning sleep, the dark lieutenant in the corner ranted on about the communist government that would follow the war. Passionately, he condemned everything about a capitalist society, including military discipline. He flayed the British political leaders as the troops would never have dared to do. 'Cannon fodder, that's what they've made of us.' Why he protested so openly, Roger couldn't imagine. The military police were always listening. 'Up the Reds!' he kept shouting, waving a red handkerchief. 'Hail communism; hail labour; hail sacrifice.' As communist Russia was Britain's ally, there wasn't much the police could do about it. He shouted so loud and so often that Roger wondered if he wasn't trying to get out of the war (like David in the Old Testament) by feigning madness. Perhaps madness was an appropriate response to a mad war. Or was his purpose to trap others? Roger knew there was rumbling in the ranks. Weary of the struggle, there was a great longing for peace among the men. 'If only the damn thing was over,' they'd say, sighing.

'You're one of Britain's exploiting rich whom I'll have to shoot after the war,' the lieutenant threatened Roger. 'Your class has to be removed.' For a moment his cold, grey eyes held Roger's gaze. 'The workers will replace you. I won't try to explain the sins of capitalist greed and degradation; you wouldn't understand. Democracy will also have to die – it's reactionary, corrupt and standards fall. The Royals have got to go too,' he went on. 'Sort them out as Lenin did in Russia. No exceptions. The same with God; Marx will replace him. Only Marx had the answer to the riddle of our times. The Americans will also have to be cleaned out of Britain after the war. There is only one way to make the change – revolution!' With the hectic imagination of a fevered brain, he went on and on threatening and foretelling like an Old Testament prophet. Assuming that everybody was deaf, his voice was so loud that he stunned those who listened to him. He took not the slightest heed of anything anybody else said.

Roger had a wild impulse to laugh. 'Did anyone ever tell you that you are quite mad?'

The lieutenant's face showed scorn. 'I was mad to have tolerated the rule of your class as long as I did.'

When he wasn't ranting, he was chewing dry tea leaves, which he kept in his greatcoat pocket; he never took the trouble to brew tea. When he wasn't chewing tea leaves, he was

281

munching dates, which he kept in his other pocket. Whenever the train stopped for fuel or water, he was the first to climb down to find out where they were. 'I expect you're too dim to realize that we're travelling in circles,' he said to Roger on one occasion when climbing back. Roger decided that the man was not as mad as he made out. He suspected that he would hear more about him again when peace came. He wondered what Charley Bradbury would have made of him.

The next day, for no reason at all, the train halted in a remote meadow by a river. A rash of wild flowers ran along the banks. The engine's steam rose in leisurely rings. All around was the smell of things growing. Palm fronds rattled overhead. Roger was told that when the rains stopped the flowers quickly shrivelled and died. That night they slept with the boxcar doors open. It was a most beautiful, star-filled night. The endless organ-like croaking of frogs and the trembling notes of cicadas filled the air.

The next morning, before the mist had cleared, the loco-motive and the engine driver disappeared. Some said the engine had been taken for repairs; others that it was needed more urgently elsewhere. The optimists said that it was a sign that the war in North Africa was drawing to a close. Nobody really worried about the missing engine; nobody was in any hurry to get to the front. The army 'ferrets' went to work bringing in olives, dates, bread and wine. Others cooked, ate, gambled, sunbathed and swam.

Camping in the meadow gave the troops an opportunity to go native. They threw off their tunics and wore their military caps half over their eyes or at the back of their heads. One of them ran around naked except for a tarboosh on his head; others sat under the trees ponderously smoking water pipes they had looted, while talking about home. A group sang an incredibly coarse rendition of 'Bless 'em All'. The more nervous wondered aloud if the river was contam-inated. 'Who gives a damn! A spell in "dock" is preferable to having your head blown off.' Anyone foolish enough to use his rank to keep the soldiers out of the water was threatened with the river itself. Except for the occasional row over food, everybody was friendly, including the non-commissioned officers, who once back in the line would give the troops hell. Other than a stately camel, which came to drink and eat the wild flowers, and which regarded them with disdain, they might have been in an English meadow on a warm summer's day. Even a mad life could be enjoyed if only one could rid oneself of the futility of war.

Having emptied a bottle of wine, Roger and the Red lay stretched out full length, almost naked on the grass, flicking flies. 'It's only a matter of time before Britain goes communist,' the Red told him. 'It will be worth all the struggle.'

'Like bloody hell!'

Suddenly, a plane came down the line, bombed and strafed the train and the bathers and was gone. The shells exploding on the open wagons shook the whole valley. Clouds of smoke and dust, and the ugly smell of gunpowder, filled the air; a fertile meadow had become a charred graveyard. After a stunned silence, the cries and the wailing began. 'My God,' Roger muttered, as he struggled to his feet; wherever he looked there was carnage; he was shaking horribly. His companion was drenched with blood. Under a blazing sun, his hands were already cold and clammy. Roger tried to speak, but couldn't; his lips made no sound. He could tell from the silent, detached look the fellow gave him that he was going to die.

Roger collapsed from shock beside a shattered tree stump. His heart thumped. He was numb with fear. A feeling of unutterable weariness came over him. How black and hopeless things seemed. Later he made his way among the wounded, giving aid and comfort where he could. Several times, he had to take out his handkerchief and wipe his eyes.

The lieutenant was quickly buried with his comrades among the flowers. His pockets revealed nothing of his past;

his mad political dreams were denied him. Roger picked a red poppy and placed it on his grave. He preferred the Red's eccentricity to death's eternal silence. That night a column of ambulances came to carry the wounded away.

Before dawn the next day the locomotive and a different driver appeared as mysteriously as the other one had departed. With flames lighting the morning sky, what was left of the train slowly trundled towards the front. Coils of smoke and sparks enveloped it. There was silence among the survivors.

That morning, a hollow-eyed, emaciated boy of four or five, dressed in tatters, suddenly appeared out of the rubble of a gutted village alongside the track, accompanied by several mongrel dogs. As the train rolled by, the child raised an appealing hand for help. '*Min fadlak*' (Please), he begged. Nothing could have moved the soldiers more. It was as if the waif symbolized for them the horrors of war. Any food that could be grabbed quickly was thrown from the train. Dogs and child fought over the spoils. '*Shukran!*' (Thanks!) the boy yelled.

It was dusk when the train crawled to a halt in a siding. Outside, English voices and gunfire broke the night silence. As Roger jumped down, new battle casualties were lifted in. Wonder of wonders, he was handed letters from home; the journey and its hardships were forgotten. On returning to his unit, he learned that the train driver who had left them in the meadow had been apprehended, tried as a German spy, and shot.

62

By the spring of 1943 Roger's brigade was fighting at the gates of Tunis, where the Afrika Korps still barred their path.

The land and air war had shifted decisively in the Allies' favour. The Germans were inferior in terms of weapons, troops and aircraft. The German prisoners they took were worn out, yet the German Army supported each other in the direst conditions and refused to surrender. Roger wondered how they had managed to keep going as long as they had.

March and April 1943 saw no let-up in the fierce battle being waged across the Majarda valley. The fighting went on day and night and the Germans shelled Roger's position so heavily that his men were forced to dig deep caves in the high river-bank. They became moles, digging tunnels and zigzagging paths. At night, clouds of mosquitoes descended upon them; malaria was common. Nobody complained; malaria was better than losing a leg. The troops were suspicious of the anti-malarial ointment handed out and used it as hair oil. Help came only from the bats, which hung in their hundreds upside down on the cave ceilings and fed on the mosquitoes. Come darkness, with the odd squeak, they were gone.

One early dawn, after fighting all night in the pouring rain, Roger sought rest in one of the caves. It was dim and dark down there, but much safer than on the surface – below ground he was safe from gunfire; the cluster of bats on the ceiling could do him no harm. Sleep offered oblivion, a temporary relief from fear and homesickness; perhaps the war would be over when he awoke. To avoid the dust falling from the shaking roof, he slipped fully dressed under a makeshift table at which some officers were planning the next attack. The candlelight lit up their features as they hunched over the maps. Tobacco smoke hung heavy in the air. The sputtering candles had a ring of coloured light around them and cast shadows into the corners. Roger used his mud-clogged boots to keep his head out of the dirt; his tunic was already filthy. Everything smelled of trodden mud and of the river outside. He was so tired that he could have slept anywhere. The deaths that had occurred during the night lay on him like a drug. If he stayed in the army for the rest of his life, he would never become immune to the gruesome slaughter and barbarity which war entailed. 'I'm damned wet,' one of his wounded men had complained in a cloud-burst as Roger had tried to staunch the bleeding. The bullet had hit the man in the face, giving him the appearance of having three eyes. With a rattle, his head had sunk back.

Roger also recalled the lonely Arab he had found at the foot of a stunted tree. The man was barely conscious. '*Sa'edni! Sa'edni!*' (Help me!) he muttered. Showing the black stubs he had for teeth, he was too weak to brush off the insects that plagued him. His limbs were horribly swollen; his grizzled face was yellow and shone with sweat; his body shook with pain. Only God could have known the man's torment. Had the poor devil ever known happiness? Had he ever known anything that was sweet and beautiful? Roger wondered as he tried to stifle the man's groans with water. He longed to offer him some comfort, but any morphine he had carried was already spent.

The man's feeble cries were renewed when he left him. Shooting would have been merciful, but Roger was stupefied with exhaustion, wet to the skin, and could bear no more killing. He had reached the point where he was no longer sure where one thing ended and another began. In soldier's language, he had begun to 'float'. Squelching and splashing about – his torch had failed him – he groped his way past the torn trees. Weeks before, they had murmured in the breeze. Now they were a chaos of earth and broken branches. How terrible, he thought, for the Arab to suffer and die alone in obscurity.

Roger had no idea how long he had slept under the table among the mud-caked boots. He was dazed when he awoke – as if he were returning from a long journey. He had dreamt that he was walking with Gloria in the rose garden at

Ansfield: she was dressed in gleaming satin and was surrounded by a glowing light. Everything about her, her eyes, her hair, her laughter and her moving body, entranced him. The breeze blew her hair over her face, he reached out and gently parted it. He saw the radiant eyes and the face of all his dreams, vividly. In the background, someone played a piano softly. They'd had tea on the balcony, served on a snow-white cloth; the cups and saucers gleamed. The dogs fidgeted at their feet, the trees rustled above their heads. How beautiful was his dream. How much he loved Gloria! Without her he would never have been able to hang on.

Roger continued to doze. Half-dreaming, half-waking, he had the sensation of bodily comfort; he felt happy and detached. He refused to get to his feet; the war could wait. He caught snatches of conversation. His fellow officers were discussing the latest cricket scores from home. There was talk of England's one-time famous cricketer, bodyline-bowler Douglas Jardine, now fighting in Burma.

As he moved a boot off his chest, the brilliance of his dream died. He was back in a world where the only law was to kill or be killed; back with death and wounds and pain and fire and ruin. He had to think hard to realize that he had lived another life before the army claimed him. It was so far away that it might never have been.

It was pointless to write home about such things; they could not be expressed in words. Only soldiers could understand the terrible reality of war and they didn't want to talk about it – except among themselves. For them it wasn't real life; the war was a stage set to be endured and then go home. The only thing that really mattered was to go home again, safe and sound. He mustn't give up now, having come so far. Nobody had to tell him that those in the line who lost heart usually died. So also did those who yearned for home too much, the old sweats said. It encouraged fate to strike a blow. It was eerie the way some men knew instinctively when the game was up. Tomorrow he was due to go on rest leave, far from the killing. Some of his companions, having been through hell, would seek revelry. For him, it was enough to sleep and forget the war.

So much had happened to him during these past years that he hardly knew himself; he had been blown about like tumbleweed. There were times in battle when he couldn't think straight. Constant fear had reduced him from the man he had been. He felt older; grey had appeared in his hair. He wondered what he was doing burrowing like a rodent into the African soil, and whether he would ever rid himself of its rotting smell. His antipathy towards Africa was deep down inside him where washing wouldn't do any good. To him, Africa was a strange, harsh land on the remote edge of the world. It was a barrier separating him from his love. God forbid that he should leave his bones here. Not when the greatest love man could have awaited him in England.

With difficulty, he wriggled out from beneath the table. He was too absorbed in thought to do more than make a gesture to the others. He put on his boots and staggered to the entrance of the cave for air and light. For a few minutes he stood there, listening to the guns, stretching, looking at the yellow water flowing by. The river was high; it was flecked in places with shafts of light; on warm days it stank. Although he had some-times sat for hours watching it go by, he had never seen a fish there. He was too prejudiced to recognize any merits the river might have. It was one more reason to leave Africa behind. What would he give to row on the sweet Thames again! For a moment, he recalled the days of his youth. A smell of cooking wafted in his direction; a recent shower had laid the dust; spring and the idea of new life were in the air. The ground was carpeted with wild flowers; the torn bushes were sprouting new leaves. The sun lay low in a leaden sky. He listened to the whine of a passing shell.

Once more he stretched his arms to the sky; his eyes rested

288

on the distant woods where he had fought the night before. At that moment an Me 109, its wings almost touching the water, glided bat-like down the winding river and blasted Roger and those seated behind him in the cave point-blank. He saw a swastika and the helmeted head of a pilot peering at him before he was hurled back on to his companions.

A handful of miles away, in Tunis, the muezzin was calling the faithful to prayer, extolling the greatness of God and the brotherhood of man.

Five days after Roger's death, in May 1943, the Afrika Korps surrendered.

63

At the end of May Johanna received a letter from Gloria.

Dear Johanna,
I'm overwhelmingly sad to have to tell you that Roger is dead. I'd have phoned you earlier had I not been full of despair. The hopes and dreams I clung to are no more. I received the telegram from the War Office while feeding Margaret. I read the message, and the room began to spin. I can't remember anything else after that except little Anthony hanging on to my skirt. 'Don't cry, Aunty Gloria' he pleaded. Moments before he'd been shouting joyfully and throwing cushions about the room. It's as well that Margaret doesn't know what she has lost. How cruel that she will never know her father. His death has added lines to Tony's face.

The award to Roger of a posthumous Military Cross for heroism shown in battle the night before his death only adds to our sorrow – what counts in life and death can never be inscribed on a medal. Roger never sought heroism. He was one of those millions who were swept up in a savage contest they never really understood. He did his best, he was brave, but he was never warlike. Nor did he hate the Germans. Hatred of people was not Roger. He once told me in a letter that the war had given him a greater appreciation of what it was to be human. It never turned him into a savage, he remained a great human being until the end. He thought war – whether justified or not – the height of human folly. It confirmed his belief in an absurd world . . .

Clutching the letter, Johanna choked with tears. She hid her face in her hands.

George conveyed the sad news to Walter Turnbull and Harvey Childers. 'Surely not,' said Turnbull and shook his head. Childers looked crushed, his voice faltered. Roger's father later established a scholarship at Arnold College in his son's name.

That day, Gloria gently removed the photograph of the crew from her writing table and put it away in a drawer. Their eyes had begun to haunt her. David Evans, Bill Clark and her husband Roger were dead. Since his death, she had been unable to look at the picture without bursting into tears.

64

In the wake of the retreating Afrika Korps, Alex Haverfield journeyed from Egypt to Tunis. He had rarely been out of sight of soldiers' graves, abandoned weapons and burned-out trucks and tanks. He wondered what the shrouded figures often seen among the graves were doing there at night. Looting?

It was in Tunis that he heard of Roger's death. He searched for his grave in the British military cemetery at Medjez-el-Bab. The ground had recently been flooded and he found Roger's mound littered with debris. The wind stirred the surrounding palms, the leaves rattled above his head. Alex straightened the temporary wooden cross, which had slipped forward in the mud. Inexplicably, he felt a growing numbness as he did so; his throat tightened. The promise to meet again, which the crew had sung one Christmas, could not now be kept. He recalled the tune with anguish. With a broken-down mosque only a stone's throw away and hungry buzzards shifting uncomfortably on a nearby wall, he thought it was a dreadful place for an Englishman to be buried.

Beyond Roger's grave, another dead soldier was being lowered into the ground. Helmets under their arms, his comrades stood around the grave. Alex caught the chaplain's words; he had come to know them by heart: 'As for man, his days are of grass. As a flower of the field, so he flourisheth. For the wind passeth over it, and it is gone, and the place thereof shall know it no more. Earth to earth, ashes to ashes, dust to dust.' Clods of earth rained down, the grave was quickly filled in. Alex stood there, head bowed, his mind flooded with memories of his friend. Silently, he commended Roger's soul to God. He took a picture of the grave, which he would send to Gloria. He avoided showing any of the desperate surroundings; they would have appalled her.

The war in North Africa over, Alex had the job of helping to incarcerate scores of thousands of German prisoners

(Italian prisoners were interned elsewhere). Some drove in from distant parts of the battlefield in their own trucks. Men who would have been shot on sight the day before were stopping and asking British soldiers the way. Having fought them to the death, the British now shared their cigarettes with them. The ideal of the brotherhood of man had been banished by the savagery of war, but it was not dead.

The silent legions of German soldiers, fifty abreast, entering the prisoner-of-war cages on the outskirts of Tunis was one of the saddest sights Alex had ever seen. Defeated and disarmed, their tunics black with sweat, and white with patches of salt, the prisoners came on and on like an incoming sea. A ragged, swaying, helpless horde, surrounded by a cloud of dust and flies, had taken the place of a proud, invincible army. The only sound was the unending shuffling of feet and the low rumble of voices. Here and there was a wisp of tobacco smoke. All the scene lacked was the beat of a muffled drum.

The British onlookers, standing in meagre shade, were also silent; there was no flush of victory on their faces.

Alex stood in the searing sun, shading his eyes while watching the human tide go by. Some of the prisoners leaned on each other; others were carried by their comrades; the seriously wounded were brought in German trucks and horse carts. What they had endured was reflected in their worn faces and bloodshot eyes. The sight repelled him. It surprised him to see so many young soldiers among them. Were these the same people who had proposed to build a new and better world?

Instead of hating the Germans, he began to feel sorry for them. He found no pleasure in seeing them suffer like this. He had known in his heart for a long time that his hatred of them was wrong. What has come over me? Alex found himself wondering. Why this sudden feeling of pity? Was this the sense of tragedy that Roger said I lacked? Is this a war that has gone on too long? The quotation from the *Iliad*, 'Glory in war is life's highest honour', began to lose its meaning for him. For the first time he saw the enemy as fellow men and wondered how he'd come to hate them. With far fewer resources, they had fought brilliantly, and to the bitter end. Behind them were the victories of Tobruk, Bardia and Bir-el-Gobi. They had come within an ace of overrunning Egypt and undoing British rule in the Middle East.

Later, he talked to a group of German officers inside the wire. Their eyes were clouded with uncertainty. 'Where do we go from here?' they asked. Alex knew that he shouldn't have answered, but he said, 'To Egypt, to a place called Quassassin, down the Suez Canal.' He didn't tell them that he'd been there and that it was hell. A *khamseen* (sand-storm) had come out of the desert like a roiling cloud, and had almost buried his unit alive – blotting out sight and sound. So powerful was it that it gave the impression of being the only thing in the world. Until the storm had blown itself out, they ate sand. Before he left the German officers, he promised to obtain aspirin for their wounded. His offer of help brought light to empty faces. 'A kind act in cruel times,' one of the German officers said in broken English. He expressed his gratitude with a smile.

While going in search of the aspirin, Alex was ordered elsewhere. 'Get along, Haverfield, can't afford to waste time.'

'No sir.' He saluted smartly and turned away. He saw the Germans staring at him through the wire. He never saw them again, yet he never forgot that he had made a promise to men in great distress and had not kept it.

The matter was still on his mind when he took part in a march-past on a bare, windswept plain outside Tunis some days later. The troops had spent the night on the plain polishing boots and brasses. Any sleep they got was where they stood. At daybreak, after everyone had washed and shaved, inspections began.

Gossip was the only relief from the flies and the hot wind. As the troops awaited the order to march, there were snatches of music and song, but they died as quickly as they had started.

Days before, an army of carpenters had erected an elaborate canvas-roofed reviewing stand; the saws and hammers had never stopped. When the last wood-shaving had been swept away, an ugly structure stood there in the middle of a dried-out salt pan. Passing tribesmen gaped at it as if they'd seen a mirage. They laughed and shook their heads. 'What will the *berrumiyin* (foreigners) do next? They invade our land, impose their laws, treat us as inferiors, turn the desert into a slaughterhouse, maim and kill our camels, waste our fields, pollute our wells, and now this! When will these fools stop their madness and go home, wherever that is?'

After an endless wait, the commanders and their staffs arrived in a cavalcade of cars. They had dined well and in comfort, and were jolly and bright-faced, at times exploding into laughter. With hounds and a glass of wine, it could have been a meeting before a hunt. Alex envied them their good breakfast. Their spotless vehicles were greeted with a sullen whistle from the ranks. No one asked the troops to cheer; cheering is best done in the early stages of war.

Ponderously, in strict order of seniority, with the aides-de-camp relegated to the rear, the generals took up their positions on the dais. Allied flags were unfurled in the breeze; a bugle sounded; briskly a guard of honour presented arms; pleasantries were exchanged; there was a bark of orders. All ashine, the army was brought to 'Atten-shun!'

With the bands crashing out 'Colonel Bogey', and the polished fixed bayonets and brasses flashing in the sun, Alex's regiment began to move forward. As they approached the dais, shoulders pulled back, ranks lined up, the soldiers' step became more spirited. For a moment, Alex felt some of his earlier excitement at military parades. As his formation came abreast of the saluting post the order rang out: 'Eeeeyes rrrright!' Through a veil of dust he caught a quick glimpse of red-banded hats, polished brasses, puffed-up chests, and a little figure touching his cap. A long, drawn-out 'Eeeyes front!' and it was over. With the bands deafening the ears of all, Alex continued to lead his men into the sun.

'No fireworks, no loot and no bloody grub,' an old sweat grunted.

Brushing off the flies that plagued them, burned by the sun, the last unit marched past two hours later. They were followed by a column of lively, ragged Arab children led by a child furiously beating a drum. 'Sod off! Vamoose!' was all they got. With the lowering of flags and the bugle sounding 'Stand down', the march-past was brought to a close.

With the North African war over, the British Army organized a thanksgiving service in a Roman amphitheatre at nearby Carthage. The troops were ordered to march again. Once more, the bands were out in force. This time, the cross took charge; the crook and the mitre prevailed. The troops were no longer animals, but children of God. More than 100,000 of them sang 'O God, Our Help in Ages Past' to the crashing of the bands. Like the sound of distant thunder, the voices welled from the ground into the sky. They ended by saying the Lord's Prayer.

> Our Father, which art in heaven . . .
> For thine is the kingdom, and the power,
> and the glory,
> for ever. Amen.

Such praise for God in such a God-forsaken place.

65

When the Kemps next heard from Alex, he had been promoted to major and was stationed at British Air Headquarters, Levant, in Jerusalem. One went where one was sent. Because of the fighting going on between the Arabs and the Jews, and the Arabs and the Jews against the British, Jerusalem was under martial law. It was an eerie experience, Alex wrote, to enter a city where only sentinels moved, and the threat of accumulated fury and hatred filled the air. He was ignorant of the centuries of sorrow and irreconcilable differences that had brought it about.

No sooner had Alex entered his sandbagged headquarters outside the Damascus Gate of the Old City, than the sentries behind him were shot dead by terrorists who slowly drove past in a taxi. The next day, when visiting Petah Tikva military airport, he waved from his vehicle to several jeeploads of Palestinian police; they returned his wave with a strange, inquiring stare. When he got back to Jerusalem he learnt that the 'Palestinian police' he'd waved to had been Jewish terrorists – liberation fighters to the Jews. They had successfully raided the armoury and killed several members of the guard.

That afternoon a bright-eyed Arab boy brought Alex his tea. Although dismissed, the boy stood there silently, fixing Alex with a stare. 'Do you know Lawrence?' he suddenly asked. T. E. Lawrence had fought in the Arab revolt against the Turks thirty years before; among the Arabs he had become a legend.

Some days later Alex left his billet in the Franciscan monastery at the top of the Street of the Prophets to go to his headquarters at the other end of the street. He was accompanied by several officers and a platoon of infantry. As martial law was in effect, no soldier walked alone. No sooner was he through the monastery gates than he remembered that he had left his papers behind. 'I'll join you in a moment,' he called as he ran back. In minutes he was out of the building again, running to catch up with the platoon. To his surprise, the narrow street was empty; nothing stirred except a stray cat. He checked his .45-revolver and quickened his pace. Air Headquarters was only several minutes away. Birdsong accompanied him.

With the Damascus Gate in sight, he was just about to relax when a wooden door creaked open across the way. A short dark man wearing a cap sidled out. Leisurely, he looked up and down the street. Several others wearing hats and long coats, in which their hands were hidden, followed behind. They watched Alex with sullen faces. He didn't know whether they were Jews or Arabs.

All that he had been taught since arriving in Jerusalem told him that he was in deadly danger: the only civilians wandering about Jerusalem without a military escort during curfew were terrorists. To capture or kill a British officer was considered a coup. He thought it pointless to turn and run, there were too many to take a shot at him; it was equally pointless to shout for help, there was no one to hear. Warily, he slipped the safety catch off his pistol and continued on his way. He did his best to keep a firm step.

He had begun to sweat with fear when he heard the rumble of a vehicle coming down the street behind him. He looked back: it was a bus full of children on their way to school; no children walked alone during curfew. Wildly, he waved for the bus to stop. He caught a glimpse of the driver's frightened eyes. With one glance, the driver took in the situation, swung the bus away – even overrunning the kerb – and accelerated. Children's faces were pressed against the windows.

Alex knew that there was only one chance of escape and he seized it. Breaking into a sprint, he got the bus between himself and the group of men across the street. He refused to die the way these men perhaps intended him to. The faster the bus went, the more desperately he clung to its side; excited children looked down at him and waved. Still clinging to the bus, he reached his headquarters at the bottom of the street in a state of near-collapse.

Two weeks later Alex was glad to be ordered to return to Cairo. There was too much cloak-and-dagger fighting going on in Jerusalem for his liking. After his narrow escapes at Petah Tikva and in the Street of the Prophets, Alex knew that the sooner he left Palestine the better.

Before leaving, he visited the Old City – strictly out of bounds to the British Army – with a fellow officer. Martial law had been lifted. They both wore mufti and carried concealed weapons. He had been brought up as a Christian and he wasn't going to miss an opportunity to visit the Church of the Holy Sepulchre, the place where Christ had been crucified and buried.

Instead of the peace he had hoped to find in the Old City's narrow, twisted streets, he felt the Jews' silent rage against the British. It was tangible.

He found peace only alongside Christ's Tomb where no voice was raised.

To hasten his departure, Alex used his rank to seek authority to cross the Sinai desert without waiting for a convoy. The British Field Police tried to dissuade him: 'Tribesmen will kill you for your boots, sir, to say nothing of your gun.' But, permission granted, he decided to go anyway; it was a risk he was willing to take.

Starting at dawn, Alex and his driver passed through the frontier post at Beersheba and plunged into the unending expanse of sand, gravel and open sky. They had checked every item of their kit; they knew that the desert was unforgiving, the careless died. The farther they went, the hotter it got. Sweat began to trickle down their backs and into their crotches; their bare knees, necks and arms glistened and their wet shirts stuck to the seats. Slowly the moisture was drawn from their bodies.

Mesmerized by the shimmering heat, they followed the track before them and pressed on, mile after mile, across the ever-changing sand. Billowing dunes stretched as far as the eye could see. Since leaving Beersheba, they had not met or seen a soul; they might have been at the end of the earth. Only the wind broke the endless silence; shadows from the high dunes sometimes crossed their path.

At one point, when Alex took over the driving, he noticed that the petrol was getting low. He stopped to fill up, keeping the engine going. A dark cloud had formed on the horizon; a sandstorm threatened. He felt a flutter of fear. After looking around, he lifted the car seat and unscrewed the cover of the tank. 'Pass the funnel!' There was no answer. He shouted louder against the rising wind: 'Pass the funnel!' There was a worried look on the driver's face.

'What's up?'

'We've left the bloody funnel behind.'

Alex refused to believe him. How could they forget the funnel when crossing the desert in a jeep? Without it, they ran the risk of getting sand into the tank and stalling the engine. Each blast of wind increased the risk.

Fortunately, Alex had an inspiration. 'Give me your greatcoat,' he demanded. He had lost his own in action. He put one of the sleeves into the tank and poured the petrol down the improvised funnel. It worked perfectly. The jacket guarded against the blowing sand. His driver looked on with a nervous smile.

That done, Alex let out the clutch and did his best to

keep the jeep crawling towards the Suez Canal. There were times when the growing storm blotted out their surroundings; times when it screamed at them and shook the vehicle. It was an all-powerful, howling force, flattening everything in its path. Alex slowed down, keeping his eyes glued to where the road should be. As the wind got stronger, they were in danger of sinking into the sand – a mistake could be fatal. Every now and then his driver leapt out and, with head bent against the blinding sand and flying grit, prodded for the road with a cane.

He had just got back into the jeep when, with a crack, a bullet shattered the rear-view mirror in front of Alex. Another bullet destroyed the windshield. Both shots were fired from behind. Neither man saw the assailant, only sand. 'My God,' Alex exclaimed, treading on the accelerator. With growing speed they fled into the storm. Mercifully, the car was not hit again and he managed to stay out of the sand drifts. It took some time for his driver to recover. His face was white with fear. 'You know, I nearly didn't come with you today. Last night I had a dream which left me with a dread of this journey. Thank God we're not dead.'

By the time they had reached the bridge over the Suez Canal the storm was over. Black pools of blood were drying on the bridge. A whiskery old man dressed in a long, loose, striped jellaba was fishing; a boy sat cross-legged beside him. They stared at Alex with vacant eyes.

'Whose blood?' he shouted, pointing.

'Engleesh,' the old man replied, spitting.

Donkey carts full of vegetables jostled by. '*Balek! Balek!*' the drivers shouted, 'Make way!'

Alex was glad to head back to Cairo where he stayed on the Staff for some time.

66

A week after they heard from Alex in Palestine, George Kemp received through the Red Cross the devastating news that Johanna's parents had been killed in an Allied air raid on Cologne a year before. Of Johanna's sister, Brigitte, nothing was known. George was told this privately and it was left to him whether or not to tell his wife. Convinced that he couldn't live with himself unless he told her, he broke the dreadful news. Johanna covered her face with her hands and burst into tears; shock and grief overcame her. For a moment, she saw her parents and her sister on the railway station at the German frontier five years earlier. George held Johanna silently, tears running down their cheeks; he felt powerless to help.

The death of her parents wounded Johanna deeply. The loneliness she had known since coming to Britain grew. For a long time after that she had crying fits, sobbing convulsively. Nothing helped. Sometimes she just buried her face in a cushion. Her refuge was her child, Harold, not her husband.

Johanna had more than her own grief to deal with; the Markham's second-born son – the child that Lydia had fought to keep through a difficult birth – had died suddenly in his cot. Lydia had gone to pick up the baby one morning and found it dead. It was an irreparable loss. Johanna travelled to Ansfield to console her friend, taking Harold with her; he was three by now and a high-spirited child. George could not get away. There was a combined memorial service for Gloria's husband, Roger – and Lydia's baby. Having known the child, Johanna couldn't face it in its coffin. She prayed to God to take it to Heaven. She wept for Roger; why should a man who was so kind and always laughing have to die?

After the death of Roger and the sad news of Johanna's parents, the war became more remote to the Kemps. It should have mattered to them greatly, but it didn't. Of course they followed the successive Allied victories against Germany and Japan. They knew that the tide of war had begun to turn; that the Battle of the Atlantic had at last moved in Britain's favour. All the newspapers were on about it. They also knew that the war in North Africa was over; in September 1943 Italy had surrendered to the Allies, and Mussolini had been overthrown. In January 1944 Rome was threatened by Allied troops. A landing had been made at Anzio. Daily, the wireless announced the havoc being caused by British and US bombers over Germany and German-occupied Europe. Berlin was now being bombed as London had been two years earlier. Thousand-bomber raids were common. Cities like Hamburg were being wiped off the map. It was difficult for Johanna not to feel for her people.

They also were conscious of the widespread heartbreak people were suffering. The human wreckage that war had left in its wake was all around them. Mourning was universal. So many young officers they had known had been killed.

They began to hear rumours from Jewish refugees about a Jewish holocaust in Europe. They found the stories difficult to believe. Johanna's father had never mentioned such a possibility. Forced emigration for Jews, second-class citizenship, these things had been feared before Johanna had left Germany, but not once had she heard talk of mass killings. That would have been inconceivable to the Germans she knew.

George was shocked by the savagery of it all. He felt the horrors of the war deeply. 'I no longer believe that everything that is being done is "in the name of humanity",' he confided to his diary. 'Humanity, where it survives, is sick.

302

Each year since 1939 we have descended further into the pit. Today, terror bombing – the mass killing of civilians – is being carried out by both sides. There has never been such a mass slaughter of women and children on this scale before. Primitive basic forces are in charge of the human lot. Nothing in ancient or medieval history can compare with what is happening today. Strategic bombing has been sidelined in favour of widespread massacre – "de-housing" we British call it. Glory in war, if it ever existed, is dead. Not victory, but obliteration of the enemy – at whatever cost to humanity – is the aim now. To exterminate the human race seems a strange way to extend civilization. I wonder whether the world will ever rediscover humanity.'

'Peace,' he told Johanna, 'is becoming an abstraction. The Allies' demand for unconditional surrender is prolonging the war. It is contrary to all the previous peace settlements. It seems that there are no ethics or morals outside of total victory. Instead, there's a growing moral indifference, often amounting to downright hypocrisy or lies. The war's become a giant absurdity.'

George had long discussions with Walter Turnbull too. 'You're looking for something that war cannot give: moderation,' Turnbull said. 'To go to war is to descend into hell. It's man's greatest evil and his greatest folly. Nothing carries with it a greater price.' In his lectures to the RAF cadets, George found it hard to conceal his true feelings.

'There's only one thing that matters in this war, George,' Max Elsfield told him a few days later, 'and that is winning. This is not a holy war, or a king's war; it's a war of survival. It doesn't matter what we do, or how brutal we get, as long as we win. The end justifies the means. You do what you have to in order to survive. Just forget what you learnt at Sunday School about rights and wrongs. There's no room for turning the other cheek in this business. We've become so destructive that I doubt we'll ever regain the values of

Western civilization. If we lose, we'll really have trouble with moral issues. Victory first, humanity second.'

George didn't agree. It would make convenience a moral right, and was against all he had been brought up to believe. But he was prepared to listen to Max who risked his life in the air every day.

The Kemps not only worried about the wider moral issues, they worried about those they loved. At least Harold prospered. As a result of the care showered upon him by his mother, his English grandmother, and Mrs Childers, the boy had grown by leaps and bounds. He was bursting with life, climbing over everything that got in his way. He loved playing with the Childers's dog Brendan. Next to his marriage, the birth of Harold had been the greatest event in George's life. He had bonded with his son in an almost magical way. There was something utterly fulfilling about watching him grow. He was captivated by Harold's bright, brown eyes; they were Johanna's eyes, full of promise, trust and innocence. He was fascinated by how quickly the child had learned to crawl, and then to totter about. The cadets who visited the Kemps loved to play with him.

67

For the Kemps, the really bright event in 1943 was Max Elsfield's marriage in August to the actress Lucy Warner. There had been rumours about it for weeks, but most of his friends didn't take them seriously. Max was the one who had said, 'Never get married. Don't tie yourself to a woman; she'll ruin you. A man in love is a fool. Happiness? Hope? Love? A perfect match? They are all delusions.' At least they were until Lucy came along.

The wedding, which took place at St James Piccadilly, was the occasion of the year; everybody who was anybody was there; a radiant Lady Elsfield saw to that. Max and Lucy had first met in Morocco. In England, Lady Elsfield had brought the couple together again at one of her soirées.

Max wore an RAF uniform tailored in Savile Row. Lucy wore white, and all that money could buy; a long silk train rustled after her. The reception was at the Savoy Hotel where Max directed everything in his restless, voluble way.

The RAF were proud of Max and were there in force. Tony Markham was best man. He had always supported Max; he'd been too decent to do anything else. He told George that the marriage was a turning point in Max's life; the warmth of Lucy's love had made an entirely new man of him. At the reception, Max danced with his wife as they had never seen him dance before. For the first time, it seemed that harmony had entered his life and they were delighted.

That same month, August 1943, Hazel Elsfield followed her brother to the altar. Against the advice of several of her friends, in a quiet ceremony, she married her Bulgarian suitor, Count Stamboliisky. Lady Elsfield was glad to have a count in the family. Others weren't so sure.

68

Whatever the course of the war, George Kemp and Walter Turnbull still began most days by walking together through Christ Church Meadow. They made an early start because George had to be on parade with the cadets at 8 a.m. By now, Turnbull had become George's political and spiritual mentor. Together they watched the seasons come and go. Both were glad to hear the cuckoo's call and see the twittering swifts return. Often they came across a rabbit sitting trembling in the grass.

On one of their walks, George confessed that the war was causing him to lose faith in the idea of an all-loving God. 'How can a God of mercy allow the war's torments to continue? He no longer motivates me as He did.'

'That is because you want to take God on your own terms,' Turnbull reproached him. 'If people are kind to each other, there is a God. If people are cruel, there is no God. The next thing you will be asking me is how tall is God and what He weighs. You can't have everything cut and dried and explainable. Why not? Because it's beyond our reach. Our existence here on earth can never be plotted and planned. We simply don't know what's going to happen next. Nor can we prove God's existence, or non-existence. We can only approach Him on His terms, and as a child. It is given only to a child to renew life and defy death.'

'So the horrors of war will go on?'

'There'll be conflict as long as people are what they are, or until we can find an acceptable and enforceable universal measuring rod of right and wrong, good and bad. This is very difficult, if not impossible to achieve. What is right for one country is wrong for another. Every age, every society thinks it knows the truth. Other than feeling joy and sorrow, happiness and pain, there is no one overall explanation for the suffering of human beings. The older I get, George, the more I realize the difficulty of achieving lasting harmony between people. We can make necessary changes in institutions, but we can't make the changes that have to come in heart and mind. On my worst days I fear that we shall have to pass through a cataclysm worse than the present one before we can see the light.'

There was silence between the two men.

'We can lessen strife and suffering, as we must, but it is not in our power to end them,' Turnbull continued. 'Life is a never-ending quest, George, in which we are condemned to struggle with the actual, instead of being able to enjoy the ideal. We rarely get what we want. Few of us reach the goals we set. Heartbreak is the human lot. The struggle between war and peace, life and death, good and evil, will go on; the pendulum will continue to swing. There can be no life without joy *and* sorrow. Both are integral to it. The trouble is that while joy is often hard to find, sorrow comes uninvited and frequently:

> When sorrows come they come not singly.
> One woe doth tread upon another's heels
> So fast they follow.

And while joy is fleeting, suffering lasts. Even to contemplate past bliss gives pain. Yet there's no sorrow that time doesn't touch and weave into something else. If we can hang on long enough, sorrow always gives way to joy and joy to sorrow. That is where life is a mystery.'

As ever, George found it impossible to follow Turnbull's thinking. Why couldn't things be explained? Talking about mystery was dodging our responsibilities. He could not understand the older man's acceptance of grief. Surely, something could be done to stop sorrow returning.

69

How uncertain life had become was brought home to George on a visit to Tony Markham at Ansfield House. He noticed how run-down the estate and the house now appeared. They'd had a long talk about the war. 'I'm disillusioned with the whole thing,' George had confessed.

'I'm not,' Tony answered, 'but there are times when I yearn for peace.' They toasted each other with brandy before going to bed.

That night, George was woken by the sound of planes and anti-aircraft fire. As he listened, a plane dropped its bombs; he heard them coming down. One hit the building, shaking the whole structure. The next thing he knew, he was on the floor beneath a pile of timber, plaster and glass. All the lights had gone out; he heard someone shouting. Where his window had been, there was a great gaping hole. He squirmed out from under the debris, found his artificial leg, and with other terrified people groped his way down the dust-filled corridors and the broken stairs to the Great Hall.

Most of the household were already there – several of them cut and bleeding. Tony led a group to put out the fires; Lydia helped to bandage the injured. Thankfully, the children were unhurt. Mrs Joad, the Markhams' old nanny who lived in a corner of the building, had been killed. Much of Ansfield House, including the RAF convalescent home, had to be evacuated. Even the seemingly impregnable oak trees in the drive had been uprooted and splintered. Of the Markhams' treasures, only the suits of armour survived undamaged. Nothing seemed permanent or inviolable any more.

70

In February 1944, the Kemps attended the wedding of Charley and Victoria at the Registrar's Office in Marylebone in London. There was no dressing-up, no reception afterwards. Few of the old Oxford or Ansfield crowd were there and none of Victoria's family. They had never received Charley, nor had they forgiven him for taking their daughter from them. It didn't matter, Charley and Victoria appeared wonderfully happy together.

Three weeks after their wedding, the Bradburys took the train from London to Liverpool to join a Foreign Office delegation sailing to Murmansk, Russia's port on the Arctic Ocean. The purpose was to increase co-operation with the Soviet government. They were both excited at the prospect of seeing the first socialist republic in the world in action. The Bradburys seemed destined to play an important role in Britain after the war.

The voyage through the Arctic Ocean began with the misery of seasickness. North of Norway their convoy was attacked by German planes and U-boats.

Having survived days and nights of repeated attacks, the convoy, one third of which was lost en route, eventually reached Murmansk. Everything there was dirty and over-crowded. Noise and tumult were all around. Worse, far from being greeted warmly as allies and survivors, the delegation was treated by the Russian officials as potential enemies. Had British Foreign Office officials from Moscow not come to their rescue, they might have remained in Murmansk for the rest of the war.

As it was, with the difficulties of the port behind them, they wrestled their way on to a train bound for Leningrad. Through the rain-streaked windows they caught glimpses of a devastated landscape; gaunt, stunted trees made a piti-less sight. There were more horse-drawn carts than trucks or cars. Most of their fellow passengers covered their faces and slept.

From Leningrad, of which they saw little, they travelled on another crowded train to Moscow. In flurries of snow, they were taken from the station to the British Embassy off Red Square. A welcoming lamp hung from a massive bracket above the entrance.

After one last scrimmage with the Russian porters over their luggage, they were given a room at the front of the tall building. It gave them an unexpected feeling of security to be in British hands again – for the first time since they had left, they could put fear aside. They were too exhausted to notice the groaning and rattling of traffic in the street below.

The view from their window in the bright light of the next morning was overwhelming. They were right opposite the Kremlin. They'd never seen such a fabulous jumble of buildings before. The extraordinary conglomeration of golden onion domes and pinnacles of churches and palaces made up for all the inconveniences they'd suffered on the journey. Victoria remembered her father cautioning her before she left that she would find nothing in Russia little or moderate. They had been so immersed in communism that the beauty of the old Russia took them by surprise.

The next week was spent settling in. The accommodation was sparse but adequate. It helped that Victoria's father, Lord Randall, was a close friend of the ambassador. Charley was given a job in embassy communications where he could use his Russian; after four years of study it was pretty good.

Having driven the Germans off their soil, the Russians were in a buoyant mood. Guns and fireworks in Red Square constantly celebrated the victories of the Red Army; bands played at the slightest provocation. The outcome of the war was not in doubt. If the Allies launched a Second Front, it could finish quickly, certainly within a year.

For several months, the Bradburys rejoiced in the Soviet experiment in living; it was exciting to see socialist theories put into practice. Yet everything in Moscow was still under tight control. Wandering away from the beaten path was frowned upon. Several times outside the embassy the Bradburys were accosted by the police, who dissuaded Charley from talking to passers-by. On an excursion into the country-side, people were more willing to talk, although the couple never went anywhere without being trailed.

The turning point of their Russian experience came one day with the arrest of an English friend on charges of espionage. The British Embassy learned of the arrest by accident. When Charley and Victoria finally located their countryman, they were able to talk to him only in the presence of guards, who resented the intervention of the British Embassy staff. The prisoner's voice was unusually weak, his speech hesitant. It was hard for them not to believe that he was saying what his jailers wanted him to say. His fate, Charley was told, would be settled by the Russian secret police; the odds were that he would simply disappear.

By now the Bradburys had come to realize that the disappearance of prisoners was an everyday occurrence. Even with a war on, such things worried them. Time and again, they ran into other political anomalies. They began to notice and resent the more despotic traits of the Russian regime. Nobody talked about equality or brotherly love any more.

Always outspoken, Charley began to express his misgivings to Russian friends. Where were the equality and the freedom from want and fear for which he had hoped and worked? Just to say, 'It's the war,' was not a sufficient excuse. There had to be a moral basis to government action. Not that anyone of any consequence took notice of him. His talk about truth and other bourgeois ideas was thought to be riotously funny. 'Truth' was what the Party decided. Eventually, the idealistic Englishman became an embarrassment to them. There matters might have rested had Charley, deaf to his wife's warnings that he should guard his tongue, not continued to express his inner thoughts in public.

Some days later he was summoned to meet Yarsovsky, an official in the Ministry of Communications. After a long wait, ignored by frowning subordinates, he was shown into his office. A long, lean man, with a much-lined face and pale, intense eyes, the Russian looked up from his work, greeted him with a nod, and motioned him to a chair. There was no shaking of hands or welcoming smile. Ignoring Charley, he returned to his writing. Framed in his window was a view of the Kremlin clock tower. From the square a gun sounded a salute; a leading general had died at the front.

Eventually, the Russian put down his pen, sighed, and eyed Charley gravely. 'Yes?' he asked curtly. He appeared tight-lipped and secretive.

'I've come at your request.'

'Ah, yes, of course.'

Although Yarsovsky spoke excellent English, on this occasion he spoke Russian. At first, it was difficult for Charley to grasp what the fellow was saying. Only gradually did he realize – however guardedly Yarsovsky chose his words – that he was being accused of disloyalty to the communist cause. There was a touch of contempt in his voice.

'But I'm wedded to socialism,' Charley protested. 'I will die as such.'

'A true socialist would never make the criticisms you do. Your words are reported to us.'

'But this is unjust.'

'For us, there is only one kind of justice: that which helps Russia to overcome Nazi aggression and further the triumph of revolutionary socialism.'

'You judge me and my country harshly. Remember, we fought against Nazi aggression while your country was Germany's ally,' Charley said, irrelevantly.

Yarsovsky responded with a cold stare. His face hardened and further conversation proved futile. Nothing Charley said made any difference. He could have gone on explaining his conduct endlessly, to no avail. The Russian was no longer listening.

Finally, Charley picked up his hat and left. There was no word of parting, no wave of the hand. Yarsovsky watched him go with a sullen face.

Later that evening Charley told Victoria all that had gone on. She remained strangely silent. She knew that his only sin was that he had spoken his mind; he always did. There were far greater critics of the Russian government in the embassy, but they didn't air their views in public. Her concern was whether the Russians had already approached the British ambassador. It worried her greatly.

After the talk with his wife, Charley fell into a meditative mood. Justice and righteousness, it seemed, were not to be obtained as easily as he had thought. Freedom – to be in possession of oneself – had not only to be defended from its enemies, but also from its friends.

A week later, in June 1944, the Bradburys met Yarsovsky at a Kremlin reception for representatives of the Allied powers. A military band played in the background. The Russian could not have been more charming or more gracious. He displayed extravagant politeness, shaking their hands as if they were old friends. He smiled faintly when he left them. Everybody there was toasting the Allied invasion of Normandy. At long last, the Second Front was under way.

71

Germany had responded to the D-Day invasion of Western Europe with flying bombs against Greater London. In September V-2 rockets followed, against which there was no defence. The street in London where George's parents lived was almost flattened by a missile. They fled to Oxford until the renewed bombing campaign was over.

One day later that month, Victoria knocked on the Kemps' door at Arnold College. She had come from Russia by sea; her husband was to follow. She was in Oxford to see the Foreign Office people there. She was subdued and was not the Victoria they had known only months before: her face had aged, her lips had taken on an unhappy line; there was a bitter, strained note in her voice when she spoke of their experiences in Russia.

'Are you disillusioned with the Marxist experiment?' George asked.

'By God, I am. It is not a government of the people, but tyranny by a handful of men who have killed freedom of conscience. They've put salt and iron into human relations. We experienced fear as we have never done before. It sounds awful, and it was awful. Anyway, it's over now. Those who gave us glowing accounts of Soviet communism before we left misled us. They believed what they wanted to believe. Up to a point, we did the same.'

'Everybody does,' said George.

'Anyway, Russia isn't like that. All the leaders want is power,' Victoria went on. 'I've been forced to the conclusion that communism is no more acceptable than capitalism. One works by fear, the other by greed. The Soviets have killed the dream Charley and I once had.'

'How does Charley feel?'

'He is as disillusioned as I am. He is crushed by the weight of his own misjudgement, by the burden of his unfulfilled hopes. Much of Russia was too dark, too deep, too overpowering for him to comprehend. He never succeeded in penetrating the fabric of Russian traditions; nor did he succeed in piercing the Slavic mind. His belief in social justice was no match for Russian power politics. As an idealist, he was tormented by the discovery of so much evil. "The problem is not socialism, the problem is the socialist," he kept saying. He put his faith in man – not God – and man failed him. It is ironic that anyone so idealistic and visionary should have ended up so disillusioned.

'It would have been better for us if Charley had remained

314

a wholehearted supporter of the communist system,' she continued. 'Instead, he finished up by being neither one thing nor the other. What he did hold on to was Tolstoy's concern with the need for spiritual regeneration. Like Tolstoy, he'd like to live a simple life close to the soil. At least his experiences have not soured his belief in the inherent good in people and the future triumph of socialism.'

'Is he being expelled?' George asked.

'It suits the Russians and our own embassy for him to leave. He is too outspoken. Without the support of my father, they would have thrown him out earlier. But his expulsion won't harm his political prospects in Britian. Unlike in Russia, British socialism has a religious bias; hating and smashing are not the British way. Anyway, he rose by leaps and bounds in the embassy in Moscow, enough to impress my father. At long last, my family has agreed to receive him when he comes home. I can't wait.'

The Kemps looked forward to hearing Charley's side of the story on his return.

72

Following Victoria's visit, Tony and Lydia Markham spent a week with George and Johanna in Oxford. By now it had become a crowded refugee centre; military personnel thronged the streets; the peace, order and mellowness of pre-war days were a thing of the past. Tony was on leave. With deep charcoal circles under his eyes, he looked as if he needed a rest. His hair was thinning; there was a sprinkling of grey above the temples. He had long since exceeded his quota of battle actions; his fighting days were over. He was awaiting a posting to the RAF Staff College at Andover in Hampshire. He wasn't excited about it, but Lydia was.

Johanna was delighted to spend time with Lydia again; her positive outlook on life, despite the loss of her second child, was contagious. Lydia talked about Ansfield. 'Not until the war is over can anything be done to restore the house. Tony's father has become insensitive to everything since the bombing. Gloria hasn't got over the loss of Roger, any more than Helen has got over losing David. Penelope has pinned her hopes on Pat Riley, but he has changed – he's becoming quieter and more withdrawn. I'm beginning to share Gloria's views about him; he won't commit himself. Although Penelope is careful not to say a word against him, I must say I find it very unsatisfactory. He has adequate funds to support a wife.'

Or two, Johanna thought to herself.

'I'm horrified at the way Lucy's handling her marriage to Max,' Lydia went on. 'Three months and bang, she goes off on an acting tour. I wonder how serious she is about the marriage? I hope Max hasn't made a mistake.'

The two couples spent a day together in the Cotswolds. The countryside was at its best: pastures and woodland were green with summer growth, the early morning sunlight bathed the region's honey-coloured stone. Clear streams stole across the land.

In one church they did some brass rubbings of plaques on wool merchants' tombs. They lunched at the Golden Fleece, an inn hundreds of years old. Through an open window they watched a man sharpening his scythe on a whetstone. They had tea at a streamside café, this time watching an old man picking apples in an orchard across the field opposite. After tea, they ambled towards the orchard along a dusty path lined with brilliantly coloured gladioli. They found the man fast asleep at the foot of a tree. There might never have been a war. They sang as they drove back to Oxford in the dark.

316

The next day they punted on the river; a holiday spirit prevailed. Lydia and Johanna wore large frothy hats and silk dresses; George and Tony wore their old rowing blazers. It was an act of pretence, but they needed it; it made them feel young again. After some horseplay, Tony finished up in the water. He was fished out drenched to the skin. The absurdity of the whole thing sent them into fits of laughter and they went on laughing until they were on the verge of tears. 'Why can't we capture this moment,' Johanna gasped to Lydia, 'and lock it in our hearts for ever?' The beauty and the peace of the river as they glided back at dusk touched their souls.

When they were alone, Tony talked to George about raids he had taken part in. George had never lost his love of the RAF. 'Over Essen,' Tony said, 'the bombers I was escorting went so high that my oxygen tube froze up. We also bombed Brest, the most heavily defended port in France, where German fighters dived on us out of nowhere. Our heavy losses were hushed up.'

'Are German cities really being destroyed, as the papers tell us?'

'It's much worse than what they tell you. At Hamburg, the whole city was in flames. Thousands upon thousands must have been cremated. The sight will haunt me for a long time. I think the Germans know they're going to be licked; they're tired of it all. After that raid I was approaching the Kent coast when my engine gave out. I got a fix from the tower at Dover and glided in with the ambulance and fire truck racing after me.'

'Don't mention any of this to Johanna,' George said. 'She's very brave, but it would only worry her. She made a wish the other day to wake up and find the war over.'

'That's what we all wish.'

'It's time the insanity ended.'

When it came time to part, the two couples hugged each

317

other. The women had moist eyes. 'God be with you,' George said to Tony. The Markhams gave a last wave, sounded their horn, and drove away. Johanna continued to stare after them until they passed out of sight. Only then did she turn and, holding little Harold by the hand, slowly make her way into the house.

73

In late September 1944, Johanna picked up the phone to find a distressed Victoria Bradbury on the line. 'Charley's ship from Archangel was torpedoed off Norway,' she sobbed. 'He was rescued and taken to a hospital in Liverpool. I'm on my way to join him there. I'll call you back after my visit.'

Johanna was about to console her friend when the line went dead.

Two days later Victoria called again. She was broken-hearted. 'Charley was dead by the time I arrived,' she cried into the phone; her voice became incoherent. Hers was the wild voice of life bitterly crying out against death. Through Victoria's tears, Johanna gathered that her father had insisted that Charley should be buried in the family crypt at Charlton. As husband of the Randall heiress, Charley was too important to be buried in some odd corner.

With a half-smothered sob, Victoria rang off.

Johanna was conscious of nothing except the sorrow in her own heart. She thought it infinitely sad that a life of such talent should have been snatched away, its promise unfulfilled.

Several days later the Kemps attended Charley's funeral in the small chapel at Charlton. Victoria looked distinguished in mourning. Even in tears, she was in charge. All the

Randalls were there to mourn Charley's passing, as custom prescribed. Victoria despised them. She had not forgotten their opposition to her husband. Weary authority showed in Lord Randall's eyes. The only time he had spoken to Bradbury was when Charley had walked out on him in London. There was an arrangement of tulips in the shape of a cross on top of the coffin. Whether Charley would have liked it or not, the cross was witness to his death as it had been to his birth. He died a happily married man, with the Church's blessing.

By Christian standards it was a fine funeral; the Randalls wanted it that way. It pleased them that one of the officiating clergy should have referred to the deceased as a patriot and a future statesman: honour was served.

Among the mourners were Charley's parents, whose journey from Scotland, Victoria had organized. She had tried to keep in touch with them since her marriage, but writing letters embarrassed them. Overcome by grief, they looked lost and nothing anyone did helped to put them at ease. Max Elsfield's presence came as a surprise to Victoria, who answered his condolences with a piercing glance. She would take her dislike of that man to her grave.

When all was done and still, a cellist began to play. The plaintive note moved them all.

'Charley was not a bad sort,' Max confided to Tony later on. 'He was just a so-and-so who thought he knew all the answers.'

'Don't be hard on him, Max, not now . . . not now.'

George and Johanna couldn't help thinking how ironic it was that Charley had to die in order to be accepted by the Randalls.

The next day Victoria suffered a nervous breakdown.

74

Less than a week later, a saddened Max called the Kemps to tell them that his sister Hazel had been killed in a flying bomb raid on London. The whole block of flats in which she was living was demolished. Life had not been kind to Hazel. It transpired that her husband, Count Stamboliisky, had abused her and had gambled, drunk and entertained much of her money away. Each day of the marriage had added to Hazel's misery.

Gloria told Johanna that she had visited Hazel after learning that her marriage was breaking up. 'Hazel showed no anger,' Gloria said, 'but her hurt gaze told me all I needed to know. I'm sure he was rotten to her. By the sound of things he was having other affairs and had tired of her.'

Max did everything he could to keep what was left of Hazel's money out of the count's hands. He hated the man as fiercely as only Max could, and would have gladly killed him for the shameful way he had treated his sister.

Shortly after Hazel's death, quite by chance, he ran into Stamboliisky in the Savoy Grill. Before anyone could stop him Max had knocked the count to the floor and was on top of him, choking him. 'God damn you for ever,' Max shouted, as he pressed his fingers deeper into the count's throat. It took several waiters to drag him off. The incident was reported to the RAF and Max was suspended and placed on rest leave.

Three days later, Count Stamboliisky was found stabbed to death in his London home. It was in all the papers and on the evening news. There was an unfinished drink on the mantelpiece, standing before a large mirror in the lounge, where the count's body had been found. The police surmised that it was the count's drink, and that he couldn't have been standing in front of the mirror without seeing his would-be assassin enter the room behind him. Had Max not been visiting Air Vice Marshal Pennington's headquarters that day, suspicion would have fallen on him.

A wild-looking Bulgarian of extreme political views was later arrested and convicted of the crime. It was said in court that Stamboliisky had lived a cloak-and-dagger life as a spy in Europe before coming to England. The Bulgarian who killed him was settling an old score.

The final blow regarding Stamboliisky came several weeks later in the courts, when it was revealed that he already had a wife in Bulgaria.

According to what Tony Markham told George, Hazel's death continued to haunt Max. 'Drowning his sorrows in drink, he doesn't seem to know if he is getting in or out of his plane. He is oblivious to the world around him. Nothing anybody does, out of kindness or discipline, makes the slightest difference. As he's on the point of ending his combat duties, his superiors look the other way. They are only too glad to be getting rid of him. He even sought a pretext to quarrel with me – something he has never done before. "Go to hell and stay there," he raged at me. "I never want to see you again." I was more sad than angry, and didn't leave him until peace was restored between us. I'm afraid his life is being reduced to tatters.'

One night, Max took Tony to dine with Lady Elsfield. 'You are quite well?' she asked formally, offering Tony her cheek. She had become a poor palsy-stricken thing who had lived beyond her time. Her former grandeur had decayed. He noticed a profound sadness in her eyes.

It was a disastrous evening. Lady Elsfield got mixed up and talked at random. Somewhere in between she had a coughing fit. That Max had been drinking showed in his slurred speech and contemptuous tone. Eventually neither mother nor son knew or cared what they were saying.

It was at the height of one of Max's tirades, with his face twitching, that Lady Elsfield suddenly clutched her chest, struggled to her feet and, striking the table, fell to the floor. She made a desperate effort to speak and then fell silent. Deeply shocked, Tony noticed how still and chill the room had become.

When Max discovered that his mother was dead, and that there was nothing he could do to revive her, he walked out of the room. 'I know you expected me to tear my hair and grovel at my mother's feet,' he explained to Tony later. 'I couldn't. She and my father made life hell for Hazel and me. They never stopped fighting. Can you imagine what it must have been like never to have been loved for our own sake? The absence of warmth between parents and children was our family's tragedy. Even when my father lived with us, he was always preoccupied with making money, which was his measure of all relations. We had everything, except love. There have been times when I concluded that our family was meant to be miserable – happiness always escaped us.'

'You're free to change now.'

'I've seen too much of the dark side of human nature to be able to change, Tony. I'd rather put up with the pitfalls I know than create new ones. As it's not in me to go down on my knees, or believe in fate, I'll have to take my chance. I don't fear death or what awaits me after death.'

'It's never too late to change, Max.'

Max looked away, silently.

75

On a wintry day in October 1944, Tony Markham and Max Elsfield took part in a bombing raid on the Dortmund-Ems Canal aqueduct near Münster. Only at the last minute had Max decided to join the raid. He and Tony had smoked together before taking off. After four years of war, they couldn't imagine being apart. In a week's time, both men would be taking up posts at the RAF Staff College at Andover. Like Tony, Max had been due for retirement from active service for some time.

Approaching France, on the return journey from Münster, Tony's plane was struck by enemy fire and fell behind. 'I'm losing pressure,' he reported matter-of-factly.

'Ditch it, ditch it, get out now, and that's a bloody order!' Max shouted.

Either Tony had his earphones off or he pretended not to hear; he continued to follow the squadron. Black stains of flak surrounded his plane.

Sure of its target, a fast-climbing Me 109 came up through low clouds and went for Tony like a shark to bait. Tony met his attacker head-on. It must have been his lucky day, for he hit the plane with his first burst; the torn fabric flapped in the wind. After hanging in the air for a moment, the Messerschmitt nose-dived to earth. Two more enemy planes appeared.

Without hesitating, Max wheeled around and flung himself into battle. Two of his pilots followed. In the ensuing mêlée, cannon shells blasted away the nose of Tony's aircraft. Gradually he eased his plane down. Max and the other pilots watched him make a forced landing.

To their horror, the plane became a ball of fire as it hit the ground.

News of Tony's death was telephoned to Ansfield later that night by Sir Hugh Massingham, commander of the air base at West Hadding. A neighbour and a close friend of Lord Markham, Massingham had taken it upon himself to convey the sad news.

Lord Markham was standing at the festively-dressed dining table proposing a toast to Lydia on her birthday when the phone rang. The dinner had been delayed in the hope that Tony might join them, as he had promised. She assumed that it was Tony calling. The call was taken in the sitting room by the butler, who entered the dining room and haltingly whispered something in his master's ear. 'I'll take the call in the study,' Lord Markham told him. Bowing to Lydia, he put down his glass and excused himself.

Massingham came straight to the point. 'I'm terribly sorry, Cecil, but Tony was killed while making a forced landing in France early this afternoon. His plane burst into flames. Several pilots have confirmed his death.'

Godfather to Tony, Massingham's voice was deep with emotion. Lord Markham sank into a chair.

When he returned to the birthday party, Lydia read his thoughts as he entered the room. She paled. Grasping the edge of the table, she slowly got to her feet.

'Not Tony?' she asked, her voice faltering.

He took her gently by the shoulders. 'My dear Lydia, Tony is dead.'

Lydia ran from the room, weeping.

Max had fought on to avenge the death of his friend with the tenacity of an animal at bay. He swooped out of battle only to wheel in again. Struck by his cannon fire, one of the German planes exploded; the other tried to get on to

324

Max's tail. Max tumbled, banked and turned, only to watch the German slide out of his sights. He tried every trick he knew, without success. Several times he fired and missed.

Moments later, the barrels of Max's guns were shot away. Those watching saw the debris flying through the air. Still in charge of his battered plane, Max swung round in a wide arc and disappeared into a cloud. Not to be denied his prey, the German followed. He had no fear of a defenceless plane. When they emerged, the German was leading. Max was above him. Before the enemy had had time to disengage, in a lightning manoeuvre, Max swooped down, closed, and crashed into his opponent. The two planes went hurtling down together, turning over and over in flames.

In the eyes of his fellow pilots, in his last intemperate act, Max had redeemed himself.

'Oh, George,' Johanna sobbed, when she heard of the fates of Max and Tony. 'Why does ugly death raise its head all the time? We used to talk about life and death, now we only talk about death.'

Walter Turnbull was just as shocked by the sad news. 'The tragedy about Max Elsfield,' he said to George, 'was that his life was spent searching for love and affection. When he did find it, it failed him. Tony Markham never even had to look.'

A crowded memorial service was held for Max at the West Hadding air base. In charge was an RAF chaplain who sat at the front of the room at a table with a green baize cover. Hands clasped, he stared into the distance. On the wall behind him was a large operational map of Western Europe. Max's friends from Ansfield and Oxford were there, but his father was not. Most of his fellow officers and ground crew attended. There were also pilots from other countries, especially from the US, who tiptoed in and whispered among themselves as if they were in church. The last to arrive was the base commander.

Just as the ceremony was about to begin, Max's wife Lucy arrived dressed in mourning. She sat apart at the back. Walter Turnbull caught a glimpse of her tear-stained face through her veil. Momentarily, their eyes met. Despite the talk about her, he felt her face expressed deep devotion.

Max in death was praised by all – even by those who had clashed with him. Death had absolved all his past wrongs. He had achieved every success. He had fought for so long that his fellow pilots had come to think of him as indestructible. One speaker said that Max's life had gained a mystic dimension! Twice he had defeated the efforts of his superiors to relegate him from fighting to Staff. The chaplain spoke of his dauntless courage, his steadfastness, his fearlessness in battle, his talents as a leader, and the circumstances surrounding his death. 'Greater love hath no man than this, that a man lay down his life for his friends.'

Lucy disappeared just as suddenly as she had arrived, the moment the ceremony was over.

The memorial service for Tony Markham was held at Ansfield parish church several days later. George and Johanna were met outside the church by Tony's widow Lydia and her four-year-old son Anthony. Gloria Blundell was accompanied by her three-year-old daughter Margaret. The children clung to their mother's hands, subdued. All were in mourning.

Johanna greeted them, clasping each of them in turn. The three women found the occasion overwhelming and dissolved into tears.

In a cold, crowded church, with the vicar's voice echoing in the rafters and the candles flickering, they honoured the man who had made the supreme sacrifice for his country and his people, who was now part of the grand communion in heaven. Servants from Ansfield, who had known Tony all his life, were deeply moved.

The altar was bare. The vicar spoke of Tony's generous,

selfless character, his inbred goodness, his gracefulness, his moral decency and the certainty of his eternal life. 'Whoever has faith in me shall have life, even though they die. And everyone who has life, and has committed themselves to me in faith, shall not die for ever.' Tony had died and was now reborn. Death had been conquered. A true and infinite peace had taken its place.

As George listened, he thought of Tony standing up in class at Eton years before, struggling with a passage from the *Iliad*. It was a drowsy afternoon; through the open windows he could hear the cricket team practising at the nets. The recollection of Tony's halting attempts to convey the sadness of the young Greek's death evoked in George a special pathos. 'In grieving for Tony,' George wrote in his diary, 'I am grieving for myself.'

Lydia, draped in black, head erect, eyes red-rimmed, sat in the Markham pew as still and as silent as a rock. Her quietly mournful gaze expressed dignity and strength. Tony wasn't dead, he had gone before. Death was a temporary separation, not an end. 'There will be no death,' says St John. The body had died, the soul lived on, unstained by hate. The revelation of the love and the fatherhood of God never left her. The idea of sitting in judgment on God the Redeemer was alien to her. George knew that she believed in eternal salvation and envied her. He had lost so much of his belief in God, without finding a satisfactory alternative. She had an assurance about life and death that escaped him. Matthew's quotation, 'Blessed are the pure in heart: for they shall see God' was written for the Lydias of this world.

She and her son Anthony sat next to a subdued Helen and Penelope. Lord Markham's head drooped; Lady Markham, her mouth narrowed by pain and disappointment, was bent forward as if she had received a blow. There were strangers there, but no one had any idea who they were; it didn't matter anymore. Tony Markham's Sergeant Weasel sat alone at the front.

The worshippers left the church with the vicar's words ringing in their ears: 'The Lord bless you and keep you; the Lord let His face shine upon you and give you peace. Amen.'

At the lunch that followed the funeral at Ansfield House it saddened George to find himself sitting where he'd sat for Tony and Lydia's wedding breakfast. Penelope and Helen sat opposite him. George found it difficult to listen to Penelope talking about Pat Riley, whose loss of an arm had only increased her love for him. He avoided talking to Helen about David Evans. He reflected on what a different world it would have been for all of them if there had been no war.

76

The following day Lord Markham received a letter from his son. On the envelope was written: 'To be delivered in the event of my death.'

> Dearest Father,
> When you read this I shall have left you. My earthly destiny will have been fulfilled. Don't weep for my passing. Think of the wonderful times we have had together over the years.
> There is something I have to tell you that I couldn't bring myself to tell you or Helen before. David Evans was to be married to a West Hadding girl called Iris Penny the day he died. She was bearing his child and he felt compelled to marry her. I forgave him his trespasses, as I know you will. In other times, it might have all worked out differently, who is to say?

Having met the woman, it was my intention – for her and for David's sake – to help her when the child was born. She is very young and alone in the world. Can I ask you to do this for me – for charity's sake and my own? I'll rest better if you do. I would not ask this favour of anyone but you. With so many of the staff away on war work, there's need of hands at Ansfield. I know you'll find Lydia, Gloria and Penelope sympathetic.

My love as ever to you and Mama, Gloria, Penelope and Helen. From my heart, I thank you all for your love and kindness. Take care of my beloved Lydia and our child. The Markham sword now passes to him.

Every blessing,
Until we meet,
Your loving son, Tony

P.S. Iris Penny's address is Flat A, No 10 Baker Street, West Hadding, Middlesex.

Letter in hand, Lord Markham slumped back in his chair, his eyes wandered around the room. Helen must never find out that David had betrayed her.

77

Back in Oxford, George felt the deaths of Tony and Max keenly. They rattled him. He felt a hidden menace of impending doom. 'I've become a spectator at the death of all I hold dear,' he recorded. 'My comrades die as if it's been secretly ordained. It's like a Greek tragedy, with the fates lamenting, but urging each of the victims on to his inevitable undoing. Talk about glory in death is all eyewash. It doesn't matter whether you are a scholar like David, a man of duty like Bill, a joker like Roger, an idealist like Charley, a gentleman like Tony, or a reckless egotist like Max – like bubbles on water, they've all died; death has won. Their earlier dreams might never have been. No matter how I twist and turn to shake it off, the sorrow of their deaths clings to me. Sometimes their voices echo in my ears. They give me no peace; they keep at me until I sweat with fear. There are times when I believe I'm being watched by them; I fear I might be losing my mind.'

George secretly hoped that Alex Haverfield would stay in Cairo where he was safe. Pat Riley was safe because he'd become a novice for the priesthood at a Benedictine monastery in Orpington in Kent. Everyone who spoke of him said he'd changed. But the idea of Pat becoming a priest had shocked everyone. The Kemps had become so accustomed to shocks that little surprised them anymore; their feelings had dulled.

In a letter to Penelope, Pat tried to explain his decision.

My dear Penelope,
This is a letter that I never dreamt I would have to write. Its chief purpose is to ask your forgiveness for all the wrongs I have done you. You will ask me why I have decided to become a priest. My answer is that I feel I have no choice. There was a long drawn-out tussle between God and myself, which God won. The hell of Dieppe made me a different man; the man who set out for Dieppe is not the man who was carried off the beach on the verge of death.

Having survived, I've decided to amend my ways and do something serious with my life. I've put my dissolute past behind me. I started out in life looking for God, but lost my way. Now God has called me back.

May God forgive me if I have given you the impression that we might share our lives. Is it too much for me to ask you to pray for my soul? I shall pray for yours. Always I shall remember you in my heart. Never will I forget the joy we knew together. Thank God you are young enough to go on with your life. If I have caused you grief, forgive me.

Your friend,

Pat

Penelope showed the letter to her sister Gloria. Gloria couldn't get over the idea that Riley – a mature man – had totally and ruthlessly destroyed her sister's girlhood dream.

78

About two months later, in early February 1945, George was surprised to hear from Mrs Haverfield that Alex had been wounded in Italy and had been flown to England. He was a patient at Queen Mary's Hospital, Roehampton. George took the news hard – Alex still had always been a favourite of his. He had assumed that Alex still had a desk job in Cairo about which he was always complaining. His mother, who had friends in the War Office, was doing all in her power to have him transferred to the Radcliffe Infirmary in Oxford where she could be with him.

A week later, Johanna arrived on duty at the Radcliffe to discover that a Major Alex Haverfield was to be a patient on her ward. For a moment she couldn't believe her ears. Tidying her hair, she ran along the corridor to greet him. The last time she had set eyes on Alex was in 1939 – six years before.

She found him in a more serious condition than she had

expected. The war and his wound had aged him. His cheeks were thinner, his eyes darker. His mother was with him, but he didn't recognize her. 'The journey hasn't done him any good,' the supervising doctor told them. 'But he's a young lion with an amazing constitution. If he were going to die, he would have died days ago. He's had all the surgery we can give him. The only question is whether his body will recover.' To Johanna, the head on the pillow didn't look like the handsome young man she had met before the war. But he's alive, she kept saying to herself, there's hope.

Between them, Alex's mother and Johanna helped to nurse him back to health. Everything had to be done for him. Every day they bathed his body, which was Herculean and sunburned. They took it in turns to feed him with a spoon at mealtimes and spent hours at his bedside, refusing to lose heart when he continued to stare at them blankly.

One morning Johanna entered the ward to find that Alex had turned a corner in his illness. There was life in his eyes again. His colour was better. His youth had pulled him through. For the first time he recognized her.

They talked, but not much. Alex was easily exhausted. She told him how life had gone on in Oxford all the years he'd been away. As he got better he spoke about the beauty of the desert and its night skies. 'I have never felt so exposed to the forces of nature. North Africa was the place where I changed my beliefs about war and peace and my hatred of the Germans. We left behind an ugly world strewn with the debris of war.' When he was tired, they were happy to share silence.

Two weeks later, with his mother and Johanna propping him up, they got Alex out of the ward on to an adjoining glassed-in balcony, where, wrapped in a blanket, he sat for an hour or two each day. The weather was unusually warm for March. Here he had long talks with his friends from Oxford and Ansfield. Gloria told him about the deaths of

Hazel Elsfield and her Bulgarian count. Sometimes the names of David Evans, Bill Clark, Roger Blundell, Charley Bradbury, Max Elsfield and Tony Markham cropped up.

After a month, Alex was taken home to Woodstock where he got stronger and fitter by the day and appeared to be on the way to full health. The doctors were amazed at the speed of his recovery. As soon as he was allowed to drive, he used his mother's car to visit the Kemps and the Childers's in Oxford. Harvey Childers walked the tow-path with him, talking boats. He was amazed that Alex had remembered so much of what he had taught him as a stroke. To Childers' delight, the boat races had begun again. It had given him new life and he loved to discuss the crews with Alex. At the end of their walk, they would return to the Master's lodgings to be refreshed with a glass of home-made bilberry wine. Both Mr and Mrs Childers had aged while Alex had been away, and so had their dog Brendan.

Alex often visited the Kemps at weekends when George was at home. He enjoyed playing with Harold, who was now five. The child gave Alex no respite; the rougher their games, the better. Alex was as optimistic about the future as George was gloomy and Johanna enjoyed his company. With Alex she felt young again. Without realizing it, she drew closer to him. In Woodstock he was forever talking about Johanna; so much so that his mother began to wonder about it.

79

One Saturday when Alex was visiting the Kemps, George excused himself to go and collect Harold from the Childers. They were always borrowing him, and he was always glad to go – not least to play with Brendan. Alex offered to go for the child, but George wouldn't hear of him breaking off the game of chess he was playing with Johanna. 'Finish your game,' he insisted. 'I'll be back in a minute.'

There was a long, expectant silence between the chess players. The clock on the mantelpiece ticked away. Johanna realized that this was the first time that she and Alex had been alone together. There had always been somebody around at the hospital, and Alex never visited them unless George was at home. She was aware of an entirely different atmosphere in the room; it had become emotionally charged and strangely intimate. It didn't seem wrong to her that this should be so.

As Alex reached across the board to move a knight, he clumsily knocked over one of Johanna's castles. His hand rested close to hers. Without thinking, she gently covered his hand with her own. For a moment neither of them spoke. They were at a loss to explain what had happened between them. Rising, Alex leaned across and gently kissed Johanna on the cheek. In doing so, he aroused her as George was no longer able to do; he satisfied an unfulfilled longing. They kissed again, this time much more passionately. Several chess pieces fell on the floor; an everlasting moment followed, interrupted finally by the voices of George and Harold in the drive.

'I found him asleep with Brendan in the dog bed,' George said as he came in carrying the child. It surprised him to see the chess pieces lying on the carpet. He was silent for a moment. 'Must have been a fierce game,' he said.

Johanna bowed her head. She blushed. 'It was my fault.' With one arm around Harold, who had run to her, she busied herself picking up the pieces.

George had a fleeting recollection of his wife as he had seen her five years earlier, when she had come to Oxford for the boat race, with her pretty lace blouse and her straw hat with its large red ribbon. He remembered her smile when he had met her off the train, and recalled the look of joy in her eyes.

Shortly afterwards Alex stood up to go. On parting, he glanced at Johanna with a hesitancy that did not escape George. She felt the overwhelming grip of his fingers as he passed through the door; it left tremors. His footsteps grated on the gravel outside.

That night Johanna lay awake for hours. She was frightened and bewildered by what had happened. Nobody needed to tell her that man and wife were one flesh. The priest had done so at her wedding, and George and Harold were her life. She couldn't abandon herself to a passing infatuation for someone else. Her family must come first. But why had she become infatuated? Why had she taken Alex's hand? Was it because she needed somebody else to love, or because of a growing discontent with George? She didn't know. David Evans had once told her that there was a reason for everything. But there was no reason for this; it had just happened. All thought had been driven from her head. She wondered why such happiness had to occur almost accidentally – like a flash of lightning in a dark sky. Was God testing her? Torn between the heart's wishes and the impossibility of satisfying them, she finally fell into a troubled sleep.

Alex never returned to the Kemps'. George did not comment on his absence; he knew what had happened; he had taken it all in at a glance. 'The truth dawned on me,' he wrote in his diary, 'when I saw the scattered chess pieces. I felt the excitement in the room. I saw it in Johanna's eyes; Alex's eyes confirmed my suspicions. At first the possibility of their falling in love was so preposterous that my mind refused to accept it. Alex wouldn't do that to me, nor would Johanna. Perhaps I am imagining it. I've become so eaten up with my own worries and depression that I've forgotten to love the most wonderful companion that a man could have. My affections for her are always in my dreams, but they cannot be lived. Instead of being angry, I have a sense of guilt, of self-hate. I have no desire to inflict my secret remorse upon her. What has spoiled our happiness? Nothing, except that it's no longer shared; and not being shared it is dead. It's not the big things that are driving me mad, but the little things, like the touch and warmth of Johanna's hand, or the tone of her voice. What use am I? I can do nothing right. I always lose. It's as if I was meant to fail. Now I am about to lose my wife. I weep at the thought of it, because I fear in my heart that she loves Alex more than me. As I cannot live without Johanna, what is the point of going on? Death fills my thoughts. Only death offers escape from my illusions. It frightens me.' Jealousy grew in him daily. His spirit was clouded with his sense of failure.

He recalled what Dostoevsky had written in *The Brothers Karamazov*, which he had read on his second visit to Cologne: 'The man who lies to himself and listens to his own lie comes to such a pass that he cannot distinguish the truth within him, or around him, and so loses all respect for himself and others. And having no respect he ceases to love . . .' Was he lying to himself about Johanna and Alex? No. If he were lying about Johanna's infidelity, then why was he so devastated by it? He had never felt so lonely.

'Is there anything you want to tell me?' he asked Johanna one day.

'About what?' She raised her eyebrows.

'About your relationship with Alex. Don't you realize what you're doing? Have you no shame?' he shouted, giving way to anger.

Johanna burst into tears and ran from the room. She knew in her heart that her love for Alex was too intense to last.

George had the urge to tell Johanna how much he loved her. Instead he went back to work, slamming the door behind him. A weariness possessed him.

* * *

336

A week later, Alex appeared unexpectedly at the Radcliffe Infirmary. There was another outburst of feeling between Johanna and himself. 'Can we go somewhere where we can talk?' he pleaded. Overwhelmed by his presence, Johanna begged to be let off duty for a couple of hours and they drove to Blenheim Park a few miles away. It was a perfect April day, with the first flowers showing. After walking hand in hand, they sat in the shade under the trees. Being a weekday, the park was empty of visitors.

Whatever Johanna and Alex may have intended when they left the Radcliffe, they gave way to their emotions once they were alone. They became insensible to everything except their passion for each other; it possessed them. With shafts of sunlight breaking through the trees, the two young lovers knew nothing but rapturous delight. Why is it, Johanna asked herself, that everything else fades in his presence? Why the magic? Why the longing? Why does his love flood my heart?

Johanna was filled with shame that night. She had betrayed her husband and broken her marriage vows, so much so that she found herself unable to appeal for help to the Mother of Christ. Her love for Alex had come upon her like a storm – a storm of her own making – and she had lost her head. As if in a dream, she had given herself to him willingly. But how could she? It was adultery – the brink of damnation. She had never known such misery. She recalled a phrase from the Bible about tasting bitter ashes.

That weekend she went to Confession; her conscience weighed her down. 'I shall refuse to give you absolution,' the priest threatened, 'if you see that man again. The lusts of the flesh have blinded you to the immortality of your soul. Go and sin no more!' The consolation she sought was denied her.

Alex had no peace either. Other than divorce, which Johanna refused to consider, there was only one way out: they would have to part. He hated living a lie behind George's back, hated seeing what he saw of himself in a mirror. The deceit had to end. To leave the country was the only decent thing to do. The next morning he called an old friend in the War Office.

80

One day in the late spring of 1945, George's college business took him close to Orpington. Why not call on Pat Riley in the Benedictine monastery? he thought.

Pat was glad to see him. He asked about Johanna and Harold. He seemed to be managing very well with his artificial arm. As it was a fine day, they walked in the gardens, chatting happily. George thought Pat had changed; there was a new contentment and calmness about him. Cowled monks passed by, the church bell began to toll, lambs frisked around them. They rejoiced that the war in Europe was almost over. The German Army was being overwhelmed; its last throw on the western front had failed; Berlin was threatened by the Russians.

Inevitably, their conversation turned to the dead members of the crew. 'What has happened is a form of madness,' George declared. 'If there is a God, He's a very capricious God. There are times when I think evil is in charge.'

'You're not the first to think that evil outweighs virtue,' Pat assured him. 'Max Elsfield did too. He thought the world was irredeemably bad. The truth is the opposite: hope is always more insistent than despair; virtue is always more persistent than vice. The Church has lasted as long as it has because it recognizes the inherent good and the inherent evil in man. It knows that life is a contest between the two, and that good will prevail.'

'Pat, I find your picture of an orderly world in which

338

virtue will triumph unsettling. It's not an orderly world – it's a mad one where these men could be cut down, one after another. All of them were crushed by events over which they had no control.'

'I agree, George. The war has robbed us of our best. In two wars our best have been consumed by the flames. Only God knows what our friends might have achieved if they had lived. When the war is over, little men will take the place of the big men who might have been. We'll come out of this war a smaller, different people than we were when we entered it.'

They went on talking about their dead comrades. For a moment, across the years, George heard the song 'We'll Meet Again . . .'

'You know, George,' were Pat's parting words, 'I think your problem is that you cannot accept death, either for yourself or for your companions. You fear it like a child going to bed in the dark. I can sense it. To some extent, we are all haunted by what we think about death. It's something peculiar to humans – the riddle of death has faced every civilization since time began. The ancient Egyptians were obsessed with it. Yet death is the inescapable reality of life; it is life's fulfilment. You've got to begin to look upon death as the other side of life. To die is as natural as to be born. Death only looks fearful when you hope to escape it. When there seems to be no hope, then you hunger for it.'

George left the monastery in the late afternoon, promising to return. Pat Riley was right, he *had* come to dread death. He was reluctant to say goodbye to his friend. He had neglected Pat ever since hearing of his affair with the Dutch girl. Now he'd make up for lost time. Of the crew, only Pat and Alex remained.

On leaving Orpington for London, an air-raid alert sounded. The shaking train slowed, but didn't stop. George put his

339

head out of the window and saw a V-2 streaking across the sky. Everyone thought that the rocket attacks had ended – there hadn't been one in days. The missile fell with a noise like thunder in the area he'd just left.

He heard that night that the rocket had exploded inside the monastery grounds, destroying several buildings. Pat had been tending the roses on the chapel wall when the rocket struck. Several monks had died with him. Pat had been killed by one of the last two rockets fired on England. Death had missed George by less than an hour. 'How has it come about,' he asked himself, 'that I who have done least, and who have probably feared death most, should still be alive?'

'Pat found his destiny, but was not allowed to fulfil it,' Johanna said when she heard the news. 'Something more has gone out of our lives, never to return.'

The next day George phoned the McTavishes in Mull to tell them of Pat Riley's death. Would they please tell Beatrix Dekker?

The Kemps were unable to attend Pat's funeral but they went down to Orpington a week later, buying a bunch of flowers on the way. As always, Johanna took great care in choosing them. They found his and other new graves tucked away in a corner of the monastery garden, away from the damage the rocket had done. The funeral wreaths had begun to fade; daisies were already growing around the cut turf; blackbirds sang in the surrounding bushes; some sheep were grazing nearby. They were told that Beatrix Dekker and Penelope Markham had stood there together, united in their grief. After Johanna had crossed herself and knelt to say a prayer, she and George stood silently, heads bowed, and thought of Pat Riley and all the others, all that they had stood for and done together, and what might have been. The thought of what might have been struck deep into Johanna's heart. She remembered the joy the crew had shared over the years. Uncontrollable tears ran down her face. All that she could do was to stare at the grave and sob freely. She just felt empty. George had to pluck at her sleeve to leave.

Honour and friendship served, they left the monastery garden as they had entered it: by a small picket gate. George glanced back as he fastened the latch. The sheep were on Riley's grave and were nonchalantly munching the flowers that Johanna had put there.

81

One day at the end of April, George returned from Arnold and told his wife that he had just lunched with Alex. On the surface, Alex and he still pretended to be the best of friends; George thought it preferable to a sordid row.

'Alex mentioned that he's about to return to the army as a battalion commander. He could have dodged it on medical grounds, but he's set his heart on going. He's fit enough.'

Johanna was too shocked to answer. No matter how she argued with herself about her responsibilities to her husband and child, she could not help being drawn to Alex.

A few days later, Alex visited Johanna at the Radcliffe to say goodbye. He looked tall and splendid in his uniform. The day was fine, and Johanna and he strolled in the grounds, eventually reaching a secluded corner. There was a stillness between them. Crocuses nodded their heads in the sun.

'Don't go now,' she pleaded, 'not when the war is almost done.' Tears in her eyes and voice, she begged him, but he was deaf to her appeal and avoided her eyes. She threw her arms around his neck. He held her close. 'You are running away from me,' she accused him.

'I can do nothing else. Every time I see George I'm aware that I'm betraying him.'

'Even if it means the end of our love?'

'I shall always love you.' He reached out and pressed her face against his, longingly. 'I shall return to you when the war is done.'

After a long silence, both unable or unwilling to articulate their thoughts, they kissed and held each other tight. Never before had Johanna seen Alex stifle tears. She buried her head in his shoulder. Later they stumbled back towards the hospital. They released each other's hand. He returned her wave as he passed through the gate. She went inside weeping; she wept quietly to herself most of that day. Later, she cycled home through the quiet rain.

Early next morning, in desperation, Johanna phoned Harvey Childers from the Radcliffe. Would he, she pleaded, intercede with Alex before it was too late? He could still be reached in London. He had given her his address. 'I know he's putting on a brave face, he doesn't have to go back in the army.'

'My dear Johanna, what good do you think you would do by insisting that he should stay? He can only do what you want him to do by losing his self-respect. I know Alex well. He is at a crossroads and doesn't know which way to turn. He feels it better at this point to get away and sort out his life alone. I'll do anything I can to help you, Johanna, but not this.'

'But Harvey . . .'

'Johanna, I'm sorry to have to say this, but you must know that Alex is torn between his love for you and his loyalty to George. For Alex, to turn to you is to betray your husband, his lifelong friend. I pity you. You are caught in a conflict between duty and love.'

There was silence on the line. Grief-stricken, Johanna slowly replaced the phone. For a moment, she held her head in her hands. She had known that her action was futile the moment she had dialled Harvey's number. Where Alex was concerned, she had no right to ask anything of him. It was horrible to feel so helpless.

Apprehensive as she was for Alex's sake, Johanna tried to keep up a front of quiet cheerfulness following his departure. She dedicated herself to looking after George and Harold, and to her work at the hospital. She avoided using Alex's name. If anyone else mentioned him, she pretended not to hear. She gave no outward sign of the battle going on inside her. Her husband needed none.

82

At the end of April 1945, Alex Haverfield flew from London to Athens. It was a wrench to leave Johanna behind. From there he flew to Crete with a military detachment to handle the surrender of the German garrison.

The Germans were ordered by wireless to lay down their arms, but refused. As the British approached the airfield at Maleme, where the enemy forces were concentrated, they didn't know for sure whether or not they would be blown out of the sky. In the bright morning light they could see Maleme's anti-aircraft guns pointing at them. Sitting on the edge of his seat, Alex thought how ironic it would be if he should die at this late moment in the war. In May 1941 Roger Blundell had fought a ferocious battle in Crete. For minutes, no one in the plane spoke. Everything seemed frozen in time. Alex found himself remembering Johanna's tears, and the strange look George had given him when they said goodbye.

Fortunately, the Germans surrendered. The British takeover went smoothly. The Germans complied with soldierly precision. It was as if they had been rehearsing the procedure for weeks. As the sombre-faced German commander saluted Alex, he offered his hand as a gesture of friendship; the war between them was over. Alex declined: shaking hands with the enemy was against King's Regulations. By 1945, whatever chivalry had existed between the British and the Germans was dead. It would have been perfectly in order for him to blow the German's head off, but not to shake his hand. Fraternizing with the enemy was a criminal offence, which could bring imprisonment. With others looking on, Alex saluted and turned away. The German's look of bitter disappointment left him with a feeling of deep regret.

The hauling down of the German flag at Maleme that day had sent a message to the whole island. The savage war between the Cretans and the Germans was over. Almost instantaneously, the guerrilla troops in the hills began to flood down on to the coastal plain. Alex watched them through his binoculars. He had never seen such a motley crowd. They were of all ages, they were dressed in rags, they wore beards, and they carried every kind of weapon. No wonder the Germans feared them. The guerrillas expressed their joy at the German surrender by filling the sky with bullets and shrapnel. A thin, bitter haze of expended cordite drifted across the hills.

Later that morning, a one-eyed Cretan turned up on a motorcycle at Maleme with a request for Colonel Haverfield to attend a feast at Khania a few miles away. He hinted darkly that a refusal to celebrate their common victory over the Germans would give serious offence.

'When?' Alex asked.

'Now.'

'How do we get there?'

'Follow me.'

With little choice, Alex and two other British officers

dropped what they were doing, commandeered a German truck with a British driver, and followed their guide; they also took guards. At that moment everything in Crete was up for grabs.

The first thing Alex saw in Khania through the veil of smoke that enveloped the town was a dark-haired brigand dragging a woman by her hair over the cobblestones; the woman's screams were muffled by the clamour going on around them. Alex knew better than to intervene; the desperado would have shot him on the spot.

The British followed their one-eyed guide into a barn, from which came a great din. Inside they found the guerrillas – still armed to the teeth – sitting at long wooden tables. Amid shouts and laughter, they were drinking wine from jugs that were refilled the moment they were empty. There was time only to take a swig and pass the jug down the table. The smell of unwashed bodies was overpowering. The arrival of the British officers was met with growls and the waving of hands; there was no let-up in the drinking or the noise. As a diversion, one of the men periodically fired a gun into the rafters. Others expressed their solidarity with Alex by clapping him on the back.

As he and his companions sat down, bread and steaming platters of lamb were brought in. The moment the food touched the table, the men jumped up and grabbed their share. They used their own knives or borrowed one quickly.

Between bites, a white-haired man rattled off something in Cretan dialect to Alex, not one word of which he understood. Assuming it to be a form of welcome, Alex reciprocated by shouting back in English, not one word of which the Cretans understood either. They expressed their appreciation of what had been said by firing a whole volley of rounds through the roof; fragments of wood fell on to the food.

While eating, Alex began to take stock of those around him. On his right was a surly-looking guerilla dressed in rags, with a beard down to his chest. He had a butcher's knife stuck in his belt, smelt to high heaven, and had lost two of his front teeth. Alex eyed his neighbour for some time before taking the plunge. 'Do you speak English?' he eventually asked.

'I . . . I'm the . . . L . . . L . . . London . . . T . . . T . . . T . . . *Times* c . . . c . . . correspondent,' the man stammered.

'You've got to be joking.'

'I wish I were.'

'But I don't understand. Do the correspondents of *The Times* usually go about dressed like you?'

'N . . . n . . . n . . . no,' he laughed, stuffing his mouth with food, 'and they probably wash more often.'

'Can you explain how you come to be here?'

'Not an explanation you'd believe.'

'Would you like to try?'

'Well, it's like this,' he stuttered. 'Roughly three years ago, I landed from a submarine at Sphakia in southern Crete. I was supposed to get a story and leave within the week; it was all arranged. Instead I was trapped on the island – as were many British, Greek and New Zealand soldiers. Following the British defeat in northern Crete, we fled back over the mountains to Sphakia in the hope of finding a ship. Instead we found German troops. Detachments of New Zealanders managed to get away, but most of us fled to the hills to join the partisans. Once in the mountains, we lived a wild existence, always on the move, sometimes killing Germans, sometimes killing each other. It was a hard life. It's over now and I am glad to be going home. I'm sure you'll believe that.'

Alex did believe him. Until late that evening, while most of those around them tried to drink themselves insensible, they exchanged news and ate and drank together. A fiddler played on and off, but the din was too great to hear him.

On leaving, Alex wished the *Times* correspondent well on his return to Britain.

'What are you going to do with yourself now the war is over?' his companion asked.

'I'll probably leave the army. I need to make a new beginning. The ideals with which I grew up haven't survived the war. The world's changed. I've changed.' For a moment he wondered what his father would have thought of this admission; he had been so firm in his beliefs. Alex recalled his father telling him that it was Britain's sacred duty to save the world. In his mind's eye, he saw the Victoria Cross hanging on the wall of his father's study at Woodstock, and the quotation from the *Iliad* about glory in war being the highest honour. Six years of war had shaken his belief in these things. He knew that it was wrong of the British to have claimed to know what the rest of the world ought to do. The world was too big and too old for them to have a lasting effect upon it.

'Well, whatever you decide, good luck with it. Cheers!' He raised his glass.

'Cheers!' answered Alex.

It was a filthy, black night when Alex and his men climbed into their truck and began their journey back to Maleme. Revellers were still shouting and firing into the air. The headlights danced merrily along the seashore and glanced off the roadside bushes. Someone was singing in a low voice in the rear of the vehicle. The roar of the engine echoed along the wet road.

Halfway to Maleme, the driver swung the truck slowly around a sharp bend. Crack! A rifle shot rang out. Alex slumped to the floor. The driver's face was bleeding freely from broken glass. For a moment, there was panic.

The vehicle brought to a halt, Alex was lifted back on to his seat. He was unconscious. By torchlight they saw that he had been shot in the chest. No one could make any sense of where the shooting had come from; there was not a soul

347

to be seen. It could have been a partisan taking a last shot at a German truck, or a madman, or a drunk; no one knew.

With one of the men holding Alex in his arms and another trying to staunch the bleeding, they raced back to Maleme, the horn sounding all the way. Alex was at once evacuated in a small plane to Athens. His friends stood at the runway and watched the tiny aircraft disappear into the dark sky. That night he underwent emergency surgery at the British military hospital. The bullet was retrieved, but he died as dawn was coming to Greece, with Johanna's name on his lips. A letter from her was found in his clothing.

83

George heard the news from Mrs Haverfield who called him at the college. She was in a terrible state. 'It's impossible,' she sobbed into the phone.

'What is impossible?'

'Alex is dead. Don't you realize what I'm saying, George, my son is dead. All for nothing. There is no God. Did you hear what I said? *There is no God*.' There was an outburst of sobbing.

A vague fear seized George. He felt the sudden shock of dismay. The last of the crew was dead; all eight had died. It took some moments for the message to sink in. He became highly nervous.

He was reluctant to tell Johanna about Alex when he went home for lunch. He entered quietly. Johanna was sitting in the bedroom drying her hair. 'You startled me,' she said.

'Alex is dead,' he blurted out, watching his own and her face in the dressing-table mirror. 'Oh no,' she gasped, 'don't say that.' She buried her face in the towel and sobbed. When

348

she was alone once more, she threw herself on the bed and wept bitterly; she had no defence against Alex's death. She knew he was the father of the child she was carrying. That night she cried herself to sleep. She had mocked God, and God had shown His wrath.

A few days later, prayers were said in the college chapel for all those Arnold men who had died in the war. Dean Stably was there; he looked awfully frail and had the eyes of a very old man. He had lost his only son at sea. As always, Walter Turnbull stressed the Resurrection and the promise of eternal life.

'I bowed my head with the rest,' George wrote in his diary, 'but in my heart I have come to doubt the promise of eternal life and immortality. It's religious hocus-pocus, meant to make you feel better. The older you get, the more you believe in it. I don't. I think we create God to help us make sense of life and see us through our trials; God is a useful explanation of life's uncertainties. We settle for imagination rather than reason. Why would a loving God permit the world to suffer like this? I cannot resign myself to grief. What purpose does it serve? What's going on is an absurd nightmare.'

With the war over in the Mediterranean, and helped by her late husband's friends in the War Office, Evelyn Haverfield was successful in having her son's body returned for burial at Woodstock.

The funeral took place beneath a grey sky. The path to the grave was running with water. Among the mourners were the Kemps. Evelyn was stricken by grief, Johanna looked inconsolable. George's earlier fears that Alex would return had been fulfilled – but not in the way he had expected. As the coffin was slowly lowered into the ground, his earlier jealousy receded. Thank God he hadn't posted his letter to Alex with its tirade of anger and scorn. His hatred of Alex had been an

349

expression of his own weakness. Dressed in black, a weeping Johanna led Evelyn Haverfield out of the graveyard. Both were too distressed to speak. The church bell tolled. George tried to keep his umbrella over the two women, but they seemed oblivious to the rain. Johanna's tears undid him so.

Evelyn and Johanna had supper together that night. Johanna felt drawn to the older woman. Taking her hand, she told her that she was bearing Alex's child. For a moment Mrs Haverfield was confused. 'Did you say . . .' she began, disbelief in her voice.

Johanna repeated the news.

'Oh, my God, it can't be true.' She was beside herself with joy, talking about life replacing death. 'I cursed God, but now I thank Him.' In tears, she reached out and held Johanna in silent companionship. The two women stayed together until late that night.

84

For George, Alex's death was the last straw. A terrible fit of melancholy engulfed him. Already afraid of dying, he was even more fearful of this kind of inscrutable death, which had picked off his friends one after another. It brought up issues he had already discussed with Turnbull. Were the deaths of his friends part of a grand design, or was it all a matter of chance, a pointless sacrifice in which virtue, truth, courage, duty, patriotism and honour were empty words? Was life an absurd lottery, as Roger Blundell had held long ago? Was chaos the norm? Or was it evil? To talk about rhyme and reason, hope and virtue, when life was tooth and claw, was absurd.

Johanna was aware of her husband's anguish. One day he'd be in the highest spirits, the next he'd be in the depths of despair. His sleep was always disturbed. In his work at Arnold he had become a plodder; everything was an effort. He was more and more indifferent to himself and those around him. Childers had already voiced his concern about George to Johanna and she in turn had had a quiet word with Dr Carter at the Radcliffe. Carter found nothing physically wrong with his patient. His private opinion was that there was something seriously wrong with the Kemps' marriage. George bore all the signs of someone who had been rejected and who was suffering from a sense of overwhelming guilt. A psychiatrist in the hospital confirmed Carter's findings. Both doctors feared that he was heading for a serious nervous breakdown. Carter began to see George more regularly.

While Johanna refused to believe that life and death were as absurd as George argued, there were occasions when she was bewildered by his contradictions. His fear of death, and his diminishing interest in life, were beginning to overwhelm her. It took an effort of will for her to retain her belief that past joys would return; that life was not an empty promise; that she was not a prisoner of fate. For her, life still had meaning and the new life within her confirmed it. Human goodness and fulfilment were not dead. She refused to surrender to her husband's despair. For her, hope kept fear at bay. 'Hope, you must remember,' her mother had told her long before, 'is the only alternative to death. To live in Christ, you must live in hope.'

85

Not long after Alex's funeral, George and Turnbull took their usual early-morning walk. They talked of the death of the crew.

'Why did they all have to die, Walter?' he asked. 'And their promise die with them. Why did God permit it?'

'God knows. Uncertainty and ambiguity are the human lot. Perhaps they are God's way of reminding us of our frailty and mortality. We humans will always be vulnerable to the tangle and the hurt of life.'

'Why do you always say God knows?'

'Because God is the ultimate truth and the ultimate purpose. Unless life is nonsense, somebody must be responsible for what is happening. Because we don't understand life is no reason to think there is no afterlife. These things are beyond human understanding. Yet there is order in the universe, take my word for it. A God whose mind you could understand would not be God. Evil, absurdity and brutishness are not the work of God but of men. Too often, tragedy is the consequence, not of God's indifference to human suffering, but of man's wickedness. It's man's self-destructive tendencies that mar life, not God. God gives, evil takes away. The struggle between virtue and evil is unending. The enormous pain in the world does not entitle us to say that there is no God. Without his grace and his solace we would all shrivel like leaves in the sun. There were times in the Great War when I thought He must have regretted creating us. If you had seen what I have seen, you would wonder why God has not already destroyed us all.'

As always, George had difficulty understanding Turnbull's argument.

'If, on the other hand,' the chaplain continued, 'the idea of God and an eternal life is so much rubbish, then it doesn't matter why or how your friends died. They died and that's the end of it. All that's left is to bury them. Rightly or wrongly, most of the human race has not held that view. The instinctive piety of man down the ages has caused him to seek God and acknowledge His works. Not even the Soviets have succeeded in killing God; no one

352

can. To live this uncertain life, as well as to make the journey into the unknown, you need something higher than yourself; something other than what man can give you. God has everything to do with our life and our death on earth.'

'That doesn't make the death of the crew any less grotesque.'

'To say that it's grotesque is to challenge God's wisdom. Their death is what the Christian Gospel is all about. Good prevails because there are people who are prepared to sacrifice themselves for others or for a faith. The blood of the Christian martyrs was the seed of the Church. You can never do anything of any consequence in life without somebody getting hurt. There always has to be a sacrifice; freedom means pain. The only way you can accept the death of your friends, or any death, is to accept it as God's will. Without God, there's nothing to hang on to. Reason alone won't do. It certainly won't explain how your particular generation came to pay the price they did – or mine, for that matter.'

George didn't like the talk about 'God's will'. It closed men's minds and gave them an excuse for every kind of weakness. Why would men fight evil if God were in charge? Let Him do it! George preferred not to reveal his thoughts. Instead he asked Turnbull whether he thought his eight friends had died in vain.

'Nobody dies in vain, George. Death not only diminishes, it enlarges. It's the dead who help the living to give the wheel another turn. Nobody dies without affecting the lives of others. The dead always walk beside us; we live in their shadows; memories linger. The deaths of your comrades will inspire and strengthen those of us who must go on ploughing to the end of the furrow. Their dreams are our dreams. Remembered or not, to die as they did, to have loved as they did, is enough; the things they stood for will never die.'

353

'I hope you are right, Walter. It would be better for everybody if you were.'

'Can you possibly imagine a world where courage is not valued? Can you tell me what we can substitute for bravery and duty? Faith, love, virtue, truth, courage, nobility, patriotism and honour are not empty words. Without them, we cannot go on.'

There was an expectant pause.

'God rest their souls, George,' Turnbull muttered. 'These men were ordinary people who rose to extraordinary heights. It was not love of glory or hope of honour that caused them to give their all, but a belief that they might save the rest of us. England expected that they would do their duty, and they did – and perished in the attempt. We are the poorer for it. To ignore their courage and self-sacrifice is to rob life of its meaning. As long as there are such people, there will be hope for the human race. May their glory never fade. "But these are deeds which should not pass away, And names that must not wither." In years to come they will be regarded as an heroic generation.'

George thought of the war memorial at Arnold College for those students who had fallen in the Great War. Sadly, his generation had hardly given the names a second glance. Yet, in a detached sort of way, they had been taught to revere those who had died for their country. 'I hope you are right,' he said to the chaplain.

Turnbull halted for a moment, blowing out his cheeks and glancing at the spring landscape around him. 'Blow the trumpets, George, sound the drums!' he ordered, as he shuffled off down the path. George followed, struggling with what had been said about death and sacrifice. He never understood what Turnbull was talking about. There was a secret side to his words. George couldn't make the spiritual leap of believing in an all-powerful God who had stood by while half the world had tried to massacre the other half. What kind of 'God's wisdom' is that? he asked himself.

That night a quarrel broke out between George and Johanna. Ridiculously unimportant squabbles happened between them almost daily. In the heat of exchange, Johanna revealed that she was carrying Alex's child. The moment she said it, she knew that she had taken advantage of a sick man. Her words struck George dumb; his anger died; he dropped his gaze and turned away.

86

The next day, Walter Turnbull waited for George outside Arnold College's main entrance, where they usually met to go for their morning walk. The rising sun had begun to shed its light on Oxford's spires.

After some minutes, Turnbull set out for Christ Church Meadow alone. George must be sleeping late, he concluded.

As he entered the Meadow, he was surprised to see George sitting on a bench where they sometimes sat and talked. His cane was lying on the ground.

Why is he out here so early, and alone? Turnbull asked himself as he drew closer. He called, but there was no reply.

A few steps away, the chaplain suddenly halted and stiffened. George was holding a revolver, which he slowly raised to his head. 'No! No! George, in God's name, no!' Turnbull shouted as he sprang forward and wrestled the gun out of his grasp. There was a loud crack as the bullet sped aimlessly into the sky. The chaplain picked up the fallen pistol and put it in his pocket.

With Turnbull supporting George, the two men started

slowly back towards the college. George was weeping; he hardly seemed aware of Turnbull's presence.

In the distance, they saw a distraught Johanna running towards them, her hair streaming behind her in the wind. 'What's the matter?' she cried.

'Nothing serious,' Turnbull called back, 'George is a little off-colour.'

'Thank God,' she gasped. 'I just awoke with a terrible feeling that he was about to die.'

Putting his other arm around Johanna, Walter Turnbull led the couple out of the Meadow. That night he had a long talk with George. 'There's nothing more that I can say, George,' he ended. 'You can either go on wallowing in self-pity and destroy yourself (to the distress of your parents and your wife and child), or you can get up off the floor, climb back into the ring and respond like a man to life's trials. You need to turn your attention from death to life. Everything I have known or experienced tells me that life is worth living. You have the choice – either to triumph over or be beaten by yourself. The help you need is not mine, but God's.'

Later on Turnbull threw the gun into the river.

87

On 5 May 1945, peace returned to the European world. The sudden transition from war to peace left a lot of people in Oxford bewildered. Relieved of an ordeal they had lived with for so long, people talked differently; an artificial merriment prevailed; feasting and revelry broke out all over the city. There were bonfires and fireworks in St Giles's. 'It is finished, it is finished, it is finished,' Oxford's church bells rang out. 'The horrors and the savagery of war are done.' On the Broad crowds sang the national anthem.

Johanna wept when she heard that the war was over; she hugged Harold and thanked God that the killing had stopped. She at once took down the blackout curtains to let in more light; she'd had her fill of gloom. Six years had come and gone. Her parents and so many of her friends had died. The Germany of her childhood had been effaced. Her father's worst fears had come true: Hitler and the Nazis had turned a thriving country into a giant graveyard. With the help of friends from the Foreign Office, she began a search for her sister Brigitte.

Through her tears, she remembered the joy she and George had known, the dreams they'd shared. It all came flooding back: their first meeting, her trip to Oxford for the boat race, the joy of their early married life. They couldn't reclaim that; it had gone for good. Time and the war had changed everything, but not her hope, which had outlived all the terror and the deaths of the past six years. It had been her refuge and her strength. With God's help they could start all over again. They must start all over again.

Three days later, George Kemp and Harvey Childers met at the boatshed. They had agreed to watch the Head-of-the-River Race together. To reach Childers, George had to push his way through a waving, cheering crowd. The towpath was lined with spectators, many of them in uniform. A group of Americans had also come to see the race. All the crowded barges were flying their flags. Arnold's barge stood out. Banners, streamers, rattles, whistles and bunting were everywhere.

Childers was fussing about among the boats when George entered the boatshed. He had just returned to the college after being away. The bike the crew had given him years before was leaning against the wall.

'You've heard about Alex, Harvey?' George called. There

was so much din outside that he had to repeat himself. 'Yes.' Childers didn't turn but kept his back to George.

The two men went out together to see the race. They heard the starter's pistol in the distance. The noise on the tow-path was deafening.

They stood on the bank apart from the milling crowd, waiting for the boats to come round the bend in the river. Neither felt like talking. Minutes later, they saw the two prows slicing through the water. Trinity was leading. Swiftly, the vessels approached the place where they were standing. To see better, they pressed forward, staring at the leading crew. The rowers were pulling madly. Perhaps because their eyes were dimmed, or perhaps because they were mortal men, both Childers and George saw Pat Riley, Tony Markham, Max Elsfield, David Evans, Bill Clark, Roger Blundell, Charley Bradbury and Alex Haverfield. They saw them as they'd been. George called and waved, but the rowers had gone.

The old man and the young man stood there quietly, staring into the past. Neither said a word. It was Trinity's day.

Eventually, George spoke up. 'They've all gone, Harvey. All of the eight.'

'Yes.'

'It's hard to believe that they've all gone.'

Childers turned slowly and faced George. He had the soft eyes of a deer; he looked tired. George wondered if his face hadn't shrunk a little. 'They haven't all gone, George,' he said quietly. 'Their bones have, but not what they stood for. For me, they'll always be as they were the night they leapt across the burning boat.' He paused, overcome by feeling, searching for the right words . . . 'In their blaze of glory.'

'Shadows of glory,' George thought, but he didn't say it. Only shadows remained.